'LIZBETH OF THE DALE

'LIZBETH OF THE DALE

Mary Esther Miller Macgregor

www.General-Books.net

Publication Data:

Title: 'lizbeth of the Dale
Author: Macgregor, Mary Esther Miller, 1876-1961
Reprinted: 2010, General Books, Memphis, Tennessee, USA

'LIZBETH OF THE DALE

Cover art
  'LIZBETH
OF THE DALE
  BY
MARIAN KEITH
  Author of "Treasure Valley," "Duncan Polite,"
"The Silver Maple," etc.
  HODDER STOUGHTON
NEW YORK
GEORGE H. DORAN COMPANY
  Copyright, 1910,
By GEORGE H. DORAN COMPANY.
  'LIZBETH OF THE DALE
  CHAPTER I
THE GAY GORDONS

On the side porch of the gray stone house sat Miss Gordon, steadily darning at the eight pairs of stockings belonging to her eight nephews and nieces. The strenuous task of being foster-mother to the eight had long ago taught Miss Gordon the necessity of doing two things at once. At the present moment she was attending to three beside the darning, and had chosen her position with an eye to their accomplishment. Here, where the Virginia creepers shaded her from the afternoon sun, she was near enough to the wall enclosing the backyard to mark that the Saturday raking and tidying of that battleground of the young Gordons suffered no serious interruption. Also, she could watch that little Jamie, tumbling about the grass in front of her, did not stray away to the pond. And, best of all, she commanded a view of the lane leading up to the highway, for a girl in a blue cotton gown and a big white hat was moving up the path to the gate between the willows, and Miss Gordon had awakened to the fact that her eldest niece needed watching.

Miss Annie had remarked a moment before, that she thought she might as well run up to the gate and see if Jerry Patterson, the mailman, was at the post-office yet; and besides, it was time Malcolm and Jean were home from the store, and she might help to carry their parcels; and, anyway, she had nothing to do, because it wasn't time to get the tea ready yet.

Miss Gordon would not have stooped to quote Shakespeare, considering him very irreligious and sometimes quite indelicate, and having forbidden the reading of him in the Gordon family. Nevertheless the unspoken thought of her mind was his–that the lady did protest too much.

Of the eight, Annie was her aunt's favorite. She was pretty and gentle and had caused Miss Gordon less trouble during the four years she had been head of her brother's house, than John or Elizabeth had frequently contributed in one day. But lately it seemed as though her greatest comfort bade fair to become her greatest anxiety. For Annie had suddenly grown up. The fact had been startlingly revealed by the strange actions of young Mr. Coulson, the school-teacher, who was probably at this moment walking across the fields towards the big gate between the willows.

At the thought, Miss Gordon closed her lips tightly and looked severe. To be sure, Annie must marry, and young Coulson seemed a rather genteel, well-made young man. He was studying law in the evenings, too, and might make his way in the world some day. But Auntie Jinit Johnstone, who lived on the next farm, and knew the minute family history of everyone in the county of Simcoe, had informed the last quilting-bee that a certain Coulson–and no distant relative of the young schoolmaster either–had kept a tavern in the early days down by the lake shore. Miss Gordon had made no remark. She never took part in gossip. But she had mentally resolved that she would inquire carefully just how distant this relative was, and then she would take means to place their Annie at a distance from the young man in an inverse ratio to the space between him and the tavern-keeper.

She peered through the tangle of alder and sumach that bordered the lane and saw her suspicions confirmed. Annie was at the gate, her blue dress set against the white background of some blossom-laden cherry-boughs, while down the road, the long limbs of this probable descendant of the tavern-keeper were bearing him swiftly towards her.

Miss Gordon's needle flashed in and out of Malcolm's sock, in a disapproving manner. She tried to look severe, but in spite of herself, her face showed something of pleasant excitement, for Miss Gordon was very much of a woman and could not but find a love affair interesting.

She had been a handsome girl once, and her fine, high-bred face was still almost beautiful. It was covered with innumerable tiny wrinkles, but her dark eyes were bright, and her cheeks bore a fixed pink flush, the birth-mark of the land of heather. Her hair, glossy black, with not a thread of gray, was parted in the middle and lay on either side in perfectly even waves. Her figure was slim and stiffly straight, her hands long and slender. She looked every inch a woman of refinement, and also a woman who would not flinch from any task that duty demanded.

And duty had asked much of her during these last few years—exile, privations, uncongenial tasks, and the mothering of eight orphans. This last demand had been the hardest. Even to their own mother, upon whom the burden had been laid gradually and gently, in Nature's wise way, the task had been a big one; but what had it been to her, who, without a moment's warning, had one day found herself at the head of a family, ranging from sixteen years to six days? Many times she had needed all her strength of character to keep her from dropping it all, and flying back to the peace and quiet of her old Edinburgh home. And yet she had struggled on under the burden for four years—four long years this spring; but even at this late day, she was overcome with a feeling of homesickness, as poignant as it had been in her first Canadian springtime.

She suspended her needle and looked about her as though inquiring the cause of this renewed longing. It was a May-day—a perfect Ontario May-day—all a luxury of blossoms and perfume. In the morning rain had fallen, and though now the clouds lay piled in dazzling white mountain-heaps far away on the horizon, leaving the dome above an empty quivering blue, still the fields and the gardens remembered the showers with gratitude and sparkled joyously under their garniture of diamond-drops. The wild cherry-trees bordering the lane and the highway, and the orchard behind the house were smothered in odorous blossoms of white and pink. A big flower-laden hawthorn grew in the lane, near the little gate leading from the garden. From its topmost spray a robin was pouring forth an ecstatic song—a song so out of proportion to his tiny body that he was fairly shaken by his own tumult—trills and whistles, calls and chuckles, all incoherently mingled and shouted forth in glorious hysteria. Miss Gordon looked up at the mad little musician and her face grew sad. She had recognized the cause of her renewed longing for home. At the little gate of her Edinburgh garden there grew just such a hawthorn, and the perfume of this one was telling her not of the joy and beauty before her, but of all she had left behind.

Miss Gordon had never seen the loveliness nor felt the lure of this new land—a garden-land though it was, of winding flower-fringed roads, of cool, fairy-dells, and hilltops with heart-thrilling glimpses of lake and forest and stream. Her harp was always hanging on the willows of this Canadian Babylon in mourning for the streets of Edinburgh. She could never quite rise above a feeling of resentment against the land that held her in bondage, and never once dreamed that, should she go back to the prim little house in McGlashan Street, with Cousin Griselda and their cats and their embroidery and their cup of tea at exactly half-past four in the afternoon, she would long for the old stone house in the far-off Canadian valley, and the love and companionship of the merry rioters who now made her days a burden.

Her grievance against Canada was due to the fact that she had crossed the ocean merely to make one short summer's visit to brother William and had been held a prisoner ever since.

It had all come about through Cousin Griselda's mistaken idea that to be truly genteel one must travel. The cousins had ever set before themselves perfect refinement and gentility as the one condition to be devoutly striven for, and the only one in keeping with the Gordon traditions. They lived in a quiet old house on a silent old street, with a sleepy old servant and two somnolent old cats. They were always excessively polite to each other and to everyone with whom they came in contact, even to the cats. Every afternoon of their lives, except Sunday, and once a month when the Ladies' Guild met at the manse, they wore their second-best black dresses, their earrings and bracelets, and sat in the parlor with the two cats and dozed and embroidered until half-past four when the tea was brought in. They always spoke slowly and carefully, and conversed upon genteel subjects. Nothing less important than the doings of the Royal Family, or at least the nobility, and, of course, once a week, the minister's sermon, was ever discussed in their tiny parlor. And as Cousin Griselda often remarked privately, Who were more able to discourse with ease upon such themes? For did there not live, right in Edinburgh, Sir William Gordon, who was almost a second cousin to both, and whose wife, Lady Gordon, had once called on them right there in McGlashan Street.

But Cousin Griselda was not content even with perfect refinement and titled relatives, and her vaulting ambition had led to the great mistake of Margaret's life. The draper's wife next door had called, and when she had gone and Keziah had carried away the three tea-cups, Cousin Griselda had remarked upon the almost genuine air of grandeur possessed by Mrs. Galbraith. Margaret had asked how it could be, for Mrs. Galbraith had no family connections and a husband in trade, and Cousin Griselda had thereupon expressed the firm conviction that it was because Mrs. Galbraith had traveled. She had been twice to London and several times to Liverpool. Cousin Griselda concluded by declaring that though a baronet in the family, and good blood were essential to true gentility, no one could deny that travel in foreign lands gave an air of distinction which nothing else could bestow.

The cousins were thoroughly disturbed in their minds thereafter and talked much of travel, to the neglect of the Royal Family. And even while the subject was absorbing them there had come to Margaret her brother William's letter from far-off Canada inviting her to visit him. The bare thought that Margaret might go, set the cousins into a flutter of excitement. To be sure, Margaret argued, Canada was a very wild and frost-bound country, scarcely the place one would choose to travel over in search of further refinement. But Griselda declared that surely, no matter where dear William's lot might be cast, being a Gordon, he would be surrounded by an atmosphere of gentility. And so, little by little, the preposterous idea grew into a reality, and by the time the cousins had discussed the matter for a year, it was finally decided that Margaret should go.

All through the twenty years of his absence, William's letters had been just as beautifully written and as nicely phrased, as they had in his student days in Edinburgh. The paper was not always what true refinement called for, but one could overlook that, when one remembered that it probably came to him on dog-sleds over mountains of snow. One had to surmise much, of course, regarding William's experience in Canada. His letters were all of his inner life. He said much regarding his spiritual condition, of his grievous lapses of faith, of his days on the Delectable Mountains and of his descents into the Slough of Despond, but very little of the hills and valleys of his adopted country. Once, shortly after his arrival, he had stated that he was living in a shanty where the bush came right up to the door. Margaret had had some misgivings, but Cousin Griselda had explained that a shanty was in all probability a dear little cottage, and the bush might be an American rose bush, or more likely a thorn, which in springtime would be covered with May.

But now William lived in a comfortable stone house, had married, and had a family growing up around him, who were all anxious to see their Old Country aunt. And so the unbelievable at last came to pass and his sister sailed for Quebec.

In the home land William Gordon had entered training for the ministry. His parents had died, owing their chief regret that they could not see their son in the pulpit, and his sister received the bitterest disappointment of her life, when he abandoned the calling. But William was largely Celt by blood and wholly so by nature and had visions. In one of them he had seen himself before the Great White Throne, worthless, sin-stricken. What was he that dared to enter such a holy calling as the ministry? He who was as the dust of the earth, a priest of the Most High God! He beat his brow at the blasphemy of the thought. It was Nadab or Abihu he was or a son of Eli, and the Ark would depart forever from God's people, did he dare to raise his profaning hands in its ministry. And so, partly to escape his sister's reproaches, he had sailed away to Canada. Here he had tried various occupations, and finally settled down to teaching school away back in the forests of Lake Simcoe. He married, and when a large family was growing up around him, and the ever-menacing poverty had at last seized them, he experienced the first worldly success of his life.

About a mile from the school which had witnessed his latest failure, there lay a beautiful little valley. Here an eccentric Englishman named Jarvis had built a big stone house and for a few years had carried on a semblance of farming. This place he called The Dale, and here he lived alone, except for an occasional visit from his wife, who watched his farming operations with disapproving eye from a neighboring town. The schoolmaster was his only friend, and when he died, while he left the farm to his wife, he bequeathed to William Gordon his big stone house and barns, and the four-acre field in which they stood. Fortune had looked for the first time upon the Gordons, and she deigned them a second glance. Through the energy of his wife and the influence of her people, the MacDonalds, who owned half the township of Oro, William Gordon obtained the position of township clerk. On the modest salary from this office, supplemented by the four acres where they pastured their cow and raised garden produce, the family managed to live; and here the young Gordons grew up, healthy and happy, and quite unconscious of the fact that they were exceedingly poor.

But someone had suffered in the fight against want, and when the worst of the struggle was over the brave mother began to droop. William Gordon had been a kind husband, but he lived with his head in the clouds. His eyes were so dazzled by distant visions that he had failed to notice that most beautiful vision at his side, a noble woman wearing her life away in self-forgetful toil for him and his children. She never spoke of her trials, for her nature was of the kind that finds its highest enjoyment in sacrifice. She was always bright and gay. Her smile and her ready laughter brightened the home in the days of her husband's deepest spiritual gloom. But one day even the smile failed. At the birth of their eighth child she went out into a new life, and the noble sacrifice was complete.

The long-expected aunt from the Old Country sailed a short time before baby Jamie's birth. So when Miss Gordon arrived, it was to an unexpected scene–a darkened home, a brother stunned by his loss, and a family of orphans, the eldest, a frightened-eyed girl of sixteen, the youngest, a wailing infant of a few days.

Miss Gordon was made of good Scotch granite, with a human heart beneath. The veneer of gentility had underneath it the pure gold of character. She seized the helm of the family ship with a heroic hand. She sailed steadily through a sea of troubles that often threatened to overwhelm her; the unaccustomed task of motherhood with its hundred trials, her brother's gloom and despair, the new conditions of the rough country–even the irony of a fate that had set her at hard, uncongenial toil in the very place where she had sought culture. But she succeeded, and had not only held her own poise in the struggle, but had managed to permeate the family life with something of her old-world refinement.

It was four long years since she had seen the hawthorn blooming in her home garden. And now the infant of that dark springtime was the sturdy boy, rolling over the grass with Collie, and the sixteen-year-old girl, with the big frightened eyes, was the tall young woman up there at the gate beside the figure in gray tweed.

Miss Gordon had stood the trial, partly because she had never accepted the situation as final. She would go back to Edinburgh and Cousin Griselda soon, she kept assuring herself, and though the date of her departure always moved forward, rainbow-like at her approach, she found much comfort in following it.

First she decided she must stay until the baby could walk, but when wee Jamie went toddling about the big bare rooms, Annie had just left school, and was not yet prepared to shoulder all the cares of housekeeping. She would wait until she saw Annie capable of managing the home. Then when Annie's skirts came down below her boot-tops, and her hair went up in a golden pile upon her head, and she could bake bread and sweep a room to perfection, the care of the next two children presented itself. Malcolm and Jean had from the first shown marked ability at school, and Miss Gordon's long-injured pride found the greatest solace in them. She determined that Malcolm must be sent to college, and William could never be trusted to do it. By strict economy she had managed to send both the clever ones to the High School in the neighboring town for the past year; how could she leave them now at the very beginning of their career?

And so the date of her return home moved steadily forward. Sometimes it went out of sight altogether and left her in despair. For even if the two brilliant ones should graduate and William should cease to be so shockingly absent-minded, and the younger boys so shockingly boisterous, and Mary so delicate, there was always Elizabeth. Whenever Miss Gordon contemplated the case of her third niece her castles in Edinburgh toppled over. What would become of Elizabeth if she were left unguided? What was to become of Elizabeth in any case, was an ever-present question.

But in spite of all the ties that held her, Miss Gordon had determined that, come what might, her homegoing was finally settled this time. It was to take place immediately after Annie's marriage. For of course Annie would marry–perhaps a rich gentleman from the town–who knew? Then, when Annie was settled, Jean must leave school and keep house, and she would sail away to Edinburgh and Cousin Griselda.

She made this final decision once again, with some stubbornness, as the breath of the hawthorn brought a hint of her old garden. She finished Malcolm's sock with a determined snip of her scissors, and took up John's.

Near the end of the long porch, a door led through the high board wall into the orchard and kitchen-garden. It swung noisily open, and a tall, broad-shouldered young woman, arrayed in a gay print cotton gown, a dusty black velvet sacque, and a faded pink hat, bounced heavily upon the porch.

Miss Gordon glanced up, and her startled look changed to one of relief and finally to severity. She bent over her darning.

"Good-afternoon, Sarah Emily," she remarked frigidly.

The young person was apparently unabashed by her chilling reception. She took one stride to the green bench that stood against the house and dropped upon it, letting her carpet-bag fall with a thud to the floor. She stretched out her feet in their thick muddy boots, untied her pink hat strings, and emitted a sounding sigh.

"Laws–a–day, but I'm dead dog-tired," she exclaimed cordially.

Miss Gordon looked still severer. Evidently Sarah Emily had returned in no prodigal-son's frame of mind. Ordinarily the mistress would have sharply rebuked the girl's manner of speech, but now she bent to her work with an air of having washed her hands finally of this stubborn case.

But Sarah Emily was of the sort that could not be overawed by any amount of dignity. She was not troubled, either, with a burdensome sense of humility–no, not even though this was the third time she had "given notice," and returned uninvited.

"Well," she exclaimed at length, as though Miss Gordon were arguing the case with her, "I jist had to have a recess. There ain't there no one could stand the penoeuvres of that young Lizzie, an' the mud she trailed all over the kitchen jist after I'd scrubbed!"

Miss Gordon showed no signs of sympathy. She felt some, nevertheless, and suppressed a sigh. Elizabeth certainly was a trial. She deigned no remark, however, and Sarah Emily continued the one-sided conversation all unabashed.

"I hoofed it every fut o' the road," she remarked aggrievedly.

Miss Gordon took a new thread from her ball and fitted it into her needle with majestic dignity.

Sarah Emily was silent a moment, then hummed her favorite song.

"My grandmother lives on yonder little green,
As fine an old lady as ever was seen,
She has often cautioned me with care,
Of all false young men to beware!

"I couldn't abide that there Mrs. Oliver another five minutes. She had too stiff a backbone for me, by a whole pail o' starch."

Miss Gordon's face changed. Here was news. Sarah Emily had been at service in town during her week's absence, and not only that, she had actually been in one of its most wealthy and influential families! To Miss Gordon, the town, some three miles distant, was a small Edinburgh, and she pined for even a word from someone, anyone, there who moved in its social world. She longed to hear more, but realized she could not afford to relax just yet.

"Perhaps you will understand now what it means to be under proper discipline," she remarked.

"Well, I wasn't kickin' about bein' under that, whatever it is. It was bein' under her thumb I couldn't abide–makin' me wear a white bonnet in the afternoons, jist as if I was an old granny, an' an apron not big enough for a baby's bib!"

Miss Gordon longed to rebuke the girl sharply, but could not bear to lose the glimpse of real genteel life.

"She has one girl an' one boy–an' that there boy! She'd dress him up in a new white get-up, 'bout every five minutes, an' he'd walk straight outside an' wallow in the mud right after. I thought I'd a' had to stand an' iron pants for that young heathen till the crack o' doom, an' I had just one pair too many so I had. An' I up an' told her you'd think she kep' a young centipede much less a human boy with only two legs to him. And then I up and skedaddled."

Miss Gordon's conscience added its protest to that of her dignity, and she spoke.

"I prefer that you should not discuss your various mistresses with me, Sarah Emily. I can have nothing to do with your affairs now, you see."

Sarah Emily lilted the refrain of her song:

"Timmy–eigh timmy–um, timmy–tum–tum–tum,
Of all false young men to beware!

"Would you like muffins or pancakes for supper?" she finished up graciously.

Miss Gordon hesitated. Sarah Emily was a great trial to genteel nerves, but she was undeniably a great relief from much toilsome labor that was quite incompatible with a genteel life. Sarah Emily noticed her hesitation and went on:

"When Mrs. Jarvis came she had me make muffins every morning for breakfast."

Miss Gordon dropped her knitting, completely off her guard.

"Why, Sarah Emily!" she cried, "you don't mean–not Elizabeth's Mrs. Jarvis."

Sarah Emily nodded, well-pleased.

"Jist her, no less! She's been visitin' Mrs. Oliver for near a month now, an' she was askin' after Lizzie, too. I told her where I was from. I liked her. Me and her got to be awful good chums, but I couldn't stand Mrs. Oliver. An' Mrs. Jarvis says, 'Why, how's my little namesake?' An' o' course I put Lizzie's best side foremost. I made her out as quiet as a lamb, an' as good an' bidable as Mary."

"Sarah Emily!"–Miss Gordon had got back some of her severity–"you didn't tell an untruth?"

"Well, not exactly, but I guess I scraped mighty nigh one."

"What did Mrs. Jarvis say?"

"She said she wasn't much like her mother then, an' she hoped she wouldn't grow up a little prig, or some such thing. An' she told me"–here Sarah Emily paused dramatically, knowing she was by this reinstating herself into the family–"she told me to tell you she was goin' to drive out some day next week and see you all, an' see what The Dale looked like."

Miss Gordon's face flushed pink. Not since the day Lady Gordon called upon her and Cousin Griselda had she been so excited. It seemed too good to be true that her dream that this rich lady, who had once owned The Dale and for whom little Elizabeth had been called, should really come to them. Surely Lizzie's fortune was made!

She turned gratefully towards her maid. Sarah Emily had arisen and was gathering up her hat and carpet-bag. For the first time her mistress noted the weary droop of the girl's strong frame.

"We needn't have either muffins or pancakes, Sarah Emily," she said kindly. "Put away your things upstairs and I shall tell Jean and Mary to set the table for you."

But Sarah Emily sprang airily towards the kitchen door, strengthened by the little touch of kindness.

"Pshaw, don't you worrit your head about me!" she cried gayly. "I'll slap up a fine supper for yous all in ten minutes." She swung open the kitchen door at the end of the porch, and turned before she slammed it. She stood a moment regarding her mistress affectionately.

"I tell ye what, ma'am," she cried in a burst of gratitude, "bad as ye are, other people's worse!"

She banged the door and strode off singing loudly:

"Timmy–eigh timmy–um, timmy–tum–tum–tum,
Of all false young men to beware!"

Miss Gordon accepted the doubtfully worded compliment for all it really meant from Sarah Emily's generous heart. But the crudeness of it jarred upon her genteel nerves. Unfortunately Miss Gordon was not so constituted as to see its humor.

She darned on, quickly and excitedly. Her dream that the rich Mrs. Jarvis should one day take a fancy to the Gordons and make their fortune was growing rosier every moment. Little Jamie came wandering over the grass towards her. His hands were full of dandelions and he looked not unlike an overgrown one himself with his towsled yellow curls. He leaned across her knee, his curly head hanging down, and swayed to and fro, crooning a little sleepy song. Miss Gordon's thin hand passed lovingly over his silky hair. Her face grew soft and beautiful. At such times the castles in Edinburgh grew dim and ceased to allure.

She arose and took the child's hand. "Come, Jamie dear," she said, "and we'll meet father." And so great was her good-humor, caused by her hopeful news, that when Annie met her shyly at the garden gate with the young schoolmaster following, her aunt gave him a stately but cordial invitation to supper. In view of the prospects before the family, she felt she could for the time at least let the tavern-keeping ancestor go on suspended sentence.

The Gordons gathered noisily about the supper table, William Gordon, a tall, thin man, strongly resembling his sister, but with all her severity and force of character missing, came wandering in from his study. His eyes bright and kindly, but with a far-away, absent look, beamed over the large table. He sat down, then catching sight of the guest standing beside Annie, rose, and shook him cordially by the hand.

The family seated themselves in their accustomed places, Annie, the pretty one, at her father's right hand, then Malcolm and Jean, the clever ones, John the quiet one, and Mary, the delicate one–a pale little girl with a sweet, pathetic mouth. On either side of their aunt were the two little boys, Archie and Jamie, and there was a plate between Mary and John which belonged to an absent member of the family. Here the visitor sat, and Sarah Emily was squeezed into a corner near her mistress. That Sarah Emily should sit with the family at all was contrary to Miss Gordon's wishes, and one of the few cases in which she yielded to her brother. She had brought Sarah Emily from a Girls' Home four years before, and had decreed that she would show the neighbors the proper Old Country way of treating a servant. Sarah Emily was far from the Old Country type, however, and William seemed to have forgotten that servants had a place of their own since he had lived so long in the backwoods. When the family would arrange themselves at table, with the maid standing properly behind her mistress, Mr. Gordon would wait for her to be seated before asking the blessing, regarding her with gentle inquiring eyes, and finally requesting her in a mildly remonstrating tone to come away and sit down like a reasonable body. And Sarah Emily, highly pleased, would drag a chair across the bare floor and plant herself down with a satisfied thud right on top of the family gentility. Miss Gordon tried many ways to prevent repetition of the indignity by keeping Sarah Emily out of the way. She disliked explaining, for William was rather queer about some things since he had been so long in this country. But Sarah Emily always contrived to be on hand just as the family were being seated. And finally, when her brother inquired anxiously if she wasn't afraid Sarah Emily had Roman Catholic leanings, since she refused to sit down at the table for grace, Miss Gordon gave up the struggle, and to the joy of all the children, Sarah Emily became one of the family indeed.

"Where's Lizzie?" asked the guest, when the pancakes had been circulated. He addressed his host, but looked at Annie. Mr. Gordon gazed around wonderingly. "Lizzie? I didn't miss the wee lamb. Where's our little 'Lizbeth, Margaret?"

Miss Gordon sighed. William never knew where the children were. "Did you forget it's Saturday?" she inquired. "Elizabeth always spends Saturday afternoon with Mrs. MacAllister," she explained to the young man.

"Mrs. MacAllister is very much attached to Elizabeth," she added, feeling very kindly just now toward her most trying child.

"Lizzie always does her home-work over there," ventured Archie, "'cause Charles Stuart does her sums for her." John gave the speaker a warning kick. Archie was only seven and extremely indiscreet, but John was twelve and knew that whatever a Gordon might do or say to his sister in the bosom of his own family, he must uphold her before all outsiders, and particularly in the presence of a school-teacher.

But the school-teacher was in a very happy unprofessional frame of mind. "Never mind," he said, "Lizzie will beat you all at something, some day!"

He knew that a good word for the little sister always brought an approving light into the blue eyes across the table. Annie smiled radiantly.

"What is Lizzie best at?" she inquired with sweet anxiety.

Young Mr. Coulson looked at his plate and thought desperately. To discover any subject in which Lizzie Gordon was efficient was enough to confound any teacher. Then he remembered the caricatures of himself he had discovered on her slate.

"She has a remarkable talent for drawing," he said generously.

Annie beamed still brighter, and Miss Gordon glanced at him approvingly. She really did hope the story about the tavern-keeper was not true.

"Perhaps Elizabeth will be a great artist some day," she suggested.

"And she'll paint all our pictures," added Jean, "and we'll be more like the Primrose family than ever." The Gordons all laughed. They generally laughed when Jean spoke, because she was always supposed to say something sharp.

Mr. Gordon had lately been reading aloud the "Vicar of Wakefield," and, as always when a book was being read by them, the Gordons lived in its atmosphere and spoke in its language.

"Father will be the Vicar," said Annie, "and Aunt Margaret"–she looked half-frightened at her own audacity–"Aunt Margaret will be Mrs. Primrose."

"And you'll be Olivia," added Jean. "I'll be Sophia, with John and Mary for my sheep, and Malcolm can be Moses and wear Annie's hat with the feather in it."

The Gordons all laughed again.

"And who'll be the Squire?" asked little Mary, gazing admiringly at her wonderful sister. "Mr. Coulson would do, wouldn't he?"

Two faces strove to hide their blushes behind the bouquet of cherry blossoms which Sarah Emily had placed upon the table in honor of her return.

There was an intense silence. Mr. Gordon looked up. Nothing aroused him so quickly from his habitual reverie as silence at the table, because it was so unusual. He beheld his second son indulging in one of his spasms of silent laughter.

"What is the fun about?" he inquired genially, and then all the Gordons, except the eldest and the youngest, broke into giggles. Miss Gordon's voice, firm, quiet, commanding, saved the situation. She turned to Mr. Coulson and remarked, in her stateliest manner, that it had been a wonderful rain, just such a downpour as they had in Edinburgh the day after Lady Gordon called–she who was the wife of Sir William Gordon–their cousin for whom her brother had been called.

Young Mr. Coulson seized upon the subject with a mighty interest, and plunged into a description of a terrible storm that had swept over Lake Simcoe in his grandfather's days–thunder and hail and blackness. The storm cleared the atmosphere at the table, and Annie's cheeks were becoming cool again, when the young man brought the deluge upon himself in the most innocent manner.

"There are signs of it yet," he went on. "Did you ever see the old log-house at the first jog in the Ridge Road?" he inquired of Malcolm. "Well, there are holes in the chimney yet where the lightning came through. I can remember my grandfather lifting me up to look at them. He kept tavern there in the bad old days," he added cordially, "but the Coulsons have become quite respectable since."

There was another silence deeper than the last. Even young Archie, smothering himself with a huge slab of bread and butter and caring little about anything else, understood that to be related to a tavern-keeper placed one far beyond the pale of respectability. Annie was looking at her lap now, all her rosiness gone. The young man glanced about him half-puzzled, and Miss Gordon again saved the day by introducing a genteel word about Edinburgh and Lady Gordon.

But, as they left the table, she decided that again her home-going must be postponed until all danger of a Gordon uniting with the grandson of a tavern-keeper was passed.

CHAPTER II
THE WILD STREAK

The valley where the Gordons lived had narrowly escaped having a village at the corner. The surrounding district held all the requirements of one, but they did not happen to be placed near enough to one another. At the cross-roads in the center of the valley stood a store and post-office. But the blacksmith's shop, which should have been opposite, was missing. In the early days the blacksmith, being a Highland Scot, had refused to work opposite the storekeeper, who was only a Lowlander, and had set up his business over on the proud seclusion of the next concession. The school, too, had got mislaid somehow, away to the south out of sight. So the valley was left to the farms and orchards, and contained only five homes in all its length.

But where man had been neglectful, nature had lavished wealth, performing great feats in the way of landscape gardening. On all sides, the vale was held in by encircling hills. The eastern boundary was steep and straight and was known as Arrow Hill. On its summit stood a gaunt old pine stump, scarred and weather-beaten. Here, an old Indian legend said, the Hurons were wont to tie a captive while they showered their arrows into his quivering body. The children of the valley could point out the very holes in the old trunk where certain arrows, missing their victim, had lodged. Away opposite, forming the western wall, rose the Long Hill, with a moss-fringed road winding lingeringly up its face. Down through the cedars and balsams that hedged its side tumbled a clear little brook, singing its way through the marigolds and musk that lovingly strove to hold it back. Reaching the valley, it was joined by the waters that oozed from a great dark swamp to the south, and swelling into a good-sized stream, it wound its way past The Dale, held in by steep banks, all trilliums and pinks and purple violets and golden touch-me-not, and hedged by a double-line of feathery white-stemmed birches.

From east to west of the valley stretched a straight road, hard and white. Old Indian tales hung about it also. It was an early Huron trail, they said, and the one followed by Champlain when he marched over from the Ottawa valley and found Lake Simcoe hanging like a sapphire pendant from the jewel-chain of the Great Lakes. It was still called Champlain's Road, and had in it something of the ancient Indian character. For it cut straight across country over hill and stream, all unmindful of Government surveys or civilized lines.

Just a few miles beyond Arrow Hill it ran into the little town of Cheemaun, and on market-days its hard, white surface rang with the beat of hoofs and the rattle of wheels. In the early morning the procession rolled forward, strong and eager for the day's bargaining, and at night it swept back bearing some weary ones, some gleeful over their money-getting, some jealous and dissatisfied because of the wealth and ease they had seen, and some glad to return to the quiet and peace of their farm homes. And there were always the few who lurched along, caring not whether they reached home or fell by the wayside, having sold their manhood over the bar of one of Cheemaun's many hotels.

And thus the tide of rural life ebbed and flowed, beating ceaselessly against the town, leaving its impress both for good and ill, bringing back on its waves treasure-trove to be swallowed by the deep of the country, and often, too, carrying on its surface some of the urban community's slime and filth.

On this May evening Champlain's Road stretched across the valley, not white and hard, but softened by the rain, and looking like a great broad lilac ribbon, set here and there with sparkling jewels made by the pools of water. The sun had slipped behind the cedars of the Long Hill and the valley was clothed in a wonderful combination of all shades of blue–the cloak Mother Nature so often throws round her shoulders after a shower. The towering elms, the glossy beeches, and the spreading maples, that grew on either side of the highway, were all bathed in the blue radiance. The old snake fences, smothered in raspberry and alder bushes, were a deep purple, and the white rapture of the cherry-trees and the orchards by the farm-houses had turned a delicate lilac. The valley had taken on heaven's own blue this evening, and smiled back at the gleaming skies with something of their own beauty.

On every side the robins shouted their joy from the treetops, the bob-o'-links tinkled their fairy bells as they wheeled above the clover-fields; and from the dainty line of white-stemmed birches that guarded the stream came the mingled even-song of the frogs and the veeries.

There was but one pedestrian on Champlain's Road this quiet evening. This was a small person who had just emerged from a farm gate at the foot of the Long Hill. Back from the gate stood an old farm-house and at its door a woman was standing. She was knitting a long gray sock, holding her ball under her arm, knitting swiftly, even while her eyes followed lovingly the little figure skipping along the lavender road. The soft blue light touched her silver hair and her white apron and turned the gray homespun dress into a royal robe of purple worthy of the owner's wearing. The little figure danced out of sight behind a clump of cedars and the woman turned from the doorway with a tender smile that ended in a sigh. One evening her own little girl had passed down the lane and along Champlain's Road to the churchyard beyond the hills, and this little one filled somewhat the dreary space in the mother's heart.

Meanwhile, the one pedestrian on the lavender road was going swiftly on. She was clothed in a blue checked pinafore and a sunbonnet of the same material, which absorbed the blue light and glowed with vivid color. Beneath the sunbonnet hung a long heavy braid of shiny brown hair, with a reddish streak down the middle of it. The pinafore was tucked up round the owner's waist to form a bag, in which were carried a pair of stockings and strong, copper-toed boots, three very wrinkled apples, a bunch of wilted marigolds, and a cake of maple-sugar. The small person clutched this bundle in her arms and held up her short skirts in a highly improper manner, while she went splashing through the puddles singing a loud and riotous song.

This was Elizabeth. And this unseemly manner of peregrination displayed just one of Elizabeth's trying peculiarities. For four years she had been faithfully taught that little girls should never go barefoot outside their own gardens, and that when they were on the public highway they must walk quietly and properly on the grass by the roadside. When she remembered, Elizabeth strove to conform to the laws of home and social usage, for she was very docile by nature; but then Elizabeth seldom remembered. When she did, it was only to recall hopelessly her aunt's many times reiterated statement that Lizzie had the wild streak of the MacDuffs in her, and what could you expect? The Gordon family had generally been genteel enough to keep this objectionable MacDuff connection hidden, but occasionally it came out in red hair, deep gray eyes, and a wild, erratic disposition. To be sure, little Elizabeth's hair was not red, but a deep nut-brown, shading to rich yellow at the ends, where it curled upwards. But down the middle of her heavy brown braid ran a thick strand of reddish gold, quite enough to account for the vagaries of her behavior. And there was no doubt about Elizabeth's eyes–those unfathomable gray eyes that looked steel blue or soft gray or deep black, according to the owner's mood. Yes, Elizabeth had the two fatal badges of the wild MacDuffs, coupled with dear knows what inheritance from her mother's people, the fighting MacDonalds, who had been the scandal of the whole countryside in the early days.

Having heard all this many, many times from her aunt, Elizabeth had finally accepted the sad fact that she had "a wild streak" in her, just as she accepted the variegated color of her hair, not without much rebellion against her fate though, and many tears of repentance, and frequent solemn pledges to walk in unstreaked propriety for the rest of her days.

At other times she recklessly concluded that it was impossible to battle against destiny. For one never knew just how one was going to act. For a very chameleon was this strange Elizabeth, always the color of her surroundings. Being just ten-and-a-half, she would act with the wisdom of an ancient sage when in company with Mrs. MacAllister, and the foolishness of a spring lamb when left to gambol with her little brother. To-night her spirit had caught the joyous note of the wonderful spring evening, and she was like the valley, gay and sparkling and noisy with delight. Besides, this was the first time she had ever been allowed to go home alone from Mother MacAllister's, and the sense of freedom went to her head.

So, along the lavender road she skipped, holding her skirts very high, splashing mud over her pinafore and even her sunbonnet, and singing loudly:

"She's ower the border an' awa
Wi' Jock o' Hazeldean!"

Mr. MacAllister had sung this song after supper, between the puffs of his pipe, as he sat on the wash bench by the door, and Mother MacAllister had told them the story, as she and Elizabeth washed up the dishes, the story of the lady of high degree who had cast aside wealth and noble lovers to hie awa wi' Jock o' Hazeldean.

Charles Stuart, who was Mother MacAllister's really, truly child, had interrupted to inquire what "ower the border an' awa'" meant, and Elizabeth had felt impatient enough to slap him had she dared. Charles Stuart was very stupid about some things, though he could spell and always got the right answer to a sum in school. Elizabeth knew exactly what it meant, though she could not have explained. It was just what she was doing now, as she leaped from pool to pool with her skirts and her pinafore in a string about her waist–fleeing in ecstasy away, away, to that far-off undiscovered country of dreams, "Ower the border."

Her joyous abandon was rudely checked. There was a quick splash from a pool not a yard ahead of her, where a stone hit the water sharply. Elizabeth stopped in alarm. She whirled round towards the low fence bordering the highway. Its innocent appearance, all draped in woodbine and fringed with alder and raspberry bushes, did not deceive her in the least. "You're a nasty, mean, mean boy, Charles Stuart MacAllister!" she cried indignantly to the thickest clump of alders. She dropped her dress and stepped to the grassy side of the road, filled with rage. Of course it was Charles Stuart. He was always in the direction whence stones and abuse came. It had ever seemed to Elizabeth the strangest injustice that a dear, lovely lady like Mother MacAllister should have been so shabbily treated both in the quantity and quality of the family Providence had given her. For while there were eight Gordons, and every one of them fairly nice at times, there was but one single solitary MacAllister, and a boy at that; yes, and sometimes the very nastiest boy that went to Forest Glen School!

She walked along with a haughtiness her Aunt Margaret might have envied and took not the smallest notice when a little turbulent fox-terrier, with many squeaks and squirms, wriggled through a hole in the fence and came bounding towards her. And she turned her head and gazed absorbedly across the fields when it was followed by a boy who pitched himself over the fence and crossed to her side.

"Hello, Lizzie!" he cried, his brown eyes dancing in his brown face in the friendliest manner. "Mother says I've got to see you home."

Elizabeth's head went higher. She fixed her eyes on the line of white-stemmed birches that guarded the stream. Neither did she deign to notice "Trip," who frisked and barked about her.

Charles Stuart came a step nearer and took hold of the long, heavy braid. "Mud-turtle, Lizzie!" he hissed. "Mud-turtle! Look out there! Your neck's gettin' that long you'll hit the telegraph wires in another minute."

Elizabeth's shoulders came up towards her ears with a quick, convulsive movement. Her dignity vanished. Her long neck, her long hair, her long fingers, and her gray eyes were features over which much teasing had made her acutely sensitive.

She whirled round, made a slap at her tormentor, which he dodged, stumbled over Trip, who was always in the way, and fell full length upon the wet grass, scattering her treasures far and wide. Trip snatched up a boot and began worrying it; Charles Stuart shouted with laughter; and Elizabeth picked herself up, sank upon a stone, and began to cry.

The boy was all repentance immediately. He gathered up the apples, the stockings, the maple sugar, and even the faded bunch of marigolds, rescued the boot from Trip, and handed them all to their owner, remembering contritely how his mother had said he must be kind to little Lizzie on the way home and, above all things, not to make her cry.

Elizabeth received her treasures with averted face. "I wish you'd go back home and leave me alone," she wailed, as she wiped away her tears with the muddy skirt of her pinafore.

"Well, I'd like to," said Charles Stuart honestly; "but mother said I'd got to see you home. Hurrah, Lizzie! Aw, come on, I won't tease you any more."

So Elizabeth rose, not without much of the dignity of a broken heart in her attitude, and walked forward in a very stately fashion indeed.

Charles Stuart did his best to make amends. He pointed out the oriole's little cradle that swung from the elm bough high above their heads. He showed her the ground-hogs' hole beside the hollow stump and the wasps' nest in the fence corner, until at last friendly relations were once more established.

They walked along side-by-side: he, splashing through the blue rainpools; she, envious and proper, stepping over the soft, wet grass. She was slightly disconcerted, too; for a Charles Stuart that walked beside you on the public highway, and did not run and hide nor throw stones, nor even pull your hair, was something to raise even more apprehension than when he behaved naturally.

But the young man was really trying to atone for his sins, for a reason Elizabeth could never have guessed, and he now sidled up to her holding something in his hand.

"Say, Lizzie?"

"What?"

"Don't you want this?" He handed her, with an embarrassed attempt at nonchalance, a very sticky little candy tablet. It was pretty and pink and had some red printing on it. Elizabeth took it, quite overwhelmed with surprise and gratitude. She was just about to put it into her mouth when she thought of Jamie. The little brother loved sweeties so. Of course she had saved her cake of maple sugar for him, all but one tiny bite; but a pink candy was ever so much better. With a hasty "thanks," she slipped it into her pinafore with her other treasures.

Charles Stuart looked disappointed. He picked up some stones, shied one at the telegraph wires, and another at the green glass fixture at the top of the pole. This last proceeding caused Elizabeth to scream and beseech him to stop. For Malcolm had said that a dreadful man would come out from town and put you in jail if you committed this crime. Charles Stuart, having accomplished his purpose in fixing Elizabeth's attention upon himself once more, desisted, and cast his last stone with a crash into the raspberry bushes by the roadside.

"Ain't you goin' to read it?" he asked, with his back towards her.

"Read what, the candy?"

"O' course."

Elizabeth paused and rummaged in her pinafore. She bundled shoes and stockings aside and fished out the little pink tablet. The legend, inscribed in red letters, was, "Be my girl." She read it aloud quite impersonally. She did not object to it, for fear of hurting Charles Stuart's feelings; but she wished that it had been, "Be my boy," instead. It would have been so appropriate for Jamie. For every day she bribed and coaxed him to be "Diddy's boy," in preference to Mary's or Jean's or even Annie's.

Charles Stuart waited for some comment, feeling that Elizabeth was certainly very dull. No wonder she could never get a sum right at school, and was always foot of the spelling class. He flung another stone to relieve his feelings; this time in the direction of a pair of chiming bob-o'-links that, far over the clover-meadow, went up and down in an airy dance. He felt he must put forth another effort to make his position clear to Elizabeth's dull wits.

"Say, Lizzie, did anybody ever–ever see you home before?"

Elizabeth stared. Surely Charles Stuart must be wandering in his mind, for how could he help knowing that his mother or father or Long Pete Fowler, the hired man, often accompanied indeed by Charles Stuart himself, had always, heretofore, seen her home?

"Of course," she answered wonderingly. "But I'm a big girl now, I'm going on eleven, and I'm too old to have anybody see me home."

This was worse than ever. Charles Stuart looked at her in perplexity. Then he came straight to the point in the wise old way.

"Say, Lizzie, I think you're the nicest girl in all Forest Glen School."

Elizabeth stared again; not so much at the remark, though it was extremely absurd, for Charles Stuart hated all girls, as at his uncomfortable subdued manner, which she now began to notice. She felt vaguely sorry for him. Charles Stuart never acted like that unless his father had been giving him a scolding. Her sympathy made her responsive.

"Do you?" she cried. "Oh, I'm so glad, Charles Stuart."

This was making fine progress. The young man looked vastly encouraged.

"I'm going away to the High School, in Cheemaun, if I pass next summer," he said, with not so much irrelevance as might appear.

Elizabeth was all interest. To "pass" and go to the High School in the neighboring town was the grand ambition of every boy and girl in Forest Glen School.

"Oh, are you, Charles Stuart? Maybe John is, too."

"Yes." He was getting on famously now. "Father says I can. And I'm going to college after."

"And what'll you be?" asked Elizabeth admiringly.

"I'm not sure," said Charles Stuart grandly. "Mother wants me to be a minister, but I think I'd rather be a horse-doctor."

Elizabeth looked dubious. She did not like to differ from Mother MacAllister, but she could not see how it would be possible to make anything like a minister out of such an uncomfortable, hair-pulling stone-thrower as Charles Stuart.

"You'd best be a horse-doctor, Charles Stuart," she advised wisely. After all, that was a very noble calling, Elizabeth felt. Once a horse-doctor had come out from town to Rosie Carrick's place and Rosie's pussy had been sick, and he had given it medicine which cured it. She related the incident for Charles Stuart's encouragement, but he did not seem very favorably impressed. Pulling pussy-cats' tails was more in Charles Stuart's line. He began to show leanings towards the ministry.

"Mother says it's a grander thing to be a minister than anything else in the world," he asserted. "But you have to know an awful lot, I guess."

"And you have to be most awful good," said Elizabeth emphatically.

"Mother says you have to be most awful good no matter what you are," said Charles Stuart, with greater wisdom.

Elizabeth nodded; but she could not allow the ministry to be belittled.

"My father was nearly a minister once, but he said he wasn't good enough, and he's the very, very goodest man that ever lived."

"It'll be easy to be good when we're grown up," said Charles Stuart.

"Oh, yes, ever so easy," said Elizabeth comfortably.

"And, say–Lizzie."

"What?"

Charles Stuart was looking embarrassed again. "I'm–I'm nearly twelve, you know."

They had reached the big gate between the willows by this time. Elizabeth flung her treasure trove upon the grass and, springing upon the gate, swung out on to the road again.

"Well, I know that," she said, wondering what such gratuitous information had to do either with being a minister or riding a gate, "and I'm going on eleven."

Charles Stuart mounted on the other side and swung, too. It was rather childish, but he was bound to be agreeable until he got something off his mind.

"Well, you know—when I'm done going to college, and we've grown up we'll have to get married, you and me. Long Pete Fowler said so."

Elizabeth did not look at all impressed. Such a proposition did not appeal to her. It was too vague and intangible. People all got married, of course, some day, but not until you were very, very old and staid, and all the joy of life had departed from it—just as everybody died some day. But, though death was inevitable, Elizabeth did not borrow trouble from that solemn fact. Besides, she had far other and greater ambitions than were dreamed of in Charles Stuart's philosophy. She was going to be grand and famous some day—just how, Elizabeth had not yet decided. One day she would be a great artist, the next a missionary in darkest Africa. But Joan of Arc's life appealed to her most strongly, and oftenest her dreams pictured herself clad in flashing armor, mounted on a prancing charger, and leading an army of brave Canadians to trample right over the United States.

So there was nothing very alluring in the prospect of exchanging all this to settle down with Charles Stuart, even though one would be living with dear Mother MacAllister, with whom one was always happy. She looked at Charles Stuart, about to speak out her disdain, when the expression of his face suddenly checked her. Even as a child Elizabeth had a marvelous intuition, which told her when another's feelings were in danger of being hurt. It gave her a strange, quite unacknowledged feeling that she was far older and wiser than the children she played with. There was always an inner self sitting in judgment on all childishness, even when she was on the highroad to every sort of nonsense by way of the wild streak.

That inner self spoke now. It said that Charles Stuart was very young and silly, but he was also very nervous, and she must not hurt him. She must pretend that she thought him very wise. It would not be very wicked, for was she not always pretending? When Jamie said, "Be a bear, Diddy," or "Be a bogey-man," Elizabeth would go down on her knees and growl and roar, or pull her hair over her face, make goggle-eyes, and hop madly about until the little brother was screaming with ecstatic terror. So when Charles Stuart said, "We'll get married," it required less effort to comply than to be a bogey-man, and she nodded radiantly, and said, "All right."

Charles Stuart looked equally radiant, and they swung back and forth smiling at each other over the top of the gate. Elizabeth began to think it would not be such a bad bargain after all. If Charles Stuart was really going to like her, how much happier life would be! For, of course, he would never plot with John to run away from her any more, and they three would play one perpetual game of ball for ever and ever.

They had swung some moments in happy silence when Charles Stuart, with masculine obtuseness, made a blunder that shattered the airy fabric of their dream. He had been looking down into Elizabeth's deep eyes, and exclaimed in honest surprise:

"Say, Lizzie, your eyes are green, I do declare!"

Elizabeth's face turned crimson. To accuse her of having black eyes, as many people did by lamplight, was horrid, horrid mean; to say her eyes were gray was a deadly insult. But to be told they were green! She had only a minute before delicately spared Charles Stuart's feelings, and now he had turned and trampled upon her most tender sensibilities.

"They're not! They're not!" she cried indignantly. "They're blue, and I won't play with you ever again, Charles Stuart MacAllister, you nasty, nasty boy!"

She flung down off the gate and swept up her treasures from the wet grass. The sight of her roused all Charles Stuart's desire to tease. She really looked so funny snatching up a shoe or stocking and dropping it again in her wrath, while Trip grabbed everything she dropped and shook it madly. Charles Stuart jumped from the gate and began imitating her, catching up a stone, letting it fall, with a shriek and crying loudly at the top of his voice, while Trip, enjoying the noise and commotion, went round and round after his tail just because he could think of nothing else to do.

This was too much for Elizabeth. Charles Stuart was heaping insult upon insult. She got the last article of her bundle crushed into her pinafore, and as the boy, going through the same motions, raised his head, she gave him a sounding slap in the face, turned, darted through the gate, and went raging down the lane, dropping a shoe, a stocking, an apple, or a piece of maple sugar at every bound. She was blinded with tears and choking with grief and anger—anger that Charles Stuart should have cajoled her into thinking he intended to be nice to her, and grief that she could have been so cruel. Oh, what a terrible blow she had struck! Her hand tingled from it yet. It must have hurt poor Charles Stuart dreadfully, and after such conduct she could never hope to be a lady. Her aunt would be disgraced, and that wonderful lady, whose name she bore, would never come to see her. She was an outcast whom nobody loved, for not even Mother MacAllister could like her now!

She could not go home, so she flung herself down upon the wet grass in a corner of the lane and wept bitterly. It was always so with Elizabeth. She was up in the clouds one moment and down in the depths the next. Her heart was breaking over the injury she had done. For the first time in her life she experienced a feeling of warm regard towards Charles Stuart, simply because she had hurt him.

She stopped sobbing, and, raising herself from the ground, peeped out through her tears to see if he were in sight. Perhaps he was stunned by the blow and was lying beneath the gate. She could see no sign of him and her heart stood still with dread. She had been vaguely conscious of joyous shouts and cries from the field behind the house and had heard the rifle-crack of a baseball against the bat, telling that there was a game in progress. She was now made aware that the joyous shouts were growing into a noisy clamor of welcome. Above the din she could hear John's roar: "Charles Stuart on our side! I bar Charles Stuart!" And there was her false lover speeding across the field towards her home, Trip at his heels! Elizabeth arose from the ground, dry-eyed and indignant. She wished she had hit him harder. Charles Stuart MacAllister was without doubt the horridest, horridest boy that ever lived and she would never speak to him again—no, not if she lived to be two hundred and went over to his place every Saturday for a thousand years. Just see if she would!

As she passed an alder clump and caught a glimpse of her aunt standing near the garden gate talking with Mr. Coulson, Elizabeth became suddenly overwhelmed with a sense of her shoeless and disheveled condition. She knew that, while untidy hair and a dirty pinafore were extremely reprehensible, bare feet put one quite beyond the possibility of being genteel. That word "genteel" had become the shibboleth of the Gordon family in the last four years. It was poor Elizabeth's chief burden in life. For how could anyone hope to live up to it when she was possessed of a wild streak?

Fortunately, her aunt was in deep conversation with Mr. Coulson, and had not spied her. She dropped upon the grass, safely hidden by the alders, and began to drag her damp stockings over her muddy feet. There would arise dire consequences from this later, but Elizabeth found the evil of the hour sufficient unto it and never added the troubles of the future. As she sat thus busily engaged, she was startled by the sound of footsteps and drew back further behind her flowery screen. The next moment Mr. Coulson strode rapidly past her and up the lane without glancing to the right or left. Elizabeth stared after him. He had passed so close she might have touched him, and how pale and angry he looked! The schoolmaster was one of the objects upon which Elizabeth showered the wealth of her devotion, and she was vaguely disturbed for him. He looked just as if he had been whipping someone in school. Then her own uncomfortable condition obtruded itself once more, and she arose. She straightened her sunbonnet, smoothed down her crumpled skirts and slowly and fearfully took her way down the lane. She dreaded to meet her aunt, knowing by sad experience that as soon as that lady's eye fell upon her, not only would all the misdemeanors of which she was conscious appear silhouetted against Miss Gordon's perfection, but dozens of unsuspected sins would spring to light and stand out black in the glare.

She peeped through the tangle of alders and saw that Aunt Margaret was now talking to Annie, with her back to the lane, and the same instant she spied a way of escape. The lane ran straight past the big stone house and down to the line of birches that bordered the stream, forming the road by which Mr. MacAllister reached his old mill, lying away down there in the hollow. Down in the lower part of the lane where the birches grew, William Gordon was wont to walk in the evenings, and here Elizabeth, with infinite relief, spied him just coming into view from beyond a curve. He was walking slowly with bent head, his long, thin hands clasped behind him. At his side was a young man, of medium height, thick-set, and powerful-looking. This was Mr. Tom Teeter, who worked the farm upon which The Dale stood, and lived only a few hundred yards from the Gordons. Mr. Teeter was an Irishman, with a fine gift for speech-making. He was much sought after, for tea-meetings and during political campaigns, and had won the proud alliterative name of Oro's Orator. Tom was now holding forth hotly upon the "onparalleled rascality and treachersome villainousness" of the Opposition in the Ontario Legislature.

Elizabeth, her eyes alight, ran swiftly past the gate towards her father. She loved each member of her family with all the might of her passionate heart; but she held for her father an especially tender regard. Her love for him had in it something of the sacred grief that clung about the memory of her dead mother, something too of mother-love itself, felt in a longing to comfort and protect him. The stoop of his thin shoulders, the silvering hair on his bowed head, and the sound of his gentle voice all appealed to Elizabeth's heart in the same way as when Jamie cried from a hurt. Whenever he looked unusually sad and abstracted, his little daughter yearned to fling her arms about his neck and pet and caress him. But Elizabeth knew better. Such conduct would be courting death by ridicule at the hands of the Gay Gordons.

She ran to him now, and, as there was only Tom Teeter to see, ventured to slip her hand into his as she walked by his side. Tom Teeter was the bosom friend of every young Gordon, and he pulled her sunbonnet and said:

"Hello, Lizzie! How's the wild streak behavin'?"

Her father looked down at her, apparently just conscious of her presence. His eyes brightened.

"Well, well, little 'Lizbeth," he said. "And where have you been?"

"Over to Mother MacAllister's. And look, I've got three apples and some maple sugar, and there's a piece of it for you, father, and I found the marigolds at the crick."

"Well, well, yes, yes." He seemed suddenly to remember something. "What was it your aunt was saying? Oh, yes, that I must go to the gate and meet you. And here you are!"

Elizabeth beamed. "Come and tell her we're home then," she said warily; and thus fortified, but still fearful, she walked slowly up the garden path to the front door, where Aunt Margaret was standing.

But to Elizabeth's amazement and infinite relief, Aunt Margaret was all smiles and graciousness, even to Tom Teeter. She took no notice of her niece's disheveled appearance, but said cordially:

"Run away in, Elizabeth. Sarah Emily has come back, and she has some news for you. I hope it will help to make you a very good, thankful little girl."

Entranced at this marvelous escape, Elizabeth flew through the old echoing hall and bounded wildly into the kitchen. She welcomed Sarah Emily rapturously, listened with wonder and awe to the news that the fairy god-mother was no dream after all, but was really and truly coming to see her, and finally went shrieking out to join in the game of ball, on Charles Stuart's side, too, all forgetful that not ten minutes before she had vowed against him an undying enmity.

CHAPTER III
A GENTEEL SABBATH

Elizabeth arose early the next morning, feeling at peace with all the world. For the first time in her life she felt herself an important member of the family. Her aunt had distinguished her by special friendly notice, and had omitted to scold her when she went to bed the night before. Besides, it was Sunday, and on the first day of the week she almost always escaped disaster. First, her aunt was more genial on Sunday, because the family was on its best behavior that day, and came a little nearer to being genteel. Then Elizabeth was clothed in a long, spotlessly clean, dun-colored pinafore, starched to the extremity of discomfort, and her spirits, always colored by her surroundings, were also subdued and confined.

The Gordons assembled for breakfast early on Sunday morning. Miss Gordon saw that the Sabbath was strictly kept, but she believed the idea of rest might be carried to indulgence, especially with young people. So, on this particular morning, breakfast was at the usual hour. Indeed, it was a little early, owing to the fact that Sarah Emily, rejoiced at her reunion with the family, had arisen betimes and broken the Sabbath by making a fine batch of breakfast biscuits. Sarah Emily always sang at her work and had aroused the household, and brought down the stern displeasure of Miss Gordon, who forbade the unholy viands to be brought to the table.

The young Gordons assembled, sniffing hungrily and regretfully at the pleasant odor. Sarah Emily caught their glances and made a sympathetic grimace.

Mary giggled, but Elizabeth looked severe. She was in her best Sabbath mood and felt that Sarah Emily was not at all genteel, nor Mary either. It really gave one such a nice feeling to know one was genteel. Involuntarily she glanced at her aunt for approbation. But Aunt Margaret was looking at Annie, with a strange expression in her eyes, an almost apologetic look Elizabeth would have thought if Aunt Margaret could ever have been in such a mood. But that was quite impossible with one who was always right. She was looking particularly handsome this morning in her black silk dress, with her jet earrings, and the knot of white lace at her throat. Elizabeth gazed at her in profound admiration, and then at Annie with some anxiety. Annie was looking pale this morning. Elizabeth wished she had not given away all her maple sugar to the little boys last night; a bite might have been such a comfort to poor Annie, and she was looking sadly in need of comfort.

When the plates of oatmeal porridge and the big pile of bread-and-butter had disappeared, Annie handed her father his Bible and psalm-book and they all joined in family worship. The little ceremony opened with the singing of a paraphrase:

"O God of Bethel, by whose Hand
Thy people still are fed."

The windows were open and the breath of the apple-blossoms came floating in. The bees, droning over the honey-suckle in the garden below, and the song sparrow on the cherry-bough above, both joined in the hymn to the great Father who had made the beautiful world.

Then Mr. Gordon read a chapter; a wonderful chapter, Elizabeth felt. She was in perfect accord with the beauty and peace of the Sabbath Day and every word went to her heart:

"The wilderness and the solitary place shall be glad for them; and the desert shall rejoice and blossom as the rose. It shall blossom abundantly, and rejoice even with joy and singing. The glory of Lebanon shall be given unto it, the excellency of Carmel and Sharon——"

Elizabeth had no idea of its meaning, but its beauty, with some vague hint of its eternal promise of love and joy, made her child's heart swell. She was dismayed to feel her eyes beginning to smart with the rising tears. She did not guess why, but she could have cried out with both joy and pain at the majestic triumph of the close:

"And the ransomed of the Lord shall return and come to Zion with songs and everlasting joy upon their heads. They shall obtain joy and gladness, and sorrow and sighing shall flee away."

She struggled with her tears. If John should see them! He would wonder why she was crying, and she could never tell him. John would not understand. That was the tragedy of Elizabeth's life. One could never tell things, for nobody understood.

She was relieved when they knelt in prayer and she could hide her tears in a corner of the old sofa. Prayers were very much longer on Sundays than on other mornings, but, though the boys might fidget a little, the most active member of the family never moved. Elizabeth's soul was carried away far above any bodily discomfort. But not even the smallest Gordon made a sound. There had been a dreadful day once when Jamie and Archie, kneeling at one chair with their heads together, had been caught red-handed playing "Put your finger in the crow's nest"; but since then their aunt had knelt between them and the crime had not been repeated.

Prayers ended, and the few household duties attended to, Mr. Gordon shut himself in his study, and the children sat out on the side-porch and studied their Sunday-school lesson, their catechism, and their portion of the 119th Psalm, which Miss Gordon had given them to memorize.

Elizabeth had no trouble with her Golden Text or the Psalm, but the catechism was an insupportable burden. She was always appearing with it before her aunt, certain she could "say it now," only to turn away in disgrace. She sat on the green bench beside John and droned over her allotted portion. John was far ahead wrestling with What is required in the commandments, while poor Elizabeth plodded behind, struggling with the question as to Wherein consisted the sinfulness of that estate whereinto man fell. She rhymed over the profound words in a meaningless jargon:

"The sinfulness of that estate whereunto man fell, consists in the guilt of Adam's first sin, the want of original righteousness, and the corruption of his whole nature, which is commonly called original sin, together with all actual transgressions which proceed from it."

She strove to keep her mind upon it, but the exaltation of the prayer-time had passed, and the vision of Mrs. Jarvis obtruded itself on her Sabbath thoughts. She drove it away–as with tightly-shut eyes and wrinkled brow and swaying body she attempted to get through the answer unaided. But she stuck fast at "the want of original righteousness" and again at "original sin," and was stumbling blindly over "all actual transgressions" when there came a wicked whisper in her ear.

"Lizzie," hissed John, "there's 'The Rowdy'!"

Elizabeth's eyes flew open, and the sinfulness of man's estate flew away. John had turned his grave face towards her, lit up with a quick smile. Elizabeth flashed back at him the same smile, a sudden gleam of white even teeth in a rather generous red mouth. Brother and sister were very much alike in their smiles, but only here, for John's face was solemn almost to dourness, while Elizabeth's countenance was full of light and animation.

"The Rowdy" was enough to provoke laughter even on the Sabbath and under Aunt Margaret's nose. He was the robin whose chief shouting-place was the hawthorn bush in the lane. John and Elizabeth had so named him because he always made such a noise, leaping about and calling "Hi, Hi! Whee! Whoo–Hoo!" in a most rowdy manner indeed.

They had named many other familiar birds in The Dale fields that spring, and now Elizabeth gave a significant nod towards the orchard to announce the song of another favorite. This robin sang from the top of the big duchess tree that peeped over the wall into the front garden. His was a plaintive, quiet song, quite unlike The Rowdy's. They had noticed the pathetic little chant one evening when the schoolmaster sat beside Annie on the front porch. Mr. Coulson had remarked that there was a robin in the orchard who was singing the anthem of the Exile of Erin. But John declared in private to Elizabeth that it wasn't anything of the kind. Anyone could hear he was saying "Oh, wirra-wurra! Wirra-wurra!" just the way old Mrs. Teeter did when she recounted her troubles of the early pioneer days, or when Oro's Orator had been fighting again. So to John and Elizabeth the robin of the duchess tree was known as "Granny Teeter." They listened to him now, complaining away to the pink apple-blossoms; and, knowing it was very wicked and dangerous to laugh just then, they held themselves in convulsions of silent mirth.

Elizabeth forgot all about the sinfulness of man's estate as well as the gorgeousness of Mrs. Jarvis's in listening for sounds of other old friends. There was a pair of meadow larks that had their nest in the pasture field just on the other side of the lane, and now one of them was mounted in his favorite elm, pouring forth his delicious notes in a descending scale of sweetness: "Dear, hear, I am near." Farther down, near the line of birches, in a feathery larch tree, sang a peculiar song sparrow, who pounded four times on a loud silver bell to attract attention before he started his little melody. Then there was a crowd of jolly bob-o'-links over yonder in the clover-meadow who danced and trilled, and a pair of blue-birds in the orchard who talked to each other in sweet, soft notes. There was a loud and joyous oriole, proud of his golden coat, blowing up his ringing little trumpet from the pine tree near the gate, and ever so many flickers, all gorgeously dressed in red and yellow and every color their gaudy taste could suggest, each with his little box of money, Elizabeth explained, which he rattled noisily, just to attract attention when he couldn't sing. But the favorite was a gray cat-bird that sang from the bass-wood tree at the back of the vegetable garden. They liked him best, because he was so naughty and badly behaved, always sneaking round the backyard, and never coming out where there was an audience, as The Rowdy did. And then he could beat everybody, and at his own song, too! He was at them all now, one after the other—robin, song sparrow, oriole, flicker, everything—with a medley of trills and variations worked in just to show that he had a whole lot of music of his own if he only cared to use it.

John's silent laughter was quite safe, but Elizabeth's was of the explosive variety. A chuckle escaped which caused Aunt Margaret to look up from her Sunday-school paper, and the two culprits immediately dived back to their tasks. Elizabeth felt how wicked she was to have allowed her thoughts to wander thus, and for a time gave such good attention to her question that she arrived at original sin with only two slips.

But Mrs. Jarvis came back again, arrayed in all the grandeur in which Elizabeth's imagination always clothed her. She planned how she would act when that great lady came. She would walk very slowly and solemnly into the parlor, just the way Aunt Margaret did, and bow very gravely. Then she would say those French words Jean always used since she had been attending the High School in Cheemaun, "Commay voo, porty voo." That was French for "Good afternoon, Mrs. Jarvis"; and of course Mrs. Jarvis would know French, and be very much impressed. She strove to weave a pious thread of catechism into the wicked fabric of her thoughts—"the sinfulness of that estate whereunto man fell"—perhaps Mrs. Jarvis would ask her to go for a walk with her down the lane, or even a drive in her carriage—"consists in the guilt of Adam's first sin"—of course she would talk only of books, and not let her see the playhouse she and Mary had made in the lane. That was very childish. She would tell how she had read "The Vicar of Wakefield" and "Old Mortality"—of course father had read them to her, but it was all the same thing—and "Hiawatha" and "The Lamplighter"—"the want of original corruption and the righteousness of his whole nature." And surely Mrs. Jarvis would think she was genteel and know that the wild streak had completely disappeared—"together with all actual transgressions which proceed from it." Elizabeth then and there solemnly vowed that she would neither run nor jump, nor climb a fence, not even the little low one between their pasture-field and Tom Teeter's, until Mrs. Jarvis's coming.

And so the morning passed slowly in a struggle between a restless body, a restless mind, and a restless soul, all tending in different directions, and at last they stood in a row before their aunt to recite their morning's task. Even little Jamie had his verse of Scripture to lisp, and was patted on the head when he stammered out:

"De people dat sat in dawkness saw a dwate night."

Everyone acquitted himself well except Elizabeth. The catechism refused to disentangle itself from the jumble of bird-voices and dream-voices with which it was mixed; and she went out to dinner with hanging head and tear-dimmed eyes.

The light lunch of cold boiled beef and potatoes was soon disposed of, and then the hour for starting to Sunday school had arrived, bringing with it a great relief, and making Elizabeth completely forget her troubles.

The Gordons had an old speckled gray horse and a queer basket phaeton, left by the eccentric Englishman in The Dale stables years before. Mr. Gordon used them to convey him to the town hall, some miles distant, where the township council meetings were held, but Miss Gordon always drove to church in this family carriage, accompanied by Malcolm, and with little Jamie on her knee, while the remainder of the family walked.

The church, like the school, lay a couple of miles south of The Dale, away at the other side of a great hill. There were two roads leading thither. The one used by the school children on week-days was called the Short Cut. It ran down The Dale lane, crossed the pond beside MacAllister's mill, went up the opposite bank, over a wild half-cleared stretch of land called The Slash, through old Sandy McLachlan's wood, and by way of his rickety gate out on to the public highway a few yards from the school. It was much shorter this way than going "down the line," though strange to say it took far longer to traverse it on a schoolday, for it was a very enjoyable road indeed, from which one was ever making side excursions after berries or nuts or wild grapes, and which admitted of endless ways of beguiling dull time, and rendering oneself late for school.

For various reasons the church-going population took to the public highway on Sabbaths. Those who drove went this way from necessity, and those who didn't went because they were always picked up before they had gone half a mile. Besides, parents had long since learned that Sabbath clothes as well as Sabbath decorum were apt to suffer from the conveniences of the Short Cut.

William Gordon alone took this solitary road on Sabbath afternoons, for he loved the loneliness and quiet of the woods. This arrangement suited everyone except Elizabeth. Her heart always suffered a pang as they all turned up the lane together, and her father went away alone in the opposite direction. Once she had begged so hard to accompany him that he had yielded, and she had walked by his side, holding his hand, in silent sympathy, all the way over the sunny fields and through the cool green shadows of the woods. She had been quiet and good and he had said she was his little comforter, but Elizabeth had never gone again. It was not that she had found the walk dull in comparison to the companionship of the regular highway, for Elizabeth would have walked through a fiery furnace with her father in preference to any other road. But that wise older self had told her that her father preferred to be alone. She could not have told how she knew, but she was seldom mistaken in her intuition and followed it. And so, though it wrung her heart to see him go alone, she merely watched him with loving eyes, until his bowed head and thin, stooped shoulders disappeared from view in the willowy ravine.

Those who walked started only a few minutes before the phaeton, for if they were not picked up by Martin's big double buggy on the Champlain Road, then the MacAllisters would take them in at the corner, or they would be gathered to the bosoms of the Wully Johnstones before they had gone many rods down the line.

The Martins were a trifle late to-day and, to Elizabeth's joy, they reached the corner where four great elms stretched out their sweeping arms to each other just as MacAllister's ample three-seated buggy came lumbering along. Charles Stuart was there on the front seat beside his father, to be sure; but Mother MacAllister was in the back seat alone. The girls climbed in, Sarah Emily and all, and Archie and John took their places in Wully Johnstone's vehicle that had just emerged from their lane on to the public highway.

Elizabeth sat in her favorite place, close up to Mother MacAllister. At first she decided she would not speak to Charles Stuart, nor look near him. Then, recalling her undignified conduct in the ball game with him, she felt ashamed. It would be no use to act haughtily now, she reflected with a sigh. "I wish I hadn't forgotten," she said to herself. "It's so much easier to forget than forgive." She finally decided to treat Charles Stuart politely but distantly. She must let him see that he had behaved very badly indeed and that, though she might be kind and forgiving, all was over between them.

Just then Charles Stuart turned in his seat and whispered, "Look, Lizzie, look at Trip!"

Elizabeth turned in the direction he indicated. Trip had as usual been forbidden to follow the family to church, but there he was trotting along the roadside, stopping every now and then to lift up one paw and look inquiringly after his master. Elizabeth returned Charles Stuart's glance and they giggled.

Trip was really a very dear and funny little dog and she was very fond of him. To be sure, he was often wild and bad just like Charles Stuart, but then he was so neat and cute and frisky and altogether lovable. He had a cunning face, queerly marked. Round one eye was a large black patch, which gave him a disreputable air, and his habit of putting his little head on one side and looking supernaturally wise, just as though he could not see out of the bad black eye, further emphasized his naughty appearance. He was the noisiest thing of his size that could be found too. He could raise more row over a groundhog's hole, Tom Teeter said, than an army would over the discovery of an ambushed enemy. But to-day he was trotting meekly by the roadside, unmindful of chipmunks or swallows, for he knew right well he was doing wrong, and felt it was safer to be quiet.

"What'll you do with him?" asked Elizabeth anxiously.

"Wait till I catch him at the church. I'll make him scoot for home, you bet."

Elizabeth looked worried. "Oh, Charles Stuart, you won't hurt him?"

"I'll make him mind me, anyhow," said Charles Stuart firmly, and Elizabeth knew from past experience that it would be useless to interfere. Nevertheless, she felt very sorry for the little dog trotting along towards sure disappointment, and once again she quite forgot that she had intended to be cold and distant to Trip's master.

The old buggy rattled along through alternate sunshine and shade. Elizabeth soon forgot Trip and sat gazing off over hill and valley, not even hearing what Annie and Jean were telling Mother MacAllister about their new dresses. She was far above such thoughts. They had dipped down into the hollow where the stream flowed brown and cool beneath the bridge and had begun to climb the big hill where the view of the lovely green earth grew wider at each step. As they went up and up, the rolling hills seemed gradually to fall away, leaving a great space of deep blue sky touched with white bunches of dazzling clouds, for there always seemed more sky in Oro than in any other place. Now the long thread of the little river lying across the valley they had left, gleamed out blue and bright, now it disappeared, and before them another gleam of blue above far-off treetops shone forth, where Lake Simcoe lay sparkling in the sunlight. There was a little green island away out on its shining floor, and Elizabeth, with her dreamy eyes fixed upon it, thought it must look like Heaven. Then it all vanished, sinking like a beautiful dream-lake behind the treetops as they descended into the wooded valley. Elizabeth sighed happily. Here the air smelt cool and sweet, a mingling of damp earth, fragrant blossoms, running water, and wood-violets. The loveliness of the world of forest and sky would on ordinary occasions have driven her to wild abandon, sent her flying over fields and fences as far removed as possible from the genteel. But to-day was Sunday, and Mother MacAllister's arm was about her, and her spirit was filled with a great content.

She softly hummed the psalm with which they so often opened the church service down there in the hollow:

"O, come let us sing to the Lord,
To Him our voices raise.
With joyful noise let us the rock
Of our salvation praise."

And from the little basket phaeton behind, Miss Gordon, watching her charges, wondered what foolish thoughts were passing through Lizzie's flighty little head. It could not even approach her consciousness that the child's very soul was raised in rapturous worship.

Down the hill slowly wound the little procession. Elizabeth looked back. Behind her aunt was Martin's buggy. She could see Susie, one of her bosom-friends, on the front seat beside her father. But she did not wave her hand, because it was Sunday and Aunt Margaret was looking.

The little church in the hollow opposite the schoolhouse came in sight as they emerged from the woods at Sandy McLachlan's gate. It was a straight, clapboard structure, painted white, and standing in a forlorn-looking little field bare of trees. At one side stretched a long shed; at the other a grass-grown graveyard with leaning headstones. Inside there were also evidences that beauty had been sacrificed to economy in the building of Forest Glen Church. It was severely plain, with bare white walls, and a flat and smoky ceiling. There was a big oblong stove, the same shape as the church, at the end near the door, and a little organ and a pulpit-table on a small platform at the other end.

The only attempt at decoration was a big bunch of cherry blossoms someone had placed upon the organ, and four mottoes, worked in colored wools and framed in Lake Simcoe shells, which hung upon the walls.

Sunday school was held during the hour before the church service, the two congregations being very much alike. For an ideal state of affairs prevailed in Forest Glen. People did not send their children to Sunday school; they took them. Noah Clegg was the superintendent, and old Sandy McLachlan assistant. Noah operated at the end where the platform stood, while Sandy officiated at the door, ushering in the pupils, and often during the session, calling out instructions to Noah from his end of the building. Sandy's chief duty was to let people into the church and keep out the dogs, which like the people showed a laudable desire to attend divine service, especially in the winter. Sandy was armed with a big stick, and if any canine approached it, woe betide him. He and Noah Clegg were fast friends, so the double-headed organization worked well. Besides it was a necessity, for, while the Forest Glen church and its minister were Presbyterians, the Sunday school had gone far ahead of the times and was a shining example of what might be achieved by Church union. Noah Clegg was a Methodist, and Sandy McLachlan a pillar in the Presbyterian church. Old Silas Pratt, who was secretary-treasurer, and his daughter who was the organist, were close-communion Baptists, and there were several Anglicans who taught classes. All denominations had a voice in the managing of the Sunday school, but an hour later, when the Rev. Mr. Murray drove out from Cheemaun, the service took on a decidedly Presbyterian color.

When the buggies from The Dale valley rumbled up to the door, Sandy McLachlan was there, stick in hand. He was a queer but intelligent old man, who lived in a little house on the edge of the woods where the Short Cut met the highway. He was quite alone in the world, except for his little grand-daughter Eppie. Elizabeth knew Eppie well, as they were about the same age, and in the same class in Sunday school. As she alighted, she caught sight of the little girl in her coarse homespun dress and heavy boots hiding shyly behind her grandfather. At the sight of Elizabeth her face broke into a radiant smile. This was her one schoolmate who was always kind to poor Eppie.

But, as Elizabeth hurried up the steps towards her, she almost stumbled over Trip who came cowering behind. There were only two or three things in the world that Trip was afraid of, and Martin's big yellow dog was one of them. This terrible brute was slowly approaching with gleaming teeth, bristling yellow hair, and terrible inward rumblings. Scarcely knowing what she did, Elizabeth caught up the shivering little terrier and rolled him under her pinafore. She looked about distractedly for Charles Stuart, but both he and John had driven the horses to the sheds. Elizabeth slowly approached the door in an agony of uncertainty. It would be dreadfully wicked to take a dog into church, even if one could pass old Sandy, but it was impossible to leave Trip out there to be rent in pieces by those terrible yellow jaws. She pressed behind Sarah Emily, striving to hide the squirming little bundle beneath her pinafore.

"Are ye goin' to take him in?" whispered Eppie in dismay.

"I–I don't know what to do," faltered Elizabeth. "Brag 'll kill him if I leave him here–and your grandpa won't let him in."

"Grandaddy 'll not be saying anything," whispered Eppie. "Jist be slippin' in by."

As they approached the big knotted stick, Miss Gordon, leading Jamie by the hand, passed in ahead of them. Sandy lowered his stick and made a profound bow. He had been heard many times to declare that Miss Gordon was the finest lady he had seen since he left the Old Country, and he knew a lady when he saw one. Miss Gordon was aware of Sandy's opinion, and as usual bowed to him most graciously, and under cover of her entry Elizabeth, breathless with dread of the fell deed she was committing, slipped inside and up to her class seat, still holding the trembling little dog beneath her pinafore.

There were already three other little girls in the class, who all gazed in amazement at the new pupil. Rosie Carrick was there, Rosie of the pink cheeks and the long curls who was Elizabeth's dearest chum. Rosie giggled at the sight of Trip, and Elizabeth felt ashamed. Rosie was the dearest girl in the world, but she would giggle at anything, even a tragedy.

"Please, teacher," said Katie Price, "Lizzie Gordon's fetched a dog into Sunday school." Katie Price always told things, and Rosie stopped giggling and whispered, "Aw, tattle-tale!"

The teacher looked down at the little dog crouching between Elizabeth's feet and Eppie's. But she did not look the least bit cross. Martha Ellen never did. She giggled harder than Rosie, and exclaimed:

"Laws! Lizzie Gordon, where did you get him?" and then straightened her big hat and glanced across the aisle towards Mr. Coulson's class. Elizabeth looked up at her in overwhelming gratitude. She had always adored Martha Ellen Robertson, but never so much as at this minute.

"Please, teacher," she faltered, "Martin's Brag was going to eat him up. He's Charles Stuart MacAllister's dog, and I can give him to Charles Stuart when he comes."

"Oh, he ain't going' to hurt anybody; are you, little doggie?" whispered Martha Ellen good-naturedly. "He'll be all right so long as your grandpa don't see him; eh, Eppie?"

Eppie smiled shyly, and then Noah Clegg's squeaky boots sounded up the aisle and Sunday school had commenced.

Elizabeth drew a great sigh of relief, and glanced about her to see if anyone appeared conscious of the guilty secret squeezed between her and Eppie. But apparently no one was. All her own family, seated about the room, seemed absorbed in their own affairs.

Each of the Gordons had a place in Sunday school, either as pupil or teacher. Mr. Gordon taught the old folk who sat on the front row of seats. Every Sabbath they were there, their hard hands folded, their gray heads and toil-worn shoulders bent, listening while the man with the sad, sweet face told them stories of One whose hands had been rent, and whose shoulders had been bowed by the burden of their sin, and Who, could they but know Him, would, under all the labor and money-getting of their narrow lives, reveal to them life's true and noble meaning.

Miss Gordon taught the Young Ladies' Bible Class, her most critical pupil being Sarah Emily, whose presence there the good lady could not but regard as an intrusion. Annie taught a class of tiny girls near the front. She had taken her place beside them and sat with bent head and scarlet cheeks. Long ago she had learned that from her position it was very easy to catch the eye of the teacher of a class of big boys across the aisle. But one swift glance at him sitting up straight, haughty, and severe, convinced her she must never expect a kindly glance from that source again. She had bidden him go, because her aunt had commanded her, but, oh, how could she have suspected that he would obey? She sat in misery, striving desperately to keep back her tears.

Ordinarily Elizabeth would have noticed her sister's distressed face, but Trip once more claimed her attention. Just across the aisle was Old Silas Pratt's class, to which John and Charles Stuart belonged. They had just entered, and, with a squirm and a grunt, the little dog jerked himself free from the nervous grip of his preserver's feet, and darted across the aisle to his master. Charles Stuart shoved him under the scat, pinning him there with his legs, and looked inquiringly towards Elizabeth. Such an improper proceeding as this entirely suited Charles Stuart's ideas, but how Elizabeth came to be a partner in it was something he did not understand.

But Sunday school was opening, and, as no one seemed to have noticed the dog, Elizabeth, greatly relieved, gave her attention to duty. Noah Clegg had sent Wully Johnstone's Johnny to look up and down the line to see if there was anyone coming, and Johnny having reported no one but Silas Pratt's brindled cow, the service commenced.

"Now, boys and girls," said the superintendent, with a fine old London accent, "we'll sing 'ymn number fifty-four:

"There is a 'appy land
Far, far away."

Noah Clegg was a good little man, with a round, cheery face, iron-gray hair, and a short, stubby beard. He wore a shiny black suit, and his new Sabbath boots, which turned up at the toes like Venetian gondolas and sang like gondoliers. He held a stick in his hand, with which he beat time, and now gave the signal to the organist to commence.

Miss Lily Pratt struck up the tune, and the school arose.

"Now, boys an' girls, an' grown-ups, too," cried the superintendent, "sing up fine an' 'earty. This is a 'appy land we live in an' we're goin' to a 'appier one; an' this is a 'appy day, an' I 'ope the good Lord 'll give us all 'appy 'earts."

The school burst into song. Everyone, from old Granny Teeter in the front row to little Jamie Gordon down in the primary class, sang with all his might. Then there was an equally hearty reading of the Lesson. This was a short extract from the Scriptures printed on their little leaflets. Noah Clegg read one verse, while the school responded with the next in rumbling unison, after which each teacher turned to his class. This was simply done by reversing the seat ahead, the back of which turned over in the most accommodating manner, enabling the instructor to sit facing his pupils.

The Lesson was read again in class, verses were recited, and then the teacher asked questions or expounded the passage. A pleasant buzz and hum arose. Now and then a voice would rise above the general rumble, for old Silas Pratt was deaf, and Charles Stuart MacAllister and Wully Johnstone's Johnny, and John Gordon and all the other bad boys in his class, shouted their memory verses into his ear louder than even necessity demanded. Then Wully Johnstone had a powerful and penetrating voice and taught so loud that everyone in the church heard him even better than he heard his own teacher.

The little girls in Martha Ellen Robertson's class were always quiet and well-behaved, partly because it was the nature of all except Elizabeth, but mostly because they were very much in love with their teacher and intensely proud of her. They felt they had good reason to be, for was it not known all over the countryside that Martha Ellen was the best-dressed young lady outside Cheemaun. Every Sunday, Elizabeth and Rosie, squeezed up against the wall to avoid the drip from the coal-oil lamp above, sat waiting for her arrival and whispering eager speculations as to what new things she would wear. They were seldom disappointed, and to-day their teacher had never looked finer. She wore a brand new white hat, with a huge bunch of luscious red cherries nodding over the wide brim. To be sure, the white embroidered dress was last summer's freshly starched and ironed, but she had a new, broad blue satin ribbon round her slim waist and tied in a big bow at her side. Then Martha Ellen always wore gold bracelets and rings; and, what was her most attractive ornament to her class, a beautiful gold watch in her belt, attached to a long gold chain about her neck. The girls often saw the watch, much to their joy, for several times during Sunday school Martha Ellen would pull it out and say in surprise, "The time's not up yet," and would continue with the lesson.

Martha Ellen was always kind, and one of the few people with whom Elizabeth expanded. Elizabeth was often wild and foolish in school, but in Sunday school that older inner self was always predominant and she was as wise and well behaved as Noah Clegg himself. For inside the church building the child's mind was held in a kind of holy fear. She spent most of her time there dwelling upon her sins and longing to be good. She did not know that the starched pinafore that scratched her neck, the tightness of her heavy braid of hair, and the stiffness of her Sunday boots contributed not a little to her inner discomfort. But she gave her undivided attention to Miss Robertson and the lesson.

She was never distracted, as Rosie so often was by Katie Price's clothes. Katie had on a new sash to-day, and Rosie sighed and poked Elizabeth and asked her if she didn't wish to goodness she had one, too. Elizabeth glanced at the sash quite unmoved. The Gordon girls never had sashes, nor finery of any kind, but why should one who knew she would some day wear a flashing suit of silvery armor and a crimson velvet cloak be envious of mere ribbons? Elizabeth did not confide this comforting assurance to Rosie, but she whispered truthfully, No, that she didn't want one like Katie Price's. She was quite unconscious of the fact that there dwelt in her mind not a little of Aunt Margaret's pride–the feeling that it was infinitely better to be a Gordon in a dun-colored pinafore than a Price in a silk sash and a flower-trimmed hat.

She soon forgot all about Katie in her absorption in the lesson. Anything savoring of religion took strong hold of Elizabeth, and even Martha Ellen's presentation of a passage of Scripture appealed to her. When the passage was re-read, Miss Robertson read a list of questions off the printed page before her. "Who was Zaccheus?" was the first question. Katie Price was looking at her sash and didn't know. Susie Martin hung her head and blushed, Eppie Turner was always too shy to speak, and Rosie Carrick ventured the remark that "he was a man." Miss Robertson passed on perfectly good-natured. "Lizzie Gordon, who was Zaccheus?" Lizzie Gordon knew all about him, and spun off information, even to his being little and having to climb a tree. "I can tell lots more," she said invitingly, as Miss Robertson held up her hand to stem the flood. But the teacher smilingly shook her head. Lizzie was getting too far ahead. "Where did he live?" was the next question read off in the direction of Katie Price, and so on they went until all the questions were read and answered, Elizabeth supplying whatever information the rest of the class failed to give. Next came the "Application," which Elizabeth enjoyed most, because it left room for discussion. The "Application" applied to each verse and was also read by the teacher. "Zaccheus was a small man. We may be small and insignificant in the eyes of the world, but none the less does responsibility devolve upon each one of us." "Zaccheus climbed a tree. We learn from this that we should all strive to climb to the loftiest that life can attain." Elizabeth put in an occasional remark, and Martha Ellen responded. This was one of the former's grown-up moments and she reveled in it. There was none of the family there to carry home the tale that Lizzie was putting on pious airs, and so expose her to Jean's ridicule; and Martha Ellen's marked appreciation drew her out to make the wisest and profoundest remarks.

Occasionally Miss Robertson would take out her gold watch and look at it in surprise, and then continue. Occasionally, also, she glanced across the aisle to the big boys' class, and once she was rewarded by a smile and a gracious bow from its teacher. Then Martha Ellen's cheeks grew pink and the cherries on her hat, Elizabeth noticed, shook just as the cherries in the orchard did when the wind swept through the boughs. She looked very much pleased, too, and glanced back to where Annie Gordon in her plain, blue cotton dress sat with drooping head, striving to give her attention to the lesson.

Miss Robertson had finally read all the "Application," and again she looked at her gold watch, while the class sat admiring it. There were still some minutes left, and, with a sigh, the teacher twisted her gold bracelets and then turned the page. "We have just time for the moral piece," she said. "The moral piece" was a little sermon at the end of the Lesson, containing an admonition to all youthful minds, and Martha Ellen sometimes used it to fill in the last few minutes. Elizabeth always listened to it solemnly, for it was full of long, high-sounding words that gave her an exalted feeling. But just now her attention was diverted by signs of dire trouble brewing across the aisle. John and Charles Stuart, all unmindful of old Silas Pratt, who was solemnly reading the moral piece, the paper held close to his eyes, were doubling up in convulsions of silent laughter; while from underneath them came ominous squeaks and rumbles and a pair of wicked eyes gleamed from the dusky shadow of the seat. Elizabeth's heart stood still. Those dreadful boys were teasing Trip, and he would burst forth soon into loud barking, and what would become of the culprit who had brought him into the church?

The moral piece was drawing to a close; old Wully Johnstone had finished his, and a hush had fallen over the school. Noah Clegg had left his class, and gone squeak, squeak on tiptoe to the platform, and was coming squeak, squeak back again with the collection box. The little girls had begun to untie their cents from the corners of their handkerchiefs.

Now, the window just above Elizabeth's head was open, and a little sparrow, emboldened by the quiet, hopped upon the sill, and fell to pecking at some crumbs left there from the last tea-meeting. He even ventured to the edge of the sill and with his knowing little head on one side contemplated, with one bright eye, the cherries on Martha Ellen's hat, as though he longed to get a peck at them.

But just across the church the wicked pair of gleaming eyes were watching the little sparrow from the dark corner. From beneath them subterranean grumblings and mutterings warned Charles Stuart that Trip was growing dangerously excited. John Gordon indicated the cause, by a nod at the sparrow, and the two boys ducked their heads in an agony of mirth. This was too much for Charles Stuart. Not stopping to consider the consequences, he leaned down and whispered, "Crows, Trip, crows!" and clutched the little dog tighter between his legs. Now Trip had been trained all spring to chase the crows from the corn, and this was his signal to charge. Not all the boys in Forest Glen Sunday school could have held him at that moment. The word "crows" changed him into a raging, squirming, yelping, snarling, exploding little powder-magazine. With a yell of wrath he burst free and leaped upon the opposite seat, knocking the moral piece from Silas Pratt's hand and the spectacles from his nose. With one explosive yelp he hurtled across the aisles, landed upon Martha Ellen Robertson's seat, slid half its slippery length, righted himself, and standing upon his hind legs, with his front paws upon the back of the seat, he burst into a storm of wild barking. Of course the sparrow was by this time away down near Lake Simcoe, but Trip still continued his uproar. He did not bark, he fairly squalled out all his long pent-up rage, leaping and dancing on his wicked little hind legs, and making noise enough to scare every bird out of Forest Glen woods.

The consternation was not confined to the birds. Everybody stood up and exclaimed in horror. Martha Ellen was so alarmed that she screamed right out loud, and ran across the aisle to Mr. Coulson for protection. Noah Clegg dropped the collection all over the floor, and Silas Pratt put on his spectacles again and ejaculated, "Well, well, well, well!" Even the daring Charles Stuart was rather dismayed at the havoc he had wrought, and as for poor Elizabeth, words could not describe how rent and torn she was between shame and terror. Sandy McLachlan was the only one who seemed equal to the emergency. He arose, exclaiming explosively, "For peety's sake!" and in two minutes the dog was flying through the doorway with yelps of terror, followed by several profane anathemas upon his wicked little head for "pollutin' the hoose o' God."

Noah Clegg gathered up the pennies and took his place upon the platform as if nothing had happened. Any rare case of insubordination in the Sunday school was never dealt with there. It was left to home discipline, which, being of the good old Canadian sort, was always salutary. So, knowing by the MacAllister's lowering countenance that dire consequences awaited his son upon his return home, Noah gave out the closing hymn, with undisturbed cheerfulness:

"Come along now, boys and girls, an' we'll sing our closin' 'ymn. Never mind the poor little puppy, there ain't no bad in him at all. Come along an' we'll sing No. 148–'Oh, 'Appy Day,' and then you'll go out an' fill your lungs full o' 'hair before church starts."

CHAPTER IV
AT THE EDGE OF THE DAWN

There were many Sabbaths indelibly impressed upon Elizabeth's memory, but none that burned its way in as did that afternoon's experience with Trip. The misery of sitting through the long church service, with the awful guilt upon her soul, and the thoughts of approaching retribution, almost made her physically ill. As yet there was very little fortitude in Elizabeth's soul. She was the only coward in the Gordon family, John was wont to say, and, though she dreamed of valorous deeds as the successor of Joan of Arc, in real life she had never yet been able to vindicate herself.

She sat through the sermon, making vows, Jacob-like, that if she ever came through this time of tribulation alive she would go softly all the rest of her days. She would live a life of complete renunciation–selfish pleasures, worldly ambitions centering round Mrs. Jarvis, even dreams of Joan of Arc she would put away forever. She would not finish that enthralling story she was surreptitiously reading in the Cheemaun *Chronicle*, the story of Lady Evelina De Lacy and the false Lord Algernon. She would never even wish she had curls like Rosie, but would be glad her hair was straight and plain; and when Mrs. Jarvis came, offering her a fortune and a velvet dress and a gold crown, she would turn away, declaring firmly that for her there could be no pleasure in such worldly joys.

The sermon had never seemed so long. Mr. Murray, a good old man, whose discourses had steadily lengthened with his years, preached on and on. Forest Glen nodded and woke up and nodded again, and finally roused itself to stand up for the closing psalm. As the people slowly and silently filed out of church, still only half-awake, Elizabeth followed her aunt with the feelings of a criminal going to the gallows. She knew that her secret was safe with John and Charles Stuart. The boys might fill her days with tribulation by teasing, but they would never stoop to tell tales. Nevertheless, Elizabeth did not for a moment consider this as an avenue of escape. The integrity of her soul demanded that she go straight to Mr. MacAllister and confess. And then everyone would know she had disgraced the name of Gordon forever, and what Aunt Margaret would say was a thought to make one shudder.

As she went blindly down the aisle, she found herself shoved against Mr. Coulson. He was looking straight ahead of him, very sternly, as though to let her know he realized how wicked and ungenteel she was. But Elizabeth had in memory many blessed occasions upon which her teacher had exonerated her in the face of damaging evidence. She had learned to put unbounded confidence in him. He was a person who understood, and there were so very few people in the world who did understand. He possessed some wonderful divining power, which Elizabeth felt would make it possible for him even to conceive of a person who could carry a dog into Sunday school and yet not be quite a social outcast.

So she slipped up close to him, so close that she forced him to look down at her. He saw the misery in the little girl's deep eyes, and forgot that she was Miss Gordon's niece. "Are you sick, Lizzie?" he asked. Elizabeth shook her head, speechless. She caught his coat and drew him aside as they came outside the door. He was so big and so strong, his very presence thrilled her with hope.

"Oh, Mr. Coulson," she whispered. "I–I–what'll I do? It was me took Trip into Sunday school!"

"Trip?" Mr. Coulson had already forgotten the little incident in his own troubles. "What about it, you poor little mite?"

"Will they put me out of Sunday school? Will Mother MacAllister be angry? Susie Martin's Brag was going to bite him, and I was afraid."

Mr. Coulson laughed. It struck Elizabeth as almost miraculous that anyone who had witnessed that awful scene in Sunday school could ever laugh again. He glanced around and saw that Miss Gordon had already driven off in the little basket phaeton.

"Come along," he said, and taking Elizabeth's hand he led her up to where the MacAllisters were climbing into their buggy. He leaned over and talked in a low tone to Mr. MacAllister and they both laughed, and the latter called, "Hey, hey, Lizzie, come awa', bairn, and jump in!" And Mother MacAllister said, as her arms went around her, "Hoots, toots, and did the lamb do it to save the little dog?" And Charles Stuart looked at her with undisguised admiration in his eyes, and said, "Aw, you goose, what did you go and tell for?" And Elizabeth's soul went straight from the depths right to the highest pinnacle of joy and thankfulness.

Then Mother MacAllister said, "Come away, Mr. Coulson, come home and have supper with father now, come away." Mr. Coulson sprang into the seat opposite, and he was no sooner in his place than Mother MacAllister cried out "Why, father, where are the girls? Come away, children. Come, Annie girl,–come, Sarah Emily! Come away, we're waitin' on you!"

Sarah Emily came forward, and with one leap landed herself upon the front seat with Mr. MacAllister and Charles Stuart; Jean climbed in beside Mr. Coulson, but Annie held back. The young man arose hastily. "Perhaps it's too crowded," he said hurriedly; "I'd better not go this time." Now this was a very absurd statement. For it had never been known that a MacAllister vehicle had ever been filled, much less crowded, and its owner turned upon the young man in wrathful amazement.

"Hoots, man! Ye're haverin'. Sit ye doon there! Annie bairn, jump in. What are ye gawkin' there aboot? Are ye scared o' the master?"

There was no other course but obedience. Mr. Coulson helped the young lady into the buggy and away they rattled up the hill. And Elizabeth, thrilled with joy over her escape, little realized that in saving herself she had done a good deed that day for two people very dear to herself–a deed the results of which lasted through a lifetime.

It all turned out so beautifully. Mother MacAllister, who never in her life was known to do such a wicked thing as go visiting on Sunday, left her guest with Charles

Stuart and his father, and went all the way over to The Dale to explain Elizabeth's case to Miss Gordon. And Annie was so radiant, and John was so admiring, that Elizabeth fairly glowed in the family felicity, and the sun went down behind the Long Hill in perfect peace and happiness.

After the excitement of that Sabbath, the days sped somewhat evenly. May budded into June, June blossomed into July, and still the long-looked-for Mrs. Jarvis did not come. Her non-appearance filled Miss Gordon with a sense of keen disappointment, but Elizabeth soon forgot all about her. She had more important things to take her attention.

The 1st of July had come, the first day of the holidays, and Elizabeth went to bed the night before unable to sleep from excitement. Mr. Coulson had bidden them farewell that afternoon. He had resigned and was going to Cheemaun to finish his law studies. Elizabeth and Rosie had cried themselves sick over the good-bys. But it was not grief that was keeping Elizabeth awake. It was the machinations of John and Charles Stuart. On the way home from school she had been made aware by certain nods and winks and significant signs between her two tormentors that some wonderful scheme was on their programme for the morrow. Elizabeth knew as well as though they had shouted it from the treetops that they were going fishing. They always ran away from her when they went fishing. She firmly determined that, come what might, she would go fishing, too.

Just why the sight of those two disappearing down the lane with rods over their shoulders always filled Elizabeth with such unbearable anguish was a question even she could not have answered. Such expeditions with the boys were sources of tears and tribulations. Elizabeth was always meeting with disaster. She was not satisfied unless she was manipulating a rod and line, and she did not know which filled her with the greatest heartrending compunction, the sight of the poor worm writhing on the hook or the poor fish. Then she was always being thrown into a panic of terror by the sight of a snake or a frog or a mud-turtle, and when real dangers did not menace, the boys supplied imaginary ones more terrible.

But, for all this, when John and Charles Stuart went abroad Elizabeth must accompany them, and, though her aunt felt that every such expedition removed her niece farther from the genteel ideal, she generally allowed her to go. For there were quieter times at home when the noisy one was away.

Elizabeth knew by experience that the two would be likely to arise at dawn and steal away, and she went to bed that night in the bare white-washed little room, which she and Mary shared, with the determination that she would lie awake until morning and be ready. By persistent pinching of her arms and tossing about, much to poor Mary's discomfort, she managed to keep herself awake for about an hour, but sleep overcame her at last, the dead, dreamless sleep of childhood, and all Elizabeth's joys and sorrows were as naught until morning.

But her restless spirit asserted itself early. When she awoke it was scarcely light. The old clock in the study downstairs had just struck three. The room was quite dark, but a faint light from the window, and a strange hum of life from the outdoor world, told her that morning was approaching.

She slipped stealthily from her bed and, trembling with excitement, ran silently down the long, bare hall to her brothers' room. It was a big chamber above the dining-room. Its only furniture was two beds; a big old four-poster, where John and Malcolm slept on a lumpy straw mattress, and a low "bunk" or box-like structure on casters, where the little boys, Archie and Jamie, lay tossed about in a tangle of bare limbs and blankets. Elizabeth brushed back her hair from her sleepy eyes, and peered into the dim room. The green paper blinds were partly raised, and she could discern through the gloom John's black head on the bolster beside Malcolm's fair one. The black head was hanging half out of bed and its mouth was wide open. Elizabeth giggled softly. She longed to stuff something into that yawning cavity; but she knew that dire consequences followed upon tampering with John. She tiptoed back to her room. The excitement was lulled and she was beginning to feel sleepy. But she suddenly bethought herself that it would be wise to look out and see if Charles Stuart were coming. She remembered with hot indignation how once John had tied a string to his toe, which he let hang out of the window, and how Charles Stuart had come in the gray dawn and pulled the string, and the two had fled away in the dusk, while she slept all unawares. If they had any such plan on foot this time, she would be even with them. She would sit at the window and watch for Charles Stuart. She tiptoed gleefully across the room, and, slipping between the green paper blind and the sash, shoved her head and shoulders out of the open window.

And then her mischievous mood fell from her like a garment, and there stole over her a feeling of awe. Elizabeth had often beheld the sunrise, and, being a passionate lover of nature, her soul had arisen with the day, radiant and full of joy. But never before had she witnessed the first mysterious birth of the dawn, and the wonder of it held her still. It was so strange and unreal. It was surely night, for the stars still hung above the black treetops, and yet it must be day, for above, below, on every side one great unbroken voice of song was pouring forth from the darkness. Or was it dark? It certainly wasn't light. The swamp, away behind old Wully Johnstone's fields, lay in blackness, and there was even a hint of moonlight sifted faintly through the gray veil of the sky. But the white line of birches by the stream stood out a soft, cloudy white, the fields were dimly distinguishable, and here and there a tree had taken form from its dark background.

But the wonder of it was the great chant the whole dark earth was raising to heaven. As June had waned Elizabeth and John had missed many of their bird companions, who were too busy raising their families to sing much. But now it seemed as though every blade of grass and every leaf on the tree was giving forth a voice. At first no separate note could be distinguished. It was one great voice, all-penetrating, all-pervading. But gradually the ear discerned the several parts of the wondrous anthem. The foundation of it seemed to come from behind the line of birches that hedged the stream, and here and there in the darkness of tree or bush an individual song arose to melt again into the grand chorus.

Elizabeth knelt by the open window, lost to everything except the mystery of music and light being woven before her. It was creation's morn again, at which the child's wondering eyes were gazing. Again the divine Fiat had gone forth, "Let there be light." And, moving in stately march to the grand processional, slowly, majestically the light was coming. Softly, almost imperceptibly, the phantom world took shape, and grew clearer as the stars grew paler. Here a bush detached itself from its gray background, yonder a tree grew up tall and stately, there the curve of a hillock swelled up from a dark valley. And as each growing maple or cedar or alder-bush took shape, from its depths there awoke a sleepy little murmur, swelling into a rapturous song and melting away again into the great anthem. Away down the dim lane, near the edge of the pond, stood a noble elm, its topmost branch towering into the gray heavens, its lower limbs sweeping the earth. As it gradually detached itself from the grayness and came forth beautiful and stately, there arose from its heart the musical accompaniment to its birth–not a sleepy little murmur, such as befitted a sumach or a bramble, but a loud, clarion note, one wild shout of joy–and out poured the ecstasy of a robin's song. There was a storm of music on all sides now, a splendid fortissimo, keeping pace with the growing light. Elizabeth, suddenly mindful of former sunrises, leaned far out to look towards the east, holding her breath. Over there might be glories that were not lawful for men to look upon, much less utter. And, yes, there was a great wonder there, no sun's rays as yet, no daylight even, but behind the black trees of Arrow Hill there shone a luminous crystal glow, a light more heart-moving than if the sun had risen in all his pomp of purple and gold. There was an awe, a mystery about this transparent clearness, a great promise of unspeakable glories to come. Elizabeth drew a long breath. She was but a child, perfectly unconscious and unthinking in all that she said and did, but she had a heart capable of being strongly moved by any hint of the Infinite. She did not guess why, did not even imagine the reason, but the tears came to her eyes with a smarting sting, and with them that feeling of overwhelming joy that was half-pain, the feeling that rushed over her so often when her father read some sublime passage from the Scriptures.

One came to her now from the psalm of the night before:

"Who coverest Thyself with light as with a garment; who stretches out the heavens like a curtain."

God Himself must be just behind that mysterious glow, little Elizabeth said to herself reverently. That shining crystal was the garment in which He had wrapped Himself, so that people might not see Him. But she saw Him. Yes, He was there, she knew, and in the uplift of the moment there came to her child's heart a vision that never faded, a vision that many years later bore her up on the wings of poesy to fame.

But Elizabeth was woefully earthbound, tied down by the cares and worries that fall to humanity. As she still hung over the window-sill, gazing enraptured at the heavens, she was brought sharply down to earth. Up near the willows at the gate she dimly descried a dark figure hastening along Champlain's Road. It paused at the gate. Instantly Elizabeth was transformed. From the rapt priestess of the dawn she descended sharply to the keen-eyed spy. That was Charles Stuart just as sure as sure! And John would be up and off in another five minutes. She jerked herself back into the room so suddenly that her head came in crashing contact with the window-frame. Elizabeth was naturally keenly sensitive to pain, but she scarcely noticed the blow. There was no time to even complain. Though her head was spinning, she began to fling on her clothes in mad haste, feverishly watching Mary lest the noise of the crash had awakened her. But Mary slept on soundly; and, reassured, Elizabeth made a frantic toilet. She wrenched herself into her clothes, pulling on garments upside down, inside out, any way that was most expeditious. Buttons would not go into button-holes, strings refused to tie, pins would not hold. But somehow she managed to get herself dressed, after a fashion. There was no time to think of washing, or combing her hair. She crushed her sunbonnet down over her untidy head, snatched up her shoes and stockings, slipped silently into the hall, and took her place behind a huge wardrobe at the head of the stairs, from which hiding-place she could command a view of John's bedroom door. By this time she was bursting with mischievous glee. Wouldn't John and Charles Stuart be good and mad when they found her following them? She knew exactly how to do it. The only way was to dog their footsteps, keeping safely out of sight until they were too far from home to send her back alone. Of course she would have to endure innuendoes all day regarding "Copy cats," but that was nothing to the anguish of being left at home.

As she stood breathless and full of mirth, she was rewarded by the sound of a door creaking, and a stealthy footstep approaching the stair. She crushed back into her hiding-place. She could not help wondering even in the midst of her excitement how John could ever move so quietly. She held her breath as the owner of the soft footfall came into view. And then it returned in a little gasp of astonishment. For it was not John at all, but Annie! Annie at this hour of the morning! Could she be going fishing, too? Elizabeth could not think of any other justifiable reason for getting up so early; Annie certainly looked as if she were on a very important mission. She went down the stairs hurriedly and silently, as though she were being pursued. Elizabeth had for an instant an impulse to call softly after her; but that wiser, older self within her arose and forbade. This ancient Elizabeth respected a secret, and said that here was one into which there must be no intrusion. She felt ashamed of herself, as though she had done something dishonorable like listening at a keyhole, as Sarah Emily had once done.

She heard the old door leading on to the side-porch creak stealthily, then pause, and creak again. Perhaps Annie was ill, and she ought to follow her. She softly tiptoed back to her room and peeped from her window. Her sister was stealing down through the orchard, her light summer dress plainly visible against its dim greenness. She stopped at the bars that led into the pasture field, and as she did, Charles Stuart came vaulting over the fence from the lane and strode towards her. And surely everybody must have been touched with a magic wand, and turned into somebody else; because it wasn't Charles Stuart at all, but Mr. Coulson, to whom Elizabeth had bidden such an agonized farewell only yesterday! He came straight towards Annie, holding out both his hands, and when he reached the bars he leaned over them and kissed her! And then, though Elizabeth was not quite eleven, she knew that she was looking upon something sacred and beautiful, something that should not be exposed to the eyes of another, and she turned swiftly and, running to the bed, hid her face in the clothes beside Mary.

She knelt there, motionless, wondering, and in a few minutes she heard the stealthy foot upon the stair again and the soft rustle of Annie's skirts. She crept into bed and pulled the clothes over her sunbonneted head. She felt she would be doing her sister an irreparable injury if she let her know anyone had witnessed that parting scene.

She lay there, trembling with excitement, until all was still again. She forgot all about the fishing expedition in this new discovery, and lay wideawake wondering why in the world Annie should kiss Mr. Coulson good-by when she had not even gone to school to him, until worn out with wonder and excitement she fell sound asleep. And outside the dawn still marched majestically onward towards the day, in time to its glorious accompaniment of song.

When Elizabeth awoke again it was broad daylight. Sarah Emily was already downstairs, setting the breakfast table, stirring the oatmeal porridge, and singing loudly about the many glittering but false young men who had sought her hand, but had been defeated in their machinations by the finest old lady that ever was seen, who lived on yonder little green.

Fortunately Elizabeth escaped inquiry by slipping from the bed and arranging her clothes in a more respectable manner before Mary was stirring. Mary was delicate, and the only one allowed to lie abed in the morning, or to refuse porridge if she did not want it, so Elizabeth's early morning adventure was not discovered. To her relief also she found John downstairs apparently not going fishing. At breakfast Annie was quieter than usual, but it was characteristic of Elizabeth that she did not by word or sign let her elder sister see that she had the smallest knowledge of the morning's farewell. John was right when he conceded to Lizzie the power of not only keeping secrets,–deathly secrets like a pet toad under the bed or rabbits in the barn,–but at the same time looking as if she had nothing to hide.

It was Elizabeth's turn to help Sarah Emily with the dishes, and after breakfast she wearily dragged her feet towards the kitchen. Tom Teeter had come over and was talking to her father as the latter hoed in the vegetable garden, and Tom always had candies in his pockets. Then Malcolm and John were building a new hen-house in the barnyard, and every stroke of the hammer shouted to Elizabeth to come. She took up the dish-towel drearily and stood looking wistfully down the sunny path that led into the orchard. She realized now that she was utterly worn out with the excitement of her morning adventure. Mary and the little boys were playing in the old wagon that stood in the barnyard. She could hear them laughing and shouting. The old pig was grunting over his trough, the hens were cackling. She really ought to go and gather the eggs. She felt just then that drying dishes was an insupportable burden. It was always so with Elizabeth. She could toil strenuously all day, building a playhouse, or engineering a new game, running, leaping, toiling all unwearied. But when household duties were laid upon her, except when she worked for Mother MacAllister, she was actually overcome with physical weariness. She leaned against the table and yawned aloud.

"Oh, Sarah Emily, don't you hate dishes?" she groaned. "We've got such stacks of them."

But Sarah Emily did not hear. Tom Teeter was standing down there between the rows of cabbages, talking to Mr. Gordon upon the "Conscienceless greed and onmitigated rapacity" of certain emissaries of the opposing political party. To all of which his neighbor was responding with: "Well, well. Deary me, now, Tom."

But Sarah Emily was firmly convinced that Tom was there for other reasons than to talk politics with her master. Sarah Emily was neither fair of face nor graceful of form, neither had a suitor ever been seen to approach the Gordon kitchen; nevertheless, she lived in the pleasant delusion that all the young men of the countryside were dying for love of her. Tom Teeter's condition she believed to be the most hopeless; and, like all other proud belles sure of their power, she flouted him; and the innocent young man, when he thought about her at all, wondered why Sarah Emily disliked him so, and took considerable pleasure in teasing her.

So Sarah Emily made frequent excursions to and from the well as he stood in the garden. She sang loudly and pretended she saw no one.

"The 'first that came courting was young farmer Green,
As fine a young gent as ever was seen."

"Oh, Sarah Emily, I'm awfully tired," said Elizabeth, when the young woman had at last settled to washing the dishes. "Don't you 'spose you could do them yourself this time. I really ought to go and help Malc and John with the hen-house."

"No, I don't, you lazy trollop," responded Sarah Emily promptly. "You don't seem to think I ever get tired, an' me with that pinny of yours to iron for Sunday, too!"

Elizabeth was immediately seized with compunction. She caught up the towel and went at her task with feverish haste. But her eyes would stray down the orchard path that led to the barn.

It was only this very morning she had witnessed that strange little scene there in the dewy, music-thrilled twilight. It seemed so unreal now that Elizabeth could almost believe she had dreamed it all. She almost wished she had. For Mr. Coulson was perfection, and Annie was a little better, and it was rather hard to think of her two paragons doing anything that people might laugh at. In the Gordon family life there was something improper attached to any display of affection, and kissing was positively disgraceful. Elizabeth dared not even kiss Jamie, much as she enjoyed it, except when the older boys were at a safe distance. She herself disliked being kissed by grown-up people. Babies and little people were different. She could remember being kissed by her aunt once, on her first arrival, but never since. She and Rosie had sobbed for an hour with their heads on the desk when Mr. Coulson made his good-by speech, but they would never have dreamed of doing what Annie did. And surely they loved him far more.

She was recalled to present affairs by Sarah Emily's snatching the plate out of her hand and demanding if she intended to rub it clean off the face of the earth?

Elizabeth took another rather sullenly. But such a mood never lasted longer than half a minute with her, and she was suddenly struck with the notion that Sarah Emily might furnish some valuable information on the subject that was worrying her. Sarah Emily had such a vast experience with young men.

"Sarah Emily," she said, rather hesitatingly, "did anybody–I mean any young man ever–kiss you?"

Sarah Emily gave an hysterical shriek. She doubled up over the table, almost dipping her face into the dish-pan, and went off into a hurricane of giggles.

"Oh, oh, you awful, awful bad girl, Lizzie Gordon!" she screamed, whereupon Elizabeth knew she had not been bad at all, but had said something that had mightily pleased Sarah Emily.

"But did they though?" she insisted, showing her even white teeth in a sympathetic laugh. "Eh, Sarah Emily?"

The young woman straightened herself and suddenly became dignified.

She darted a withering glance at Elizabeth. "Not much, they didn't!" she cried righteously. "Jist let me ketch any o' them–yes, jist any one o' the whole gang up to any such penoeuvres. I'd soon fix 'em!"

There was so much scorn in her demeanor that Elizabeth was disconcerted.

"Why?" she asked anxiously. "Ain't it nice, Sarah Emily?"

"No, it ain't!" snapped Sarah Emily emphatically.

Elizabeth was much taken aback. It was surely not possible that Annie could do anything impolite or ungenteel–Annie, the only one in the family whom Aunt Margaret never scolded. She was puzzled and troubled. There was no one to whom she could take the matter for advice. Elizabeth had no close confidant. John was the nearest, but there were so few things John understood. Then one never dared tell Mary anything. Mary did not mean to be a tell-tale, but somehow everything she knew always oozed out sooner or later. Yes, this was a puzzle Elizabeth must work out alone.

"Well," she said at last, determined to uphold Annie at all costs, "it's all right in stories, anyhow. I mean when people are going to get married some day. I read about it in that story about Lady Evelina in the *Chronicle*. Now, if you were going to get married to Tom Teeter, Sarah Emily—-"

Sarah Emily exploded in another spasm of shrieks and giggles. She leaned against the wall, overcome with laughter, wiping her eyes, and declaring that if Lizzie didn't hold still she'd be the death of her.

Elizabeth became impatient. Her older self rose up, protesting that Sarah Emily was very silly, indeed.

"Oh, bother you, Sarah Emily," she cried, "you're a big goose!"

Sarah Emily made a leap towards her. "You jist say that again, Lizzie Gordon, and I'll give you a clout over the head that'll make you jump."

Elizabeth dodged round to the other side of the table, and promptly said it again–said it many times, dancing derisively upon her toes and waving her towel; sang it, too, in the most insulting manner to the tune of "My Grandmother Lives, etc."

Then ensued a mad chase around the table, attended with uproar and disaster. A plate fell crashing to the floor, the dish-pan was upset, the water splashed in all directions, and the small figure with shrieks of laughter dodged this way and that, followed by the big clumsy one shouting vengeance.

And then there suddenly fell a great silence as from the heavens. The door had opened, and Miss Gordon was standing in it. Elizabeth stood rigid in a pool of dish-water, and instinctively felt to find how many buttons of her pinafore were undone. Sarah Emily promptly turned away and went vigorously to work, presenting a solid wall of indifference to her mistress, in the form of a broad pink calico back with a row of black buttons down the middle.

Elizabeth was not so incased in armor. One swift glance of shame and contrition she gave towards her aunt, and then hung her head, waiting for the blow to fall. Miss Gordon had never seemed so remote and so chillingly genteel.

"Elizabeth," she said in a despairing tone, "how is it that I can never trust you for even a few minutes out of my sight? You grow more rebellious and unmanageable every day. I have given up my home, and slaved and worked for you all, and you alone show me no gratitude. I can never make a lady of you, I see. How any child belonging to a Gordon could be so entirely ungenteel—-"

On and on Miss Gordon's quiet, well-bred voice continued, every word falling like a whip upon Elizabeth's sensitive heart. She writhed in agony under a sense of her own sinfulness, coupled with a keen sense of injustice. She had been bad–oh, frightfully wicked–but Aunt Margaret never arraigned a culprit for any particular crime without gathering up all her past iniquities and heaping them upon her in one load of despair.

She listened until she could bear no more, and then, darting past her aunt, she tore madly upstairs in a passion of rage and grief. Miss Gordon's genteel voice went steadily on, adding the sin of an evil and uncontrollable temper to Elizabeth's black catalogue. But Elizabeth was out of hearing by this time. She had shut herself, with a sounding bang, into the little bedroom where she and Mary slept, and flung herself upon the mat before the bed. Even in her headlong despair she had refrained from pitching herself upon the bed, which Annie and Jean had arranged so neatly under its faded patch-work quilt. Instead she lay prone upon the floor and wept bitterly. Anger and a sense of injustice came first, and then bitter repentance. She loved her aunt, and Sarah Emily, and she had injured both. She was always doing wrong, always causing trouble. Aunt Margaret could not understand her being a Gordon at all. Probably she wasn't one. Yes, that was the solution of the whole matter. She was an adopted child, and not like the rest. She was sure of it now. Hadn't Aunt Margaret hinted it again and again?

Elizabeth always went through this mental process during her many tempests of anguish. But always, through it all, the older self sat waiting, sometimes quite out of sight, but always there. And in the end she brought up a picture of Elizabeth's mother–the bright little mother whom she never forgot and who used to say, "Little Lizzie is more like me than any of my children." That assurance always came to Elizabeth. No, her whole family might forsake her, but her mother was always her very own. Her mother could never, never have been so cruel as merely to adopt her. Next, as always, came contrition, and deep self-abasement. She stopped crying and lay still, wondering why it was she could never be good like Annie, or even Jean. Then there was Constance Holworth, the lonely girl in the Sunday-school library book. She never got into a temper. And if she ever did, or even thought the smallest wrong thought, she always went down to the drawing-room and said sweetly, "Dear mamma, please forgive me." Even Elizabeth's imagination could not draw a congruous picture of herself speaking thus to Sarah Emily without some strange result. Besides, they had no drawing-room, and evidently one needed that sort of chamber for the proper atmosphere. Elizabeth wondered drearily what a drawing-room could be. Most likely a room in which one sat and drew pictures all day long. This reminded her of her own drawing materials lying in the bottom drawer, one of her birthday presents from Mrs. Jarvis. She half arose, with the thought that she might get out her paint-box or the old faded doll that Mary and she shared, then sank back despairingly upon the mat again. What was the use trying to solace a broken heart with such trifles?

But when she grew up and became a great artist, and drew pictures as big as the Vicar of Wakefield's family group, and all the Gordons came to her drawing-room to wonder and admire,–Sarah Emily and Aunt Margaret the most eager and admiring of all,–then, though she would be very kind to them all, she would never smile. She would always wear a look of heart-broken melancholy, and when people would ask what made the great Miss Gordon, who was Mrs. Jarvis's adopted daughter, so very, very sad, Mrs. Jarvis would explain that dreadful afflictions in her childhood had blighted her whole life. And then Sarah Emily and Aunt Margaret would go away weeping over the havoc they had wrought.

Elizabeth gained so much comfort from these reflections that she came up from the depths of despair sufficiently to take note of her surroundings. The window looking out upon the orchard was open, and from the pasture-field there arose a great noise–whistling, shouting, rattling of tin pails, and barking. She sprang up and darted to the window. That double racket always proclaimed the approach of Charles Stuart and Trip. Yes, there they were, the former just vaulting over the bars, the latter wriggling through them. Charles Stuart had a big tin pail and a small tin cup, and, just as sure as she was a living, breathing person, he and John would be off in two minutes to pick strawberries in Sandy McLachlan's slash!

Elizabeth went down the stairs three steps at a time. Miss Gordon was sitting by the dining-room window, Annie at her side. Both were sewing, and Annie's cheeks so pink and her eyes so bright that her aunt looked at her curiously from time to time. They were interrupted by the bursting open of the door, and like a whirlwind a disheveled little person, wild-eyed and tear-stained, in a dirty, streaked pinafore, flung herself into the room.

"Oh, Aunt Margaret! The boys are going pickin' berries. Can't I go, too? Oh, do let me go?"

Elizabeth stood before her aunt twisting her pinafore into a string in an agony of suspense.

Miss Gordon looked at the turbulent little figure in silent despair, and Annie ventured gently:

"It would be nice to have strawberries for tea, aunt, and Lizzie could help John."

Miss Gordon sighed. "If I could only trust you, Elizabeth," she said. "But I wonder what new trouble you'll get into?"

"Oh, I promise I won't get into any!" gasped Elizabeth in solemn pledge, all unconscious that it was equivalent to a promise from the wind not to blow.

"It's no use promising," said Miss Gordon mournfully. "You know, Elizabeth, I have warned you repeatedly against the wild streak in you, and yet in the face of all my admonitions you still persist in acting in an unladylike manner. Now, when I was a little girl, I never went anywhere with my brother, your dear papa, except perhaps for a little genteel stroll——"

Elizabeth could bear no more. The last prop of endurance gave way at the sight of John and Charles Stuart marching calmly past the window, rattling their tin pails.

"Oh, Aunt Margaret!" she burst out in anguished tones, "couldn't you–would you please finish scolding me when I get back. The boys are gone!"

Miss Gordon paused, completely baffled. This strangest child of all this strange family of William's was quite beyond her.

"Go then," she said, with a gesture of despair. "Go. I have nothing more to say."

Elizabeth was tearing down the garden path before she had finished. To be cast off as hopeless was anguish, but it was nothing to the horror of being kept at home to be made genteel. In a moment more, with shrieks of joy, she was flying down the lane, towards two disgusted looking boys reluctantly awaiting her at the edge of the mill-pond.

CHAPTER V
A ROYAL TITLE

"The Slash" was the name given to a piece of partially cleared land lying between the mill-pond and Sandy McLachlan's clearing. The timber on it had been cut down and it had grown up in a wild luxuriance of underbrush and berry bushes. The latter had from time to time been cleared away in patches, and here and there between the fallen tree-trunks were stretches of green grass, where the wild strawberries grew. The Slash was the most delightful place in which to go roaming at large and give oneself up to a buccaneer life. On schooldays, though the Gordons passed through it morning and afternoon, there was little opportunity to linger over its treasures. But the memory of its cool, flowery glades, its sunny uplands, its wealth of berries or wild grapes or hazel-nuts as the season of each came round, always beckoned the children on holidays. The Gordon boys had long used it as a playground. Here they could indulge in games of wild Indians and pirates, setting fire to the brush-wood, cutting down trees, and engaging in such other escapades as were not sufficiently genteel to be carried on under their aunt's eye. So on holidays thither they always repaired, either with the excuse of accompanying Charles Stuart to the mill, or carrying a pail or a fishing-rod to give the proper coloring to their departure.

But on this first summer holiday John and Charles Stuart found themselves, upon setting out, hampered by a much worse encumbrance than a berry-pail.

"Lizzie Gordon!" said her brother sternly, "you ain't comin'."

"I am so!" declared Elizabeth, secure in permission from the powers at home. "Aunt said I could."

John looked at Charles Stuart, and Charles Stuart winked at John and nodded towards the opposite edge of the pond. Elizabeth knew only too well that those significant glances meant, "We'll run away from her and hide as soon as we're into The Slash."

"No, you can't then," she cried triumphantly, just as though they had spoken. "I can beat you at running, Charles Stuart MacAllister."

This was a fact Charles Stuart could not contradict. Elizabeth was the wind itself for speed, and many a time he and John had tried in vain to leave her behind. But her brother knew a manoeuvre that always brought capitulation from the enemy. He turned away and walked for some paces at Charles Stuart's side, then glanced back at Elizabeth resolutely following.

"Aw, you're a nice one," he exclaimed, "followin' boys when they're goin' swim-min'!"

Elizabeth stopped motionless in the pathway. One might bear slights and indignities, even positive opposition, but the insinuation that one was vulgar enough to go swimming at all, much more with boys, was an insult no human being could stand. She turned away slowly, and, as the two inexorable figures went on down the willow path into the ravine, she dropped upon the earth and burst into despairing sobs. To be left so cruelly was bad enough, but what hurt most was John's horrible innuendo. It fairly scorched Elizabeth's soul.

She was lying prone upon the clover-starred grass, weeping bitterly, when she was aroused by a rustle in the willows. A face was looking through the green tangle.

"Aw, hurrah, Lizzie," Charles Stuart was saying, "come on. We're only in fun. We ain't goin' swimmin' at all."

"I won't," wailed Elizabeth. "John doesn't want me; he never does, and I'm going right back home."

Through her vanishing tears she had seen John approaching, and had suddenly became conscious of the fact that if she returned home weeping she would be questioned and matters might not be so comfortable for John. That the young man recognized the danger himself was evident, for he added his olive branch to Charles Stuart's. "Hurrah, Lizzie. Don't be such a baby. Come along. We can't wait."

But Elizabeth was a woman to the very tips of her long, tapering fingers, and finding herself in a position of power was not going to capitulate at once. It was delightful to be coaxed, and by the boys, too. So she merely sat up and, gazing back up the lane, sighed in a hopeless way and said, "You don't want me, I know you don't, I might as well go back."

"Come on, you silly," cried John, now thoroughly alarmed. "Come on now. Mind you, we won't wait. Hurrah, Charles Stuart, and she can stay if she likes."

They started down the ravine again; and, seeing that her air of grieved dignity was liable to be lost in the willows, Elizabeth got to her feet and went scrambling after them.

Down at the bottom of the hollow, where the little stream widened into a lazy brown pond, lay Mr. MacAllister's saw-mill. It ran for only a few months in the spring and early summer and was now closed. Only, away down the valley where the road wound into the lumber yard, the banging of boards told that someone was preparing to haul away a load.

None of The Dale children ever passed the mill without a visit, and of course Charles Stuart always explored it all with a fine air of proprietorship. So they scrambled over the silent place with its sweet smell of running water and fresh sawdust. They beat a clamorous tattoo upon the big circular saw, they went down to the lower regions and explored the dark hole where the big water-wheel hung motionless, with only the drip, drip of water from the flume above. They rode on the little car that brought the logs up from the pond, and in as many ways as possible risked life and limb as boys must ever do.

In all these hazardous ventures Elizabeth joined. She was desperately frightened, but knew she must win her spurs at the outset or run the awful risk of being left behind even yet. Her conduct proved satisfactory, and by the time they reached the other side of the pond, and had climbed the steep bank, clinging to the bracken and dog-wood, friendly relations had been once more established. When the boys had once got over the disgrace of feeling that a girl was tagging after them, and took Elizabeth on her own merits, these three generally got on very amicably. She was often a great nuisance, but on the whole they got as much fun as trouble from her panics over snakes and field-mice, and, when out of sight of The Dale, they voted her as good a fellow as the rest.

So away they went over The Slash, tearing through underbrush, and pausing occasionally to glance over the patches of grass for strawberries. They soon decided that there were so many they could soon fill their pails, and John suggested they sit down and eat the lunch Charles Stuart had brought, for he was sure it must be dinner-time by the look of the sun.

Mother MacAllister, with a motherly thought for the Gordons, had put up a substantial repast of bread and pork and generous wedges of pie and a pile of cookies big enough to make glad the heart of any boy. This, supplemented by some thick slices of bread and butter which John had begged from Sarah Emily, made a great feast. They grew very merry over it, and when it was finished, up from the bottom of John's pail came a book–the real reason for the berry-picking expedition. Just whether it would be forbidden by their aunt or not, John and Elizabeth had not run the risk of inquiring. It was a tremendously funny book, so funny that the last time they had read a chapter–it was up in the hay-mow on a rainy Saturday–Elizabeth had laughed so loud that they had almost been discovered. John could go off into one of his silent fits of laughter in the same room as Aunt Margaret and never be discovered, but Elizabeth was prone to scream and dance, and when anything funny seized her Sandy McLachlan's slash was only at a safe distance from home.

So, as the book was so very enjoyable, they had decided that it had better be read in private. Elizabeth had some conscientious scruples, which she had been bold enough to utter, but they were silenced by John's quoting no less an authority than Mr. Coulson. The schoolmaster had been overheard saying to Tom Teeter that he had spent all one Saturday forenoon reading "Innocents Abroad." And he had told Annie some of the funny stories in it, hence John had begged it from Malcolm, who had borrowed it from a High School boy in Cheemaun.

So the three sat them down in a shady nook, against a mossy log, and listened with delight while John read. They took turns at reading aloud; Charles Stuart was the best reader, and Elizabeth the worst. She either read very slowly and stumbled over all the long words, or else so fast one could not follow her. But Charles Stuart was a wonderful reader, one of the best in school. Indeed, Mr. Coulson declared that Charles Stuart would make a greater public speaker than Tom Teeter some day, if he set his mind to oratory.

But to-day it was John's turn to read, and when the extracts were not too funny he progressed fairly well, toiling along in a quiet monotone. When the story became very laughable, however, he proved a great trial to his listeners. Before he could utter the joke, his voice would fail and he would collapse into helpless laughter. When importuned by his audience to speak out and let them know what the fun was, he would make agonized attempts to utter the words, failing again and again, until Charles Stuart would snatch the book from him. Sometimes the sight of John struggling to utter in anguishing whispers the thing that was rendering him helpless was far funnier than Mark Twain himself, and Elizabeth and Charles Stuart would roll over on the grass in shrieks of laughter long before they heard what the joke was about.

But such irresponsible conduct could not continue, and when the cool part of the day had been consumed in the shade, they had to turn out in the blazing noon-day sun to hunt for strawberries. The three adventurers would have preferred the shade and Mark Twain, or else a dash through the woods, but they were true Canadians, born with that innate idea that he who does not work should not eat. So to work they went of their own free will. The strawberries were plentiful, and soon the tin cups, heaped with their luscious loads, were being carried to the pails beneath the bass-wood bushes. Elizabeth never grew weary picking strawberries. This was a task infinitely removed from being shut into a hot kitchen with a dish-towel, while the boys played in the barnyard. The glory of the day, the sense of freedom from restraint, the beauty of the rosy clusters, hiding shyly beneath their pretty leaves, all combined to make work seem play. She picked so furiously that she was a spur to even Charles Stuart, accustomed as he was to hard work at his farm-home, and lest they be beaten by a girl the boys toiled strenuously.

By the time the afternoon sun had begun to wane, the big pails were filled and shaken down and filled again, the pickers had eaten almost as much more, and surfeited, hot, and thirsty they found themselves on the edge of the slash that bordered the woods.

Down the leafy pathway which led towards the school they could see Sandy McLachlan's log house standing in its little clearing.

"Hurrah over and ask old Sandy for a drink," cried Charles Stuart. "I'm chokin'."

Elizabeth followed them into the woods, full of delight. It would be such fun to visit Eppie in the afternoon, just as if they were grown-up ladies, and she had come to stay to tea.

There was a strange, deserted air about the little place. There was nobody in the tiny garden, where Eppie's sunflowers and sweet peas stood blazing in the sunshine. There was even no sign of life about the little log house. They went up the hard beaten path to the door. It was open, and they peeped in. Eppie's pink sunbonnet was lying on a chair and the crumbs of the late dinner were still scattered over the bare pine table.

"They must be down at the barn," said Charles Stuart. "I'm goin' to have a drink, anyhow."

A rusty tin dipper hung over the well, and they helped themselves. The sound of the pump brought a little figure round the corner of the old log barn.

At the sight of Elizabeth, Eppie came running up the path. She was barefooted, as Eppie always was except on Sundays, and wore a coarse, gray wincey dress and a big apron. Poor Eppie's clothes were all much too large for her, for the little girl had no woman's deft hand to dress her. She shyly slipped past the boys and took hold of Elizabeth's hand. Her big, pathetic eyes shone with joy. "Oh, Lizzie, I'll be that glad to see you," she whispered in her old-fashioned way. Perhaps it was her long dress, but somehow Elizabeth always had the impression that poor Eppie had always been old and grown-up. "Come away down to the barn and see grandaddy," she added, including the boys. "There's two men down there an' they're goin' to take grandaddy's house away from him, only the master says he won't let them."

Here was exciting news. The boys ran on ahead, and Elizabeth and Eppie quickly followed, the former plying her hostess with wondering questions.

A smart horse and a shiny top-buggy were standing in the barnyard. In the vehicle two men were seated, and beside them stood old Sandy and Mr. Coulson. The schoolmaster was using the first two or three days of his holidays in which to bid farewell to his Forest Glen friends. Elizabeth had heard him say he would do so, yesterday in school, and as she caught sight of him she could not help thinking he must have said good-by to hundreds and hundreds of people that day, since he had started so early. The speculation passed dimly through her mind as to how many of them he had kissed.

But her chief feeling was one of joy at the sight of him, and keeping hold of Eppie's hand she went round to the side of the horse where he stood. Elizabeth was shy and frightened in the presence of strangers, unless some unusual encouragement brought her older self to the fore, when she could converse with the ease of an accomplished society woman. But the sight of these smart-looking strangers, evidently from town, filled her with discomfort, and she shyly drew up behind Mr. Coulson.

"But, Mr. Oliver," he was saying, "there must surely be some justice in his claim. Why, Mr. McLachlan has lived here for twenty years, and changed the place from dense woods to what you see now."

The elder man in the buggy, a stout, good-natured looking fellow, lazily blew a whiff of smoke from his cigar and smiled in a superior way. "Mr. Huntley," he said, turning to the young man at his side, "when Mr. Coulson enters your office, I'm afraid you're going to have trouble drilling him into the mysteries of meum and tuum as interpreted by the law."

"Yes, as interpreted by the law," repeated Mr. Coulson rather hotly. "The law sometimes speaks in a foreign language. If I thought my study of it was going to warp my ideas of right and wrong I'd go back home and pitch hay for the rest of my life."

The young man in the carriage looked at him closely. He was a handsome young fellow, about Mr. Coulson's own age, with a clever, clean-cut face. "There's something in your contention, John," he said, "but I'm acting for my client remember, and he has his ideas of right and wrong, too. He's paying for the place."

The young teacher's face fell, and old Sandy McLachlan, who had been watching him with eyes pitifully anxious, came a step nearer.

"They will not be turning me off?" he asked, half-fearfully, half-defiantly. "I would be working on this place for twenty years. Mr. Jarvis would be telling me it will be mine, as long as I live. And what will become of me and my little Eppie?"

"Well, well, Mr. McLachlan," said the jolly-looking man, not losing a whit of his jollity at the sight of the old man's distress. "Well, well, we won't discuss the matter any further to-day. You won't be disturbed until the fall anyway. And Mr. Huntley here will see that justice is done, whatever happens. He's one of the cleverest young lawyers in Cheemaun, you know."

"Hech!" interrupted old Sandy, his eyes blazing. "Yes, it is that I will be fearing. The Lord peety the man that will be falling into the hands of a clever lawyer!"

The comfortable-looking man seemed to take this as a grand joke. He laughed heartily and dug his elbow into the side of his young companion. "Hear that, Blake? Ha, ha! you lawyers deserve all you get. Ha! ha! that's good!"

The young man at his side did not reply to the raillery. He was looking past Mr. Coulson at the group of four children, standing open-mouthed, gazing at the men, and breathlessly listening to every word. He was particularly struck with the smallest one, a little girl in a torn, berry-stained blue pinafore and a sunbonnet of the same material. Her two small brown hands held in a tight grasp the hand of old Sandy's granddaughter, her cheeks were crimson, and her big eyes were blazing with an expression of mingled wrath and fear.

"Whose youngsters?" he asked, nodding towards them. "They don't all belong here, do they?" Mr. Coulson turned, and for the first time noticed the berry-pickers. "Hello! Charles Stuart and John Gordon and Lizzie herself!" he cried. "Been picking berries, eh?"

"Who's the little brown thing with all the eyes and hair?" asked Mr. Huntley.

Mr. Coulson took Elizabeth's hand and drew her up to the side of the buggy. "This gentleman wants to know your name, Lizzie," he said.

"It's 'Lizbeth Jarvis Gordon," said that young lady with great dignity. She was not the least bit shy or frightened now. Had she liked this Mr. Huntley she might have been, but she was filled with a longing to stand up boldly and denounce him as a cruel monster who was trying to turn Eppie and her grandfather out of Forest Glen. She looked straight into his face with big, accusing eyes.

"Jarvis!" said the young man in surprise. "That's a familiar name. Where did you get it, Miss 'Lizbeth Jarvis Gordon?"

Elizabeth gave that haughty turn to her long neck, which the conduct of Charles Stuart and John so often called forth. She looked away straight over the fence-tops. It might be rude, it certainly was not genteel, but she positively refused to converse with a scoundrel who would ill-use Eppie.

Mr. Coulson looked down at her averted face and tightly closed lips, and an amused look flitted over his countenance. He understood this peculiar little Lizzie fairly well, and lately had been feeling very sympathetic towards her, for special reasons of his own.

"She's a namesake of Mrs. Jarvis," he explained. "But you're not in favor. There's a deep friendship here, you understand." He nodded significantly towards Eppie, standing back pale and tearful.

"Oh, I see. And I'm the ogre in the fairy-tale." The young man laughed. "Well, well, Queen Elizabeth, I hope we'll meet again under more friendly auspices. In the meantime, here's something to remember me by." He dived into his pocket, and the two boys behind Elizabeth gave a gasp of astonishment. He was holding towards her a shining silver American dollar!

And then, for the first time in his life, John Gordon felt a thrill of pride in Lizzie. For the little girl stepped hastily back, her hands clasped tightly behind her. Her face grew crimson with shame and anger. Why, no one was ever given money to except the beggars and crossing-sweepers she had read about in the Sunday-school library books! And she–a Gordon–to be offered a coin, as if she were a charity orphan, and by such a horrid, horrid, bad man as this! She flashed him one look of deeply offended dignity, and, catching hold of John's coat, slipped behind him.

The man named Oliver burst again into loud laughter, and slapped his companion on the back.

"Ha! ha! Blake! Turned down that time, all right. Queen Elizabeth's a mighty haughty young lady!"

The young man pretended to laugh, but he really looked annoyed, as he crushed his scorned money back into his pocket, and took up the reins. He did not glance again at the haughty Queen Elizabeth, but nodded curtly to old Sandy. "Good-by, Mr. McLachlan. Don't forget to drop into my office when you're in town. Good-by, Coulson. See you Monday, I suppose."

And, giving his horse a sharp cut with the whip, he went whizzing off down the lane.

"Lizzie Gordon," said Mr. Coulson, catching hold of her sunbonnet and giving her a little shake, "you gave that young man a severer rebuke than I managed in half-an-hour's hard talk. Now, cheer up, Sandy. Things aren't hopeless yet."

"Och, and it iss not hopeless I will be," said the old man, with a stately air. His face lit up, and his eyes took on a far-away look. "I haf never seen the righteous forsaken nor his seed begging bread. That will be the word of God, Mr. Coulson, and not even the lawyers can be breaking that. I will not be righteous, oh, no! The Lord forbid that I say such a word, for it is the evil tongue I will be hafing that will be uttering ungodly words when the dogs will be coming into the house o' the Lord–and a curse on them for pollutin' the holy place! But, indeed an' indeed, it is a miserable sinner I will be. But my father would be a great man of prayer, and versed in the Scriptures, and for his sake the Almighty will not be letting the wee thing come to want. Oh, no, indeed."

There was a sublime faith in the old man's heart that rose above worldly disaster. His little granddaughter crept up to him and laid her little brown hand on his coarse shirt-sleeve.

"The place will be ours, anyway; won't it, grandaddy?" she whispered tremulously. "They couldn't be turning us out, could they?"

As he looked down at her, the old man's mood changed. His fighting blood was rising.

"Eh, them lawyers!" he cried fiercely. "I will be begging your pardon, Mr. Coulson," he added apologetically. "But it will be a great peety that a fine man like yourself would be hafing anything to do with the tribe. But if they had jist been hafing the Gaelic, I would haf been giving it to them. Och, but it will be a peety about the English. It would be but a poor spoke, indeed."

"Well, Sandy, let us hope that there are some honest lawyers. I'm going into Mr. Huntley's office on Monday, and I'll do my best for you. Don't worry."

When the farewells had been said, and Elizabeth had comforted Eppie in parting, the berry-pickers found to their joy that Mr. Coulson was to accompany them for a short distance, on his way to Wully Johnstone's. They had many eager questions to ask him. What were those men doing? the boys demanded. How dared they try to turn old Sandy away? What had they to do with his place, anyway? Mr. Coulson explained that they could not understand it all, for law was a very complex thing indeed. But all this property of Sandy's, as well as Tom Teeter's land, and everything between here and The Dale, had once belonged to Mr. Jarvis, and now belonged to the lady for whom Lizzie was called. Mrs. Jarvis had come to Cheemaun this summer and had asked her lawyer to sell all this property. And now it would appear that old Sandy's farm was for sale, too. For Sandy had no deed of his property; in fact, had merely worked it for Mr. Jarvis, who, Sandy declared, had told him that all south of the Birch Creek belonged to him. But it wasn't in writing, and lawyers did not believe anything they didn't see.

The children listened dismayed, and each proffered his own opinion as to the line of conduct old Sandy should pursue. Charles Stuart would barricade the gates and put up a palisade round the whole farm, the way they did in the old Indian days. Yes, and he would buy a gun and shoot dead anyone who set foot on his property. John heartily agreed with the plan, introducing modifications. A palisade would require all the soldiers in the County of Simcoe to man it. Instead, he would lay mines and torpedoes and deadly man-traps up the lane and all through the bush, so that no approach could be made to the house.

The two walked on ahead, consumed with excitement over the warlike plans, and Elizabeth and Mr. Coulson fell behind. He saw the distress in the little girl's face, and made light of the situation. Eppie would be all right, she need not worry. No one would touch her, not even Mr. Huntley, who was after all not such a bad young man. And, to change the subject to something brighter, he said:

"It's just fine luck you came along this way. I'm going away to-morrow, and I thought I shouldn't see you again."

"But I was up when you were at our place this morning," said Elizabeth, and no sooner were the words out than she could have bitten off her tongue for its indiscretion. She did not need the startled, dismayed look in the young man's eyes, or his crimsoning face, to tell her she had made a shocking mistake, for the older inner self rose up in severe accusation.

"Oh, Mr. Coulson!" she stopped in the pathway and regarded him with deep contrition. "Oh, I didn't mean that! I–I mean I couldn't help seeing. I was watching for fear John would run away on me, and go fishing. And nobody else saw–and Annie doesn't even know. And you know I wouldn't ever, ever tell, don't you?"

She looked up at him with such desperate anxiety that he could not but have confidence in her. His own face cleared.

"You're sure nobody else saw?" he whispered.

"Oh, yes, certain," breathed Elizabeth. "I–I–" she stopped, overcome by the tears of shame that were filling her eyes.

Her teacher took her hand. He could never bear to see a little girl in distress. "There now," he said. "It's all right, Lizzie. But you know, little girl, this is something I can't explain to you, because you are too little to understand. You will know all about it some day. But listen." He stopped and looked at her closely. "I know we can trust you, little Lizzie," he said.

Elizabeth looked up at him through her tears. It was entirely the wise old Elizabeth that was there.

"Yes," she said solemnly, "I wouldn't tell."

He slipped his little notbook from his pocket and scribbled in it. It might be just as well to warn Annie. The two boys had disappeared round a curve in the leafy pathway ahead. He folded the note carefully and handed it to her. "You won't lose it, Lizzie?" he asked. "And you'll give it to Annie when there's no one around?"

"Yes! yes!" cried Elizabeth. She slipped it into the pocket of her blue pinafore, and smiled up at him. She felt wonderfully grown-up and important. Mr. Coulson was putting confidence in her. They had a secret between them, he and she. She said good-by to him at the place where the path to Wully Johnstone's branched off, and away she ran after the boys, dancing with joy.

When the weary and hungry berry-pickers reached home they had an exciting tale to tell and many questions to ask. Tom Teeter came over after tea to give his opinion upon poor old Sandy's case. Jake Martin across from him was trying to buy Sandy's land, folk said, and if Martin did such a thing, then he, Tom Teeter, considered him a more penurious and niggardly miser, that would skin his neighbor's grasshoppers for their hide and tallow, than he had already proven himself to be.

Mr. MacAllister had dropped in, too, as he very often did of an evening, and suspended his work to discuss the question of the moment. Mr. MacAllister's double business of farmer and mill-owner, while not at all taxing his physique, was too much for his mental powers, and he was frequently compelled to have recourse to Mr. Gordon for help. Mr. MacAllister had a peculiar method of calculating the selling price of lumber, which he very appropriately termed "the long way of figgerin'." It was so long that it frequently covered boards and shingles, and even the walls of the mill, before the final number of dollars and cents appeared, the result being that the lumber sawn was all out of proportion to the number of figures required to compute its value.

So Mr. Gordon was frequently appealed to, and with a few magic strokes he would reduce the Long Way to its proper size. On this evening the problem was put aside for the discussion of poor Sandy's affairs. Mr. Martin was known as a hard man throughout the countryside, and Mr. MacAllister gave it as his opinion that if Sandy had Jake Martin and the lawyers after him, he might as well get out of the country. There was no hope for a man when the law got him. For the law was a scheme used by smart folks in town to cheat people out of their earnings.

Mr. Gordon said, "Well, well, well," and, "Indeed and indeed," and hoped things would not be quite so bad. But his sister looked worried in her stately, reserved fashion. To be sure, this business might bring Mrs. Jarvis to her door, who could tell, especially as Mr. Oliver and Mr. Huntley had both seen Elizabeth. But what an Elizabeth to be described to that lady! On the whole, she was worried, and when the visitors were gone she followed her brother into his study and asked to see the paper signed by the late Mr. Jarvis, stating that they had really a lawful claim upon The Dale. And she was not surprised, though much dismayed, to find that her unbusinesslike brother had no such document in his possession.

CHAPTER VI
SCHOOLDAYS

The Forest Glen School opened on a ripe, warm day near the end of August. The Dale Valley lay basking in the sunshine, with that look of perfect rest and content that comes from labor well done. Where the fields were not heavy with the harvest, the barns were bursting with it. The orchard trees bent to the earth with their wealth of red and golden spheres. The wild grape-vines along the roadside were hung with purple clusters. On sunny slopes the golden-rod waved its yellow plumes, the herald of autumn, and near, its companion, the aster, raised its little lavender stars. Summer was at its maturity, warm, ripe, and dreamily restful, with as yet no hint of days less fair.

But dreams and rest were far from the minds of the Gay Gordons as they met the gathering clans in the lane to take their journey down the short-cut to school. Charles Stuart was there, and a crowd of Martins, and even Wully Johnstone's youngsters, who had come half a mile out of their way to join the crowd.

Miss Gordon stood at the door, holding little Jamie by the hand, and watched the happy troop, ladened with schoolbags and dinner-pails, go down the lane. Jamie cried because his "Diddy" was leaving him, and there would be nobody to play with, but Miss Gordon saw them depart with feelings of unmixed pleasure. In a few days Malcolm and Jean would start for the High School in Cheemaun, and what a relief the long, quiet genteel days would be with only Annie for a companion!

Down the lane gayly passed the joyous procession. For the rising generation of Forest Glen had not yet become sophisticated enough to consider school a hardship. Instead, it was a joy, and often an escape from harder work. To the Martins, at least, it was. Jake Martin was indeed a hard man, as the country-side declared, and nowhere did his hand lie heavier than on his own family. There was a Martin to match each Gordon and some left over, and not one of them but already showed signs of toil beyond their young strength. Dairy-farming, market-gardening, poultry-raising, and every known form of making money on the farm was carried on by the Martins on an extensive scale, and everyone, from Mrs. Martin down, was a slave to their swelling bank account. The older boys and girls had already left school to work at home, and those who did go always hurried back to plant or weed or dig in the fields as the season demanded. Susie was Elizabeth's comrade, being of the same age. But there was none of the light and joyous thoughtlessness of Elizabeth's character in poor Susie's life. The little girl's hands were already hardened by the broom, the churn-dasher, and the hoe, and the only emotion Susie ever displayed was fear lest she might be late in reaching home, and so miss five minutes' work and suffer punishment at the hands of her father. Elizabeth often wondered what it would be like to have a father one was afraid of, and was very kind and gentle with Susie, though she considered her a complete failure as a playmate.

As they passed the mill, John and Charles Stuart and Wully Johnstone's Johnny seized the car and took a couple of tumultuous rides down to the water's edge, but the Martin boys went on steadily and solemnly. Their father would be sure to hear if they paused to play on the way to school.

The pond lay cool and brown beneath the shade of the alders and willows. Away up at the end, where the stream entered from its jungle of water-reeds and sunken stumps and brown bullrushes, there grew a tangle of water-plants all in glorious blossom. There were water-lilies both golden and waxy-white, and blue spikes of pickerel-weed, and clumps of fragrant musk. And over the surface of the golden-brown water was spread a fairy web of delicate plant life, vivid green, and woven of such tiny forms that it looked like airy foam that a breath would dissolve. On its outer edge was an embroidery of dainty star-blossoms, like little green forget-me-nots scattered over the glassy surface.

The green and golden vista of flowers that led away up from this fairy nook, with the green and golden water winding between the blossoming banks, always called aloud to Elizabeth whenever she crossed the ravine by the mill-path. She never looked up the creek without longing to explore its winding pathway, right up to the depths of Wully Johnstone's swamp. And yet, strange Elizabeth, when she had once gained her desire, it had given her anything but enjoyment. She and Charles Stuart and John had built a raft from old mill slabs that spring, just when the creek was choked with blue fleur-de-lis and pink ladies'-slippers. They had gone way up stream on a voyage of discovery, bumping over sunken logs, crashing into rotten stumps, and ruthlessly destroying whole acres of moss and water-reeds. It had all been just as lovely as Elizabeth had dreamed, but there were other things upon which she had not reckoned. There were black water-snakes coiled amongst the rushes, and horrible speckled frogs sitting up on water-lily leaves; frogs with awful goggle eyes that looked at you out of the darkness of your bedroom for many, many nights afterwards. There were mud-turtles that paddled their queer little rafts right up to yours, and poked their dreadful snaky heads right up at you out of the water. And besides all the creepy, crawly things that swarmed down in the golden-brown depths and made your hair stand on end when your bare feet touched the water, there were thousands of frightful leggy things that wore skates and ran swiftly at you right over the surface. Even the air was filled with blue "darning-needles" and stingy-looking things, that buzzed and danced about your ears, so that there was no safety nor comfort above nor below. And so Elizabeth had returned from her first visit to her Eldorado full of mingled feelings. And all the time she was learning that great lesson of life: that the fairy bowers which beckon us to come away and play give pure pleasure only when viewed from the stony pathway that leads up to the schoolhouse of duty. But that was a lesson Elizabeth took many years to learn.

So she merely glanced up the creek and sighed as they climbed the hill. She said nothing to Susie of all it meant to her. For Susie, though a very dear girl, was not a person who understood.

Over The Slash they went, through old Sandy McLachlan's woods, down his lane to the highway, and with a last glad rush right into the schoolyard.

Eppie joined Elizabeth at her barnyard gate. Childlike, they had both practically forgotten the fear that had hung over Eppie's head early in the summer, and were happily unconscious that the little home in the woods was already another's.

Forest Glen School stood near the road; so near, indeed, that the porch actually encroached upon the Queen's Highway. But there was plenty of room behind the building. For beyond a lumpy yard, innocent of a blade of grass, stretched miles of Wully Johnstone's swamp, which had been appropriated by the pupils as a playground. This seemed only just, for remains of the forest still held possession of much of the school-grounds proper. Nobody objected to the stumps, however, because they were useful as bases in the ball games, and young Forest Glen had once raised a storm of protest when a visiting lady from town had suggested to Mr. Coulson that he have them removed on Arbor Day. There was a battered old woodshed at the back, its walls covered with carvings, its roof sagging wearily from the weight of many generations of sliders who had shot down its snowy surface to the top of the hill behind. Near it stood a crippled old pump that had brought up water for these same generations of sliders, and was still bringing it up, which perhaps explained its disheartened appearance.

The Dale contingent always arrived early at school, and on this first day they had still more than half an hour at their disposal. The boys rushed into a game of ball, but the girls gathered in groups about the gate to watch for the new teacher. For this one was new in every sense of the word–a lady in fact, and Forest Glen had always heretofore had a man; and the older girls were filled with pleasurable excitement.

Miss Hillary was to board at Martha Ellen Robertson's place, the big, white house not a quarter of a mile down the road. All eyes were fastened upon the red gate to see her emerge, and many were the speculations as to whether she would be tall or short, old or young, plain or pretty, and above all what she should wear.

She appeared at last, and the chief questions were at once settled. She was tall, she was young, she was pretty, and she wore a most beautiful dark-blue dress with a trim white collar and cuffs. She had pretty dark hair, just waving back from her little ears, and shaded by a dainty blue hat, trimmed with a wreath of white daisies. The girls gravitated towards the center of the road, Elizabeth and Rosie at the head of the group. Elizabeth fell in love at first sight. She had vowed with sobs last June that she would never, never love a teacher again, and here she was ready to declare that this one was the most wonderful and beautiful creature she had ever seen.

As the new teacher approached, she smiled in a stately fashion and said, "Good-morning." As she entered the school, the boys drifted farther away from the building and the girls drifted nearer. Some of them even ventured into the room, to see her hang up her hat and take off her gloves. Elizabeth was foremost among the latter. She longed to go up to her and offer her assistance in the many new difficulties which she saw the teacher might meet. She would have liked to show Miss Hillary from the first that she was really quite grown-up and genteel. She would help her with the names in the school register, show her where the chalk was kept, and how the backs came off two of the blackboard brushes, but could be kept on if you just held them right, and how the bottom board of the blackboard might fall if you weren't careful; and ever so much more valuable information. Miss Hillary would have profited much more even than Elizabeth thought, if she had accepted that young lady at her most grown-up estimate; and Elizabeth would have profited even more. But, unfortunately for poor Elizabeth, Miss Hillary was not one who easily understood.

The new teacher rang the bell and the school assembled, the big boys straggling in last and flopping into their seats with a bored and embarrassed air. The room was very quiet, the unaccustomed surroundings impressing everyone into unaccustomed silence. For the place had been all scrubbed and white-washed, and there were wonderful new desks and seats that folded up all of their own accord when you stood up, as if they worked by magic. There was a strange smell of varnish, too, that added much to the feeling of newness.

As soon as prayers were over, the new teacher arose and delivered her opening speech. Her manner was still distant and stately. She wished to speak to them particularly, she said, on deportment, for she had discovered that the children of rural communities were sadly deficient in manners. Elizabeth quite lost the purport of the little address in her admiration of the beautiful, long, high-sounding words with which it was garnished. Elizabeth loved long words. She wished she could remember just one or two of the biggest, and she would use them when Mrs. Jarvis came. Suddenly a fine plan was born in her fertile brain. All unmindful that Miss Hillary had given strict commands to everyone to sit straight with folded arms, she snatched her slate and pencil. She would write down the finest and most high-sounding of those words, and how pleased and surprised Aunt Margaret would be when she used them. She would look them up in the dictionary just as soon as she could get a breathing-spell. There were "ideals" and "aspirations" and "deportment" many times, and "disciplined"–which last Elizabeth spelled without a "c." There were "principles" and "insubordination," and "contumacious," over the spelling of which Elizabeth had such a very bad time, and "esprit de corps," which, fortunately, she gave up altogether, and ever so many more, which flew over her head like birds of paradise, brilliant and alluring, but not to be caught. Some, Elizabeth could remember having heard her father use, and, proudly recognizing them as old friends, let them pass.

She was utterly absorbed in her task, her pencil flying over her slate, squeaking madly, when right in the midst of "irresponsible" with one "r" and several other letters wanting, she paused. It was a poke from Rosie that disturbed her. Elizabeth was accustomed to being poked by Rosie, for her seat-mate always attracted one's attention this way; but her pokes were always eloquent and this one betokened alarm and urgency. For a moment or more Elizabeth had been vaguely conscious that there was a lull in Miss Hillary's talk and a strange silence over the room, but she had merely taken the opportunity to stick syllables on the ends of certain words which haste had compelled her to curtail. She was in the act of fixing up "contumacious," and making it a little more un-English if possible, when the poke awoke her to her surroundings.

She looked up. All eyes were upon her–disapproving and ashamed Gordon eyes, others amused or only interested, and, worst of all, the new teacher's, stern and annoyed. Elizabeth's pencil dropped from her paralyzed fingers. It broke in three pieces–the beautiful, long, new pencil with the gold paper covering, which Mr. Coulson had given her at parting; and Miss Hillary said, oh, so coldly, and sternly:

"There is one little girl in the class who has been paying no attention whatever to anything I have been saying. That little girl will please come forward and take the front seat."

Elizabeth turned pale, and John and Mary hung their heads. Oh, wasn't it just like Lizzie to do something to disgrace the family–and right on the first day of school, too! The culprit arose, and slowly made her way forward, trembling with fear. This wonderful new creature whom she adored was after all an unknown quantity, and Elizabeth was always afraid of the unknown. She went up the aisle all unseeing. She did not even notice Rosie's glance of anguish as she left.

She stood before the teacher's desk with hanging head. "Sit down," Miss Hillary said coldly, and Elizabeth turned to obey. Now in olden times there had been a row of benches in front of the platform upon which the classes sat before their teacher, but these were gone and instead were those magic folding seats, all closed up tight. Elizabeth, still blind with fear, went to sit down upon a bench where no bench was, and instead sat down soundingly upon the floor. A titter of laughter ran over the room, and she sprang to her feet. She was quite unhurt, except her dignity, but even this she did not notice. The funny side of anything, though the joke was on herself, was always irresistible to Elizabeth. Miss Hillary might kill her the next moment, but for the present she must laugh, and laugh she did aloud, showing her gleaming teeth in a short spasm of merriment. But the fun vanished as quickly as it had come. She had no sooner struggled into the unwilling seat, and looked up at her teacher, than she froze again with apprehension.

Miss Hillary had arisen and was looking down at her, a red spot on either cheek, her eyes angry and flashing. Elizabeth could not know that the young teacher was in terror of the pupils, terror lest they take advantage of her being a woman, and was nervously on the outlook for signs of insubordination. She was almost as afraid of this mischievous-looking, little brown thing as the little thing was of her, and even suspected her of planning the ridiculous tumble for her own and the school's amusement. Miss Hillary was weak, and displayed the cruelty that so often characterizes weakness in a place of power.

"What is your name?" she demanded sternly.

"'Lizbeth," faltered the culprit. "'Lizbeth Gordon."

"How old are you?"

"Ten," whispered Elizabeth. She always said, "Going on eleven." But now, feeling keenly that she had acted in a shocking manner, to be ten did not sound quite so bad. A mature person on the road to eleven would never, never be called to the front the first day of school!

"Well, Elizabeth Gordon," said Miss Hillary, "any big girl of ten should have learned long ago that it is very rude and unladylike to sit writing when her teacher is talking to her. I want you to remain in this front seat, where I can watch you, until you have learned to be mannerly. To ignore your teacher is extremely reprehensible, but to laugh over your conduct is positively impertinent."

Poor Elizabeth crumpled up in a forlorn, little, blue-checked heap. "Rude and unladylike!" Those were the condemnatory words her aunt so often used, but the anguish they awoke was as nothing to the awful shame that descended upon her soul in the avalanche of those unknown words. "Impertinent," she remembered to have heard somewhere before. It meant something deadly–but what shameless depths might not be revealed by "reprehensible"? And, oh dear, oh dear, she had intended to be so wise and so grown-up, and be her teacher's right hand. The beautiful teacher she loved so! That was the tragedy of poor Elizabeth's life, she was always hurting someone she loved. What a dreary twist of fate it was that when one's intentions were the best one was always most–"reprehensible"! The tears came dripping down upon the blue pinafore. She remembered with dismay that she had no handkerchief. She had forgotten hers in her hurry, and Mary had said she might use hers if she needed it. But she dared not even look in Mary's direction, knowing there were rows of curious eyes down there all turned upon her. So she wiped the tears away on her pinafore, a proceeding which Aunt Margaret had characterized as positively vulgar, but Elizabeth knew that in Miss Hillary's opinion of her nothing mattered any more.

The new teacher finished her interrupted address, and began the regular work of the school. Elizabeth was forgotten, and slowly came up from the depths of despair, mounting on the wings of future glory. Miss Hillary would be sorry some day–some day when she, Elizabeth Gordon, high on her white charger, with her velvet cloak streaming behind, rode swiftly past the schoolhouse, never glancing in. Yes, Miss Hillary might weep and wring her hands and declare she had made an awful mistake in regard to Lizzie Gordon, but it would be too late.

Vastly encouraged by these dreams, the heroine of them dried her tears, and sat listening to what was going on about her. Miss Hillary was calling each class forward, taking down their names, and testing their abilities in reading, spelling, and a few other subjects. The primary class was on the floor, and Archie was standing, straight and sturdy, right before his sister. Elizabeth did not dare raise her head, but she peeped at her little brother from under her tangle of hair. She did hope Archie would lift the name of Gordon from the mire in which she had dragged it.

Archie was certainly conducting himself manfully. He spelled every word the teacher gave him, added like lightning, and read loud and clear: "Ben has a pen and a hen. The hen is in the pen. I see Ben and the hen and the pen."

Miss Hillary looked pleased, and Archie went up head. "What is your name?" she asked kindly, and he responded, "Archie Gordon." The teacher glanced towards the culprit on the front seat. There was a strong family resemblance amongst all the Gay Gordons, and Elizabeth fairly swelled with restored self-respect.

The classes filed up, each in its turn, standing in a prim line with its toes to a chalk-mark Miss Hillary had drawn on the floor. Nothing exciting happened until Mary's class was called, and then Elizabeth turned cold with a new fear. Just as they reached the chalk-line, only half a dozen of them, Miss Hillary said: "As this Junior Third is so small a class, for convenience I believe I shall put the Senior Thirds with them. Senior Third class, rise! Forward!"

Now, Elizabeth was in the Senior Third. Strangely precocious in some ways, she was woefully lacking in many branches of school work, and barely kept a class ahead of Mary. The fear that Mary would overtake her was the one thing that spurred her to spasmodic efforts. And now, like a bolt from the blue, came the dreadful news. She and Mary were to be in the same class!

The Seniors arose and filed reluctantly forward. Rosie poked Elizabeth as she passed. Elizabeth understood Rosie's pokes better than other people's plainest statement. This one said: "Isn't this a dreadful shame? How shall we ever live it down?" And then a sudden stubborn resolution seized Elizabeth, and she sat up straight with crimsoning cheeks. She would not go up into Mary's class, no she wouldn't! The teacher had said she must sit there until she had learned to be mannerly. Well, she would then! She hadn't learned yet, and she likely never would. And she would sit there on that front seat until she was older than old Granny Johnstone, who spoke only Gaelic and had no teeth, before she would go up in the same class with Mary! Mary was a good speller, and might get ahead of her, and oh, how John and Charles Stuart and Malcolm and Jean would talk if Mary beat her at school! Elizabeth grew hot at the bare thought.

The big class had just arranged itself when one little girl held up her hand. It was Katie Price, of course. Katie always told on everybody, and was only in the Junior Third herself. "Please, teacher," said Katie, "Lizzie Gordon's in the Senior Third." "Lizzie Gordon?" The teacher looked round vaguely. The swelling list of new names was puzzling her. "Where is Lizzie Gordon?"

Elizabeth did not move. To be forgotten utterly was the best she hoped for; to be noticed was the worst thing that could happen. Mary indicated her sister by a nod, and Miss Hillary grew haughty again.

"Oh," she said, "never mind her at present. We will let Lizzie Gordon remain where she is for the rest of the morning." And on she went with her work, while Lizzie Gordon, the outcast, too wicked even to be included in a disgraced class, sat and hung her head in a very abasement of soul.

She came out of the depths once at a thrilling remark of the teacher. The double-class crowded and shoved this way and that, and Miss Hillary said, just as they were about to return to their seats: "There are four or five too many in this class. I shall examine the Seniors thoroughly this afternoon, and shall allow the best four to go into the Junior Fourth."

Elizabeth fairly jumped off her penitent form. Her hopes soared to the highest pinnacle.

She would be one of the four! She must! Not only would it mean escape from Mary, but she would be but one class behind John and Charles Stuart! Yes, she would pass in spite of fate. If only Miss Hillary would not examine them in arithmetic or spelling or grammar it would be easy. She was equally deficient in all three, with a few disgraces in favor of spelling. But who knew but she would ask questions in history or literature! Or even make them write a composition! Elizabeth could not help knowing that in this one last subject at least she far surpassed her classmates.

Perhaps they would have to write one, and when the new teacher read it she would say: "Lizzie Gordon, you are too good for the Junior Fourth even. You may go into the Senior Fourth with your brother John and Charles Stuart MacAllister."

Elizabeth fairly ached for some distinction that would reinstate her in the teacher's good opinion. She began to build airy castles and grew positively happy with hope. She was thankful even for the unkind fate that had brought her to the front seat, for now Mary would never be able to say, "Lizzie and I were once in the same class, and she's a year and four months older than I am." Noah Clegg had said last Sunday that people should be thankful for trials, as they often brought blessing. Elizabeth devoutly agreed with him. She closed her eyes and thought how thankful she should be that she had been snatched as a brand from Mary's class. No one could pray in school, of course, and sitting up straight, that would be very wicked. But she resolved that when she said her prayers that night she would add a word of fervent gratitude for her escape.

The Senior Fourth class was assembling now, the highest in the school. Elizabeth gazed in longing admiration at John and Charles Stuart. How glorious it must be away up there, and preparing for the High School, too! Miss Hillary was asking names again, "Sammy Martin, John Gordon." She paused and smiled. She had been growing more genial as the morning advanced and Forest Glen showed no signs of mutiny.

"There seems to be a Martin and a Gordon for every class," she remarked, and Elizabeth's heart leaped. Perhaps this was a hint that instead of two Gordons in the Third class there would be one in the Junior Fourth. "Charles Stuart MacAllister" was the next name. Miss Hillary smiled again. "Are you the Pretender?" she asked, and the Senior Fourth all laughed at Charles Stuart's expense.

"I do not like double names," she added pleasantly. "They are too cumbersome." Elizabeth stored up the word greedily. "I shall call you Stuart, as there are four other Charlies here."

When recess was over, so good-humored had Miss Hillary become that she apparently forgot that Lizzie Gordon was to be taught how to be mannerly, and sent her to her seat to take part in the examination. Elizabeth slipped in beside Rosie, breathless with relief. Rosie had been preparing her welcome. She had sharpened the three pieces of the broken pencil to points fine and delicate as needles, she had piled all her friend's books in a neat row, and put a pink tissue-paper frill like her own around her ink-well. Elizabeth sighed happily. It was such a privilege to have a Rosie for one's friend.

Miss Hillary had paused in her work to give a little address on the proper way to wash one's slate, and to Elizabeth's joy and pride she held up Rosie as a shining example. Rosie had a big pickle bottle of water, and a little sponge tied to her slate by a string. Everything about Rosie was always so dainty. Elizabeth had a slate-rag somewhere, but someone had always borrowed it when she needed it, so she generally re-borrowed or used Rosie's sponge. Elizabeth wished she had been nice like Rosie and Miss Hillary had commended her. But somehow she never had time for scrubbing her desk and decorating it with rows of cards and frills of colored paper, as Rosie so often did. There were so many things to do in school. She was thankful, however, that she was not like big, fat Joel Davis across the aisle there, who spat on his slate and rubbed it with his sleeve. It was his action, one which Miss Hillary characterized as disgusting and unsanitary, that had called forth the little talk. And she ended up with the announcement that once a week she would give a short talk on "Manners and Morals."

Elizabeth scented a new word. "Disgusting" she knew, Aunt Margaret often used it. It meant the opposite to genteel. But "insanitary" was a discovery. She tried to store it in her mind, not daring to move her tightly folded hands towards her slate. Perhaps it was something like insanity, and Miss Hillary meant that anyone who didn't use a slate-rag and water-bottle was crazy.

But the examination was on, and the Senior Thirds, anxious and hopeful, were soon at work. Arithmetic came first, and only the anticipation of better things to come, and the forlorn hope that the problem might somehow turn out right by chance, kept up Elizabeth's spirits. There were three problems, and she could make nothing of them, though she added, subtracted, divided, and multiplied, and covered her slate with figures in the hope of achieving something. She worked in some statements, too, for Rosie had advised her that written statements always looked nice, and would probably make the teacher think the question was well done anyway. So in the complex problem inquiring how many men would eat how much salt pork in how many days, Elizabeth set down carefully:

If 18 men eat 36 lbs. in 1 day,
Then 1 men eat 36 lbs. X 18 men.

It might not be right, but it looked well anyway. Rosie telegraphed her answer on her fingers, but Elizabeth shut her eyes tight and turned away. Not if she were to be put into Archie's class would she stoop to such methods to gain marks.

Spelling was not much better. There were ten awful words, all from a lesson Elizabeth had long ago given up, "Egypt and its Ruins." There were "pyramids" and "hieroglyphics," and many others quite as bad, and when she was through with them they presented an orthographical ruin which might put any of the fallen temples of Egypt to shame.

But all her trials were forgotten when at the end Miss Hillary announced a composition on "A Summer Day." The joy of it drove away even the remembrance of the eighteen men and their allowance of pork. Elizabeth seized a sheet of paper, and doubling up over the desk wrote furiously.

Rosie sighed at the sight of her flying pen. There was no pleasure for Rosie in writing essays. She had already written carefully and slowly, "A summer day is a beautiful time, summer is a nice season," then she stopped and enviously watched Elizabeth spattering ink. That young poetess was reveling in birds and flowers and rain-showers and walks through the woods, with the blue sky peeping at one through the green branches.

She paused only to consult her dictionary. She was working in the list of words culled from the morning address. She would show Miss Hillary that if she hadn't manners, at least she had forethought. She was compelled very reluctantly to discard some of the list, as they failed to appear in the dictionary under their new arrangement of letters. She sighed especially over "contumacious"; it was so beautifully long. But there were plenty of others. "The flowers do not grow in a disciplined way," she wrote– the word still innocent of a "c."–"The birds have high aspirations. Their deportment is very nice, but it is not always genteel." Here Elizabeth had a real inspiration. A quotation from Shelley's "Skylark" came into her mind. John and Charles Stuart had memorized it one evening, and the glorious rhythm of it had sung itself into her soul. There were some things one could not help learning. Then, too, as it was from the Fourth Reader, Elizabeth felt that Miss Hillary would see that she was familiar with that book and feel assured she was ready for it. So she wrote such stanzas as she remembered perfectly, commencing:

"Sound of vernal showers
On the twinkling grass,
Rain-awakened flowers,
All that ever was
Joyous, and clear, and fresh, thy music doth surpass."

There were many misspelled words, but the quotation was aptly inserted, and she added the note that the skylark was so joyous he often acted in an insanitary manner.

She was still writing swiftly when Miss Hillary said, "Fold papers." Elizabeth had barely time to finish her second poetic contribution. It was from her own pen this time, one verse of a long poem she had written in secret evenings, after Mary had gone to sleep:

"Oh beautiful summer thou art so fare,
With thy flours and thy trees that grow everywhere,
The birds on the bows are singing so gay,
Oh how I love them on a bright summer's day!

"P.S.–This pome is original–that is, made up by the author.

"Lizzie Gordon."

Rosie had finished long ago and had carefully inscribed at the conclusion of her essay:

"Rosamond Ellen Carrick,
Forest Glen,
Ontario,
Canada,
North America,
Western Hemisphere."

All of which helped to lengthen out her too brief contribution. She was now ready to assist her friend in her last hasty scramble. Elizabeth had no blotting-paper–she never had. Rosie provided a piece and the composition was ready at last. Elizabeth sighed over it. There were so many clever things she might have put in had she only had time. There was "viz.," for instance, instead of "that is," in the last sentence. "Viz." sounded so learned.

When the afternoon recess came, Miss Hillary called Elizabeth to her. She had an essay before her, and she was looking puzzled, and not nearly so stern.

"Elizabeth," she said gently, "what were you writing on your slate this morning when I was speaking?"

Elizabeth's head drooped. In a shamed whisper she confessed that Miss Hillary's wonderful vocabulary had tempted her. She dared not look up and did not see that her teacher's pretty mouth twitched.

"Well," she said in a very pleasant tone, "you did not behave so badly after all. But remember, you must always sit still and listen when I am talking."

Elizabeth's head came up. Her face was radiant, her gray eyes shone starlike.

"Oh, Miss Hillary!" she gasped, overcome with gratitude at this giving back of her self-respect. Miss Hillary picked up the next essay, and the little girl turned way. But she could not leave without one word of hope.

"Oh, Miss Hillary," she whispered again, "do you think you could let me pass? If you'll only not put me in Mary's class, I'll, I'll–I believe I could learn to spell!" she finally added, as the most extravagant promise she could possibly make.

Miss Hillary smiled again. She looked kindly at the small, anxious figure, the pleading face with its big eyes, the slim, brown hands twisting nervously the long, heavy braid of brown hair with the golden strand through it.

"Well, I shall do my best," she said. "You can certainly write, even if you can't do arithmetic. Now run away and play."

And, wild with hope and joy, Elizabeth dashed down the aisle and out of the door, so noisy and boisterous that for a moment her teacher felt constrained to call her back and give her another lesson in deportment. For Miss Hillary did not yet understand.

CHAPTER VII
THE AGE OF CHIVALRY

Many years later there came days in Elizabeth Gordon's life when she achieved a certain amount of fame, but never at their height did any day shine so radiantly for her or bring her anything of the exaltation of that moment when she and Rosie tremblingly took their places side by side at the foot of the Junior Fourth class.

For a time Elizabeth strove to live up to her lofty position. The fear of even yet being sent back to Mary's class, which Miss Hillary held over her as an incentive to working fractions, drove her to make desperate efforts even to learn spelling. Rosie helped her all she could, and Rosie was a perfect wonder at finding royal roads to learning. If you could spell a word over seventeen times without drawing your breath, she promised, you would be able to repeat it correctly forever after. Elizabeth tried this plan with "hieroglyphics," but reached the end of her breath, purple and gasping, with only fourteen repetitions to her credit. She attributed her failure to spell the word the next day to this, rather than to the fact that, in her anxiety to accomplish the magic number, she had changed the arrangement of the letters several times.

But as the days passed, and the danger of being returned to the Third class disappeared, Elizabeth relaxed her efforts and returned to her habitual employment of drawing pictures on her slate and weaving about them rose-colored romances. Another danger was disappearing, too. Miss Hillary, finding that Forest Glen School was not hatching rebellion, gradually became less vigilant, and there was in consequence much pleasant social intercourse in the schoolroom.

Of course Elizabeth, like the other pupils, found that one could not always be sure of the teacher. She might never notice a slate dropped upon the floor, provided one took care to drop it on a day when she didn't have a nervous headache. But on the other hand, if one chose one's occasion injudiciously, she might send one to stand for half an hour in the corner, even though one was a big girl, now going on twelve.

But Rosie found the key to this uncertain situation, also. Rosie's farm joined the Robertsons', where Miss Hillary boarded, and the small, observant neighbor discovered a strange connection between her teacher's headaches and the actions of a certain young gentleman from town. She explained it all to Elizabeth one day, behind their slates, when the complex fraction refused to become simple.

Rosie was very solemn and very important. Martha Ellen Robertson had told her big sister Minnie all about it, and Rosie had heard every word. Miss Hillary had a fellow, only Elizabeth must promise for dead sure that she'd never, never tell. Because, of course, anything about a fellow was always a dreadful secret. This young man was very stylish and very handsome, and he lived in Cheemaun, and, of course, must be very rich, because everybody was who lived there. He came out nearly every Sunday in a top-buggy and took Miss Hillary for a drive. Minnie and Martha Ellen both said it was perfectly scand'lus to go driving Sundays, and the trustees ought to speak to her. The young man wrote to Miss Hillary, too, for every Wednesday she went to the post-office, and Mrs. Clegg said she 'most always got a letter. But sometimes she didn't; and the important point for themselves was just here–Rosie grew very impressive–they had to watch out on Mondays and Thursdays, if the young man didn't come, or if the letter failed, for then sure and certain Miss Hillary would go and get a headache and be awful cross and strict. Yes, it was true, because Jessie Robertson, and Lottie Price, and Teenie Johnstone, and all the big girls said so. And Jessie Robertson had promised to tell them so they could be careful, and Lizzie could just look out and see if she wasn't right.

Elizabeth did look out, and found as usual that Rosie was correct. Rosie was so wonderful and so clever that, though she was only half a year older than her friend, the latter lived in constant admiration of her sagacity. For, as far as worldly wisdom was concerned, Rosie was many, many years older than the precocious Elizabeth.

The young man of the top-buggy soon became a fruitful source of gossip in the schoolroom, especially amongst the older girls. Jessie Robertson, who lived right at the base of supplies, issued semi-weekly bulletins as to whether they might expect a headache or not, and Forest Glen conducted itself accordingly.

So, having settled exactly the periods of danger, and finding that often Mondays and Thursdays were days of happiness and license, Forest Glen settled down securely to its intermittent studies.

Elizabeth soon ceased to trouble much even over spelling, and she and Rosie gave themselves up to the fashion of the hour. And every hour had its fashion. For like most rural schools, amongst the girls at least, Forest Glen was a place of fads and fancies.

No one ever knew just how or why a new craze arose, but there was always one on the tapis. At one time it was pickles. No one could hope for any social recognition unless one had a long, green cucumber pickle in one's dinner-pail–the longer the pickle the higher one's standing. Fads ranged all the way from this gastronomic level to the highly esthetic, where they broke out in a desire for the decorative in the form of peep-shows. A peep-show was an arrangement of flowers and leaves pressed against a piece of glass and framed in colored tissue-paper. Every girl had one on her desk; even to dirty, unkempt Becky Davis. Elizabeth was not a success at such works of art. She was a wonder at inventing new patterns, and gained recognition from even the big girls by suggesting a design of tiny, scarlet maple leaves, green moss, and gold thread. But when it came to construction, she left that to Rosie and took to drawing new designs on her slate. No one could compete with Rosie anyway. She had something new and more elaborate each morning.

But the craze for peep-shows was superseded early in Miss Hillary's reign by an entirely new fad, such as had never manifested itself before in any marked degree in the school. Miss Hillary, quite unwittingly, started it herself.

It was a warm, languorous afternoon in October, and time hung as heavily over the heads of the pupils as the mists hung over the amethyst hollows and sunny hills of Forest Glen. It was Thursday and Miss Hillary was writing at her desk. Lottie Price, the biggest girl in school and the most curious and observing, wrote a note to Teenie Johnstone to say she bet anything the teacher was writing to her fellow. Lottie knew, because Miss Hillary often looked straight at you and didn't see you at all. That was a sure sign. In the back seat, John Gordon and the Pretender, as everyone now called Charles Stuart, were silently but busily whittling away, constructing part of a wonderful new kind of ground-hog trap. Elizabeth had filled one side of her slate with an elaborate picture of a castle on a hill, a stream, a lake, a ship, and an endless vista of town and road and church-spire stretching away into the distance. She had never heard of that school of artists that painted the classic landscapes, but she belonged to them as surely as any of the old Italian masters. She was now drawing Mrs. Jarvis in a trained gown standing on the steps of the castle, while Elizabeth Joan of Arc Jarvis Gordon, blowing a bugle, came riding down a perpendicular mountain-path on a stiff-legged steed. Rosie had just housecleaned her desk for the second time that day. She had rubbed all the ink-spots off the top and put a new paper frill around the ink-well. She was re-arranging her books once more and had them in an unsteady pile on the edge of her desk, when Elizabeth leaned over to her side, to display her finished landscape. Rosie's arm came against the toppling pile of books, and they went crashing to the floor.

Miss Hillary looked up. The two culprits sat up very straight and made a frantic show of figuring on their slates. For Jessie had reported no letter that morning, and who knew what might happen? The teacher arose frowning, and Rosie made a desperate dive towards the truant books, but Miss Hillary stopped her. Then, to the amazement and relief of the two tremblers, she began to rebuke, not Rosie, but Joel Davis! Joel was a big, sleepy, fat boy who sat opposite the two little girls, and the books had bounced over towards his seat. No boy was a gentleman, Miss Hillary stated, who would allow a lady to pick up anything that had fallen. She was grieved, after all the lessons she had given in manners and morals, to find that one of her pupils could be so lacking in refinement. Joel would, therefore, please gather up Rosie Carrick's books, and put them on her desk, as a gentleman should always do for a lady.

Joel scratched his shaggy head in perplexity, and gazed sleepily at his teacher, then at the debris of books and pictures and tissue-paper squares that littered the floor. He muttered growlingly that a kid like Rosie Carrick wasn't no lady anyhow; but he good-naturedly scooped up an armful of the fallen, and without moving himself unduly reached them out towards their owner. The school giggled, poor Rosie blushed, and in a spasm of embarrassment strove to take them. Between them the books once more descended to the floor in an avalanche of gayly-colored cards and papers. Rosie stooped for them, so did Joel, and their heads bumped together. The young gentleman, now blushing as furiously as the young lady, grasped the books in a promiscuous heap and slammed them down upon Rosie's desk with, "There now, butter-fingers." The school laughed aloud, and Rosie curled up behind the pile of books and cried with vexation. Joel Davis was such a horrid, horrid, dirty, fat boy that it was just real nasty mean of Miss Hillary to let him pick up her books, so it was. Elizabeth, all sympathy, patted her comfortingly, and twisted one of Rosie's curls round her fingers as she whispered soothing words.

But Miss Hillary was again talking, and she slid over to her own side of the seat and gave scared attention. It was time she gave another talk upon manners and morals, the teacher declared, and Elizabeth's heart sank. She knew she had no manners to speak of, and on Sundays she was often doubtful of her morals. And when Miss Hillary gave semi-monthly lectures on these two troublesome subjects they caused her acute misery. But to-day the address was chiefly to the boys. Evidently it was only the masculine side of the school that was lacking in manners and morals. Miss Hillary declared she must strive to inculcate a spirit of chivalry in them, and teach them the proper attitude towards girls.

Elizabeth gave a sigh of relief. This was no concern of hers, except that she devoutly hoped it might make John and the Pretender stop pulling hair. So she gave her attention to softly taking down the longest words the little lecture contained. Miss Hillary had gone sufficiently far on the road of understanding to make this safe. She sometimes even glanced approvingly at her disciple's flying fingers when she uttered a polysyllable of more than usual distinction. Rosie came from behind her shelter of books, and, wiping away her tears, attempted to help Elizabeth. There was a word that Lizzie had missed, she cautioned. Something like "shivering"–a spirit of shivering or "shivaree." But Elizabeth, in the midst of "gallantry," shook her head. That was just chivalry. She knew all about that. It was a glorious word that took in Ivanhoe, and the ladye that went ower the border and awa', and Joan of Arc, yes–and Elizabeth herself. But there was no use trying to explain it to Rosie, for, though Rosie was the dearest dear that ever sat with anybody in school, there were many things that even she did not understand.

Meanwhile, the talk on manners and morals had drawn to a close and Elizabeth went back to her classic landscape and Rosie to her house-cleaning. But the effect of the lecture did not end there. Hector McQueen, who was the handsomest boy in the school, as well as the only one who was really well-behaved, gave Rosie Carrick the tin dipper before he drank himself, at the pump the next day. Wully Johnstone's Johnny followed by opening the gate for Sissy Clegg one morning, which was quite gratuitous, for Sissy always climbed the fence anyway. Soon the older boys were vying with each other in acts of gallantry. The spirit of chivalry had been awakened and it took effect in a way the teacher had not anticipated.

For a time Elizabeth was all unconscious of the turn affairs were taking. John and Charles Stuart were not the kind who attracted attention by acts of elaborate politeness, and other boys did not enter into her world. So it was a great surprise to her one morning, when Rosie whispered, as she packed away her latest peep-shows in the desk, that the girls were not going to make any more; they were going to have beaux instead.

"Bows?" queried Elizabeth absently, all absorbed in a winding river, a moat, and a drawbridge. "Aunt Margaret won't let me have one, I know. Will they wear them on their hair?"

Rosie dived down behind her slate and her curls shook violently with convulsive giggles. Elizabeth had no idea what the joke was, but laughter was always contagious, and she got behind her slate and giggled, too; so loud, indeed, that Miss Hillary–it was Monday and the top-buggy had not come out from Cheemaun–rapped sharply on her desk and looked very severe. The giggles subsided immediately, but when a safe interval had elapsed Rosie explained the nature of the bows, and another spasm ensued.

"What are they going to have them for?" asked Elizabeth, drying her eyes on her pinafore. She could understand one desiring a bow on the hair, but what would be the function, either useful or ornamental, of the kind Rosie indicated was hard to understand.

Rosie twisted one of her curls coyly. "Oh, just because," she explained. "All the girls are getting them."

Elizabeth became interested. "Have you one, Rosie?" she whispered, and Rosie tossed her curls and giggled, but gave no answer. Elizabeth looked puzzled. Often Rosie seemed so old and wise and far away, making her feel as if she were Jamie's age.

"How do you get one?" was the next question.

"Oh, my goodness!" giggled Rosie. Such ignorance did not admit of any enlightenment. "They just–come," she explained vaguely.

The Junior Fourth class was being called forward and there was no more opportunity for explanations. But, as they passed up the aisle, Elizabeth noticed Rosie flirt her curls and glance towards Hector McQueen's seat, and Hector's admiring eyes followed Rosie all the way to her class. "Is yours Hector McQueen?" Elizabeth whispered as soon as they reached their scat again, and Rosie nodded radiantly. Elizabeth was both proud and pleased. She did not know much about boys, apart from John and Malcolm and the Pretender. All outside this list were classed in her mind as "other boys," and were an unknown waste. But Hector McQueen, everybody knew, was quite the nicest boy in school. It was just like Rosie to carry off the prize.

As the days went on, Elizabeth, now fully awake to the fashion of the hour, noticed that Rosie had been quite right–"all the girls" had beaux. Even big, untidy Becky Davis was receiving attentions from Noah Clegg, Junior. She furthermore discovered that your beau brought you apples and butter-nuts to school. That you trimmed his hat with colored maple leaves at recess, and always chose him as your partner in games; that he wrote you notes in school, when Miss Hillary was answering her Wednesday letter, and you wrote back; and, above all, that the other girls wrote your name and his side-by-side on a slate, struck out all the common letters, and over the remainder chanted, "Friendship, Love, Hatred, Marriage." If the result on both sides was satisfactory, there was nothing more to be desired.

Elizabeth noticed all this commotion and felt rather forlorn. Personally she would have preferred very much not to have a beau. It was something quite unnecessary; but then one hated to be different, and she was the only girl in her class, except Eppie Turner, who was too shy to speak to a boy, who was in a beauless state. Rosie, in her loyalty, felt Elizabeth's undesirable condition and strove to better it.

"I'll tell you, Lizzie," she advised one day. "You pick out a boy and I'll cancel your names and then you can have him for your fellow."

Elizabeth looked about her reluctantly. This was a most distasteful task. Yet, when pickles were the fad, though green cucumbers made her deadly sick, she had always had one in her desk; so surely a beau could not be worse. Rosie followed her eyes trying to assist. "You must have somebody older than yourself," she admonished, as her chum's eyes rested fondly on the row of little fellows in Archie's class. Elizabeth sighed; to have Rosie's little, curly-headed brother Dicky for one's beau would have been perfectly lovely. She glanced further down the aisle. Rosie indicated those who were "taken." The rights of property were strictly observed and there were no flirts in the Forest Glen School.

Suddenly Rosie exclaimed joyfully: "Why, I know who you'll have, Lizzie, Charles Stuart MacAllister, of course. Nobody's took him or your John, but you couldn't have your brother." But Elizabeth shook her head hopelessly. No, never, never. She would go down to history as the only unbeaued girl in Forest Glen School forever and ever before she would have Charles Stuart. Why, she had tried him. Yes, she really, truly had, long ago last summer. He'd been her beau for most nearly an hour. But it hadn't worked at all. He had told her she had green eyes right after she had promised to marry him, and she didn't like him anyway. Rosie looked disappointed. Couldn't she just cancel their names anyway? But Elizabeth was obdurate. No, she couldn't. Besides there was one boy whom she liked just a teenty, weenty bit, if Rosie would promise really, truly she'd never, never tell. Rosie snuggled up to her joyfully, making wholesale promises that sure certain, cross her heart, she'd never think of it again. Well–Elizabeth made her confession hesitatingly–it was–Charlie Peters.

Rosie drew back with a gasp of dismay and bit her lip. Now every girl in Forest Glen School knew that when another girl took her lower lip between her teeth and looked sideways, girl number one had done or said something requiring a deadly reproof. Elizabeth was startled. "Why not?" she asked anxiously.

Rosie looked at her helplessly. Lizzie was so queer about some things. Poor, dirty Charlie Peters! What in the world had possessed her? He was a quiet, sickly boy, who came from a place away back in the swamp where his father worked a portable saw-mill. He was always unkempt and ragged; his long, straight hair clung round his pale face and his right sleeve hung empty, his arm having been cut off in the mill when he was quite little. Elizabeth could not explain the fascination that poor Charlie's empty sleeve had for her, nor the great compassion his pale face and his pitiful efforts to write with his left hand raised in her heart. But he aroused far more interest in her mind than all the "other boys" put together. Rosie argued the matter, but at last consented. A dirty, ragged sweetheart was perhaps after all better than none. "Besides it doesn't matter much," she concluded practically. "'Cause it's only to tease you about, and cancel your names." She added cautiously that Lizzie had better not tell anybody else, it would be a secret between them, thus loyally saving her friend from public disgrace.

Elizabeth consented, and Rosie wrote Elizabeth Jarvis Gordon and Charles Henry Peters on her slate and performed the necessary ceremony. It turned out quite satis- factorily, and Rosie's next duty was to chant the usual incantation over the buttons of her friend's pinafore:

"Rich man, poor man, beggar man, thief,
Doctor, lawyer, merchant, chief."

There were just eleven buttons, which brought the ominous result, "beggar man." Rosie gave herself up to renewed dismay, but Elizabeth grew more joyful every moment. It would be very romantic to marry a beggar man, and likely poor Charlie would have to be one, seeing he was so sick and had only one arm. It would be just like the story in the *Chronicle*, of the lovely Lady Evelina, who ran away with the coachman, and he turned out a count! She accordingly set to work at her slate, and drew a picture of herself riding up in all her grandeur of velvet-cloak, armor, and spear to rescue a ragged, one-armed boy from an enemy's camp. Elizabeth's instincts were right, the touch of self-sacrifice she dimly divined was necessary to make an act of perfect heroism.

For the next few days Rosie lived in distress, lest Elizabeth's unfortunate love affair became public and both she and her chum be disgraced. But, before disaster could descend, Elizabeth's clouded destiny changed to one of dazzling splendor in the most miraculous way.

One morning there appeared in school, with Noah Clegg, Junior, a new boy; a wonderfully handsome boy, in a black velvet suit and broad white collar, altogether such a magnificent creature as had never before been seen in Forest Glen.

He had not been in school ten minutes before everybody knew all about him, Hannah Clegg proudly giving the information. He was from Cheemaun. His name was Horace Oliver, and his father was a rich lumberman. The Cleggs had supplied Mrs. Oliver with fresh butter and eggs for years, and Hannah herself had been at their house, which was a very magnificent mansion on the hill overlooking the lake. He had a sister older than himself, whose name was Madeline, and she had four silk dresses besides dozens of other kinds. And this Horace had been sick, so when Hannah's father and mother went into town with the butter and eggs on Saturday they had brought him back with them to stay on the farm and drink plenty of milk until he should get strong again.

The new boy was the center of interest during the morning. The girls were all admiration, and the Cleggs rose in popular favor, to be the envied of all the school. Enthusiasm amongst the boys was much milder. John Gordon and Charles Stuart MacAllister were scarcely enthusiastic at all. John privately informed his friend that any fellow of twelve–and he must be that if he wasn't thirteen–who would wear a white collar and velvet rig-up like that to school must be a baa-lamb, and ought to stay home and sit on his mother's knee. The Pretender discovered, to their further disgust, that the stranger could play a piano. This innocent accomplishment raised a strange feeling of irritation in the breast of Charles Stuart. He mentally resolved to watch the new boy, and if he showed signs of becoming too popular he would take him out behind the woodshed and settle him.

But to the school, as a whole, the new boy was all that could be desired. Even Miss Hillary shared in the popular adulation and smiled upon him at every chance. He was such a nice boy, no teacher could resist him. He had evidently been brought up on morals and manners, for when Miss Hillary dropped her brush he sprang from his seat and handed it to her before she could stoop for it.

Altogether things went very pleasantly that first day, so pleasantly that in the afternoon Lottie Price dared to hold up her hand and ask if they mightn't have a spelling match. Now no one had ever heard of such a thing on any day but Friday, and Jessie Robertson and Teenie Johnstone nudged each other. Lottie Price was the most disagreeable girl in Forest Glen School; indeed, all the Prices were noted for their capacity for making mischief. Lottie had not spoken to the girls in her class for three days, and her two chief rivals understood this move for a spelling match. Jessie whispered to Teenie that it was just like Lottie Price. She was the best speller in the school and wanted to show off before the new boy.

To the surprise of most, Miss Hillary smilingly granted the request. Jessie, however, nodded her head significantly. She wasn't surprised, not she. Why, the top-buggy had come early in the morning yesterday and stayed both to dinner and tea, and she thought it was just horrid mean of Lottie Price, so she did. She had done it just because she knew Jessie couldn't spell.

Meanwhile, the spelling match was being arranged. Of course, Lottie was sent as captain to one side, and then Miss Hillary asked would the school choose a boy for captain on the other side. A swarm of hands went up, and almost unanimously the new boy was chosen.

This was indeed a triumph for Lottie, and as the two took their places she swept a glance of disdain towards a seat where two young ladies sat gazing with averted faces far out of the window.

Rosie was "mad at" Katie Price, so she also stared in the opposite direction. But Elizabeth never had time nor opportunity to quarrel with anyone, and she gazed at Lottie with frank admiration, and wished she could spell half so well. It seemed such a pity that the grand stranger should find out so soon how stupid she was. She was always chosen the very last in a spelling match, except when Mary or Rosie happened to be a captain and selected her for private reasons.

The captains were in place, and Miss Hillary smilingly nodded to Lottie. Since the age of chivalry had dawned, the girl-captain in a spelling match was always given the first chance to select. Lottie hesitated. She had her beau, but he could not spell, and her bosom friend, but they had vowed never to speak again so long as they both should live. Miss Price was too wise to allow sentiment to injure her campaign, but too bad-tempered to permit any magnanimity to assist it. Therefore, she called Hannah Clegg. No one ever quarreled with the Cleggs, not even the Prices; they were too good-natured. Besides, Hannah was a fair speller.

Miss Hillary nodded approvingly and turned to the boy, who was standing regarding the sea of strange faces in a puzzled manner. He had been relying upon Hannah as first choice. Miss Hillary came to his aid. "Now, Horace, you are in a rather difficult position, as you do not know who are our best spellers. So you may call up anyone you like who will help you in your further selection." The visitor's face brightened. He looked right across the school and electrified everyone by calling out, "Elizabeth Jarvis Gordon."

The owner of the name could not believe her ears. She had to be poked twice by Rosie before she finally arose and took her place beside the velvet boy, overcome with wonder. It was as though one had suddenly been called out to be a Joan of Arc without any warning. Lottie Price giggled. Everyone knew Lizzie Gordon couldn't spell c-a-t without a couple of mistakes, and she saw her victory assured.

But there was one thing Elizabeth could do, and that was name all the spellers in the room. Who knew them as well as she, when each one was a reproach to her? When the velvet boy's turn came, he looked at her and she proved a fine support. Rosie came first, of course, but then Rosie not only knew every word in the Complete Speller, but was a Complete Speller herself in curls and a pink pinafore. John and

Charles Stuart were next. Elizabeth was devoutly thankful she could ask them with a clear conscience. She longed for Susie Martin and Eppie Turner also, but Susie had had five mistakes yesterday, and Eppie seven; it wouldn't be fair to the velvet boy. An exalted position, she realized, brought heavy responsibilities. She really made a very fine campaign, for she had almost all the Senior Fourth girls at her command, seeing that Lottie disdained to call them. She whispered their names to Horace, and as he summoned them to his ranks Lottie's face grew dark with anticipation of defeat.

At last everyone in the three highest classes was on the floor and the battle began. From the first the sullen face of the lady-captain, and her rapidly thinning ranks, showed upon which side the laurels were likely to rest.

Of course Elizabeth fell at the second volley, but as she left, overcome with humiliation, the velvet boy whispered: "Never mind. It was a beast of a word." Further comfort came to her when he himself went down on the next word and smiled at her sympathetically. But they left behind them plenty of veterans to carry on the war, and at last Lottie was left alone and there still stood on the other side a splendid array of six, headed by John Gordon. It was the hour for closing, and Miss Hillary announced the spelling match won by Horace Oliver; and Lottie Price almost tossed her head out of the window, the girls declared, as she passed Jessie and Teenie on her way to her seat.

When school was dismissed, the new boy paused at Elizabeth's seat, where she and Rosie were putting their books together.

"I remembered your name," he said triumphantly.

"How did you?" asked Elizabeth, amazed.

"Papa told us. Do you remember my papa? He was out here one day last summer with our lawyer. His name's Mr. Huntley. Mr. Huntley calls you 'Queen Elizabeth.'"

It was all clear to Elizabeth now. So that jolly, fat man, who didn't seem to care whether Eppie and her grandpa kept their farm or not, was the velvet boy's father; and the nasty man who was trying to take it from them was his friend. And, further, this must be the dreadful bad boy whom Sarah Emily called the "Centipede," and for whom she used to iron all day, and whose mother was so proud and haughty. She felt rather disillusioned. She wished, too, that he hadn't said "papa." She was afraid John and Charles Stuart would do something violent if they heard him.

But when Elizabeth reached home that afternoon, and Mary related all the day's exciting experiences, to her surprise, her aunt seemed almost joyful. She even smoothed Elizabeth's hair, and said she had behaved very discreetly. Mrs. Jarvis might hear about her from the little boy, when she returned, and perhaps something might happen. Further, she was sure the little Oliver boy was a gentleman and had a genteel bringing-up. Elizabeth looked vastly pleased, but John hung his head and scowled, and Sarah Emily snorted quite out loud. When supper was over, Annie drew Elizabeth away from the others and questioned her.

"Did the Oliver boy say anything about Mr. Huntley—or—or anyone else?"

Elizabeth understood perfectly. There was a strong tie between these two since the younger sister had delivered a certain precious note with such care and discretion. Elizabeth knew who "anyone else" meant. No, the velvet boy had not said anything about other people; but to-morrow she would ask him.

The velvet boy proved a source of valuable information, being very willing to talk. Of course, he knew Mr. Coulson. He had often seen him in Mr. Huntley's office; he was fine fun and could tell dandy stories. And Mrs. Jarvis, for whom Elizabeth was called, was his mamma's aunt. She was ever and ever so rich, and was away in the Old Country now, just pitching her money around, mamma said; and she might have taken her and Madeline along. Aunt Jarvis was very fond of Madeline, and mamma said she would be sure to leave her and Horace all her money when she died, though why she couldn't give them a little more of it now, was something she couldn't understand.

All this information and more, Elizabeth carried home, distributing it judiciously where it was most appreciated. She found that any news of Mrs. Jarvis warded off a scolding, and when a torn pinafore or unusually untidy hair made her dread her home-coming, she made Horace walk with her as far as Eppie's bars and gathered from him sufficient news of the great lady to insure her a welcome from her aunt.

Meantime in school she was living in a new world. She was wonderfully popular. There was no more talk of a poor makeshift for a beau like Charlie Peters. All the girls in the school canceled her name with that of the velvet boy, and Rosie was so proud because Katie Price was so envious that she fairly hugged Elizabeth for joy.

But the latter was not altogether happy. Of course it was fine to be the chosen one of the boy from town, but there were drawbacks. Horace was not strong enough to play baseball, and his mamma had forbidden him to play shinney, so he always stayed with the girls at recess, which was often very inconvenient when Elizabeth and Rosie wanted to teeter by themselves or stay indoors and tell secrets. Then, too, John and the Pretender teased her unmercifully. They called her beau "Booby" Oliver and said he should have been a girl. She took his part valiantly, but she did wish he wouldn't say "papa" and "mamma," it made her ashamed of him.

On the whole, Elizabeth was not sorry when his two-weeks' visit to the Cleggs' ended and he went back to Cheemaun. Rosie did not regret his departure either; he had served his day. For there was no doubt the age of chivalry was drawing to a close. Winter was coming on and the mantle of squire of dames was slipping off the boys' shoulders. The spirit of chivalry did not thrive in the day of snowballs.

The first news of the change in affairs came to Elizabeth, as usual, through Rosie. The latter confided to her friend that she didn't believe she liked Hector McQueen half so well as she used to. He had just been horrid mean only that morning. He had thrown a snowball right at her. Of course he didn't hit her, but she was mad at him, so she was, and if he wrote her a note she just wouldn't answer it, see if she would.

This was but one indication of the decay of chivalry. There were many others, and at last it was swept away altogether in a new fashion that shortly broke out. Jessie Robertson's uncle from Vancouver came home, bringing all the Robertsons presents, Jessie's being an autograph album. She brought it to school and each of her friends proudly inscribed their names therein, attached to verses sentimental or otherwise.

Within a week every girl in the Fourth Book had an autograph album, even if it were only one made of foolscap and trimmed with tissue-paper such as Rosie made for Elizabeth. It proved far more interesting and twice as tractable as a beau. A new era dawned in Forest Glen, an age of learning, when one racked one's brains to compose a poem for a friend's book, and the age of chivalry was forgotten.

CHAPTER VIII
A BUDDING ACTRESS

During those golden autumn months, the spirit of chivalry had been manifesting itself in other parts of Forest Glen beside the schoolroom. That in which the grown-up part of the community shared centered round Sandy McLachlan's little clearing.

The lawyers had made a bad mess of poor Sandy's affairs, the country declared. He had virtually lost his farm, as far as the law went, and all because of some technicality regarding the lack of a fence on all sides, one which the rural mind considered highly absurd. And not only that, but the place had been sold to Jake Martin, who had given Sandy notice to leave early in October.

But the old man was hard to move. Sure of his rights, and convinced of the injustice of all legal proceedings, he clung tenaciously to his little property. It was not a place anyone need grieve over losing, an observer might say—a few acres of stumpy, cleared land, an indefinite piece of forest, and an old log cabin. But it was Sandy's home—the only one he had known since he left his father's fisher-hut on the wind-swept shore of Islay. And every stone and tree on the rough little place, and the very birds that sang in the evening from the dark circle of forest were very dear to the old man's heart. From the doorway he could see down the leafy lane to the church and beyond it into the grassy graveyard with its leaning headstones. There was one there, an old moss-grown, wooden slab, once painted white. It marked two graves, those of Sandy's wife and his daughter, their only child, who had been Eppie's mother.

Yes, it was hard to think of leaving it all, and he was fiercely determined to stay.

His friends did their best to help him. Mr. Coulson took the liberty of writing to Mrs. Jarvis, the owner of the property, begging her to notice Sandy's claim. But there came no answer, and Mr. Huntley, the lawyer, laughed at him, saying by the time he had done business with that lady as long as he had he'd know better. Mr. MacAllister offered Sandy work in the mill, with pay commuted the long way. Noah Clegg invited both him and Eppie to share his home until such time as he could look about him for a new place. For, though the two Sunday-school superintendents were wont to sit up all night arguing fiercely on points of doctrine, in the day of affliction all differences were forgotten. Jake Martin even loudly declared himself powerful sorry, but then business was business, and he supposed there would always be shiftless folk like Sandy in the world who could never get on.

Wully Johnstone came next. He strolled over through the woods one afternoon and casually remarked that that old house of his by the spring was just fair totterin' for lack of care, and he wished to peace some obleegin' body would move intil it an' save him all the worry.

But Sandy would accept no man's hospitality, however delicately offered. He was proud, even for a Highlander, and not Noah Clegg himself, who was his closest friend, might extend to him charity.

Besides, as time went on, it would appear that he stood in little need of it. When the Jarvis property had been put up for sale, Mr. Martin had looked with a longing eye upon the Teeter farm, where The Dale stood. But Tom's claim had been safely established, and great was his wrath when he heard of his neighbor's machinations. Oro's Orator was a fighter in other beside forensic fields. He had a true Irish resentment against the law, and understood that somehow Jake Martin, in league with the lawyers, had outraged justice; therefore, he, Mr. Teeter, would ignore the lawyers and settle Jake, see if he wouldn't. Mr. Martin had voted Tory at the last election anyhow, and was badly in need of being settled.

So there broke out a war in Forest Glen which raged all autumn. When Jake Martin finally appeared at Sandy's door to formally assert his ownership, Mr. Teeter met him. He carried an ancient piece of firearms that had not been loaded since the day, some thirty years before, when the last bruin of Forest Glen had come ambling up out of Wully Johnstone's swamp.

Mr. Martin, not knowing how harmful the weapon might be, but being only too well aware that the man behind the gun was always to be feared, retired precipitately, and the whole countryside laughed long and loud over the victory.

He returned to the farm many times, but Tom seemed always to be on hand. Finally Mr. Martin declared, after they had come to blows the second time, that he would have the law. Mr. Teeter joyfully invited him to have all he could get of it; but the enemy hesitated. He knew his case was not looked upon with favor by his neighbors, and he dreaded to fly in the face of public opinion. For a lawsuit, as everyone in the countryside knew, was held as a disgrace, no matter how righteous one's case might be. And besides, the lawyers were apt to take so much money that a thrifty man like Jake naturally hesitated before approaching them.

So all autumn he went on making ineffectual efforts to remove the obstructions from his property, and times were very lively indeed; so lively that Auntie Jinit McKerracher, who led public opinion, declared it was clean scand'lus to have such goin's on in a Christian land; and Granny Teeter wrung her hands and said "Wirra wurra" many times a day over the Orator's waywardness.

At last, to save his reputation, Mr. Martin compromised. He would graciously allow Sandy to remain on his lawful property, he announced, till springtime. But, just as soon as the snow was gone, Tom Teeter had better watch out. For it was a penitentiary job he'd been at, and if there was any law in Canada, Mr. Martin was going to have the benefit of it.

So the countryside settled down for the winter, and as Christmas approached the Martin-Teeter conflict ceased to occupy the public mind. Even in the schoolroom it was soon forgotten, and this was a great relief to Elizabeth. For, of course, Eppie's trouble could not but directly affect her. Elizabeth and Rosie had both stood loyally by Eppie, declaring it was a dreadful shame the way Jake Martin and the lawyers acted. But this loyalty entailed an estrangement from poor, hard-working Susie; and Elizabeth's tender heart was torn between her two friends. She realized that Susie was right in taking her father's side. For, of course, one must stand by a father, no matter how bad he was, she argued. Elizabeth's position was a difficult one, and she was vastly relieved when the matter was dropped, and she and Rosie, with Eppie and Susie as their opponents, played puzzle during school hours and tag during recess, as of yore.

But all outside affairs of whatever moment would soon have been forgotten in any case. Every other interest was speedily swallowed up in the excitement over the Christmas concert Forest Glen was to have at the closing of school.

It was Jean Gordon and Wully Johnstone's Bella who imported this newest fad, bringing it all the way from Cheemaun High School. They generally kept Forest Glen posted as to what was the latest school fashion; and about the beginning of winter it appeared that concerts in which one took part were necessary to one's intellectual existence. Forest Glen at once decided it must have one, and Lottie Price, seeing a chance to distinguish herself as a reciter, once more took at the flood the tide that would sweep her on to glory, and boldly proffered a request for public closing exercises.

Miss Hillary graciously consented. Indeed, Miss Hillary was in a gracious mood almost all the time now. For, since sleighing had come, a smart, red cutter, the successor of the top-buggy, came out from Cheemaun with such regularity and frequency that the schoolroom was a place of peace and idleness.

As soon as preparations for the concert were set on foot, Elizabeth and Rosie became completely absorbed in them. The former became so busy she had scarcely time to draw pictures. They were both in a dialogue, and Rosie was to sing a solo besides. So how could one find time to worry over vulgar fractions?

The Dale contingent were all honored by being each given a special part in the performance. Archie, of course, was too young to participate; but Mary was to sing "Little drops of water, little grains of sand," in company with Wully Johnstone's Betty. John was to give a reading, and Charles Stuart and Teenie Johnstone were in Elizabeth's dialogue.

The Martins alone were not amongst the artists, and Elizabeth's heart ached for Susie. As soon as the dismissal bell rang, and everyone else ran to his or her allotted corner to be "trained," the poor Martins sadly made their way to the pegs where hung coats and dinner-pails, and hurried away home to work. No wonder they did not succeed at school. Mr. Coulson had always said the no-play rule of Jake Martin was making dullards of his children, just when he was over-anxious that they should be made very sharp and so be great money-makers.

There had been Christmas concerts in Forest Glen before, but never one like this. Other times one had to get up one's own programme, but now the teacher drilled and trained the performers until they became overwhelmed with the thought of their own importance. Besides, several young ladies of the place, Martha Ellen Robertson amongst them, came down to the school every afternoon and helped, and Elizabeth found an especial joy in being "trained" by her Sunday-school teacher and noting her daily change of finery.

Sometimes, as the date of the concert approached, groups would meet in the evenings for practice, and one night the half-dozen who were in Elizabeth's dialogue assembled at The Dale.

Miss Gordon would never have consented to such an irregularity as late hours for her family, but that the occasion served to heal a slight breach between them and the Wully Johnstones.

Since the first snowfall, her neighbors had been driving their two High School pupils into Cheemaun, and, of course, had taken Malcolm and Jean with them. The Wully Johnstones had not heretofore shown any leanings towards education, but, since Miss Gordon had set the pace by sending her nephew and niece to the High School, learning became highly fashionable about The Dale. Wully Johnstone declared his boys and girls were as smart as any Gordons living and they would show the truth of the same.

Such sturdy young Canadians as these High School pupils were, thought little of a few miles' walk morning and evening. But the girls were developing into lengthening skirts, and Miss Gordon thankfully accepted the ride through the deep snow for Jean. Nevertheless, she was troubled over receiving constant favors from even such good neighbors as the Johnstones, for she had not yet learned that in the Scottish-Canadian countryside a horse and vehicle on the highway is practically common property.

So one evening, when Miss Gordon took tea at Mrs. Johnstone's, she had politely hinted that she and her brother would like to offer some remuneration for the kindness shown the children. Mrs. Johnstone's hospitable feelings were very badly hurt indeed, but she said nothing, being a peaceable body. But her sister-in-law, Mrs. Janet McKerracher, known all over the neighborhood as "Auntie Jinit," was the real head of the Johnstone household. And, being a lady of no little spirit, she declared, when Miss Gordon had gone, that the mistress of The Dale was an uppish bit buddie, and it was jist fair scand'lus to treat a neebor yon fashion.

Miss Gordon was very much grieved when she discovered her lack of tact, and, seeing a chance to make amends, she relaxed her rigid laws for one evening and permitted the gathering at The Dale. And a few evenings earlier she sent Malcolm with a graciously worded note, asking Mr. and Mrs. Johnstone and Mrs. McKerracher to accompany the young people.

The invitation was as graciously accepted. The elder folk came and sat around the fire and watched the young folk fill the house with noise and merriment, and the breach was healed. The MacAllisters were there; and Miss Hillary and all those from Forest Glen who were taking part were driven up in the Robertsons' sleigh.

It was like a magic evening out of a fairy tale to Elizabeth. There was a roaring fire in both the parlor and dining-room; all doors between the rooms were opened, giving a spacious effect, and every lamp and candle in the place was alight. The big, bare house seemed like some great festive palace to Elizabeth, and, as she sat on the stairs watching their guests file in, she felt sure she could realize exactly how Lady Evelina felt when she stood in her father's banqueting hall and received a glittering array of lords and dukes and earls. But surely no Lady Evelina of song or story ever experienced the rapture felt by Elizabeth when Rosie came dancing up the steps.

To Miss Gordon the evening proved highly satisfactory. The atmosphere of festivity made her feel young again, and the reconciliation with the Johnstones, common folk though they undoubtedly were, was very grateful to her warm heart, and above all she was vouchsafed a surprising revelation. Elizabeth proved to be the vision revealed. There was hope that Elizabeth was not stupid after all.

The dialogue in which she figured was one Martha Ellen Robertson had chosen from the "Complete Temperance Reciter," and was intended to inculcate a lesson of a highly moral character, namely, the folly of marrying a drunkard. Martha Ellen had indulgently chosen her pet pupil as heroine. Elizabeth was a haughty belle who persisted in the face of all opposition in marrying Charles Stuart, who staggered through the whole three acts with a big, green catsup bottle in each pocket. Rosie Carrick and Teenie Johnstone did their best to dissuade the mistaken one from her strange infatuation, even setting the good example of choosing Willie Carrick and Johnny Johnstone, exemplary young men, as their sweethearts, but all in vain. The haughty belle would listen to no one, and at the end of act three, now a weeping drudge, she trailed off the stage, with the maudlin owner of the catsup bottles staggering ahead. Then Rosie and Teenie, holding the hands of their two virtuous youths, recited in unison a little verse bearing upon the unwisdom of being a haughty belle and marrying the victim of a catsup bottle.

Though the little scene was well-meant, and held within its simple story a deep truth, the incongruities of it, chiefly those contributed by the childish actors, might have made the dialogue extremely laughable had it not been for the acting of the leading lady. Elizabeth proved a star from the moment she set foot upon the stage. She was radiantly happy there. All unconsciously she had found a method of complete self-expression that was not forbidden, and the joy and relief of it lifted her to brilliant success. She was playing at something in a legitimate fashion at last; pretending, when it was the right and proper thing to pretend, with one's father and aunt and teacher looking on with approval. It was next best thing to being Joan of Arc. From the day of her power, when she haughtily turned away the virtuous William and the exemplary John, who severally came seeking her hand, to that of her humiliation, when she knelt before Charles Stuart and besought him with tears to give up catsup bottles, her whole course was one of complete triumph. Teenie Johnstone forgot her lines three times in watching her, and Charles Stuart said he wished she wouldn't go at it quite so hard, she made him feel queer all over. And at the end of one stormy scene, Rosie ran to her and said: "Oh, Lizzie, it was awful! I thought you must be really, truly crying!" And Elizabeth did not confess that she had been really and truly crying, and was now rather ashamed and quite amazed at herself.

Mrs. Wully Johnstone was quite overcome, and Auntie Jinit declared it jist garred her greet to look at the bairn, she did it jist too well. And Miss Hillary turned to Miss Gordon and said, "She will make a great actress some day, perhaps," and Miss Gordon held up her shapely hands in horror and answered: "An actress! I'd rather see her in her grave."

Elizabeth noticed that Mother MacAllister was the only one who did not praise her; she who was always so ready with commendation whenever it could be truthfully expressed. So she slipped up to her and whispered, "Do you like it?" and Mother MacAllister looked rather wistfully at the crimson cheeks and shining eyes. She stroked the little girl's hair gently. "It would be a very pretty little piece, hinny," she said softly. "But you must not be letting yourself get too much excited over it, little Lizzie. It'll make you forget your sums."

But otherwise Elizabeth's triumph was complete. She noticed her aunt's approving looks, and overheard her saying to Martha Ellen Robertson that the child really had talent.

But such a condition of affairs could not last long with Elizabeth. An atmosphere of approval was not for her to dwell in long. Her downfall came speedily.

When the practice was over, they all sat around the room and Miss Gordon bade Sarah Emily and the two older girls pass the grape cordial and the Johnny-cake, which were all in readiness. It was at this moment that Miss Hillary turned to Mr. Gordon.

"You must be chairman at the concert," she said engagingly. "It will be so fitting, as you are secretary-treasurer."

Mr. Gordon, who had been sitting at a table with Mr. MacAllister, intent on reducing the Long Way, looked up, ran his fingers through his long hair, and laughed.

"What, what?" he said. "Me for chairman! Never, never. I'd forget what night it was on. Thank you very much for the honor, Miss Hillary, but you can do better than that. Here's Mr. Johnstone, now, he's just the man."

Mr. Johnstone spat at great length into the stove damper, to cover his embarrassment.

"Hut tut, sic like havers!" was all he said, and motioned with his thumb over his shoulder towards his next-door neighbor.

Mr. MacAllister, just emerged from the depths of the Long Way, looked at her in a dazed fashion.

"For peety's sake," he said, "can ye no dae better than ask all the auld buddies in the countryside; an' the place jist swarmin' wi' young callants. There's Tom Teeter, now, he'd jump at the chance, only ye'd hae to gag him atween pieces."

"It's too great a risk to run," laughed Miss Hillary. She knit her pretty brows in perplexity. "Perhaps Mr. Clegg will take pity on me."

"There's yon gay chiel that comes oot frae toon," resumed Mr. MacAllister slyly. "Mebby ye'd hae mair influence ower him."

The young schoolmistress blushed and tried not to smile; Sarah Emily ducked her head into her apron and giggled, and a titter went round the room. And then Elizabeth, quite unconscious of any joke, spoke up eagerly.

"Oh, Miss Hillary, won't you ask that lovely gentleman that comes to see you to bring Mr. Coulson out and let him be chairman!"

Miss Hillary blushed harder than ever and laughed; so did Annie Gordon and Martha Ellen Robertson. Mr. MacAllister laughed, too, and slapped his knee, and said yon was a fine idea, and all the younger folk exclaimed in delight. And so it was promptly settled there and then, and Elizabeth understood when Annie passed her the Johnny-cake again.

But she did not understand why she was sternly ordered to bed by her aunt just the moment the company was gone; and wondered drearily why it was that this one day of triumph should end in tears.

The next morning she found matters no better, for the day had scarcely begun before Aunt Margaret singled her out to be talked to solemnly on the sin of being bold and forward, and speaking up when older people were present. Elizabeth partially brought the rebuke upon herself. Remembering only the joys of the night before, she arose early and in the exuberance of her spirits pulled Mary out of bed and tickled her until she was seized with a fit of coughing; and Mary's cough was a serious affair. Next she visited the boys' room and started a pillow-fight with John.

The noise brought Miss Gordon from her room. It was a chill winter morning, and the lady's temper was not any too sweet. Elizabeth fled to her room and began dressing madly. Her aunt slowly entered, seated herself on the little bench by the window, and, while her niece dressed and combed her hair, she gave her a long and aggrieved dissertation upon genteel conduct for little girls.

"And now," she concluded, as Elizabeth gave way to tears and showed signs of collapsing upon the bed, "I want you to learn two extra verses of your psalm before you come down to breakfast. And I do hope and trust it may lead you to be a better girl." She arose with a sigh, which said her hopes were but feeble and, bidding Mary follow her, descended the stairs.

When they were gone, Elizabeth got out her Bible, and sat by the frosty window, looking out drearily at the red morning sunshine. She wished with all her might that she had never been born. Likely she would die of grief soon anyway, she reflected, and never act in the dialogue after all. Yes, she would get sick and go to bed and be in a raging fever. And, just like the little girl in her latest Sunday-school book, who had been so badly used, she would cry out in her ravings that Aunt Margaret was killing her because she wasn't genteel.

Somewhat solaced by these gloomy reflections, she took the hairpin Annie had loaned her to pin up a lock of her heavy hair, and began tracing out pictures on the window-pane. There was already a magic tapestry there, woven by the frost-fairies; ferns, and sea-weed and tropical flowers of fantastic shapes, and wonderful palm branches all exquisitely intertwined. To these Elizabeth added the product of her imagination. Lords and ladies rode through the sea-weed, and Joan of Arc stood surrounded by palms. She had almost forgotten her woes in their icy beauty, and had quite forgotten the task her aunt had set, when Annie came flitting into the room. Annie's step was lighter than ever and her eyes were radiant. "Come down to breakfast, Lizzie," she whispered. "We're nearly through, and I've saved some toast for you. Aunt said if you said the verses before school-time it would do."

Elizabeth sprang up joyously, and hand-in-hand the two ran downstairs.

"Annie," said her little sister, gazing up at the glowing countenance, "you make me think of a girl in a story book. You look like Lady Evelina."

Annie laughed. "Why?" she asked.

"Oh, I don't know. But I guess it's because your eyes are so shiny. It says in that story in the *Chronicle* that Lady Evelina's lover rode past, and she looked out of her something or other, casement, I think, but I guess it was just a window, and it says her face flushed like a wild rose and her eyes shined like twin stars. Say, what are twin stars, Annie?"

"Oh, Lizzie," whispered her sister, her face flushing deeper than a wild rose, "for pity's sake don't let aunt hear you saying things like that. You know she doesn't like you to read that continued story." With which wise counsel, and an appreciative pat of her little sister's arm, Annie led the way to breakfast.

The night before the concert Elizabeth and Mary could scarcely go to sleep. There was another source of insomnia beside the prospect ahead. They had both cajoled Annie into putting their hair up in curl papers, because all the girls, even to Becky Davis, were going to do something new and wonderful with their hair. So the two victims of fashion slept in half-wakeful discomfort, until Elizabeth's heavy locks overcame their bounds and gave her relief and rest. But there was great disappointment in the morning, for while Mary's short, flaxen hair stood out round her head in a very halo of frizzly curls, Elizabeth's hung heavy, straight, and limp, and had to be braided in the usual old fashion.

However, she was never prone to think much of her personal appearance, and merely gave a sigh as Mary stood before the glass looking quite like a fairy.

"My, but your hair is so nice," said Elizabeth.

"Well," said Mary, as with a smile of satisfaction she surveyed what was visible of her small self in the little mirror on the wall, "I suppose I do look awful grand. But I must try and not think about it," she added piously; "aunt says so."

Since the night the practice had been held at The Dale, Miss Gordon, strange to say, had displayed a growing disinclination to attend the concert. And when the evening finally came she decided to remain at home. It was only for children, after all, she remarked at the tea-table, and she and Annie would just stay at home together by the fire; adding that she didn't suppose even Malcolm and Jean would care to go to anything so childish. But even the quiet Malcolm protested mildly, and his sister did the same vigorously. Such an expedition as going from home after dark was too rare to be missed. "Why, Aunt Margaret!" she cried, for Miss Jean was an independent young lady, by virtue of being the cleverest of the family. "Why, Aunt Margaret, I never dreamed we'd have to stay home, and I'd just love to go–and Annie wants to go, too; don't you, Ann?"

One glance at Annie's despairing face was enough to convince anyone that to miss the concert would be a more bitter disappointment than it would be even to Elizabeth, who was fidgeting about in her chair, with scarlet cheeks and shining eyes, scarcely eating anything. Miss Gordon glanced at her eldest niece apprehensively, and hesitated. Then her brother spoke up.

"Well, well," he said indulgently, "you must just all go. Archie and Jamie and I will keep house, and you'll tell us all about it when you get home."

Miss Gordon was too genteel to oppose her brother publicly, and accepted the situation with much chagrin. She determined, however, that she would keep Miss Annie close to her side all evening. And after all, she argued, probably the young man had forgotten all about her by this time. It was a way young men had, she reflected, with a sigh for a dream of her youth to which she never referred. She sighed again as she looked at Annie's bright face, and wondered if she had done wrong in separating these two. Annie never by the slightest hint let her know her real feelings. And herein lay the great misfortune of Miss Gordon's life. She loved the girl passionately, and would have made any sacrifice she felt was for her good, but Annie lived by her side day after day, and gave her not the smallest confidence. Her aunt, in her mistaken worldly ambition, had forever shut between them the door of true companionship.

They were all ready, in various stages of excitement, when the MacAllister sleigh came jingling up to the door. In the winter, sleighs generally took the sawlog road along the short-cut to Forest Glen, and the Wully Johnstones had promised to come round that way, too, and pick up anybody who was left.

To Elizabeth, this driving abroad after nightfall was like taking a voyage to a new planet. It was so wonderful and mysterious, this new, white, moon-lit world. Away in the vast blue dome the stars smiled faintly, outshone by the glory of the big, round moon that rode high above the black tree-tops. The billowing drifts along the road blazed under a veil of diamonds, and the strip of ice on the pond, where Elizabeth and John had swept away the snow for a slide, shone like polished silver. The fields melted away gray and mysterious into the darkness of the woods. Here and there a light twinkled from the farm-houses of the valley. The sleigh-bells jingled merrily, and the company joined their own joyous notes to them and sang the songs that were to be given at the concert. The woods rang with their gay voices as they passed old Sandy McLachlan's place. Sandy still held possession, and was looking forward hopefully to some providential interference in the springtime.

The old man and Eppie were plunging down the snowy lane. The horses were pulled up and they were hauled joyously aboard; and in a few minutes the happy sleighload dashed up to the schoolhouse, which stood there looking twice its usual size and importance, with the light blazing from every window.

CHAPTER IX
THE FAIRY GOD-MOTHER ARRIVES

They found the schoolhouse already rapidly filling. To Elizabeth, the little room presented a scene of dazzling splendor. The place was indeed transformed. It was decorated with festoons of evergreens and wreaths of paper flowers; and lamps twinkled from every window-sill. Across the platform was stretched a white curtain, constructed from Mrs. Robertson's and Mrs. Clegg's sheets, while from behind this magic screen–hiding one could not guess what wonders–shone all the lanterns owned by the population of Forest Glen, and across its glowing surface flitted gigantic shadows.

Martha Ellen Robertson, in a brilliant pink satin waist, and all her jewelry; and Miss Hillary in a new white dress, were already hurrying up and down the aisle marshaling their forces. As the artists appeared they arranged them on the row of improvised benches at the front, charging them to sit there quietly until their turn came for stepping behind the magic curtain.

Elizabeth and Rosie found each other immediately, and sat close together on the very front row. Rosie was a perfect vision in a white dress, with a string of beads around her neck and her curls tied up by a broad pink ribbon. Elizabeth, in her Sunday pinafore, starched a little stiffer than usual, gazed at her in boundless admiration. She had supposed, before leaving home, that Mary would be the most beautiful creature present; but Mary's pale flaxen curls and colorless pinafore were lost in the gorgeous display on all sides. Katie and Lottie Price were the grandest. They fairly bristled with ribbons and lace; but indeed all the girls were so gayly dressed that the Gordons looked like little gray sparrows in a flock of birds of Paradise. Mary sighed and looked around miserably at the gay throng; but little did Elizabeth care. She sat on the front bench, with Rosie on one side and Eppie on the other, and rapturously swung her feet and laughed and talked, all oblivious of her dun-colored clothes. It was quite impossible not to be wildly happy at such a grand festive gathering. The schoolroom seemed some wonderful place she had never seen before. The middle section of the sheets was drawn back, displaying the platform with the teacher's desk and the blackboard, all fairly smothered in cedar and balsam boughs and tissue-paper roses, and smelling as sweet as the swamp behind the school. It was such a bower of beauty that Elizabeth could scarcely believe she had stood there only yesterday, striving desperately to make a complex fraction turn simple.

The crowd was steadily gathering, and the noise steadily increasing. Right at the back a group of boys were bunched together, laughing, talking, and whistling. Elizabeth was ashamed to see that John and Charles Stuart were amongst those whom Miss Hillary was vainly striving to bring up to the performers' seats of honor.

In the midst of the pleasant hum and stir there arose a commotion near the door. A group of strangers was entering. At the sight of them, Miss Hillary plunged behind the curtains, and Rosie and Elizabeth could see her through a division in the sheets, anxiously arranging her hair before the little mirror. Then the wise old Rosie nodded her head significantly, and standing up, peered between the rows of people's heads. "I knew it was him!" she cried triumphantly. "I knew just by the way Miss Hillary jumped,"–and so it was–the owner of the red cutter! Then Elizabeth, forgetting her aunt's eye, jumped up too, and almost cried out with joy, for the man with him, the tall one with the handsome fur collar and cap, was none other than Mr. Coulson! There were two ladies with him, too–but she did not notice them in her delight. He was recognized at once by his old pupils, and they all set up a storm of clapping. The older people, gathered around the stove, crowded about him, shaking his hand and clapping him on the back. Then the Red Cutter came with him up to the curtains and introduced him to Miss Hillary. And all the other young ladies who were helping in the concert shook hands with the old teacher, and Martha Ellen laughed and talked so loud that Elizabeth was delighted and wondered what had pleased her so. Next, Mr. Coulson spied the row of little girls gazing up at him with eager eyes, and he pulled Rosie's curls and Elizabeth's braid, and kissed Mary and pinched Katie and patted all the others on the head. Then he boxed the boys' ears, and told Miss Hillary they were a bad lot, and he didn't see how she put up with them, and altogether behaved so funnily that they fairly shouted with delight. Suddenly he turned abruptly, and, marching up to the platform, took his place at the desk.

Elizabeth was greatly disappointed. She had expected he would at least shake hands with Annie. She curled round Rosie and peeped through the rows of people to catch a sight of her sister. Annie, strange to say, did not look in the least disappointed. She was laughing and chatting with Jean and Bella Johnstone, and looking just as gay and happy as possible. Elizabeth gave up the problem. It was really no use trying to understand the queer ways of grown-up folks.

Mr. Coulson stood up to make his chairman's speech and to tell them he was very glad to come back to Forest Glen. Elizabeth thought his address was wonderfully clever, her partial eyes failing to notice that he was big and awkward, that he did not know what to do with his hands, and that he was more than usually nervous. There was another pair of eyes, besides Elizabeth's, that, when they dared lift themselves, looked upon his blundering performance with tender pride. But Miss Gordon gazed at him coldly, thanking herself that she had put an end to all nonsense between him and Annie before it was too late. The grandson of a tavern-keeper, though he might rise to have good morals, could never reach the height of genteel manners.

At last the chairman's halting remarks were concluded, and the programme fairly started. First came a chorus by all the girls of the school, and such of the boys as could be coaxed or driven to the platform; the masculine portion of the artists having suddenly developed an overwhelming modesty. But the girls were all eager to perform;

and they sang "Flow gently, sweet Afton" with great vigor, and, as Mr. Coulson said afterwards, "just like the robins in springtime."

As they burst into the second verse, Elizabeth, who stood directly behind Mary, and had to view the audience through the halo, was surprised to see a boy down near the stove making vigorous signs to attract her attention. She stared in amazement, and almost stopped singing. It was Horace! There he was in a brand new velvet suit, smiling at her with the greatest glee, and pointing her out to his companions. He sat between two ladies, the very two Elizabeth had seen enter with Mr. Coulson. One was a tall, thin lady in a sealskin coat, probably Horace's mamma, as he called her. The other lady was very stout and wonderfully dressed. Elizabeth could scarcely see her face for the enormous plumed hat she wore. She seemed to be a very grand lady, indeed, for, every time she moved, jewels glittered on her hat or at her throat.

Elizabeth quite forgot the words of the song watching her, and was absently singing: "There oft as mild evening weeps over the Tea, There daily I wander as noon rises high," when Rosie poked her back to consciousness.

When they had come down from the platform and the stir of preparation for the next number was going on behind the billowing sheets, Elizabeth felt herself pulled vigorously from behind. She whirled about; Horace was beside her, all smiles.

"Hello," he cried cordially. "Say, you sang just jolly, Lizzie."

"Hello!" responded Elizabeth, forgetting in her delight that this was not a genteel salutation. "I'm awful glad to see you, Horace." This was quite true; since he did not appear in the role of beau any more, she was genuinely pleased at the sight of her old playmate. Rosie expressed the same sentiment rapturously. Susie and Katie followed, and even Eppie faltered out some words of welcome.

"How did you come to be here?" Elizabeth asked.

"Mr. Coulson told me there was a concert, and I just coaxed mamma to let me come until she was nearly crazy and just had to let me. I can manage her all right. Papa's different, though. He wouldn't let me come with Mr. Coulson alone, and I wanted to!" His handsome face curled up in a pout. "They always tag round after me as if I was a kid. But Mr. Coulson fixed it up. Say, he's a dandy. He came over and coaxed papa to let me come, and he got Aunt Jarvis to come, too. That's Aunt Jarvis next the stove. She likes Mr. Coulson awful well and said she'd come to oblige him, and then mamma said she'd come, too. Madeline intended to come, too, but she was going to a party. She goes to one 'most every night. I wish I could, but I always get sick. Say, Lizzie, I've got a new dog, and I hitch him to my sleigh, and oh, say, he's the dandiest fun——"

But Elizabeth was not listening. She was too much overcome by the wonderful news. Mrs. Jarvis, the fairy god-mother, who had always seemed unreal, was really and truly there in the flesh! She could scarcely believe it.

Horace, finding his audience inattentive, moved away, chatting volubly to all his old friends, and the next moment Jean came crushing her way through the crowd to Elizabeth's side, her eyes shining with excitement.

"Lizzie, aunt sent me to tell you to do your very, very best. Mrs. Jarvis is really and truly down there," she whispered excitedly. "And she says to be sure and smooth your hair just before your dialogue, and don't for the world let your boot laces come untied. And when it's all over, aunt says you're to come down with her and be introduced."

Elizabeth did not hear a word of her sister's admonitions. She realized only that Mrs. Jarvis was there to watch her act in a dialogue! Her heart stood still at the thought, and then went on again madly.

Meanwhile, Mary had spread the news of the town visitors, and all the girls were in a flutter.

"It's too bad," Katie Price whispered to Rosie, "that Lizzie Gordon's got that awful lookin' pinny on. Mrs. Jarvis 'll be ashamed of her. And her hair ain't curled even."

"She can beat anybody in the school at speakin' a dialogue, anyhow," declared Rosie loyally. "And Martha Ellen's goin' to dress her up in long clothes anyway, so it don't matter."

The concert was going steadily on, each performer showing signs of the epidemic of excitement that the arrival of the town visitors had produced. Lottie Price stopped short three times in reciting "Curfew must not ring to-night," and had to be helped from behind the sheets by Miss Hillary. No one felt very sorry, for, as Teenie Robertson said, "Lottie Price was just showing off, anyhow, and it served her right." But everyone else seemed to go wrong from the moment the strangers were announced, and to Elizabeth's dismay even poor Rosie did not escape.

The programme partook largely of a temperance sentiment, and Rosie's song was "Father, dear father, come home with me now," a selection which at the practices had almost moved the spectators to tears. Joel Davis, because he was the biggest boy in the school, and hadn't anything to do but sit still, acted the part of Rosie's father. He sat at a table with three or four companions, all arrayed in rags, and drank cold tea from a vinegar jar. Rosie came in, and taking Joel by the sleeve, sang:

"Father, dear father, come home with me now,
The clock in the steeple strikes one,
You said you were coming right home from the shop,
As soon as your day's work was done."

Then from behind the curtain some of the bigger girls, led by Martha Ellen Robertson, sang softly:

"Come home, come home,
Please, father, dear father, come home."

Rosie sang another verse at two o'clock, and still another at three, singing the hands right round to twelve, and still the obdurate Joel sat immovable and still drank tea.

It had been considered, even by Miss Hillary, one of the best pieces on the programme, and Elizabeth was almost as excited over it as she was over her dialogue. And to-night Rosie looked so beautiful in her white dress and pink bow that Elizabeth felt sure Mrs. Jarvis would think her the sweetest, dearest girl in the whole wide world.

But what was the dismay of all the singer's friends, and the rage and humiliation of the singer's mother, when she emerged from Miss Hillary's hands and stood before the audience! All her glory of sash and beads and frills was swallowed up in Mrs. Robertson's shawl–the old, ragged "Paisley" she wore only when she went to milk the cows or feed the chickens! Miss Hillary had even taken the pink ribbon out of the poor little singer's curls; and Rosie confided to Elizabeth afterwards, with sobs, she had actually bidden her take off her boots and stockings and go barefoot! Rosie had been almost overwhelmed by this stripping of her ornaments, but she found spirit enough remaining to rebel at this last sacrifice. And, as Elizabeth indignantly declared, even a worm would turn at being commanded to take off its boots, when they were a brand new copper-toed pair with a lovely loud squeak! But even the copper toes were concealed by the trailing ends of Mrs. Robertson's barnyard shawl, and the poor little worm was none the better for her turning.

The song was a melancholy failure. Rosie sang in such a dismayed, quavering voice that no one could hear her, and everyone was relieved when she finally broke down and had to leave before the clock in the steeple had a chance to strike more than ten.

Rosie's mother had sat through the pitiful performance, fairly boiling over with indignation, and as soon as the Paisley shawl, heaving with sobs, had disappeared behind the sheets, she followed it and "had it out" violently with Miss Hillary. Wasn't her girl as good as anybody else's girl, was what she wanted to know, that she had to be dressed up like a tinker's youngster before all those people from town? Miss Hillary tried to explain that the play's the thing, and the artist must make sacrifices to her art, but all in vain. Mrs. Carrick took Rosie away weeping, before the concert was over, and Miss Hillary sat down behind the sheets and cried until the Red Cutter had to come up and make her stop.

One disaster was followed by another. Elizabeth suffered even more agony in the next number, for this was a reading by John. Why he should have been chosen for an elocutionary performance no one could divine, except that he flatly refused to do anything else in public, and his teacher was determined he should do something. With Elizabeth's help, John had faithfully practiced in the privacy of his room, but had never once got through his selection without breaking down with laughter. It was certainly the funniest story in the world, Elizabeth was sure—so funny they had not submitted it to Aunt Margaret. It was about a monkey named Daniel that had been trained to wait upon his master's table, and Elizabeth would dance about and scream over the most comical passages, and had been of little assistance to her brother in his efforts at self-control.

At first the elocutionist did fairly well, reading straight ahead in his low monotone, and, hoping all would be well, Elizabeth ceased to squirm and twist her braid. But as John approached the funniest part, he forgot even the elegant strangers. Daniel grew more enchanting every moment; grew irresistible at last, and the droning voice of his exponent stopped short—lost in a spasm of silent laughter. He recovered, read a little further, and collapsed again. Once more he started, his face twisted in agony, his voice husky, but again he fell before the side-splitting antics of Daniel.

The audience had not caught any of the monkey's jokes as yet, but they fully appreciated the joke of the performance; and as the elocutionist labored on, striving desperately to overcome his laughter and always being overcome by it, the schoolhouse fairly rocked with merriment. Elizabeth, who had begun to fear no one would hear all Daniel's accomplishments, was greatly relieved, and laughed louder than anyone else. John was enjoying himself, and the audience was enjoying itself, and she was so proud of him and so glad everyone was having such a good time!

But, as the reader finally choked completely and had to retire amidst thunderous applause before Daniel's last escapade was finished, she was brought to a realization of the real state of affairs by glancing back at her aunt. Miss Gordon was sitting up very straight, with crimson checks, and an air of awful dignity which Elizabeth's dismayed senses told her belonged only to occasions of terrible calamity. Annie, too, was looking very much distressed, and Jean and Malcolm wore expressions of anger and disgust. Elizabeth's heart sank. Evidently John had disgraced the family, poor John, and she thought he had made such a hit! This was awful! First Rosie and then John! There came over her a chill of terror, a premonition of disaster. When those two stars had fallen from the firmament, how could she expect to shine with Mrs. Jarvis sitting there in front of her?

Had she guessed how much her aunt was depending upon her, she would have been even more terrified. Miss Gordon was keenly alive to the fact that this evening might make or mar Elizabeth's fortune. Mrs. Jarvis had from time to time recognized her namesake by a birthday gift and had often intimated that she should like to see the little girl. Miss Gordon had dreams of her adopting Elizabeth, and making the whole family rich. And now she was to see the child for the first time, and under favorable auspices. Elizabeth certainly showed talent in her acting. The others were like wooden images in comparison to her.

As the curtains were drawn back for the dialogue in which she figured, Miss Gordon drew a great breath. If Mrs. Jarvis didn't feel that she must give that child an education after seeing how she could perform, then all the stories of that lady's generosity, which she had heard, must be untrue.

But, alas, for any hopes centered upon Elizabeth! Miss Gordon told herself bitterly, when the dialogue was over, that she might have known better. The vivacious actress, who had thrown herself into her part at home, making it seem real, came stumbling out upon the little stage, hampered by Annie's long skirts, and mumbled over her lines in a tone inaudible beyond the front row of seats. Poor Elizabeth, the honor of performing before Mrs. Jarvis had been too much for her. She did her part as badly as it was possible to do it, growing more scared and white each moment, and finally forgetting it altogether. Miss Gordon hung her proud head, and Mrs. Oliver exclaimed quite audibly, "Dear me, how did that poor child ever come to be chosen to take part?"

Elizabeth had not awakened from her stage-struck condition when the concert was over, and her aunt, with set face, came to straighten her pinafore, smooth her hair, and get her ready for presentation to the ladies from town.

Many, many times had Elizabeth pictured this meeting, each time planning with greater elaboration the part she should act. But when at last she stood before the lady in the sealskin coat, realizing only what a miserable failure she had been, she could think of not one of the clever speeches she had prepared, but hung her head in a most ungenteel manner and said nothing.

Her aunt's voice sounded like a forlorn hope as she presented her.

"This is your namesake, Mrs. Jarvis," she said.

Mrs. Jarvis was a tall, stately lady, with a sallow, discontented face. Her melancholy, dark eyes had a kindly light in them, however, and occasionally her face was lit up with a pleasant smile. She was richly but quietly dressed, and in every way perfectly met Miss Gordon's ideal. Her companion was something of a shock, however. Mrs. Oliver was stout and red-faced, and was dressed to play the part of twenty when Manager Time had cast her for approaching fifty. Miss Gordon would have pronounced any other woman, with such an appearance and a less illustrious relative, not only ungenteel but quite common, and the sort of person Lady Gordon would never have recognized on the streets of Edinburgh.

But Mrs. Jarvis was Mrs. Jarvis, and whoever was related to her must surely be above the ordinary in spite of appearances.

Mrs. Jarvis was looking down at Elizabeth with a smile illuminating her sad face. "So this is the little baby with the big eyes my dear husband used to talk so much about." She heaved a great sigh. "Ah, Miss Gordon, you cannot understand what a lonely life I have led since my dear husband was taken from me."

Miss Gordon expressed warm sympathy. She was a little surprised at the expression of grief, nevertheless, for she had always understood that, as far as the companionship of her husband went, Mrs. Jarvis had always led a lonely life.

"Mr. Jarvis was always very much interested in Elizabeth," she said diplomatically. "I understand it was he who named her."

"She doesn't seem to have inherited your talent for the stage, Aunt Jarvis," said the stout lady, laughing. "Horace, did you hear me telling you to put on your overcoat? We must go at once."

Miss Gordon looked alarmed. It would be fatal if they left without some further word.

"I am sure Elizabeth would like to express her pleasure at meeting you, Mrs. Jarvis," she said, suggestively. "She has been wanting an opportunity to thank you for your many kind remembrances."

She glanced down at her niece, and Elizabeth realized with agony that this was the signal for her to speak. She thought desperately, but not a gleam of one of those stately speeches she had prepared showed itself. She was on the verge of disgracing her aunt again when Mrs. Oliver mercifully interposed.

"Aunt Jarvis," she cried sharply, "we really must be going. The horses are ready. Come, Horace, put on your overcoat this instant, sir."

But Master Horace was not to be ordered about by a mere mother. He jerked himself away from her and caught his aunt's hand.

"Aunt Jarvis," he said in a wheedling tone, "we're coming out here to visit Lizzie's place some day, ain't we? You promised now, don't you remember?"

Mrs. Jarvis patted his hand.

"Well, I believe I did, boy," she said, "and we'll come some day," she added graciously, "provided the owners of The Dale would like to have us."

Miss Gordon hastened to reply. "The owners of The Dale." That sounded like the reprieve of a sentence. "Indeed we should all be very much pleased," she said, striving to hide her excitement. "Just tell me when it would be most convenient for you to come. You see, since leaving my old associations in Edinburgh, I have dropped all social duties. You can understand, of course, that one in my position would be quite without congenial companionship in a rural community. So I shall look forward to your visit with much pleasure."

Mrs. Jarvis appeared visibly impressed. Evidently Miss Gordon was not of common clay. "Now let me see," she said, "perhaps Horace and I might drive out."

"I don't see how you can possibly find time, Aunt Jarvis," cried Mrs. Oliver, who was forcing her unwilling son into his overcoat. "We have engagements for three months ahead, I am sure!"

Miss Gordon drew herself up rigidly. She had heard enough of Horace's artless chatter the summer before, to understand his mother's jealousy. Mrs. Oliver lived in a panic of fear lest the money that should be her children's might stray elsewhere.

There was further enlightenment waiting. Mrs. Jarvis deliberately turned her back upon her niece.

"You are so kind," she said to Miss Gordon with elaborate emphasis, "and indeed I shall be exceedingly glad to accept. Horace and I shall come, you may be sure, provided he has not too many engagements; and then," her words became more emphatic and distinct, "we shall have more opportunity to discuss what is to be done with little Elizabeth." She turned to where her namesake was standing, her kindly smile illuminating her face.

"What do you want most in the world, little Elizabeth?" she asked alluringly.

Miss Gordon held her breath. This surpassed even her brightest dreams!

"Elizabeth," she said, her voice trembling. "Do you hear what Mrs. Jarvis is asking you?"

Yes, Elizabeth had heard, and was looking up with shining eyes, her answer ready. But as usual she was busy exercising that special talent she possessed for doing the unexpected.

She had been glancing about her for some means of escape from her embarrassing position, when she had espied Eppie. The little girl, muffled in her grandfather's old tartan plaid, for the cold drive homeward, was slipping past, glancing wistfully at Elizabeth, the center of the grand group from town. Elizabeth instantly forgot her own troubles in a sudden impulse to do Eppie a good turn. This was an opportunity not to be lost. She caught her little friend by the hand and drew her near.

"Oh, Mrs. Jarvis!" she cried, grown quite eloquent now that she had found a subject so near her heart, "I'd rather have Eppie stay on the farm than anything else in the wide, wide world!"

"Elizabeth!" cried her aunt in dismay, "what are you saying?"

Mrs. Jarvis looked down with a puzzled expression at the quaint little figure wrapped in the old plaid. But she smiled in a very kindly way.

"What is she talking about?" she inquired.

Elizabeth hung her head, speechless again. She had been importuned to speak only a moment before, but, now that she had found her tongue, apparently she had made a wrong use of it.

Horace came to the rescue. He spoke just whenever he pleased, and he knew all about this matter. He had not been Elizabeth's and Rosie's chum for two weeks without hearing much of poor Eppie's wrongs.

"That's Eppie, auntie, Eppie Turner, and that's her grandpa over there," he explained, nodding to where old Sandy stood with a group of men. "Mr. Huntley sold his farm, and he won't leave it."

Mrs. Jarvis glanced at the bent figure of the old Highlander, and then at the shy face of his little granddaughter; those two whose lives could be made or marred by a word from her. But this was not the sort of charity that appealed to Mrs. Jarvis. It meant interfering in business affairs and endless trouble with lawyers. She remembered that romantic young Mr. Coulson had bothered her about either this or some affair like it not so long ago.

"Horace, my dear," she said wearily, "don't you know by this time that the very mention of lawyers and all their business gives your poor auntie a headache?" She patted Eppie's cheek with her gloved fingers. "A sweet little face," she murmured. "Good-by, Miss Gordon. I shall see you and your charming family very soon, I hope."

She shook hands most cordially, but Miss Gordon was scarcely able to hide her chagrin. Elizabeth had let the great chance of her life slip through her fingers! The good-bys were said, even Mrs. Oliver, now that her aunt had for the moment escaped temptation, bidding the lady of The Dale a gracious farewell.

And not until Miss Gordon had collected her family and was seated in Wully Johnstone's sleigh, ready for the homeward drive, did she remember that in her anxiety over Elizabeth she had not once within the last dangerous half-hour given a glance towards Annie!

CHAPTER X
GREAT EXPECTATIONS

For the remainder of the winter, Elizabeth lived under the shadow of Mrs. Jarvis's expected visit. And though she was supposed to be the one who should benefit chiefly from it, a shadow it indeed proved. Did she tear her pinafore, burst through the toes of her boots, run, leap, scream, or do any one of the many ungenteel things she was so prone to do, the stern question faced her: What did she suppose Mrs. Jarvis would think of a big girl, going on twelve, who could conduct herself in such a shocking manner? Elizabeth mourned over her shortcomings, and longed to be proper and genteel. At the same time, while she condemned herself for the traitorous thought, she had almost come to look upon the expected visit as a not altogether unmixed blessing. For the Mrs. Jarvis of reality was not the glorious creature of Elizabeth's dreams. Her queens were one by one abdicating their thrones. The beautiful teacher was steadily growing less worshipful, in spite of much incense burned before her, and now even the fairy god-mother was proving but mortal. She had laid aside her golden scepter at that moment when, with perfect faith, her namesake had looked up to her as to a goddess and asked for a blessing upon Eppie. But as yet Elizabeth's soul refused to acknowledge the loss of either idol; and she lived in a state of excitement and worry over the impending visit.

At school she escaped from the thraldom of being the lady's namesake, for Miss Hillary of course made no allusion to the fatal name of Jarvis, and the Red Cutter averted nearly all other troubles. So, in the reaction from home restrictions, Elizabeth gave herself up almost entirely to drawing pictures and weaving romances. For Joan of Arc never disappointed one. She was always great and glorious, being composed entirely of such stuff as dreams are made of, and Elizabeth turned to her from fallible mortals with much joy and comfort.

But Mary's reports of school-life always showed the dreamer at the foot of her class, and Miss Gordon grew apprehensive. Mrs. Jarvis might arrive any day, ready to repeat the glorious offer she had already made to that improvident child. But if she found her dull and far behind her classmates, how could she be expected to offer anything in the way of higher education?

"Elizabeth," her aunt said one evening as the family were gathered about the dining-room table, all absorbed in their lessons, except the troublesome one, "I do wish you had some of Jean's ambition. Now, don't you wish you could pass the entrance next summer with John and Charles Stuart?"

Elizabeth glanced across the table at those two working decimals, with their heads close together. Mr. MacAllister had come over to get advice on the Long Way, and had brought his son with him.

"Oh, my, but wouldn't I love to!" she gasped.

"Then why don't you make an effort to overtake them? I am sure you could if you applied yourself."

"But I'm only in the Junior Fourth yet, aunt, and besides I haven't got a–something Jean told me about. What is it I haven't got, Jean?"

Jean, in company with Malcolm, was absorbed in a problem in geometry.

"I don't think you've got any common sense, Lizzie Gordon, or you wouldn't interrupt," she said sharply.

"I mean," persisted Elizabeth, who never quite understood her smart sister, "I mean what is it I haven't got that makes me always get the wrong answer to sums?"

"Oh! A mathematical head, I suppose. There, Malc, I've got it. See; the angle A.B.C. equals the angle B.C.D."

"Yes, that's what's the matter," said Elizabeth mournfully. "I haven't a mathematical head. Miss Hillary says so, too."

"But you might make up for it in other things," said Annie, who was knitting near. "It would be lovely to pass the entrance before you are quite twelve, Lizzie. Jean is the only one, so far, that passed at eleven. You really ought to try."

After this Elizabeth did try, spasmodically, for nearly a week, but gradually fell back into her old idle habits of compiling landscapes and dreaming dreams.

Miss Gordon questioned Miss Hillary next in regard to the difficult case. There was an afternoon quilting-bee at Mrs. Wully Johnstone's, to which some young people had been invited for the evening, and there she met the young schoolmistress. As a rule, the lady of The Dale mingled very little in these social gatherings. The country folk were kind and neighborly, no doubt; and, living amongst them, one must unbend a little, but she felt entirely out of her social element at a tea-party of farmers' wives–she who had drunk tea in Edinburgh with Lady Gordon. But Auntie Jinit McKerracher had asked her on this occasion, and even Lady Gordon herself might have hesitated to offend that important personage, particularly as there had so lately been danger of a breach between the families. So, suppressing her pride, Miss Gordon went, and sat in stately grandeur at the head of the quilt, saying little until the young schoolmistress appeared. She, at least, did not murder Her Majesty's English when she spoke, though her manners were not by any means quite genteel.

Miss Gordon opened the conversation by inquiring after the attainments of her family in matters scholastic.

They were all doing very well indeed, Miss Hillary reported. She spoke a little vaguely, to be sure. The Red Cutter appeared with such pleasant frequency these days that she was not quite sure what her pupils were doing. But she remembered that the Gordons were generally at the head of their classes, and said so, adding the usual reservation which closed any praise of the family, "except Elizabeth."

Miss Gordon sighed despairingly. "Elizabeth does not seem as bright as the rest," she mourned. "I cannot understand it at all. Her father was extremely clever in his college days; indeed, his course was exceptional, his professors all said. All our family were of a literary turn, you know, Miss Hillary. Sir William Gordon's father–Sir William is the cousin for whom my brother was named–wrote exceedingly profound articles, and my dear father's essays were spoken of far and wide. No; I do not at all understand Elizabeth. I am afraid she must be entirely a MacDuff."

It did not seem so much lack of ability, Miss Hillary said, as lack of application. Lizzie always seemed employed at something besides her lessons. But perhaps it was because she hadn't a mathematical head. Then she changed the subject, feeling she was on uncertain ground. She was secretly wondering whether it was Rosie Carrick or Lizzie Gordon who never got a mark in spelling.

Elizabeth was made aware, by her aunt's remarks that evening, as they sat around the table for the usual study hour, that she had been transgressing again; but just how, she failed to understand. Miss Gordon talked in the grieved, vague way that always put Elizabeth's nerves on the rack. To be talked at this way in public was far worse even than being scolded outright in private. For one never knew what was one's specific sin, and there was always the horrible danger of breaking down before the boys.

Before retiring she sought an explanation from Mary. Yes, Mary knew; she had overheard aunt telling Annie that Miss Hillary had complained about Lizzie not doing her sums. This was a blow to Elizabeth. It was not so dreadful that anyone should complain of her to Aunt Margaret; that was quite natural; but that Miss Hillary should do the complaining! Her teacher persistently refused to sit upon the throne which Elizabeth raised again and again for her in her heart. Miss Hillary did not understand– did not even care whether she understood or not, while her pupil's worshiping nature still made pitiful attempts to put her where a true teacher could have ruled so easily and with such far-reaching results.

But the unmathematical head was not long troubled over even this disaster. It was soon again filled with such glorious visions as drove out all dark shadows of unspellable words and unsolvable problems. Elizabeth's ambition reached out far beyond the schoolroom. There was no romance or glory about getting ninety-nine per cent. in an arithmetic examination, as Rosie so often did, after all, and Elizabeth could not imagine Joan of Arc worrying over the spelling of Orleans. So she solaced herself with classic landscapes, with rhymes written concerning the lords and ladies that peopled them, and with dreams of future glory.

And so the days of anxious waiting for the great visit sped past; and in the interval Elizabeth might have fallen hopelessly into idle habits had it not been for the one person who, quietly and unnoticed, exercised the strongest influence over her life. To the little girl's surprise, Mother MacAllister was the one person who held out no hopes concerning Mrs. Jarvis. It seemed strange; for Mother MacAllister was the most sympathetic person in the whole wide world, and, besides, the only person who could always be depended upon to understand. But she did not seem to care how rich or great or glorious that great lady was, and took no interest whatever in the hopes of her coming visit. But she did take a vital interest in her little girl's progress at school, and one day she managed to find the key to those intellectual faculties which Elizabeth had kept so long locked away.

It was a Saturday afternoon, and the two comrades–the tall, stooped woman with the white hair and the beautiful wrinkled face, and the little girl with the blue-checked pinafore, the long, heavy braid, and the big inquiring eyes–were washing up the supper dishes. They were alone, for Charles Stuart and his father and Long Pete Fowler, the hired man, were away at the barn attending to the milking and the chores. The long bars of golden light from the setting sun came slanting down through the purple pines of the Long Hill. The snowy fields were gleaming with their radiance–rose pink and pure gold with deep blue shadows along the fences and in the hollows. The old kitchen, spotlessly clean, was flooded with the evening light–the yellow painted floor, the shining kettle sputtering comfortably on the stove, and the tin milk-pans ranged along the walls all gave back the sunset glow. This was the hour Elizabeth enjoyed most–the hour when she and Mother MacAllister were safe from the teasing and tormenting of Charles Stuart.

She was wiping the cups and saucers with great pride and care. They were the half-dozen blue willow-pattern cups and saucers which Mother MacAllister had saved from the wreck of her once complete set. They were used only on rare occasions, but to-night Elizabeth had been permitted to set them out. She never tired of hearing their romantic story, and Mother MacAllister told it again, as they washed and wiped and put them away on the top shelf of the cupboard.

They had been Mother MacAllister's finest wedding present, given just before she left the Old Country, years and years ago, when she and Father MacAllister were young, and there was no Charles Stuart. They had packed the precious blue dishes in a barrel with hay, and had brought them safely over all the long way. The stormy sea voyage of two months in a sailing vessel, the oft-interrupted train and boat journey from Quebec to Toronto, the weary jolting of the wagon-trail to the Holland Landing, and the storms of Lake Simcoe–the blue dishes, safe in their hay nest, had weathered them all. But the great disaster came when they were near home, just coming along the rough wagon track cut through the bush from Cheemaun–Champlain's Road, they called it even then. And such a road as it was, little Lizzie never saw–all stumps and roots, and great mud-holes where the wagon wheels sunk to the axle. There were two wagons tied together and drawn by a team of oxen, and the barrel of precious dishes was in the first one. And just as they were coming bumping and rattling down Arrow Hill, the hind wagon came untied and went crashing into the front one. And the tongue went straight through the barrel of blue dishes–from end to end–smashing everything except these few cups and saucers that had laid along the sides.

Elizabeth wiped one of the cracked cups very carefully and a lump arose in her throat. She always felt the pathos of the story, though Mother MacAllister expressed no regrets. But somehow, as the woman held one of the treasured dishes in her hard, worn hands, the tenderness in her eyes and voice conveyed to the child something of what their loss typified. They seemed to stand for all the beauty and hope and light of the young bride's life, that had been ruthlessly destroyed by the hardness and drudgery of the rough new land.

"They are to be yours when you grow up, you mind, little Lizzie," Mother MacAllister said, as she always did when the story of the blue cups and saucers was finished. Elizabeth sighed rapturously. "Oh, I'd just love them!" she cried, "but I couldn't bear to take them away from here. The cupboard would look so lonesome without them. I suppose I wouldn't need to, though, if I married Charles Stuart, would I?" she added practically.

Mother MacAllister turned her back for a few minutes. When she looked at Elizabeth again there was only a twinkle in her deep eyes.

"You would be thinking of that?" she asked quite seriously.

"Oh, I suppose so," said Elizabeth with a deep sigh, as of one who was determined to shoulder bravely life's heaviest burdens. "Of course aunt thinks Mrs. Jarvis may take me away and make a lady of me, but I don't really see how she could; do you, Mother MacAllister?"

"I would not be thinking about that, hinny. Mother MacAllister would be sad, sad to see her little girl carried away by the cares o' the world and the deceitfulness of riches."

"I hope I won't ever be," said Elizabeth piously. "Sometimes I think I'd like to be a missionary, cause girls can't be like Joan of Arc now. But it says in the g'ogerphy that there's awful long snakes in heathen lands. I don't believe I'd mind the idols, or the black people without much clothes on, though of course it wouldn't be genteel. But Martha Ellen says we shouldn't mind those things for the sake of the gospel. But, oh, Mother MacAllister! Think of a snake as long as this room! Malcolm heard a missionary in Cheemaun tell about one. I think I'd be too scared to preach if they were round. And I couldn't take your lovely dishes away amongst people like that anyway; so sometimes I think I'll just marry Charles Stuart when I get big."

Mother MacAllister busied herself arranging the dishes on the top shelf of the cupboard. Her twinkling eyes showed not the slightest resentment that her son should be chosen only as an alternative to savages and boa constrictors.

"Well, well," she said at last, very gently, "you and Charles Stuart would be too young to be thinking of such things for a wee while, lovey. But, indeed, it's Mother MacAllister prays every day that you may both be led to serve the dear Master no matter where He places you. Eh, eh, yes indeed, my lassie."

Elizabeth swung her dish-towel slowly, standing with eyes fixed on the pink and gold stretch of snow that led up to the glory of the skies above the Long Hill.

"I'm going to try when I grow big," she whispered.

"But you don't need to be waiting for that, little Lizzie," said Mother MacAllister, and seeing this was an opportunity for a lesson, added, "Come and we will be sitting down for a rest now, until the boys come in."

The dishes were all away, the oil-cloth covered table was wiped spotlessly clean and the shining milkpans were laid out upon it. There was nothing more to be done until Charles Stuart and Long Pete Fowler came in with the milk. So Mother MacAllister sat down in the old rocker by the sun-flooded window with her knitting, and Elizabeth sat on an old milking-stool at her feet. And there in the midst of the golden glow reflected from the skies, while one pale star far above in the delicate green kept watch over the dying day, there the little girl was given a new vision of One who, though He was rich, yet for Elizabeth's sake became poor, who, though He stretched out those shining heavens as a curtain, and made the glowing earth His footstool, had lived amongst men and for thirty-three beautiful years had performed their humblest tasks.

"Run and bring the Book, Lizzie," Mother MacAllister said at last, "and we'll jist be readin' a word or two about Him."

Elizabeth had not far to run. The old Bible, with the edges of its leaves all brown and ragged–and most brown and ragged where the well-read psalms lay–was always on the farthest window-sill with Father MacAllister's glasses beside it. She brought it, and, sitting again at Mother MacAllister's feet, heard story after story of those acts of love and gracious kindness that had made His life the wonder and the worship of the ages.

And didn't little Lizzie want to do something for Him? Mother MacAllister asked, and Elizabeth nodded, unable to speak for the great lump in her throat. And then the wise woman showed her how He was pleased with even a tidy desk at school, or a sum with the right answer or all the words correct in a spelling lesson.

The memory of that golden afternoon never left Elizabeth, never ceased to illuminate her after-life. Always a shining sunset recalled that winter evening; the view from the broad, low window of the glorious staircase of earth leading up to the more glorious heavens, the reflection from it all flooding the old kitchen, lighting up the sacred pages, and the beautiful face and white hair bent above her. And, best of all, the memory of the lesson she had learned that evening at Mother MacAllister's knee never lost its influence over her life. It was part of the glory and the most radiant part, that vision of the One who is the center of all beauty and joy and life.

Sometimes in later years the brightness of the vision waned, often it almost faded from view; but there always remained a gleam towards which Elizabeth's soul ever looked. And one day the vision began to brighten, slowly and imperceptibly, like the coming of the dawn, but as surely and steadily, until at last its glory filled her whole life and made it beautiful and noble, meet for the use of Him who is the Father of Lights.

Meantime, without any warning or apparent reason, Elizabeth suddenly began to learn her lessons. No one but Mother MacAllister understood why, but everybody saw the results. The connection between Elizabeth's heart and brain had been made, and that done she even began to develop a mathematical head. It was no easy task getting over her idle habits; and it was so easy when a complex fraction proved stubborn to turn one's slate into an easel. But the Saturday afternoon talks always turned upon the subject of the vital connection between fractions and the glories of the infinite, and every Monday Elizabeth went back to her tasks with renewed vim. And soon she began to taste something of the joy of achievement. It was fairly dazzling to feel oneself slowly creeping up from the foot of the class, and she found a strange exhilaration in setting herself against a rival and striving to outspell her in a match. Here was glory right ready to hand. She was Joan of Arc herself, riding through the arithmetic and slaying every complex fraction that lay in her path.

Miss Gordon witnessed the transformation in Elizabeth with amazement, and with devout thankfulness that by the judicious use of Mrs. Jarvis's name she had at last succeeded in arousing her niece's ambition. Rosie saw and was both proud and puzzled. It seemed so queer to see Lizzie working in school. Mary gave up all hopes of ever catching up to her, and John and Charles Stuart were sometimes seized with spasms of alarm lest by some unexpected leap she might land some morning in their class.

Elizabeth's days were not too full of work to preclude other interests, and just as the winter was vanishing in sunshiny days and little rivers of melting snow, two very great events occurred. Just the last day before the Easter vacation, Miss Hillary bade Forest Glen farewell and rode away for the last time in the red cutter. Elizabeth and Rosie left their decimals and the Complete Speller to take care of themselves for fully an hour, while with their heads on the desk they wept bitterly. For, after all, Miss Hillary was a teacher, and parting with even the poorest kind of teacher, especially one who was so pretty, was heart-breaking.

That was bad enough, but on the very same day old Sandy McLachlan came to the school and took Eppie away. Fortunately, her two friends did not know until the evening that Eppie, too, was gone forever; but when they did discover it, Elizabeth's grief was not to be assuaged.

The next morning Eppie and her grandfather drove away from Forest Glen. Jake Martin had not resorted to the law as he had threatened, neither had Tom Teeter relaxed his vigilance. The old man's Highland pride had at the last driven him forth. The hardest part of it all had been that the thrust that had given him his final hurt had come from his closest friend. Noah Clegg was the warmest-hearted man in Forest Glen and would have given over his whole farm to Sandy if he would have accepted it. But, as Tom Teeter declared hotly, Noah had no tact and was a blazing idiot beside, and a well-intentioned remark of his sent old Sandy out of the community. Noah was not a man of war and was so anxious that his old friend should give up his untenable position peaceably that he had very kindly and generously explained to Sandy that it would be far better for him to come and live on a neighbor that wanted him than on a man like Jake Martin, who didn't.

That very day, proud, angry, and cut to the heart, Sandy packed his household goods and left the place. There was much talk over the affair and everyone expressed deep regret—even Jake Martin. But he wisely refrained from saying much, for Tom Teeter excelled all his former oratorical nights in his hot denunciation of such a heartless crocodile, who could dance on his neighbor's grave and at the same time weep like a whited sepulchre. Long after the countryside had given up talking of poor Sandy's flitting, they discussed Tom's wonderful speech.

Elizabeth and Rosie had one letter from Eppie. They were living in Cheemaun, she said, and grandaddy was working in a big garden nearby and she was going to a great school where there were six teachers. Elizabeth's sorrow changed to admiration and envy; and soon the excitement of having a new teacher drove Eppie from her mind.

And still the winter slowly vanished and spring advanced, and still Mrs. Jarvis did not come. Vigilance at The Dale was never relaxed through the delay, however. Everything was kept in a state of preparation, and Miss Gordon ordered her household as soldiers awaiting an onset of the enemy. Sarah Emily had a clean apron every morning, and the house was kept in speckless order from the stone step of the front porch to the rain-barrel by the back door of the woodshed. Even the barnyard was swept every morning before the younger Gordons left for school, and every day their Sabbath clothes were laid out in readiness to slip on at the sight of a carriage turning in off Champlain's Road.

But the days passed and no carriage appeared, neither did a line come from the expected lady explaining her tardiness. Hope deferred made Miss Gordon's nerves unsteady and her heart hard towards the cause of her daily disappointment. By some process of unreason which often develops in the aggrieved feminine mind, she conceived of Elizabeth as that cause, and the unfortunate child found herself, all uncomprehending as usual, fallen from the heights of approbation to which her progress at school had raised her, to the old sad level of constant wrong-doing.

And so the days passed until once more May came down Arrow Hill with her arms full of blossoms, and turned the valley into a garden. Dandelions starred the green carpet by the roadside, violets and marigolds draped the banks of the creek with a tapestry of purple and gold. The wild cherry-trees fringed Champlain's Road with a white lacey hedge, heavy with perfume and droning with bees. The clover fields flushed a soft lilac tint, the orchards were a mass of pink and white blossoms, and the whole valley rang with the music of birds from the robin's first dawn note to the whip-poor-will's evensong.

Elizabeth tried not to be wildly happy, in view of her shortcomings, but found it impossible. May was here and she, too, must be riotously joyful. The boys were wont to be off on fishing expeditions once more, and over hill and dale she followed them in spite of all opposition. One radiant afternoon John and Charles Stuart went, as usual, far afield on their homeward journey from school. They crossed the creek far below the mill and, making a wide circuit round the face of Arrow Hill, came home by way of Tom Teeter's pasture-field. They had chosen this route on purpose to rid themselves of Elizabeth, but she had dogged their footsteps; and now arrived home with them, weary but triumphant. As they approached the old stone house, she remembered that she bore dismaying signs of her tumultuous journey. She had met with many accidents by the way, among others a slip into a mud-hole as they crossed the creek. So, when they reached the low bars that led from Tom's property into The Dale field, she allowed the boys to go on alone, while she sat upon the grass and strove to repair damages.

As she was scraping the mud from her wet stockings and struggling to re-braid her hair, she heard voices coming from Tom Teeter's barnyard. Glancing through the tangle of alder and raspberry bushes she was overjoyed to see Annie standing by the strawstack talking to Granny Teeter. Annie was the old woman's especial pet, and often went over to keep her company when Tom was in town or on an oratorical tour. Elizabeth sighed happily. She would wait and go home with Annie. One was almost always safe in her company.

So she sat down on the end of a rail, teetering contentedly. The rattle of a wagon could be heard on Champlain's Road. Tom was driving in at the gate, coming from town. He would be sure to have some sweeties, and would probably send them home with Annie. Granny was hobbling about the barnyard, a red and black checked shawl round her head and shoulders, a stick in her hand, which she used as much to rap the unruly pigs and calves as for a support. She was complaining in her high querulous voice about her turkeys, the *contrary* little bastes, that would nivir stay to home at all, at all, no matter if ye give them the whole farm to ate up. Tom rode up and stood talking with them, and Elizabeth, watching him through the raspberry bushes for signs of a package of candy, saw him take a letter from his pocket. Then he pointed to the straying turkeys going "peep, peep" over the hillside, and, as Granny turned to look at them, he slipped the letter into Annie's hand. Elizabeth remembered having seen Tom do this once or twice before, when he came over of an evening. She wondered what this could be about, and decided to ask Annie as soon as she came. Suppose it should be a letter from Mrs. Jarvis, saying she had started!

Her sister was a long time in coming, and when she did appear at last, walking along the path, she came very slowly. She was reading the letter and smiling very tenderly and happily over it.

"Hello, Annie!" shouted Elizabeth, scrambling up on the fence top. The letter disappeared like a flash into the folds of Annie's skirt; and at once Elizabeth's older self told her she must not ask questions about that letter, must not even allude to it. Some faint recollection of that early dawn when she had seen the farewell in their orchard drifted through her mind.

"Why, Lizzie," said her older sister, "how did you come here?" She caught sight of the books. John carried the dinner-pail on condition that Elizabeth bore the school-bag. "Haven't you got home yet?"

"No. The boys went 'way round, miles below the mill to hunt moles, and I got into the creek. And just look at my stockings, Annie!"

"Oh, Lizzie!" cried her sister in distress, "what will aunt say?" then added that which always attached itself to Elizabeth's misdemeanors, "What would Mrs. Jarvis think if she were to come to-day?"

"Oh, bother! I don't believe she'll ever come for years and years," said Elizabeth recklessly. "Do you, Ann; now, really?"

"Ye-s, I think she might soon be here now." Something in her big sister's voice made Elizabeth look up quickly. Dimples were showing in Annie's cheeks. Her eyes were radiant.

"Oh, *do* you think so? Well, Horace promised to come anyway, but what makes you think she'll come soon?"

Annie shook her head, still smiling. "Aw, do tell me," coaxed Elizabeth. "Did aunt get a letter?"

"No," the dimples were growing deeper, the eyes brighter, "but if she's coming at all she's coming this week, because–because the year's nearly up." She added the last words in a whisper and looked startled as soon as she had uttered them.

"Because what?" cried Elizabeth, bristling with curiosity.

"Nothing, nothing," said Annie hastily. "It's," she was whispering again, "it's got something to do with our secret, Lizzie, and you mustn't ask me like a good little girl. And you won't tell what I said, will you?"

Elizabeth was quite grown-up now. "Oh, no, I won't ever, ever tell. But you're not quite sure she's coming, are you? 'Cause I never finished working the motto she sent me."

"No, I'm not quite sure. But I think she will."

Elizabeth nodded. She understood perfectly, she told herself. That letter was from Mrs. Jarvis, but having something to do with Annie's secret–which meant Mr. Coulson–its contents must not be disclosed.

She went to work at her lessons that evening and forgot all about the letter and Mrs. Jarvis, too. Decimals were not so alluring since the May flowers had blossomed. A thousand voices of the coming summer called her away from her books. But Elizabeth was determined to finish a certain exercise that week, for Mother MacAllister was looking for it. Malcolm and Jean were sitting down on the old pump platform doing a Latin exercise. Elizabeth could not understand anyone studying there, with the orioles building their nest above and the vesper-sparrows calling from the lane. So she took her books up to her room, pulled down the green paper blind to shut out all sights and sounds, lit the lamp, and there in the hot, airless little place knelt by a chair and crammed her slate again and again with figures.

Miss Gordon had been darning on the side porch, but had left her work a moment and gone out to the kitchen to request Sarah Emily to sing–provided it were necessary to sing at all–a little less boisterously. Tom Teeter was in the study with Mr. Gordon, and, to show her indifference, Sarah Emily was calling forth loud and clear the chronicles of all those "finest young gents that ever were seen," who had come a-courting all in vain.

The singer being reduced to a sulky silence, the mistress of the house passed out on a tour of inspection. She glanced approvingly at the two eager young students in the orchard, calling softly to Jean not to remain out after the dew began to fall. The little boys were playing in the lane. Mary was with them, but the absence of noise showed that Elizabeth was not. Miss Gordon moved quietly upstairs. The door of Elizabeth's room was closed; she tapped, then opened it.

Elizabeth's face, hot and flushed, was raised from her slate. The lamp was flaring, and the room was stifling and smelt of kerosene. But she looked up at her aunt with some confidence. She half-expected to be commended. She was certainly working hard and surely was not doing anything wrong.

For a moment Miss Gordon stood staring. She was seized with a sudden fear that perhaps Elizabeth was not quite in her right senses. Then she noted the extravagant consuming of kerosene in the day-time.

"Elizabeth," she said despairingly, "how is it possible that you can act so strangely? Is the daylight not good enough that you must shut yourself up here? Take your books and go downstairs immediately, and blow out the lamp and tell Sarah Emily to clean it again. Really, I cannot understand you!"

Elizabeth went tumultuously down the stairs. No, her aunt didn't understand, that was just the trouble. If she ever showed any signs of doing so, one might occasionally explain. She flung her books upon the kitchen table and went out to the back kitchen door and, sitting down heavily upon a bench there, gave herself up to despair. She gazed drearily at Malcolm and Jean and listened to the laughter from the lane without wanting to join either group. Mr. MacAllister had come over a few minutes earlier, bringing the Pretender as usual. John and the latter were upstairs. Elizabeth knew they were planning to run away from her on the Queen's Birthday, but she did not care. She told herself she did not care about anything any more. Her heart was broken, and if Mrs. Jarvis were to drive in at the gate that very moment she would not take ten million dollars from her, though she begged her on her bended knees.

Miss Gordon went back to her darning on the side porch, and worked at it feverishly, wondering if the child were really in her right mind. She had much to worry her these days, poor lady. Her ambition for the family threatened to be disappointed. Mrs. Jarvis was evidently not coming. Malcolm and Jean would probably graduate from the High School and there their education must stop. And Annie was acting so strangely. She could not but remember that it was just one year ago that evening that she had bidden Annie dismiss her undesirable suitor. And now, rumor said the young man bade fair to be highly desirable, and no other lover had as yet appeared. Of course, Mr. Coulson had gone, declaring his exile would last a year, and then he would return. But Miss Gordon had little faith in young men.

Annie had not fretted, only for a day or so–that was the strange part–but their life together had never been the same. There were no pretty, sweet confidences from her favorite, such as used to make Miss Gordon feel young and happy, and lately Annie had been so silent and yet with a face that shone with an inner light. Her aunt felt lonely and shut out of the brightness of the girl's life. Much she wondered and speculated. But Annie's firm mouth closed tightly and the steady eyes looked far away when the young school-teacher's name was mentioned.

Well, it was a blessing the girl did not fret, the aunt said to herself, for there was little likelihood of his returning. He had probably forgotten all about her since last winter–young men were like that. She sighed as she confessed it, remembering one who had declared he would come back–but who had remained away in forgetfulness.

As she sat there in gloomy meditation, a rumbling noise made her look up. A carriage was coming swiftly along Champlain's Road, one of those smart buggies that came only from the town. It stopped at the gate, and the driver, a young man, alighted. Elizabeth saw him, too, and suddenly forgot her despondency. She had seen Annie but ten minutes before, walking across the pasture-field towards Granny Teeter's. She arose with a spring and went tearing through the orchard, bringing forth indignant remarks from her studious brother and sister as she flashed past. Annie had just reached the gate leading from the orchard. Elizabeth flung herself upon her.

"Oh, Annie!" she gasped, radiant and breathless. "Somebody's coming. And you'll never, never guess, 'cause it's Mrs. Jarvis, and she's brought Mr. Coulson!"

CHAPTER XI
THE DREAM OF LIFE

"Miss Gordon is wanted in the Principal's room at once."

The Science Master of Cheemaun High School put his head in at the door of the room where the "Moderns" teacher was instructing his class in French grammar. There was a flutter among the pupils as a tall young lady in a neat dark-blue dress arose. The flutter had something of apprehension in it. Miss Gordon was a prime favorite—and this was not the first time she had been summoned to what was known amongst her schoolmates as The Judgment Hall.

"Oh, Beth!" giggled the fair, plump young lady who shared her seat. "He's found you out certain!"

"You're in for it, Beth!" whispered another. "Old Primmy's seen your picture!"

Miss Gordon's deep gray eyes took on a look of mock terror. She went out with bent head and a comical air of abject humility that left the room in a titter. The "Moderns" teacher frowned. Miss Gordon was irrepressible.

Nevertheless, when she found herself passing down the wide echoing hall alone, the young lady was seized with misgivings. For which of her misdemeanors was she to be arraigned this time? There was that dreadful caricature she had drawn of the Principal—the one with the shining expanse of bald head towards which swarms of flies and mosquitoes, bearing skates and toboggans and hockey-sticks, were hurrying gayly, while upon poor old Dr. Primrose's one tuft of hair shone the conspicuous sign, "This way to the Great Slide."

Now, what on earth had she done with that picture? Oh, yes, Horace Oliver had borrowed it to show to Parker Raymond. Perhaps Park had lost it—he was such a careless fellow—and Dr. Primrose had found it! And there was that poem, too, the one on little Mr. Kelly, the Science Master. It was a long, lugubrious effusion, telling of the search by a heart-broken chemistry class for a beloved teacher, who had unaccountably disappeared. It described them as wandering about weeping pitifully, looking into desks and ink-bottles, and under books; until at last they discovered to their horror that a careless girl had dropped her pen-wiper upon him and smothered him! That poem had circulated through the class, causing much merriment. And where was it now? The poetess could not remember. Suppose someone had dropped it and Mr. Kelly had found it? He was so small, and so sensitive about his size. No wonder Miss Gordon went very slowly to the Principal's room.

Usually her days were all unalloyed joy. High School, except for occasional skirmishes with troublesome teachers, was a delight. For Elizabeth Gordon had arrived at a place in life where one could have a good time without hurting anyone; there was so much fun in the world, laughter was so easy—and nobody seemed ever to be in trouble any more. Even as she tapped at the door beyond which probable retribution lay, she smiled at the nodding lilac bush with its bunch of amethyst blossoms that waved a greeting to her from the open window. Miss Gordon's mind was prone to wander thus from the subject in hand to such sights, her teachers often found. The song of a yellow warbler in the school maples, the whirl of scarlet leaves across the window pane, or the gleam of snow on the far-off hilltops, would drive away every item of knowledge concerning the value of $(a+b)2$ or the characteristics of a parallelogram.

The door swung suddenly open and the Principal's bald head shot into view. His eyes were stern. Evidently he had come in war and not in peace.

"Ah, Miss Gordon!" he said, briskly. "Yes, Miss Gordon! Just step this way a minute!"

He held open the door and Miss Gordon stepped in, leaving all her courage on the other side. She slipped sideways into a chair and looked up at him with scared attention. Evidently it was the picture.

"Miss Gordon," said the Principal, seating himself in his revolving chair, which creaked in a way that reminded Miss Gordon horribly of stories of the guillotine, "I am making out the list of those whom I consider competent to write on the final examinations, and I feel it my duty to notify you that I cannot see my way clear to include your name."

Elizabeth fairly crumpled up in her chair. This was awful–the thing she had most feared had come upon her at last. She sat speechless.

"Your papers on mathematics are quite hopeless," he continued, growing more querulous because his pity was aroused. "It's out of the question that you should write. I've done my best to show you that you should give less time to English subjects and devote more to Algebra and your Euclid." He arose and blustered up and down the room.

"You haven't a mathematical head," he was saying for the third time when a sharp rap upon the door interrupted. Dr. Primrose, looking very much relieved, opened it. Miss Gordon turned away to the window to hide the rising tears.

There was a short, hurried conversation at the door, and the teacher turned to his victim. He had a big, warm heart that was vastly relieved at the prospect of escape from a most unpleasant duty.

"Ah, Miss Gordon," he said briskly. "Here are two gentlemen to see you. You have permission to go home early this afternoon, by special request. Kindly bear in mind what I have told you."

He stepped quickly aside, and ushered in two tall, young men, at the same time closing the door behind him.

At the same instant all Miss Gordon's troubles were shut out with him, and her face lit up with rapturous delight. She skipped across the room with a joyful scream.

"Oh, John, John Gordon, you dear old sneak; why didn't you tell me you were coming to-day?"

She flung her arms about his neck and gave him a sounding kiss. John Gordon had been a whole year in college, but he had not yet become sufficiently grown-up to accept a salute from his sister. He drew back rather embarrassed, but his blue eyes shone in his dark face. He was tremendously glad to see Lizzie again, and could not quite hide the fact.

The other young man seemed equally pleased. "I say, Lizzie!" he exclaimed, as she joyously shook both his hands. "You're grown about a yard. And her neck's longer than ever, isn't it, John?"

"You mean old Pretender," she said with a pout; nevertheless, she did not look offended. Miss Gordon had quite changed her views regarding the possession of a long neck. Estella Raymond, her dearest chum, who was short and plump, had declared many times that she would give ten thousand dollars–not specifying how she was to come by such a sum–if she could have a neck one-half as long and slim and graceful as Beth Gordon's.

"Never mind, she's getting better looking, I do declare," the Pretender added. "How's everybody?"

"Oh, just splendid–that is, they were when I was home last. I don't go every Friday, you know. When did you come? Am I to go home with you?"

"We just got here on the noon train," her brother explained, "and we swarmed up to Annie's and she gave us the dinner of our lives."

"Say, it didn't taste much like boarding-house hash, did it?" cried Mr. MacAllister fervently.

"And John Coulson's going to stand a treat for the whole family, and drive us all out to The Dale–the Kid and all. And you're to come along. Scoot and get your hat."

Elizabeth danced away down the hall to the cloakroom dizzy with joy. Examinations, mathematics, principals of High Schools, all unkind and troublesome things had vanished in a rosy mist. The old delight of getting "off with the boys," was as strong at seventeen as at ten. The boys themselves seemed to have changed their minds in the intervening years as to the advisability of allowing Lizzie to "tag after them." John's deep blue eyes, looking after her dancing figure, showed the love and pride in his sister which he was always so careful to hide, and his companion looked with somewhat the same expression and withal a little puzzled–as one who had seen something unexpected which had dazzled him.

It was but the work of a moment for Elizabeth to put on her hat and gloves. She did not linger over the correct adjustment of the former as she so often did. Miss Gordon was prone to look much in the mirror these days. It was always the fixing of a bow or a frill of lace or some other ornament that took her attention. She scarcely looked, as yet, at the shining wealth of nut-brown hair, with the golden strand through it, nor at the deep gray eyes, nor the straight line of teeth that gleamed when she laughed. Miss Gordon was not interested in these, but she could become absorbed in the arrangement of ribbon at such length that her sister, Mrs. John Coulson, sometimes worried for fear Lizzie was growing vain.

As she hurried to the main entrance where the boys stood waiting, a group of young ladies came straying out of the classroom for the afternoon recess.

"Beth Gordon!" cried the fair, plump one, making a dive at her friend. "Are you expelled or are you off for a holiday, you mean thing? Who's out there?" She craned her short neck. "Goodness, what swells! Are they waiting for you?"

"It's only our John and Stuart MacAllister, they've just got in from Toronto, and I'm going home with them."

"MacAllister and Gordon! Goodness gracious! I'm going to ask them if they've ever met Ted Burns at 'Varsity. Ted's just crazy to get me to correspond with him."

She tore down the hall and was soon in hilarious conversation with her two old schoolmates, while Elizabeth remained behind to explain her sudden departure.

"Just look at Estella!" cried a tall sallow girl, regarding that vivacious young lady with disgust.

"How is it she always has so much attention from boys?" asked Elizabeth Gordon, half-wistfully.

"My goodness, you're so innocent, Beth! Can't you see she runs after them and demands attention. I wouldn't stoop to the means she employs not if a boy never spoke to me again, would you?"

Elizabeth was silent. Somehow she could not help thinking it would be most enjoyable to have two or three swains always dancing attendance on one, the way they did on Estella Raymond, even though one did have to encourage them. Of course Estella did resort to means that were not quite genteel—but then boys seemed to always come about her, anyway, as bees did about a flower; while Madeline Oliver never had a beau. Elizabeth had to confess that she hadn't one herself—except Horace, who, of course, didn't count. She sighed. It really would be nice to be like Stella, even though one hadn't Madeline's dignity.

"Good-by, girls!" she called gayly. "I'll bring you some lady's-slippers if they're out," and she ran out to the group on the steps.

It took some time for the two young men to tear themselves away from Miss Raymond's gentle hands. They were further delayed by her following Elizabeth to the gate, her arm about her waist, while she implored her darling Beth to come back soon, and kissed her twice before she let her go. They got away at last, and the three went down the leafy street.

They were a very different looking trio from the one that used to stray over field and through woods about The Dale, fishing, berry-picking, nutting, or merely seeking adventure. They had not been separated very long. During the boys' first year in the High School, Elizabeth had worked madly, and when she managed to graduate from Forest Glen, Mother MacAllister had insisted that Charles Stuart take the buck-board and the sorrel mare and that the three inseparables drive to and from the town to school.

For though Mrs. Jarvis had really appeared in the flesh at The Dale for that one visit, she had never repeated it nor her munificent offer to discuss Elizabeth's future. Her talk had all been of Annie, and what a good match young Mr. Coulson would make. And Miss Gordon had to be content, never guessing that the astute young man whose cause the lady championed, and not her own influence had brought Mrs. Jarvis to The Dale.

So Elizabeth's fortune had not been made after all, but she had managed to get on quite well without a fortune, it would seem. Her High School days had been days of perfect joy. Even when the boys had graduated and gone to Toronto, she had managed to be happy. For Annie lived in Cheemaun by this time, lived in a fine brick house too in the best part of the town, and Elizabeth had spent this last year with her. And now nearly five years had passed, and not Mrs. Jarvis, but Mr. Coulson had become the family's hope.

Miss Gordon had long ago become reconciled to the tavern-keeping ancestor. It would appear that social lines could not be strictly drawn in this new country, and when one lived in Canada apparently one must marry as Canadians married. For it would appear also that here Jack was not only as good as his master, but might be in the master's place the next day. And certainly John Coulson was a model husband, and a rising lawyer besides. On the whole, Miss Gordon was perfectly satisfied with the match she now firmly believed she had made for her niece. Each year she grew more absorbed in her ambition for William's family. They were all responding so splendidly to her efforts. She would raise them to social eminence, she declared to herself, in spite of William's neglect and Mrs. Jarvis's indifference. With John Coulson's help Malcolm had secured a position in the bank of a neighboring town. Jean was teaching school in Toronto, and because Jean must needs do the work of two people, she was reading up the course Charles Stuart was taking in the University and attending such lectures as she could. Even Elizabeth, through Annie's goodness, was getting such learning as she was capable of taking. And John was at college learning to be a doctor. That was the hardest task of all, the sending of John to college. And only Miss Gordon knew how it had been accomplished. She had managed it somehow for the first year, and John was to earn money during his first summer vacation for his next year.

Down the long leafy street Elizabeth was moving now between the two tall figures. There was so much to tell, so many questions to ask, and she talked all the time. To the boys' disgust they could extract from her very little information respecting any person except the one supreme personage who now ruled her days—Annie's baby. She was overcome with indignation that Annie had not already displayed him. What if he was asleep! It was a shame to make anybody wait five minutes for a sight of such a vision. Why, he was the most angelic and divinely exquisite, sweetest, dearest, darlingest pet that ever gladdened the earth. He was a vision, that's what he was! Just a vision all cream satin and rose-leaf and gold. Elizabeth described him at such length that the boys in self-defense uttered their old, old threat. They would climb a fence and run away—and Elizabeth, whose long skirts now precluded the possibility of her old defiant counter-threat to follow them, desisted and bade them "just wait."

They were climbing the heights that formed the part of the town called Sunset Hill. It was a beautiful spot, with streets embowered in maple trees and bordered by lawns and gardens. At the end of each leafy avenue gleamed Cheemaun Lake with its white sails. Sunset Hill was not only the prettiest residential part of the town, it was the region of social eminence; and it were better to dwell in a cot on those heights and have your card tray filled with important names, than exist in luxury down by the lake shore and not be known by Society. The houses on Sunset Hill were all of red brick with wide verandas supported by white pillars—the wider the veranda, and the thicker the pillars, the greater the owner's social distinction. For some years this form of architecture was the only one accepted by people of fashion, until Mr. Oliver, who was a wealthy lumberman, inadvertently put an end to it. He too built his new house on Sunset Hill, and Mrs. Oliver, just to outpillar the other pillars of society, had her veranda supported by groups of columns, three in a group. Thereafter builders lost courage, seeming to feel that the limit had been reached. Shortly after, a daring young contractor put up a gray stone house with slim black veranda posts, and no one raised a protest. And fashion, having been chased in this manner from pillar to post, so to speak, Society turned its attention to other than architectural fields. But the dull red bricks of Sunset Hill with their white ornamentations mellowing in the keen Canadian winters, stood thereafter as a title clear to unquestionable social standing.

It had always been a source of great satisfaction to Elizabeth that John Coulson had taken Annie to a white-pillared home on Sunset Hill; for Madeline and Horace lived in the finest home there, and Estella, though on the wrong side of Elm Crescent, the street that, curving round Sunset Hill, divided it from the vulgar world, dwelt in a very fine residence indeed. Elizabeth had learned many things besides French and Chemistry in Cheemaun High School.

They found a big carriage drawn up before the door of Annie's house, and Annie already in it holding the Vision, now merely a bundle of lace and shawls. Elizabeth grasped the bundle from her sister's arms and proceeded to display its many charms. "Oh, John, just look at him! Look, Stuart, see him's dear dear itty nose, an' him's grea' big peepers! Isn't he the darlingest pet——"

The boys attempted to be sufficiently admiring, but just as they were lamely trying to say something adequate to the great occasion, to Elizabeth's dismay, the Vision opened its mouth and yelled lustily.

"Betsey, you're a nuisance!" said John Coulson, with that indulgent look he always bent upon the young sister-in-law, who had been such a help to him in those days when he sorely needed help. "Come, tumble in, everybody. All aboard for The Dale,–Champlain and Cheemaun R. R.!" The Vision was quieted, the travelers sprang in, the whip cracked, the wheels rattled, the horses pranced, and away they spun down the leafy streets–down, down, to the long level stretch of Champlain's Road that ran straight out into the country.

There was much to be told of college pranks and college work, and the telling of it lasted until the horses climbed Arrow Hill and the old familiar valley lay stretched before them.

"Yook, yook, Dackie!" chattered Aunt Elizabeth, clutching the Vision, whose big blue eyes were gazing wonderingly from the depths of his wrappings. "Yook at de pitty pitty wobin! A teenty weenty itty wobin wed best!"

There was a groan from the front seat.

"Do you often get it as bad as that, Lizzie?" asked John anxiously.

"Remember The Rowdy, Lizzie?" asked Charles Stuart, "the fellow that used to sing in the hawthorn bush?"

"I should think I do–and Granny Teeter. Listen, there is The Rowdy's lineal descendant, for sure!"

It seemed to be The Rowdy's very reincarnation, singing and shouting from an elm bough by the roadside.

"That's a gay bachelor all right," said John Coulson, who, because he was so supremely happy in his married life, had to make allusion to his condition as often as possible, even if only by way of contrast.

"He sounds more like a widower," said Elizabeth gloomily; "one that had been bereaved about a year."

"Hush, hush, Betsey!" cried her brother-in-law. "Remember whose land he's on."

"That's just what I am remembering."

"You don't mean that Jake's beginning to 'take notice,' surely?" asked John Gordon, in wicked delight. For only the spring before poor worn-out Mrs. Martin had suddenly ceased her baking, churning, and hoeing, and had gone to her long rest in the Forest

Glen churchyard, and already rumor said that Jake was on the lookout for another baker, churner, and hoer.

"I'm afraid he is," said John Coulson. "There he is now prowling round his asparagus beds. He's probably got his eye on Betsey."

Elizabeth was not prepared to answer this sally. She was looking out eagerly for some glimpse of Susie. All the elder Martins had left home just as soon as they were old enough to assert their independence. But Susie's strength had given way before the hard work, and she lay all day in bed, or dragged her weary limbs about the house, a hopeless invalid, and her father's chief grievance in life. Elizabeth's warm heart was always filled with a passionate pity for Susie, and she rarely visited home without running across the fields to brighten a half-hour for the sick girl.

Just at this moment there arose from the fields opposite the Martin farm a rollicking song—loud, clear, compelling attention, and poured forth in a rich baritone.

"O, and it's whippity-whoppity too,
And how I'd love to sing to you,
I'd laugh and sing
With joy and glee,
If Mistress McQuarry would marry me,
If Mistress McQuarry would marry me!"

The last line was fairly shouted in a way that showed the singer was anxious to be heard.

"Tom's trying to outsing the robins," cried John Coulson, pulling up his horses. Mr. Teeter was coming across a rich brown field behind his harrow. John Coulson waved his hat.

"Hello, Tom, I tell you they lost a fine singer when they made an orator out of you! Give us a shake!"

Tom was over the fence in a twinkling, and shaking the newcomers' hands.

"Sure it's awful college swells ye're gettin' to be, wid your high collars. Have ye made up yer mind to be a preacher yet?" He looked at Charles Stuart.

"No, I haven't," said Charles Stuart hastily.

"Well ye ought to be ashamed o' yerself, wid the mother ye've got. So ye heard me singin' now?" His eyes gleamed with mischievous delight. "I was shoutin' for a purpose." He jerked his thumb over his shoulder in the direction of the man working in the Martin fields. "Look at that say-sarpent wigglin' over there. It makes him so mad he could set fire to me." He laughed so explosively that the horses started. "He's coortin'. Yes, siree, but he don't like to have it advertised."

"Who's the poor woman?" asked Mrs. Annie in distress.

"Auntie Jinit McKerracher! They say she throwed the dish-water on him the last time he went sparkin'. Hi! young shaver!" This to the Vision, who had insisted upon sitting erect, and was now looking about him. "Oh, he's the broth of a boy, sure enough, Lizzie. Now ye'll be sure all o' yez to come over and see mother; don't ye dare go back widout. I suppose yous two didn't hear anything o' poor Sandy and the wee girl in Toronto, did ye?"

John shook his head. "We heard they were living with Eppie's father. He kept a corner grocery store in the east end, but we couldn't find them."

"Eh, eh," sighed Tom, "poor Sandy. A fine old fellow. Eh, I hope he's not in want." He shook his fist towards his neighbor. "An' jist go on robbin' widows an' tramplin' on orphans till ye perish in the corruption o' yer own penuriousness. Yes, an' me lady Jarvis too!" he cried, abruptly finishing his apostrophe. "She'll have to answer for old Sandy an' the wee thing, see if she don't." The company smiled in spite of his earnestness, all but Elizabeth. She regarded him with big solemn eyes. "Now yous 'll be over to see mother early, mind," he added as he swung one leg over the fence.

As they drove away they heard his song rising again loud and clear–

"O, and it's whippity-whoppity too,
And how I'd love to sing to you."

"Tom's a great lad," laughed John Coulson. "He'll never grow old. I wonder why he never married," he added, returning to his favorite topic.

"Does Sarah Emily still think he's pining for her?"

"She's sure of it," said Elizabeth. "And poor old granny is so angry that Tom won't get married. 'Aw wirra wurra, if Tom'd only git a wife now.'" She wrung her hands and imitated old Granny Teeter's wail to perfection. "'Sure an' he nades a wife to tind to the chickens an' the pigs an' the turkeys–the contrary little bastes that'll niver be stayin' at home, at all at all.'"

The young men laughed, and John Coulson looked admiringly at her. John Coulson was too apt to encourage Lizzie in this sort of thing, Annie felt. She smiled indulgently at her sister, but said nothing. Mrs. John Coulson alone knew why poor unselfish Tom had never married, but hers was a loyal friendship and she had kept his secret as faithfully as he had once kept hers.

And now they had come prancing out from behind the screen of elm trees, and The Dale lay spread out before them–the big gate between the old willows, the long lane bordered by blossoming cherry-trees, and the old stone house with its prim flower beds in front. Their homecoming was a few days earlier than expected, and Mr. Gordon was all unconsciously hoeing at the back of the field, but Sarah Emily spied them as they pulled up at the gate, and came running round the house shouting in a most ungenteel but warm-hearted fashion that the folks was come home.

Elizabeth sprang from the carriage and ran down the lane to meet Mary. Though she came home often, the joy of reunion with her family never palled. There was no place like The Dale for Elizabeth, no folk like her own folk. She did not even notice in her joyous hurry that Charles Stuart had left and was striding homeward down Champlain's Road.

Mary came running out to meet her. She was a tall girl now, taller than Elizabeth, but her delicately beautiful face was wasted and pale, except for two pink spots on her cheeks. Miss Gordon was just behind her. She had not grown much older looking in the past few years, and unconsciously had lost some of her stately rigidity. She looked extremely handsome, her face flushed and alight with happiness. She did not kiss the visitors, except Baby Jackie, but her eyes shone with welcome. As she greeted John, she laid one hand for a moment on his shoulder. She looked at him closely, noting with pride the new air of gentility even one year at college had given the boy. But as she took Annie's boy into her arms Miss Gordon's face grew positively sweet.

She had not the privilege of bearing the precious bundle far. Sarah Emily, who had rushed back to the house to don a clean apron, met her at the door, and snatching the Vision fled upstairs with him, inquiring loudly of the blessed petums if it wasn't just Sarah Emily's ownest, darlingest love.

Mr. Gordon came hurrying in from the field, and after he had made them all welcome over again, he followed John about in a happy daze, saying again and again that if only Mary and Malcolm were here–no, no, Archie and Lizzie–tuts, it was Malcolm and Jean he meant,–if they were only home now, the family would be complete–"almost complete," he added. And then his eyes once more took on their far-away look, and he slipped away into the study, whither Elizabeth softly followed him.

In the late afternoon the younger boys came home from school, and the excitement had to be all lived through again. They all wandered about the old house, everyone following in the wake of the baby. The Dale rooms were not the bare, echoing spaces they once were. Just two years before, Cousin Griselda had passed quietly away, and her little annuity, as well as the property in McGlashan Street, had passed to Miss Gordon. The latter had experienced much real grief over her loss, and had taken pains in the intervening time to impress upon all her family that this bereavement was part of the sacrifice she had deliberately made for them. Nevertheless, the Gordons had benefited some from the slight addition to their income, and there were many comforts in the big stone house which had been absent in the early days. Early in the evening Mother MacAllister and Charles Stuart came over, and Granny Teeter returned their visit, bringing with her Auntie Jinit McKerracher, who had dropped in. Elizabeth and Mary and Sarah Emily, when they were not quarreling over who should nurse Baby Jackie, managed to set the table for a second late tea. A grand tea it was too, with the big shining tablecloth Aunt Margaret had brought from the Old Country, and the high glass preserve dish that always had reminded Elizabeth in her early years of the pictures of the laver in the tabernacle court. It was a great day altogether, and Elizabeth enjoyed so much the old joy of straying down the lane and over the fields with John and Charles Stuart, that when John Coulson drove up to the door, and Annie with the Vision, once more a bundle of shawls, was put into the carriage, she was glad she was to remain at home till Monday.

The Coulson family drove away, with a bunch of early Dale rhubarb, and green onions, under the carriage seat, along with a fresh loaf of Mother MacAllister's bread, and a roll of Auntie Jinit McKerracher's butter, and a jar of Granny Teeter's cider. When they were gone, John went into the study for a talk with his father alone, and Elizabeth and Mary repaired to their little room to discuss the week's doings. It was not the bare room it once was; the girl's deft hands had decorated it with cheap but dainty muslin curtains, pictures, and bric-a-brac. Elizabeth went down on her knees to clear out a bureau drawer for the clothes she had brought.

She laughed as she brought up some old treasures. Here was a pair of white pillow covers that Mrs. Jarvis had sent her on her thirteenth birthday. There was a motto outlined on each, and silk threads for working it had accompanied the gift. But Elizabeth had finished only one, and put a half-dozen stitches into the other. "Look at those!" she cried, half-laughing, half-ashamed, as she hung them over a chair. "I wonder when I'll ever get them finished." Mary picked them up, and examined them. "You really ought to do them, Lizzie. They'd be so pretty for our bed done in the pale blue silk." She read the mottoes aloud, "I slept and dreamed that life was beauty," and the second, "I awoke and found that life was duty." "It's just like you to drop a thing in the middle and not finish it." Mary was growing more like her Aunt Margaret every day in her stately prim manner.

"I didn't drop it in the middle, Miss Wiseacre," said her sister. "Can't you see I started the Duty one. It's ten stitches past the middle!" She caught them up, bound "the beauty one" about her head, stuck the other into her belt for an apron, twisted her face up into a perfect imitation of Auntie Jinit McKerracher, and proceeded to give Mary the latest piece of gossip, in a broad Scotch accent, ending up as Auntie Jinit always did, "Noo, ah'm jist tellin' ye whit ah heered, an' if it's a lee, ah didna mak it!"

Mary laughed till the tears came. Lizzie was so absurd and so funny. But the fit of laughter at her antics brought on a fit of coughing, and a voice called from the foot of the stairs–"Mary, Mary, are you sitting up in that chilly room? Come right down to the stove at once."

Mary went coughing down the stairs, and Elizabeth listened unconcerned. Mary had always been coughing and always been chased to the stove ever since she could remember. She folded her head-dress and put it into the drawer. She glanced at its inscription, "I slept and dreamed that life was beauty." She was sleeping these happy days, and dreaming too that life was all joy. The other pillow-cover slipped from her belt and lay on the floor. Her careless foot trampled it. It was the one that read, "I awoke and found that life was duty." The significance of her unconscious act did not reach her. She hummed a gay song learned at school, as she crammed the pieces of embroidery into a drawer. They were merely embroidery to Elizabeth, and so was life. She had not yet read the inscription traced over it by the finger of God, and knew not its divine meaning.

But in the silence of the little room, the remembrance of Dr. Primrose's fell message suddenly returned. It was the first time she had recalled it all that long, happy day. Well, there was no use worrying, she concluded philosophically. Sufficient unto the day was the evil thereof, and she ran down the stairs singing.

The summer holidays soon came, and Elizabeth left Cheemaun under a cloud. She had failed, while the rest of the family had succeeded. Everyone came home bearing laurels but her, and her aunt keenly felt the one shadow over the family glory.

Nevertheless, for Elizabeth the vacation passed gayly. She seemed to be the only one who did not grieve over her lack of success. She was indeed the only really Gay Gordon, so studious and hard-working had they all become.

Elizabeth somehow seemed the only one also who managed to play all the time. She had the faculty of turning everything into play. John hired with Tom Teeter for the summer, and Charles Stuart toiled all day in his own fields. Jean came home laden with books, and studied both night and day. Even Malcolm in his two weeks' vacation busied himself in the garden with his father. But Elizabeth seemed to have no definite place assigned her in the domestic economy. Mary had such light duties as her health permitted, but she refused all her sister's offers of assistance. Lizzie was sure to get the darning all tangled and spoiled, and if one left her any sewing to do, one might see her next moment chasing Jamie down the lane, with the unsewed article left hanging over a raspberry bush. Yes, Lizzie was no good, as Sarah Emily declared when she ventured into the kitchen, and the only time she appeared at an advantage was during Annie's weekly visits when she excelled everyone in her care of the baby. Even her aunt had to admit her superiority here. She was as careful, as wise and responsible as Miss Gordon could wish, and she often wondered how the reckless, nonsensical girl could be so suddenly transformed. But then Miss Gordon was still far from understanding her niece.

Elizabeth's days were very full in spite of her idleness. There were her weekly visits to Mother MacAllister, frequent calls on poor Susie lying in pain on her hard bed, and even an occasional call upon Rosie away down in Forest Glen. Rosie hailed Elizabeth's visits with delight, though she was too busy to return them. The Carricks were toiling night and day, sewing, and preserving fruit, and "hooking" mats and quilting quilts. For in the fall, just at the season when a wedding trip to the Toronto Autumn Exhibition was looked upon as the most fashionable social departure in the countryside, Rosie and Hector McQueen, who had never outlived the days of chivalry, were to be married! It made Elizabeth feel old and queer and dreadfully sorry for Rosie all at one moment just to think about it.

Elizabeth was sometimes possessed with the feeling that she was outside everybody else's life. Of course there was John. He was her chum and her soul's companion, but the rest of the family seemed to live in a world full of interests into which she could not enter. Jean was burning with ambition. She talked only of her studies, of her progress and aspirations in the teaching profession, and of Miss Mills, with whom she studied. Miss Mills was a mathematical wonder, Jean declared, but in Elizabeth's opinion, she was a tough mathematical problem clothed in partially human flesh. She wondered much at Miss Mills, and at Jean too, and tried to catch her enthusiasm. But she could see nothing in Jean's life over which to grow enthusiastic.

Another person who seemed to have grown away from her was Charles Stuart. The Pretender had changed within the last few years. He was a tall, broad-shouldered young man now, and his dark eyes did not dance so mischievously in his handsome face. They wore something of the expression of dreamy kindness that lay in the depths of his mother's gray eyes. He was generally very quiet too, given to sitting alone with a book, and Elizabeth often found him dull and stupid.

Mother MacAllister sometimes seemed worried over him, and Elizabeth wondered much what could be the reason. Had the Pretender been wild and bad as he used to be she could have understood, but he seemed so quiet and steady.

One evening she came near divining the reason for her anxious looks.

Elizabeth still kept up her Saturday afternoon visit to Mother MacAllister, and to-night they had had the blue dishes for tea. As she wiped them and arranged them on the high shelf of the cupboard, Mother MacAllister went down cellar to attend to her milk. Elizabeth finished her work and picked up a book Charles Stuart had left on the window. It was a theological work, and as Mother MacAllister came out of the cool cellar, the girl looked up joyfully.

"Then Stuart is going to be a minister after all, is he?"

The mother's beautiful eyes grew eager, hungry. "Would he be saying that to you, lovey?" she asked in a half-whisper.

"No. But this book; it's a theological work. I thought from it——" Elizabeth's heart was touched by the expression on Mother MacAllister's face. It had grown very sad. She glanced at the book and shook her head. "No, no, dearie," she said, and there was a quiver in her voice that made the girl's heart contract. "I am afraid it is books like that one that will be keeping young men away from the truth."

Elizabeth patted her arm in silent sympathy. She knew Mother MacAllister's great ambition for her boy. And Charles Stuart was such an orator too–it seemed too bad. She picked up the book again, glancing through it, and thought surely Mother MacAllister must be mistaken. It seemed such an entirely good sort of book, like "Pilgrim's Progress," or something of that sort.

"What are you going to be?" she asked as Charles Stuart walked home with her in the golden August, evening along Champlain's Road.

"I don't know," said the young man. "Sometimes I think I'd like to go in for medicine. But my four years in Arts will put me hopelessly behind John. I really haven't decided what I'll do."

"I remember you used to be divided between the ministry and veterinary surgery," reminded Elizabeth.

He laughed. "I think there is about equal chances between them still," he said, and Elizabeth's older self saw he did not wish to pursue the subject. She was very sorry for Mother MacAllister, but on the whole she still thought Charles Stuart was wise in choosing some less exacting profession than the ministry.

But the joyous holidays, driving over the country with John and Charles Stuart, wandering on berry-picking tramps with Archie and Jamie, or spending hours of adoration before the Vision, could not last forever. Malcolm's departure after his short vacation saw the beginning of the end. The last week of August came and Jean packed her books and went back to her teaching, her studies, and her beloved Miss Mills. And then September ripened into October, and college days had come.

As the day of the boys' departure approached, Elizabeth felt as though she had come to the end of all things. Her own High School days were over, ended in failure; she was not needed at home, she was no use away from home, and she had a vague feeling that she was not wanted anywhere.

The night before the boys left, Charles Stuart came over to say good-by, and before he went home Mr. Gordon led family worship. He read the 91st Psalm, that one he always chose for the evening reading the night before any of his loved ones left the home nest. He had read it often by this time, but it never lost its effect upon the young people's hearts. It made a grand farewell from the father to his children, a promise to both of perfect security in the midst of all dangers.

"He that dwelleth in the secret place of the Most High shall abide under the shadow of the Almighty.... Surely He shall deliver thee from the snare of the fowler and from the noisome pestilence. He shall cover thee with His feathers, and under His wings shall thou trust.... Thou shalt not be afraid for the terror by night, nor for the arrow that flieth by day.... For He shall give His angels charge over thee to keep thee in all thy ways."

The spell of the wonderful words was still over the young folks' hearts as Elizabeth and John walked up the lane with Charles Stuart. The latter was particularly quiet. Elizabeth had noticed that his eyes were moist and his voice very husky when he had bidden her father good-by. She herself was very, very sad and lonely to-night, and the weird beauty of the moonlit valley only added to her melancholy.

The night was still young, and up above the Long Hill there lingered the gold and pink of the sunset. Above the black pines of Arrow Hill a great round moon hung in the amethyst skies. And low over the valley there stretched a misty veil of gold and silver, a magic web woven by the fingers of the moonrise held out in farewell to touch the fairy hands of the sunset. It was such a night as could intoxicate Elizabeth. As the boys stood making arrangements for their early morning drive to Cheemaun, she leaned over the gate and looked down the long ghostly white line of Champlain's Road, hearing only the soft splash of the mill water-fall coming up through the scented dusk. She scarcely noticed Charles Stuart's farewell; nor his lingering hand-clasp. When he was gone she went upstairs to her room, and long after Mary and the rest of the household were asleep, she sat by the window. And for the first time she strove to put on paper the thoughts that were surging in her heart, demanding expression.

Elizabeth had written many, many rhymes, but they had all been gay and nonsensical. She had never tried before to express a serious thought. And to-night, she did not guess that her success was due to the fact that her heart was aching over the parting with John.

CHAPTER XII
LEFT BEHIND

And so the barque Elizabeth was left stranded while the stream of progress swept onward, bearing her friends. After the boys had left, the languorous October days passed very slowly at The Dale, and Elizabeth's energies of both body and mind soon began to cry out for a wider field of activity.

She was hourly oppressed with a sense of her own uselessness, a feeling her aunt's aggrieved manner tended to foster. Her heart smote her as she saw everyone at work but herself. She tried to help her father with his township affairs, but he met all her offers of assistance with his indulgent smile, and the remark that little girls could not understand business, and she must not bother her head.

Neither could she find any regular occupation about the house. Sarah Emily, who had conceived a great respect for Elizabeth since she had been living in the town, refused to let her soil her hands in the kitchen. It was too much of a come-downer, she declared, for a lady educated away up high the way Lizzie was to be sloppin' round with an apron on. Why didn't she sit still and read books, the way Jean did?

And Sarah Emily's will was not to be disputed. She was even more than usually independent these days, for without doubt a real suitor for her hand had appeared at The Dale kitchen. He was none of those "finest young gents as ever was seen," that existed only in Sarah Emily's imagination; but a real, solid, flesh-and-blood young farmer, none less than Wully Johnstone's Peter, now the eldest son at home, and to whom the farm was to eventually fall. Since Peter had openly avowed his intentions, Sarah Emily had been thrown into alternate fits of ecstasy over her good fortune,– which she strove to hide under a mask of haughty indifference–and spasms of dismay over the wreck she was making of poor Tom Teeter's life. That Tom was in a frightful way, she could not but see; for, as she confided to Elizabeth, it fairly made her nerves all scrunch up to hear him sing that awful doleful song about wishin' she would marry him.

Elizabeth suggested to her aunt, that as Sarah Emily was likely soon to give notice finally and forever, that she should be the one to take up the burden of the housekeeping. But Miss Gordon seemed unwilling that Elizabeth should find any settled place in the household. Mary was quite sufficient help, she said, and when Sarah Emily left of course another maid must succeed her. There really was nothing for Elizabeth to do, she added, with a grieved sigh.

She was equally averse to any proposition on the part of the girl to go away and earn her own living. Now that there was no hope of her ever becoming a school-teacher, Miss Gordon said, with a heavier sigh than usual, there was really no other avenue open for a young lady that was quite genteel.

And then Elizabeth would sigh too, very deeply, and wish with all her soul that she had had just sufficient mathematics in her head to meet the requirements of the cast-iron system of the Education Department, which unfortunately required all heads to be exactly alike.

Meanwhile, her nature being too buoyant to allow her to fret, she managed to put in the days in a way that made even her aunt confess that the old house was much brighter for her presence. Mary was her constant companion, glad of any contingency that kept Lizzie near her. But beyond the home-circle she found little congenial friendship.

She visited Mother MacAllister once a week, of course, and was some real help to her, as she was to poor Susie Martin. But she had outgrown her schoolmates, or grown away from them, even had her aunt approved of her associating with them. The Price girls had spent all their father's substance in riotous dressing, and were now in domestic service in Cheemaun. Rosie was living away up north on the McQueen farm, a new, practical, careful money-making little Rosie. And Martha Ellen Robertson even was gone. Martha Ellen was married and now lived on an Alberta ranch and had many gold watches and all the dresses she could desire. The only familiar sight in Forest Glen for Elizabeth was Noah Clegg. He was still superintendent of the Sunday school, still wore the same squeaky Sabbath boots, and though he had never quite regained his old-time cheerfulness since the day his assistant left, he still smilingly urged his flock to "sing up an' be 'appy."

Elizabeth often wondered what had become of old Sandy and Eppie. She had not quite outgrown her childish desire to right poor Eppie's wrongs, and often, even yet, she told herself that some day she would intercede with Mrs. Jarvis, and Eppie would be brought back to Forest Glen.

But in spite of her buoyant nature Elizabeth was not happy. Great new aspirations were springing up in her heart. She had submitted to a well-known magazine her little verses, born of that night of moonrise and sunset, when the boys said good-by. They had not been accepted, but the reviewer, a lady of some insight, had written the young poetess a long and encouraging letter. Miss Gordon must read and study nature, she advised, and she would do something some day. So Elizabeth tried to obey. Studying nature was like breathing and came very easily, and reading was always a joy; but she grew restless in spite of it all, not knowing what was the matter with her.

"I wish I could go away and do something, John Coulson," she said to her brother-in-law on an afternoon which he and Annie and the baby were spending at The Dale. "I'm no use here. I have horrible suspicions that I'm a cumberer of the ground."

"You're surely not going to develop into a new woman, Betsey," said John Coulson with alarm. "One never knows which way the wild streak is going to shoot off next."

Elizabeth was kneeling by the old dining-room sofa, upon which the Vision rolled from side to side, waving his bare pink toes in the air. She had just been busy saying over for the fifth time, "Dis 'itty pig went to market," and had evoked such gurgles and coos and giggles from the owner of the "'itty pigs," that it was hard to give her attention elsewhere.

"Maybe I am," she said at last, looking up at him with serious gray eyes. "I don't know. But I do know I don't want to sit on a cushion and sew a fine seam forever and ever like the lady in Baby's book. The rest are working hard. I wonder if I couldn't earn my living somehow."

John Coulson looked at her gravely. He generally treated his young sister-in-law as a joke, but evidently she wanted to be taken seriously.

"What do you think you would like to be?" he asked gently.

Elizabeth chucked the Vision under the chin, rolled him from side to side, and kissed each separate dimple in his plump hand before answering.

"Oh, I don't care. I'd just as soon be one thing as another."

"Well, well," John Coulson's eyes twinkled again. "Have you no ambition at all, Betsey Bobbett?"

Elizabeth looked across at him, her eyes half-veiled by her long lashes, in that way she had when she wished to hide her thoughts. The forced reticence of her childhood had grown to be a fixed habit, and for all her love for her brother-in-law, which had grown steadily with the years, she could not confide in him. For Elizabeth had ambitions, though her aunt would have found it hard to believe in them. They were quite as radiant as her old dreams of Joan of Arc, though different. They were such conflicting aspirations, too, that she was puzzled by them herself. She was filled with vague golden dreams of one day overturning the world and righting all wrongs, and making all Eppies rich and Susies happy, and giving all Mother MacAllisters their rewards. And side by side with these glorious visions lived the desire, very real and very deep, to be like Estella Raymond and have a half-dozen boys expiring for love of her. Elizabeth would have died rather than confess this wish–even to herself. Nevertheless, it was there, and back of it lay another, still hazy, but also very real, the ambition to be an Annie and have a John Coulson and a brick house with white pillars and a Vision lying on a sofa waving ten pink rosebud toes in one's face. But these were things one would not breathe, so Elizabeth answered lightly.

"I guess I haven't–much. I think I'd like to teach school–maybe. At least I'd like it just as well as anything else, but you see I can't, now."

"My, but you're enthusiastic. But isn't there something you'd like better than anything else?"

Elizabeth's long lashes drooped again. That was forbidden ground. She shook her head, and poked the Vision's ribs until he screamed with laughter.

"Some of the girls in your class have gone to Toronto to learn nursing. Would you care about that?"

"I suppose that would do to earn my own living; only John makes me sick when he talks about operations. Look, Sweetie; pat-a-cake, pat-a-cake, baker's man."

"I suppose you wouldn't like to hammer a typewriter in my office? I need a girl, but perhaps Aunt Margaret wouldn't think it was genteel."

"That would do, if I wouldn't bother you too much; and I'd just love to be with you, John Coulson, only–oh, oh, look at the darling pet swallowin' him's own pinky toes. Oh, John Coulson, just look!"

John Coulson laughed indulgently.

"Oh, Betsey!" he said in despair, while his eyes were very kind, "you're no use in the world. We'll just have to get you married."

Nevertheless, he thought much about the girl after his return home and talked over her case with his wife. "Send her a note and tell her to come here for a week," was his final decision. "We must do something for the poor kid."

So Annie very willingly wrote her sister, and on the day her letter arrived at The Dale Elizabeth received another. This one was from Estella. It was an ecstatic letter, as everything emanating from Estella generally was. It chronicled page after page of her trials with her beaux. An embarrassment of riches was what troubled Estella. She did wish Beth would come to Cheemaun and take some of them off her hands. But of course Beth didn't care about boys, she had forgotten. Madeline Oliver was just as bad, boys never looked near her. And speaking of Madeline, what did Beth think? Since they'd left school she had been putting on frightful airs, and was just perfectly, dreadfully horrid to all the girls except the Annsleys and the Delafields and a few others of those nobs on Sunset Hill. Madeline seemed to forget she'd ever known half her old chums. And Mrs. Oliver gave Bridge parties in the afternoon now, and didn't ask half the people she used to ask. And it was all on account of Mrs. Jarvis. She had just come back from the Old Country, and the Olivers were making a terrible fuss about her. They said she intended to spend the winter in California, and Madeline was working to get taken with her. And the Olivers had given a great big reception last week for Madeline's coming out, and such airs Beth never saw, and Mrs. Jarvis was there dressed like a queen. And she, Estella, had asked Madeline if she wasn't going to ask Beth Gordon to her party, seeing she'd been called for Mrs. Jarvis, and Madeline just tossed her head and said, "Oh, Aunt Jarvis never thinks about her now." And Horace was there; it was down in the ice-cream parlor where Frank Harper had taken her–really, he was getting perfectly awful he called so often–and Horace spoke up and said he bet his Aunt Jarvis would just like jolly well to see Beth, and he'd a good mind to drive out and fetch her in; and Madeline looked crosser than ever. And so now, here was Estella's plan. She was just going to show Madeline Oliver, see if she wasn't! She was going to "come out," and mamma was going to give a reception–one far bigger and grander than the Olivers' had been, too. And they were going to ask Mrs. Jarvis, of course, and Mrs. Oliver daren't refuse because papa had a hold on Mr. O. in business, and the whole family would just have to come. And darling Beth was to come, too–with Mrs. Coulson, and wear her white dress and the blue bows in her hair, and Mrs. Jarvis would see her, and be certain sure to love her. She couldn't help it. And between them they'd spite that nasty Madeline, see if they wouldn't. Horace himself had said he knew his aunt would like to see Beth. He told her that, going home one evening from choir practice. Horace had done that twice, and Frank Harper and Will Drummond were both just wild about it. But of course there was nothing at all between her and Horace, and if Beth minded the tiniest bit she'd never speak to him again as long as she lived, etc., etc.

The letter went on in this strain for many more pages. Elizabeth laughed and handed it to her aunt, anticipating some fun when Miss Gordon gave her opinion of it. But to Elizabeth's intense surprise the lady made no comment upon the writer's manners and heartily approved of her niece accepting the invitation. Elizabeth had fully expected Estella to be pronounced entirely ungenteel, and no sort of person to associate with a Gordon. But Elizabeth did not yet understand her aunt, any more than her aunt understood her.

So very joyfully an acceptance of both invitations was written, and Miss Gordon helped Elizabeth prepare for her visit to Annie's with hope once more rising in her heart. Surely, surely, upon this occasion, this one unsuccessful member of her family would grasp opportunity before he passed her for the last time.

They were debating as to how Elizabeth was to reach town, for both the gray horse and the old phaeton were now tottering on the verge of dissolution, when Auntie Jinit McKerracher came across the brown shaven fields, to make a call and an offer. Auntie Jinit had heard of Elizabeth's proposed visit to Cheemaun, for the lady knew minutely the downsitting and the uprising of everyone in the valley. She, too, was bent on a journey thither, on the morrow,–on important business, she said mysteriously,–and she invited Elizabeth to accompany her.

The offer was gladly accepted, though Miss Gordon would have preferred that her niece make a more dignified entry into the town than could be accomplished in Wully Johnstone's old buck-board with the bunch of hay sticking out behind, and Auntie Jinit leaning far forward slapping the old gray mare with the lines. But little cared Elizabeth. She was going on a tour into the unknown–she was to enter Cheemaun society, and it mattered little to her how she got there, she was sure to have a good time.

The day they set out was a glorious October morning, warm and bright, with a hint of that soft blue-gray mist on the horizon which in the afternoon would clothe the landscape in an amethyst haze. Auntie Jinit's old gray horse ambled along easily, and Elizabeth gave herself up to hilarity. To go abroad with Mrs. McKerracher was to have one's entertainment insured. She was a highly diverting lady, with a youthful twinkle in her eye contradicting the shining gray hair that, parted demurely in the middle, waved down over her ears. There was youth, too, in her round plump face and the soft flush of her cheeks. Plainly Auntie Jinit had been a pretty girl once and had not yet outlived the memories of that potent fact.

As the white road dipped into the first hollow, where the crimson leaves of the maples and the gold of the elms softly floated down from the blue above, there arose from a barnyard on their right the sound of loud, uproarious singing.

"Oh, and it's whippity whoppity too,
And how I'd love to sing to you!
I'd laugh and sing,
With joy and glee,
If Mrs.–ti-dee-dilly-dee-dilly-dee!"

The singer had fortunately caught sight of the familiar gray horse, with the accustomed bunch of hay sticking out behind, and had saved his life by an adroit improvisation. For Tom had been in the habit of substituting another name for "Mrs. McQuarry," and though he might take liberties with his neighbor across the way, well he knew the dire consequences of taking Auntie Jinit's name in vain.

Elizabeth crumpled up with silent laughter; but either Mrs. McKerracher did not notice, or designedly ignored the singer. She was looking in the opposite direction, examining with a critical eye the trim fields of Jake Martin's prosperous-looking farm.

"Yon's no a place to be sneezed at, Lizzie," she remarked tentatively.

"The place is lovely, Auntie Jinit," Elizabeth returned, with marked emphasis. "Only–only——"

Auntie Jinit gave a little giggle. There was a queer mixture of girlish coquetry and masculine strength about her that was disconcerting. Elizabeth paused, afraid to go on.

Auntie Jinit gave her trim bonnet-strings a jerk, flapped the old gray mare with the lines and began her confidences in a business-like manner.

"Ye're a wise lassock, Lizzie," she said, by way of introduction, "an' ah'm gaun to hae a bit private crack wi' ye. Ye're aunt's brocht ye up weel, an' ah ken ah'm takin' nae risk in confidin' in ye. Some o' the neeighbors 'll be sayin' ye're a' that prood, but ah've always stood up for the Gordons, an' said ye were nae mair prood than ye ocht to be. Noo, aboot this business. Ah wanted tae get yer help." The girlish manner had returned, she hesitated and gave Elizabeth a half-shy, half-sly glance over her shoulder. "It's aboot him–yonder, ye ken." She jerked her thumb over her shoulder towards the receding farm-house. "There's a pint o'-o' beesiness ah'd like ye tae see Maister Coulson aboot, Lizzie–if ye would'na mind obleegin' an' auld neeighbor buddy."

Elizabeth's risibilities were nearly upsetting her composure.

"Yes," she faltered, "I–I'll do anything I can for you, and I'm sure John Coulson will, too, in your–business."

"It's no jist what a buddy might ca' beesiness, exactly." There was another coquettish glance and a toss of the pink roses in Auntie Jinit's bonnet. "But it's a thing a lawyer buddy would ken a' aboot. An' ye ken, lassie, a modest buddy like me disna like to talk aboot sich like things to a–a man, hersel'." She gave another glance, quite shy this time. Her companion was silent, afraid to speak lest her laughter break forth. The contrast between Auntie Jinit's staid, middle-aged appearance, and the gay, naughty glance of her eye was almost too much for a frivolous person like Elizabeth.

"Ah want his advice, ye ken, because ah dinna ken jist whit's the best to dae. Ah ken whit ah want to dae,"–another coquettish toss of the roses,–"but ah'm no so sure jist whit's best–aboot–merryin', ye ken."

"Yes," said Elizabeth faintly.

"He's tarrible took wi' me, mind ye,"–she looked archly at her listener,–"but ah'm no sae saft as to be took wi' men, ma' lass. Ah've seen lots o' them in ma' day." She paused and smiled reminiscently as though reviewing past conquests; and, looking at her bright eyes and pink cheeks and the waves of her once abundant hair, Elizabeth could not but imagine that many hearts lay strewn along Auntie Jinit's past.

"Ye see, it's this way, lassock: Ah've jist got to mak' ma' way in the warld. Wully is a kind brither, but the hoose is too fu' already. An' the bairns are aye merryin' here an merryin' there, an' yon daft Peter 'll be bringin' yon harum-scarum girl o' yours in ane o' thae days–not but that she's a guid honest lass, but ah dinna see whit he wants wi' an Eerish thing like yon; an' the land jist owerrun wi' guid Scotch lassies that ye ken a' aboot wha their faethers an' mithers were."

"But Sarah Emily will make Peter a fine wife, Auntie Jinit," exclaimed Elizabeth loyally. "Aunt Margaret has spared no pains to make her clean and tidy and saving—-"

"Hoots havers! Ah ken yon. But there's nae cleanin' nor scrubbin' nor washin' that'll scour the Eerish oot o' a body, lass, mind ye that. But niver mind her. Ye see, when Wully an' Betsey gets auld ah'll be left on their hands. Aye, an' ah'll be auld masel then, and, it's high time ah wes pittin' ma best fit foremost an' settlin' masel." She paused, and the shrewd, business-like air fell from her. Her eyes grew somber, she looked far away down the crimson and golden vista of Champlain's Road.

"Ah'd no be left this way, lassie, gin ma' lad, Tam, had been spared me. He wes oor only bairn, an' ah sometimes think the Lord surely micht a' left me him. But He kens best," she sighed brokenly, "aye, aye, He kens best. But it wes a hard day for me the last time they brocht ma Tam to me. He'd jist gaed awa wi' the lads aefter his supper, an' it wes no an oor, till they brocht ma bairnie hame drooned. An' ah couldna even see his bonny face. He'd fallen aff a bridge, an' bruised it that bad. Aye, aye,"–a big sigh came again convulsively,–"an' his faether not deid a month. Ma Tam wes sax feet in his socks–a bonny lad, an' eh, eh, sik a guid laddie to his mither."

Elizabeth felt a lump rising in her throat. She stroked the black alpaca arm next her in silent sympathy. Auntie Jinit fumbled in her black leather bag, and brought out a neatly folded handkerchief with which she wiped away the tear that had slipped down her cheek. There was a long silence.

"So ye see, Lizzie, lass," she said at length, her voice still thrilled with the sorrow of her great motherless, "ye see, lassie, ah've naebody but Wully an' Betsey to look to. Ma Jeams left me a wee bit siller, but it's no enough gin a wes pit oot in the warld, an' if Wully slips awa' ah canna say whit'll happen–so ah must look for a hame, ye ken. An' there's this ane ah kin have." She tossed her head towards the receding farm-house. The coquettish all-sufficient air was returning.

"Oh, yes; but, Auntie Jinit," said Elizabeth very gently, "you know–he–Mr. Martin, you know, he's a little–well, the neighbors say he's rather disagreeable at home."

"Hits!" said Auntie Jinit lightly. "He couldna be ony waur than the man ah had. Ah'm no feared but ah'll manage *him*." She drew her mouth up into a firm line, and Elizabeth looked at her, forced to admiration. Certainly Mrs. McKerracher was a many-sided woman–and one perfectly capable of taking care of herself. "But ah'm wantin' ye, lassie," she lowered her voice, "jist to speak quiet like to Maister Coulson. Ah want to know jist how *he's* fixed." She pointed with her thumb towards the big, red brick house of Jake Martin. "He tells me braw tales aboot his siller, but ah'm jalousin' he's no tae be trusted. The first time he cam' sparkin', he tauld me he wes jist fufty-sax, an' then ah catchet him up aboot hoo auld he wes the time he cam' to these pairts, an' anither time ah got it oot o' him hoo lang yon wes afore the railroad wes pit in to Cheemaun, an' a rin it up in ma mind, an' ah calcalate he was saxty-siven. Noo yon's a tarrible descreepancy, ye ken, so ah says to masel, ah'll be up sides wi' ye, ma lad. Naebody's got the better o' Jinit Johnstone yet, an' naebody's gaun tae; an' ah thocht Maister Coulson could jist tell me if the lads hae ony hand on the ferm–lawyer bodies kens a' aboot thae things–an' whit a wife's portion is, gin he should slip awa. An' ax him tae, whit ma rights 'll be. Ah've got a buggie, ye ken, an' a coo o' ma ain', foreby a settin' o' Plymouths, an' ah'm to have a horse, he says, to drive to Cheemaun–ah got that oot o' him in writin' an' he didna ken whet ah wes up to. But ah'd like to ken jist hoo much ah'm to expact. Ah'm no goin' to leap an' look aefterwards."

Elizabeth listened with mixed feelings. Auntie Jinit was not so much to be pitied after all. It would seem that Nemesis was after Jake Martin all right; but suppose she caught Susie too, and the younger one still at home? What would become of Susie if her stepmother secured her "rights"?

"I–I hope," she ventured hesitatingly, "that you'll get all you want, Auntie Jinit, but poor Susie and Charlie have slaved there for years and it would be cruel to turn them out."

The woman turned and looked at Elizabeth with a flash of her brilliant eyes. "An' d'ye think ah'd do yon?" she exclaimed indignantly. "Eh, eh, lassie, it's no Jinit Johnstone wad ill use a bairn. If there's onything we kin dae in this warld we suld dae it, and there's Jake Martin's bairns need a mither if ever onybody did–aye, for they niver had ane yit, ah misdoot–jist a pair drudge that hadna the spunk to protect her ain. But ah'm no that kind. Aye, but ah'm no!"

Elizabeth, looking at her, could not doubt her–neither could she doubt that Susie and the younger Martins would fare well at Auntie Jinit's hands.

"What about church, Auntie Jinit?" she asked teasingly. "Mr. Martin won't go to Dr. Murray since Tom Teeter goes–you'll have to turn Methody!"

The lady gave her a reassuring look out of the corner of her eye. "No likely," she said, with a setting of her firm mouth. "Dinna ye fear for me. He's gaun to Maister Murray–an' no sik a late date neither." She smiled slyly and her eyes twinkled. "He ses tae me, ses he, 'Ah dinna like ye in black,' ses he, 'Ah'd like to see ye in somethin' that's mair spicy,' ses he. An' ses ah, 'Weel, if ah hed a nice braw husband to gang to the kirk wi' me foreby, it's a braw spicy goon ah'd be wearin'–an' ah'm thinkin' o' gettin' a gray poplin the day, mebby.' An' he's promised to come–gin ah merry him–but ah'm jist no sure yet."

It was impossible to describe the air of youthful coquetry and mischief mixed with hard determination and assurance of triumphant power that beamed in Auntie Jinit's eyes. The most successful society belle, accomplished in all the arts of refined flirtation, might have envied her that glance.

Elizabeth arrived at Annie's white-pillared house bursting with mirth. She described the interview to John Coulson at the mid-day meal in such a diverting manner that he roared with laughter, and declared he would undertake Auntie Jinit's cause and tie up Jake so tight financially that he would never be able to spend five cents again without permission.

Elizabeth took full possession of the Vision during her visit. It was well she was willing to accept the position of nurse, for he welcomed her with leaps and squeals of joy, and wept loudly and bitterly whenever she dared leave him. His mother was relieved greatly by her sister's help. For Mrs. John Coulson was suffering from the chronic housekeeping malady, an incompetent maid. A faithful servant of two years' standing had gone off in a temper the week before because her mistress had announced that henceforth they should have dinner at six o'clock in the evening. Everyone on Sunset Hill had evening dinners and Annie had long felt the disgrace of their mid-day meal. But social eminence, she discovered, was dearly bought, for the faithful Bella immediately departed, declaring "she'd wash pots and pans for no living woman on nights when her gentleman friends was calling." Her successor was a leisurely young lady with an elaborate dressing of hair, who could not have got dinner a minute earlier than six o'clock in the afternoon in any case, and the Coulsons were now fashionable and uncomfortable.

During the week preceding Estella's reception, the young lady visited Elizabeth frequently to report progress. Preparations were going forward on a grand scale, and the plan to "show the Olivers" had expanded into "showing Cheemaun" what might be done in the way of an up-to-date social function.

Others of Elizabeth's old schoolmates called, but Madeline Oliver was not one of the number. Horace, however, had not forgotten his old allegiance, and often dropped in of an evening with a box of candy to sit on the veranda with Elizabeth and tell her how badly his father was using him in still keeping him at school. When Elizabeth was perfectly honest with herself she was forced to confess that Horace bored her, and she wished he would stay away and let her play with Baby Jackie. On the other hand, it was very nice to sit on their white-pillared veranda with him and see the other girls pass. For, as Estella had pointed out, it was so poky and slow to be like Madeline Oliver and never have a boy come near you, and whatever Beth did, she warned, she was not to get like that.

"But boys don't like me," Elizabeth explained dolefully, "and Horace is awfully tiresome; now, Stella, isn't he?"

"Why, no, I think he's heaps of sport if you just know how to take him, Beth," Estella declared. "But you don't know how to treat boys. Now, when you're sitting here on the veranda in the evening, and any of the fellows pass, why don't you call to them, and ask them something, or go down to the gate and talk about the lacrosse matches or the regatta. All the boys like to talk sport. You just try it."

But Elizabeth did not follow this wise advice. It had quite the wrong effect, for when she sat alone on the steps of an evening, and some of her old boy schoolmates passed, the remembrance of Estella's admonitions made her turn her back and pretend she did not see them, or even rise and retreat indoors. But she had plenty of company, for she was very popular with her girl friends, and Horace saved her from Estella's entire disapproval.

"I was telling Aunt Jarvis you were here, Beth," he said one evening as he passed the chocolates to Mrs. Coulson. Annie looked interested. "I suppose Mrs. Jarvis would not recognize Elizabeth now," she said tentatively.

"She said she'd like to see her. Why don't you come and call on aunt, and bring her?" asked the boy.

But Mistress Annie knew better than that, and made some vague excuse. She well knew that Elizabeth would not be a welcome visitor just now at the house with the triple pillars. And so the days went by, and though the lady on whom Elizabeth's hopes were supposed to depend was only a few streets away, she did not see her, and Mrs. Coulson, remembering her aunt's admonitions, was forced to wait for the reception.

CHAPTER XIII
GETTING INTO SOCIETY AND OUT

At last the day of Estella's coming-out–the day Elizabeth was to meet her fairy godmother once more–arrived. When the Vision was finally tucked away into his crib for his afternoon nap, and the leisurely young lady warned again and again to watch him carefully, Elizabeth dressed in the required white gown with the blue ribbons, and, with Annie looking very sweet and youthful in John Coulson's favorite shade of dove-gray, set off down the shady streets towards the Raymond home.

It was a hot, still afternoon, one of those days that seem left over from August which so often descend upon the coolness of October. The long rows of maples that bordered the street hung their scarlet banners motionless in the sultry air. The sky, a hazy warm blue, seemed much nearer the earth than usual. Away down at the end of each leafy avenue Lake Cheemaun lay like a silver mirror. As they crossed a dusty street on the hilltop, Elizabeth could see a little crimson and golden island reflected perfectly in the glassy depths. Another street gave a picture of a yellow elm, with an oriole's empty nest depending from a drooping branch. It hung over the roadway, making a golden curtain through which gleamed the blue and silver.

Elizabeth sighed happily, and, as was her habit, fell into the mood of the day, listless, languorous. She strolled along, all unmindful of the dust on her new slippers, and of Estella's reception, until her sister recalled her to the business of the afternoon by declaring that they must hurry, for they were already late.

"It's fortunate I wasn't asked to play cards, or we'd have to be there sharp at four."

"I suppose Stella 'll turn it into a garden-party, won't she?" murmured Elizabeth, gazing far down the street at a motionless sail on the silver mirror–standing like a painted ship on a painted lake. "It's so lovely out of doors."

"A garden-party, oh, no! That's dreadfully old-fashioned," said Annie solemnly. "No one in Cheemaun would dare to give one now. This is to be a Bridge–partially, but Mrs. Raymond is asking a great many other people who are old-fashioned like me, and won't play, so they are to come late and remain in the drawing-room while the players sit in the library."

"It's like dividing the sheep from the goats," said Elizabeth frivolously. "Aren't you sorry just to be a sheep, Ann? It's so old-fashioned." Annie laughed uncertainly. She never quite understood Elizabeth, and felt she ought to rebuke her frivolity. "No, I'm not. What would become of Baby if his mother——"

"Turned goat? But say, I'd love to learn just to see what it was like to go out every day and be a–what is it?–a social success. I believe that is what Aunt Margaret would like."

Annie rebuked her gently. She was always just a little afraid of Lizzie. The wild streak seemed to be in abeyance lately, but it might break out in a new form any day.

Their arrival at the Raymond home forbade her admonishing her at any length. It was a beautiful house–a fine red brick with white porch pillars, of course, and surrounded by a spacious lawn dotted with shrubbery and flower-beds. Its only drawback was its position, it being placed on the wrong side of Elm Crescent, the street bordering Sunset Hill. In consequence the Raymonds had suffered somewhat from social obscurity, and this At Home was partially to serve the purpose of raising them nearer the level of the proud homes on the hilltop.

Elizabeth became suddenly shy and nervous as she followed her sister up the broad steps and saw the rooms crowded with fashionably dressed people. She was not generally conscious of her clothes, but she could not help feeling, as she glanced over the sea of bonnets and hats and white kid gloves, that her muslin dress and blue ribbons must look very shabby indeed. And somehow Annie had become transformed. Upon starting out she had appeared to be the very pattern of fashionable elegance. Now she looked like a demure little gray nun. Elizabeth felt that neither of them was likely to make any impression upon Mrs. Jarvis, and began to hope devoutly that she would not meet the lady.

There seemed little fear of it. The rooms were crowded and stifling hot. The Raymond house had plenty of doors and windows, but good form in Cheemaun society demanded that all light and air be excluded from a fashionable function. So the blinds were drawn close, and Estella and her mother stood broiling beneath the gas-lamps, for though the former was half-suffocated with the heat, she would have entirely suffocated with mortification had she received her guests in the vulgar light of day.

By the time Elizabeth and her sister arrived, the sheep had been thoroughly divided from the goats. From the drawing-room on the left side of the spacious hall a babel and scream of voices mingled with the noisy notes of a piano poured forth, but in the library on the right there was a deathly silence, except for the click, click of the cards on the polished tables.

The guests were met at the door by an exceedingly haughty young woman with a discontented face beneath a huge pompadour of hair. "Will you come upstairs and lay off your wraps?" she demanded frigidly.

"Why, Katie!" cried Elizabeth, recognizing her old schoolmate, even in her unaccustomed garb of a black silk gown and white cap, "I'm so glad to see you."

But Miss Price was not going to forgive Lizzie Gordon for being a guest at a house where she was a servant. Had their positions been reversed Katie would have been quite as haughty and forbidding as she was now. "How d'ye-do," she said, with an air her young mistress, now setting her foot upon the social ladder, might well have envied. "You're to go upstairs," she commanded further.

"But we haven't anything to take off," protested Mrs. John Coulson, nervously, afraid she was omitting some requisite part of the ceremony. "We'd better not if Mrs. Raymond doesn't mind."

The young woman relaxed none of her haughtiness. "She said to take everybody up," she remarked disdainfully.

They were interrupted by a very large Hat coming violently out of the library door.

"Goodness, it's not her!" gasped the occupant of the hat, a tiny woman with a brisk, sharp manner. She turned to the room again. "No luck! It's Mrs. Coulson." She spoke as if Mrs. Coulson had made a mistake in coming. "You didn't see that Mrs. Oliver on your way down, did you?" she demanded of the unwelcome one.

No, they had not seen her. Mrs. Coulson answered apologetically, and the big Hat flounced back into the library and sat down heavily in its chair. The Hat was bitterly disappointed, and no wonder. She had come to the Function sure of the prize, being one of Cheemaun star players, but had met with a succession of incompetent partners. At present Mrs. Oliver, a fine old Bridge warrior, should have been sitting opposite her, but Mrs. Oliver was late, which was criminal, and the Hat's partner was a nervous young matron who had left two sick babies and her wits at home. Consequently the aspirant for the prize had lost game after game and was now losing her temper. One of her opponents, a frivolous lady whose score-card was decorated with green stars, giggled and whispered to the hapless partner not to mind, the Hat was only an old crank anyway; old maids always got like that. She would have continued in the same strain but for a look of deep rebuke from her own partner. The partner was a stately, middle-aged lady, a president of the Cheemaun Whist Club, and a second Sarah Battle. She had suffered much from the silly inattention of the winner of the green stars, she frowned majestically, not because she objected to the young woman's condemnation of the Hat, but because she considered it much worse form to talk during a game of cards than during prayers in church.

Again deep silence fell, and they all went furiously to work once more in the breathless heat.

Elizabeth was very much interested, but Mrs. John Coulson drew her away towards the palm and fern-embowered door of the drawing-room. She was somewhat disappointed at the news of Mrs. Oliver's non-appearance, for that meant that neither was Mrs. Jarvis present. The fates did seem to be against Lizzie certainly.

They were once more delayed. A couple of ladies who had just entered were about to make their way to the drawing-room door, but had been encountered by Miss Price, and a rather heated argument was in progress. The ladies belonged to the old school, and were not acquainted with the intricacies of a fashionable function. The foremost was a fine, stately matron who had been Sarah Raymond's stanch friend ever since the days when they had run barefoot to school together. And while under her sensible black Sabbath bonnet there still remained much warm affection and sympathy with all Sarah's doings, at the same time there was developing not a little impatience with what she termed Sarah's norms. She had just caught sight of the card-players in the library, too, and was righteously indignant that she, an elder's wife, should have been bidden to such a questionable affair. So she had not much patience left to waste on Miss Price when that haughty young lady insisted upon her going upstairs. "We've nothing to take off, young woman," she declared at last; "can't you see that? Do you want us to undress and go to bed?" And with that she brushed Katie aside and proceeded on her way. A dapper little man in a dress-suit, the only man anywhere in sight, popped out from behind a great palm and demanded, "Name, please, madam?" Elizabeth regarded him with awe. He represented the zenith point of Estella's ambition. They always had such a functionary at swell receptions in the city, she had explained to Elizabeth, a man who announced the names of the guests to the hostess. No one had ever had anything so magnificent in Cheemaun. Of course he had to come up from Toronto to do the catering anyway, because Madeline had had him at her reception, and Estella was going to go just a little farther, and didn't Beth think it was a perfectly splendid idea–so grand and stylish?

Beth supposed it was. But of what use would he be. "I thought a man like that was to tell the hostess the names because she wouldn't know them," she had ventured very practically. "But you know every cat and dog in Cheemaun, Stella."

Stella was disgusted with Beth's obtuseness. "Style was the thing after all," she explained. "People who gave social functions never bothered about whether things were any use or not. That wasn't the point at all."

Elizabeth had not attempted further to see the point, as the Vision had claimed her attention, and she now looked at the young man with some pride. Evidently Estella was doing things up magnificently. But the ladies whom he addressed were differently impressed. Mrs. Colin McTavish's patience was exhausted. The idea of anyone in Sarah Raymond's house asking her her name! She looked down at the dapper little man with disdain. He was a forward young piece, she decided, some uppish bit thing that was dangling after Stella, most likely. "Young man," she said severely, "where's your manners? Can ye no wait to be introduced to a body?"

The young man looked alarmed. He glanced appealingly at Mrs. John Coulson, and Annie, with her more perfect knowledge of Estella's ways, whispered tactfully:

"He wants to call out your names, Mrs. McTavish; he's doing it for everybody."

Mrs. McTavish stared. "And what for would he be shouting out my name?" she demanded. "If Sarah Raymond doesn't know my name by this time she never will. Come away, Margit," she added to her companion, and the two passed in unheralded.

"Mrs. Coulson! Miss Gordon!" piped the little man, and Elizabeth found herself shaking hands with Mrs. Raymond and Estella. Or was it Estella?

The young debutante, in a heavy elaborate satin gown, stood with a fixed and anguished smile upon her face, squeezing the fingers of each guest in a highly elevated position, and saying in a tone and accent entirely unlike her old girlish hoydenish manner:

"How do you do, Mrs. McTavish, it was so good of you to come. How do you do, Mrs. Cameron, it was so good of you to come. How do you do, Mrs. Coulson, etc., etc."

A wild desire for laughter with which Elizabeth was struggling was quenched by a feeling of pity. She wondered how many hundred times poor Estella had said those words during that long hot afternoon, and wondered how long she herself could stand there in that awful heat and repeat them in that parrot-fashion, ere the wild streak would assert itself and send her flying out of doors. Estella was made of wonderful stuff, she reflected, admiringly. Mrs. Raymond had succumbed long ago and stood drooping and perspiring, scarcely able to speak, and quite unable to smile.

Elizabeth felt queer and strange when Estella shook her two fingers just as she shook everyone else's and with the same smile made the same remark to her. She tried to say something to bring back her old schoolmate, but Estella turned to the next person and she found herself shoved on. And shoved on she was from that time forth, conscious only of heat and noise and fag and a desire to get away.

She found herself at last, after having been shoved into the dining-room for ice-cream, and shoved out again, packed into a corner behind Annie. The latter had been pinioned by a fat lady who, for the last quarter of an hour, had been shouting above the din a minutely detailed account of a surgical operation through which she had lately come, omitting not one jot of her sufferings. Elizabeth felt faint. The rich sweetmeats of the tea-table, the heat, the noise, and the lady's harrowing tale, were rendering her almost ill. She looked about her desperately. Just behind her was a French window. It was open, but the heavy lace-bordered blind was drawn down to within a couple of feet from the floor. All unmindful of the conventionalities, Elizabeth stooped and peeped out. The breath of fresh air revived her. The sight of the garden, and beyond, the free stretch of the out-door world went to her head like wine. She jumped up, her eyes sparkling with a sudden glorious thought. One more glance around the buzzing hot sea of flowery hats and white gloves made the thought a resolution.

"Ann!" she whispered recklessly, "I'm going to jump through this window and run away! I am so!"

"Lizzie!" gasped Mrs. Coulson in dismay. The fat lady was still under the surgeon's knife and talked on undisturbed. Annie's heart sank. One glance at the gleam in Elizabeth's eyes showed her the wild streak was uppermost. "What are you saying?" she faltered, but before she could remonstrate further Elizabeth had acted. With a lightning-like motion she dropped upon her knees, and, fortunately concealed by the crowd and the heavy curtains, she darted cat-like beneath the window-blind and disappeared.

She found herself upon a secluded side of a veranda, and still on all fours; she gave a mad caper across the floor, and staggered to her feet, her hat flopping rakishly over one ear.

Then she stood, motionless with dismay. Right in front of her, half-reclining in a veranda chair, was a lady, a richly dressed lady of very sedate appearance, who was gazing with startled eyes at the tumultuous apparition.

"I–I beg your pardon," gasped Elizabeth. "But I couldn't stand it another minute."

The two looked at each other for a moment, and then the stately woman and the hoydenish girl, with one accord, burst out laughing.

Elizabeth flung herself upon a chair and rocked convulsively.

"It–it's the first time I've ever got into society," she said between gasps; "and now I've gone and got out of it again."

"And a peculiar manner of exit you chose," said the lady, wiping her eyes on a lace handkerchief. "But I must confess I ran away too."

"You?" cried Elizabeth, amazed.

"Yes. I came here with my niece, I am sure an [Transcriber's note: line missing from source book?] hours ago. She disappeared into the card-room, and I slipped out here. I didn't come in your original manner, however." She laughed again.

"I should think not," said Elizabeth, sitting up and straightening her hat. She was now quite at her ease, since the lady was proving so delightfully sympathetic. "I am afraid I'm not truly genteel, or I shouldn't have bolted at my first sight of high life."

"How will you feel when you have been to hundreds of such affairs, all exactly alike, I wonder?" asked the lady wearily.

Elizabeth shook her head. "I couldn't stand it. My aunt thinks I need the refining influence of good society, but it doesn't seem to have had that effect upon me," she added rather mournfully.

The lady laughed again. "Well, as receptions go, it seemed to me a very pretty one indeed, and Miss Raymond is a beautiful girl."

"Oh, Stella's lovely," cried Elizabeth enthusiastically, "and everything is just grand, far more splendid than anything I ever saw before. You see, I never was at anything but a High School tea or something of that sort," she added artlessly. "But the refreshments made me ill; really, I was quite sick."

The lady looked both amused and interested, and Elizabeth rattled on:

"You see, I got my ice-cream in a mould–a little chicken; what was yours?"

"A rose, I think–some sort of flower."

"Oh, that would be lovely!–to eat a rose. But mine was a chicken, and before I thought I cut his poor little pink head off with my spoon. And it reminded me of the day when we were little and my brother John made me hold our poor old red rooster while he chopped his head off with the ax, and of course it made me sick, and I just had to run away."

"You mustn't let your imagination play tricks with your digestion that way."

"It shows that the refined part of me must be just a thin veneer on the outside," said Elizabeth, her eyes twinkling. "I don't believe my insides are a bit genteel, or I'd never have thought of the rooster."

"Well, you are a treat," said the lady–"Miss–Miss–why, I don't even know your name, child."

"It's Elizabeth Gordon," said the owner of the name, adding with some dignity– "Elizabeth Jarvis Gordon."

"Elizabeth Jarvis Gordon!" repeated the lady, half-rising, an expression of pleasure illuminating her face, "Why–surely, my little namesake! Don't you remember me?"

"Oh," cried Elizabeth, overwhelmed by the memory of her indiscretions. "It isn't–is it–Mrs. Jarvis?"

"It really is!" cried the lady very cordially. She drew the girl down and kissed her. "And I'm delighted to meet you again, Elizabeth Jarvis Gordon, you're the most refreshing thing I've seen in years!"

CHAPTER XIV
WHEN LIFE WAS BEAUTY

No. 15, Seaton Crescent, Toronto, was a students' boarding-house. Mrs. Dalley, the landlady, declared every day of the university term that they were the hardest set going for a body to put up with. Nevertheless, being near the college buildings, she put up with them, both going and coming, and No. 15 was always full. A short street was Seaton Crescent proper, running between a broad park which bordered the college campus, and a big business thoroughfare. At one end street-cars whizzed up and down with clanging bells, and crowds of busy shoppers hurried to and fro; at the other end spread the green stretches of a park, and farther over stood the stately university. buildings. A street of student boarding-houses it was, and No. 15 stood midway between the clanging and the culture.

But Seaton Crescent presented much more than a double row of boarding-houses. Passing out of its narrow confines, it curved round one side of the park bordered by a grand row of elms. Here the houses were mansions, set back in fine old gardens that had smiled there many a summer before the boarding-houses were built. The last house in the row, Crescent Court, was of a newer date. It was a pretentious apartment house, set up on the corner commanding a view of the campus and the park. Just far enough removed from the boarding-house region was Crescent Court to be quite beyond the noise of the street-cars and the shoppers, and consequently its inmates felt themselves far removed from the work-a-day world.

In one of its front rooms, a little rose-shaded boudoir, luxuriously furnished, sat a lady. She had been handsome once, but her face now bore the marks of age–not the beautiful lines of years gracefully accepted, but the scars of a long battle against their advance. She wore a gay flowered dressing-gown much too youthful in style, her slippered toes were stretched out to the crackling fire, and a cup of fragrant tea was in her hand. Her cosy surroundings did not seem to contribute much to her comfort, however, for her face had a look of settled melancholy, and she glanced up frowningly at a girl standing by the window.

"I sometimes think you are growing positively frivolous, Beth," she complained. "I don't understand you, in view of the strict religious training both your aunt and I have given you. When I was your age, all church-work appealed strongly to me."

The girl looked far across the stretches of the park, now growing purple and shadowy in the autumn dusk. Her gray, star-like eyes were big and wistful. She did not see the winding walks, nor the row of russet elms with the twinkling lights beneath. She saw instead an old-fashioned kitchen with a sweet-faced woman sitting by the window, the golden glow of a winter sunset gilding her white hair. There was an open Bible on her knee, and the girl felt again the power of the words she spoke concerning the things that are eternal. She breathed a deep sigh of regret for the brightness of that day so long ago, and wondered if her companion's accusation was true.

"I didn't mean to be frivolous," she said, turning towards the lady in the chair. "I do want to be some use in the world. But all the girls who are getting up this new charitable society are–well, for instance, Miss Kendall belongs."

"And why shouldn't she? There's nothing incompatible in her being a fine bridge-player and doing church-work. You must get rid of those old-fashioned ideas. Take myself, for instance. You know I never neglect my social duties, and nothing but the severest headache ever keeps me from church."

The wistful look in the girl's eyes was being replaced by a twinkle. "But you know a Sunday headache is always prostrating," she said daringly.

The lady in the deep chair looked up with an angry flash of her dark eyes; but the girl had stepped out into the light of the fire, revealing the mischievous gleam in her dancing eyes. She knew her power; it was a look the elder woman could rarely resist. For with all their vast differences in temperament there had grown up a warm attachment between these two, since that day, now several years past, when they had run away together from an afternoon tea.

The lady's frown faded; but she spoke gravely.

"Beth, don't be so nonsensical. You know it is your duty to me–to yourself, to join the Guild. We have not established ourselves socially yet. Toronto is ruined by pandering to wealth. I've seen the day when the name of Jarvis was sufficient to open any door, but times have changed, and we must make the best of it. But you are culpably careless regarding your best interests. Now, I particularly want you to cultivate Blanche Kendall; the Kendalls are the foremost people in St. Stephen's Church, and if you join this society it will make your position assured. Only the best people are admitted. Mrs. Kendall assured me of that herself. Now, don't trifle with your chance in life."

"A chance in life? That's what I've been looking for ever since we came to Toronto," said the girl, gazing discontentedly into the fire. "But I don't think it's to be found in St. Stephen's Church. I hate being of no use in the world."

The elder woman looked amused in her turn, now that she felt she was gaining her point.

"You talk like a child. Will you never grow up, I wonder?"

"Not likely," said the girl in a lighter tone. She stepped across the room and picked up a fur-lined cloak from a chair. "My body got into long dresses too soon, my soul is still hopping about with a sun-bonnet on, and you really mustn't expect me to be proper and fashionable until I've turned ninety or so. Is there any reason why I shouldn't run over and have dinner with Jean and the boys to-night?"

"Certainly there is. Didn't I tell you Mr. Huntley is just back from the West? He's coming to dinner."

"But you won't want a frivolous person like me round. He'll want to talk business to you all evening."

"That doesn't matter. You ought to be interested in my business. Besides, he's a charming bachelor, so I want you to behave nicely."

"I couldn't think of it. I feel sure I'd make a better impression if I stayed away, anyway." She was gathering the dark folds of her cloak about her light evening dress as she spoke. "He might feel embarrassed if we met again. The last time he laid his fortune at my feet and I spurned it with scorn."

"What are you talking about, you absurd child? Did you ever meet Blake Huntley in Cheemaun?"

The girl came back to the fire, her eyes dancing. "No, it was in prehistoric times–at Forest Glen. I remember I was dressed mostly in a sunbonnet and the remains of a pinafore–and I think I was in Highland costume as to shoes and stockings. Mr. Huntley evidently felt sorry for me and offered me a silver dollar, which was too much for my Gordon pride. Even Aunt Margaret approved of my refusing it, though she felt it might have been done in a more genteel manner."

The lady in the lounging chair laughed, and her astute young companion saw her chance. "I'm going to run over and see Jean and the boys just for five minutes," she said in a wheedling tone. "I shall be back in time for dinner."

"Well, see that you are." The elder woman's voice had lost all its fretfulness. She looked quite pleased. "You must remind Blake Huntley of your former acquaintance. What was he doing at The Dale?"

"He had come to see about"–the girl hesitated–"selling old Sandy McLachlan's farm." Her big gray eyes looked steadily and solemnly into her companion's.

The lady poured herself another cup of tea. She gave an impatient shrug. The old subject of Eppie Turner's wrongs had become unbearably wearisome. "Well, don't air any more of your romantic ideas concerning her. You'll never find her anyway. And don't stay long at No. 15. You go there so often I shall soon begin to suspect you have lost your heart to that bonny Prince Charlie–he's handsome enough."

"Charles Stuart?" The girl laughed aloud at the absurdity. "The poor Pretender! Don't hint your horrible suspicions to him, please, he'd never get over it."

"I'm glad you think it ridiculous. In view of the chances you are likely to have this winter, you'd be a fool to think of him. I hope you have some ambition, Beth."

The girl had turned away again and was carefully tucking a magazine into the folds of her cloak. Her long eyelashes drooped–that old subject of her ambition was still forbidden ground.

"Yes, I have a burning ambition at this very minute to go and see Jean and John," she said lightly, and whipping her cloak about her slim figure she waved her hand in a gay farewell and danced away out of the room.

The lady by the fire sighed. "Was there ever such a monkey?" she said to herself, and then she smiled. And as the girl ran down the stairs, she also sighed and said to herself: "I wonder how much longer I can bear this life. Pshaw, what does it matter anyway?" And then she laughed.

The short autumn day had closed and lights twinkled along the street and blazed on the busy thoroughfare–violet electric stars half-hidden high in the trees and golden gas lamps nearer the earth. The glow of one shone on the girl as she mounted the steps of No. 15 with a graceful little run. It showed her tall and willowy, lit up her sweet face, and the gray, star-like eyes that looked out from beneath heavy masses of nut-brown hair, and was reflected from them with a gleam as of bronze.

She opened the door, as one familiar with the place, and hurried up the steps of the stairs.

"I'm prowling round as usual, Mrs. Dalley," she called to the landlady who was passing through the lower hall.

The woman's tired face brightened. She liked this Miss Gordon and was always glad when she dropped in to see her brother and sister. She was ever willing to listen to complaints concerning maids and medical students.

"Dear, dear, it must be nice to be you, Miss Gordon," she sighed, "nothing in the wide world to do. I've been clear distracted this afternoon with that new maid. I dismissed her at last. She would not even carry the plates to the table properly, and as for the way she washed the dishes! Really, Miss Gordon, I tried to do my duty by her. I scolded and explained till I was hoarse. But I believe the hussy was just stubborn. I felt sorry to dismiss her, as it was Mr. MacAllister who asked me to give her a trial. Don't say anything to him about it, please, Miss Gordon. I hate to tell him I had to send her away."

Miss Gordon laughed. "Has Mr. MacAllister turned into an intelligence office? Or is he squire of domestic dames?" She retreated up the stairs as she spoke. It was not safe to get caught in the full tide of Mrs. Dalley's talk, one might find a whole evening swept away by it.

"Charles Stuart is so queer," she soliloquized. "I wonder what he's up to now."

She tapped briskly upon a bedroom door at the head of the stairs, then shoved it open. A young woman with loose raiment, untidy hair, and a green shade over her eyes looked up from her studies. She raised a book and aimed it threateningly.

"Lizzie Gordon, don't dare show your idle and frivolous head in this place. Miss Mills is coming down in five minutes, and we are going to grind for an hour before tea."

"The mills of the Gordons grind at most inconvenient seasons," said the visitor giddily. She entered just as though she had been cordially invited, concealing the magazine beneath her cloak. "I'll stay until the wheels begin to rumble, anyway. Any letters from home?" She rummaged through the books and papers that littered the table, keeping her magazine carefully hidden.

"Just that note from Malc. He was home for Sunday. Jamie's started to the High School, and Archie's in John Coulson's office. Is that really another new dress, Lizzie?"

Elizabeth, absorbed in Malcolm's business flourishes, made no reply. "Mrs. Jarvis spoils you," her sister continued. "You've had your hair done at the hair-dresser's again, I do believe. Do you know that light streak in it has almost disappeared, hasn't it?"

Elizabeth folded the letter. The gray star-eyes were very tender. "I'm so glad Mary's cough is better. My hair?" She patted the heavy brown braids. "Yes, of course. That means that the wild streak is gone. I'm perfectly genteel, I assure you, Jean. I left all my improprieties scattered over the continent of Europe last summer, and have come home prepared to give up all my penoeuvres."

"I wish you wouldn't use those foolish expressions of Sarah Emily's, dear, they sound so illiterate."

Elizabeth put down the letter and gave her sister's ear a pull.

"Jean Gordon, you are becoming so horribly particular I'm scared of you. Every time I come over here I spend the day before getting out an expurgated edition of everything I intend to say, and even then I fall into rhetorical pits."

"You're hopeless," sighed Jean. "What were you at to-day, a tea?"

"Yes, some kind of pow-wow of that sort. I'm at one every day." She moved about the room straightening photographs and arranging cushions. "Do you know, Jean, I'm so tired of it all I feel like running away back home sometimes."

"Dear me, you don't know how fortunate you are. You'd soon discover, if you got home, that life at The Dale would be dreadfully monotonous."

"It couldn't be more monotonous than fashionable life. Those receptions are all so horribly alike. There is always a woman at one end of a polished table cutting striped ice-cream, and another at the other end pouring tea; with a bouquet between them. If I ever so far forget my genteel upbringing as to give a Pink Tea I'll put the bouquet at one end and make the ice-cream cutter sit in the middle of the table with her feet in the tea-pot."

"Don't be absurd. If you dislike it all so thoroughly, why do you do it?"

"Mrs. Jarvis does it, and I have to go with her. After all, that's the way I earn my living."

"That's the way I'd earn my death in a month," said her sister, looking proudly at the pile of books before her. "Are there no girls amongst those you meet who have a purpose in life?"

"None that I've discovered, except the supreme purpose of getting ahead of her dearest friend. Society is just like the old teeter we used to ride at school. When Rosie Carrick was up, I was down, and vice versa."

Jean Gordon looked at her younger sister seriously. Jean took everything in life seriously, and plainly Lizzie was determined to continue a problem in spite of her brilliant prospects. She did not understand that the girl's old desire for love and service had grown with the years, and her whole nature was yearning for some expression of it. It was this desire to get back to the old simplicity of life that drove her so often to her brother and sister in their cramped boarding-house.

"Why don't you read some improving books," said Jean primly. "I wish I had your chance. If Mrs. Jarvis had taken a fancy to me I'd be a Ph.D. some day."

Elizabeth regarded her in silent wonder. The hard life of student and teacher which Jean still pursued was telling on her. She was pale and stooped, and deep lines marked her forehead. To Elizabeth her life seemed a waste of strength. She could never get at Jean's point of view.

"And what would you do then—even if you should turn into a P.D.H., or whatever you call him?"

"Why, just go on studying, of course."

"Until you died?" whispered Elizabeth, appalled at the thought of a life-long vista of green eye-shades and Miss Millses and mathematics.

Jean opened her book. "You can't understand," she said patiently. "You haven't any ambition."

It was the old, old accusation under which Elizabeth had always lived. She thought of Annie's cosy home which three Visions now made radiant, of John Coulson's love and devotion, and her heart answered the accusation and declared it false. She wondered if other girls were as silently ambitious as she, and why this best of all ambitions must be always locked away in secret, while lesser ones might be proudly proclaimed upon the house-tops.

"Evidently I haven't," she said, pulling her cloak about her with a laugh. "I'm a butterfly. Gracious! I believe I hear the Mills rumbling. I'm going to get out of the way."

"Wait and talk to her. She'll fire you with a desire to do something. She's the brainiest woman that's ever come under his tuition, Professor Telford says."

"I haven't a doubt of it," said Elizabeth, with a look of alarm. "That's just the reason I'm scared of her. She's always in a sort of post-graduate attitude of mind when I'm round, and it makes me feel young and foolish. Good-night. I'm going up to molest the boys."

"Don't bother them long, Lizzie–there's a good girl. John needs every minute."

But Elizabeth had caught her cloak around her and was already fleeing up the second flight of stairs. She barely escaped Miss Mills, who was coming down the hall. Miss Mills did not approve of Jean Gordon's fashionable sister, and Elizabeth feared her clever, sarcastic tongue.

John and Charles Stuart shared a bedroom and sitting-room on the top flat. Elizabeth tapped on the door of the latter room, and in response to a "come in," entered. They were already at work. Her brother was doubled up over a table close to a reading-lamp; the Pretender was walking the floor notbook in hand. They were men now, these two, both in their last year at college. John Gordon had the same dark, solemn face of boyhood, lit by that sudden gleaming smile which made him so resemble his sister. Charles Stuart had changed more. He was graver and quieter, and a great man in his year at 'Varsity by reason of his prowess on the public platform. Everyone said MacAllister would be sure to go into politics, but Charles Stuart, remembering the wistful look in a beautiful pair of eyes away back in the old home valley, would never say what would be his calling.

Elizabeth burst radiantly into the room and was received with joyous acclaim. No matter how busy these two might be, there was never any doubt of her welcome here.

"Miss Gordon, I declare!" cried the Pretender, making a deep bow. He handed her a chair and John pulled her into it.

"Hello, Betsey! I say it's a great comfort and uplift to Malc and me when we toil and moil and perspire up here, to remember there's one lady in the family anyhow. It keeps up a fellow's self-respect."

"I hope you're going to be nice to me," said Elizabeth, turning to the other young man. "It's a great strain on a frivolous person like me belonging to a clever family. Jean's grinding at the Mills, and I came up here for relaxation, and now John's throwing witticisms at me."

"Jean's studying too hard," said Charles Stuart. "It is enough to drive those girls out of their minds the way they go at it."

"Well, I hope they won't go that distance. It's hard enough to have them out of temper all the time," said Elizabeth. Charles Stuart was always so staid and solemn, she took an especial pleasure in being frivolous in his presence. She knew he disapproved of her fondness for dress, so she turned to her brother.

"How do you like my new frock, Johnny?" she asked.

She slipped out of her cloak, dropping the magazine into a chair with it, and walked across the room, with an exaggerated air of haughty grandeur. The soft gray folds of the gown swept over the carpet. There was a hint of rose-color in it that caught the lamp-light. Elizabeth glanced teasingly over her shoulder at the Pretender, who turned abruptly away. He was a very poor sort of Pretender, after all, and he feared the mocking gaze of those gray eyes. They might read the secret in his own and laugh at it. He picked up the magazine she had dropped and began turning over its pages, just to show his lofty disapproval, Elizabeth felt sure.

John proceeded to make sarcastic remarks upon her appearance, while his admiring eyes belied his tongue. But Elizabeth and John had never outlived the habits of their reserved childhood, and found it necessary always to keep up a show of indifference lest they reveal the deep tenderness between them. Lizzie looked frightfully skinny in the dress, he announced, and her neck was too long by a foot. Besides, as her medical adviser, he felt it his duty to tell her that she would likely get tangled up in that long tail and break some of her bones.

"I'll bet a box of chocolates you can't tell the color of it," Elizabeth said. She was glancing nervously at Charles Stuart. He was surely near the place in the magazine. The guessing grew lively, John finally giving his verdict that the dress was "some sort of dark white," when Elizabeth saw Charles Stuart pause and read absorbedly.

"It's your turn, Stuart," she cried, to gain time. "John's color-blind."

Charles Stuart glanced up. It was no easy task this, examining Elizabeth's gown, under the fire of her eyes.

"Another new dress," he said evasively. "I suppose that woman has been taking you to another Green Tea this afternoon."

From the day Mrs. Jarvis had made Elizabeth her paid companion, Charles Stuart had taken a strong dislike to the lady, and always spoke of her as "that woman."

"A 'Green Tea,'" groaned Elizabeth. "Charles Stuart MacAllister! It sounds like something Auntie Jinit would brew at a quiltin'. It's positively shameful not to be better acquainted with the terms of polite society."

"Well, here's something I *can* appreciate," he said, still avoiding her glance and turning to the magazine again. "Listen to this. It's as pretty as the dress."

Elizabeth stiffened. It was her poem. He walked over to the lamp and read it aloud. It was that old, old one of the moonrise and sunset she had written long ago, now polished and re-dressed in better verse; a pretty little thing, full of color, bright and picturesque, nothing more. But it was Elizabeth's first success. The *Dominion* had accepted it with a flattering comment that had made her heart beat faster ever since. But the young poetess was far more anxious as to what "the boys" would think of it than the most critical editor in all broad Canada.

Charles Stuart knew how to read, and he expressed the sentiment of the pretty verses in a way that made Elizabeth look at him with her breath suspended. They sounded so much better than she had dared hope.

John looked up with shining eyes. "I've seen that very thing at home, at The Dale, in the evening." He turned sharply and looked at his sister's flushed face and downcast eyes. "Hooroo!" he shouted. "A poetess! Oh, Lizzie. This is a terrible blow!" He fell back into his chair and fanned himself.

"Do you really truly like it, John?" the author asked tremblingly.

John stretched out his hand for the magazine, and Elizabeth, watching him as he read, drew a big breath of joy. She could tell by his kindling eye that he was both proud and pleased. But, as she expected, he expressed no praise.

"There's a good deal of hot air in it, Lizzie," he remarked dryly. "And say, you and Mac must have been collaborating. He had that very same expression in his speech last night–'member, Mac, when you brought down the house that time when you flung something 'against the eternal heavens,' or some such disorderly act. Here's Lizzie up to the same business."

The young orator looked foolishly pleased, and the young poetess pulled the critic's ears. But her heart was light and joyous. John liked her poem, and that was more to her than the most flattering praise from the public. For Elizabeth was much more a woman than a poet.

"You're a barbarian, John Gordon," she cried. "He doesn't know a finely turned phrase from a dissecting-knife; does he, Stuart? But really, it sounds far better than I thought it could. You read so well."

"When did you take to rhyming, Lizzie?" asked her brother. "I really didn't know it was in you."

But Elizabeth was watching Charles Stuart anxiously. He had taken up the magazine again and was reading it absorbedly. She waited, but he said nothing. But those dark, deep eyes of his, so like his mother's, had a wistful look, a look that reminded Elizabeth of the expression in Mother MacAllister's on the occasion of her last visit home. She regarded him, rather troubled. What was the matter with her little verses? She knew Charles Stuart was much more capable of a sound judgment than John; she knew also that his kindly heart would prompt him to say something pleasant if he could.

There was an awkward silence. Happily it was broken by the sound of stumbling footsteps in the passage without. The door opened noisily and a wild-looking head, with long, tangled hair, was poked into the room. It emitted in sepulchral tones:

"I say, Gordon, will you lend me your bones?"

The wild eyes caught sight of Elizabeth, and the visitor backed out suddenly with a look of agony, crashing against the door frame as he disappeared.

"It's Bagsley!" cried John, springing up. "Hi, Bags, come back here!" He whistled as if for a dog.

"He's scared to death of girls," said Charles Stuart; "better get under the table, Lizzie."

"Hurrah, Bagsley!" cried John cordially, "you can have 'em. Here, they're under the bed!"

A tall young man, incredibly thin and disheveled-looking, sidled into the room, moving around Elizabeth in a circular course like a shying horse. He stumbled over a chair, begged its pardon, floundered into the adjoining bedroom, and dived under the bed. He reappeared with his arms full of human bones, and shot across the room, muttering something like thanks. As he fled down the dark hall, he collided with a piece of furniture, his burden fell, and with a terrific clatter rolled from the top of the stairs to the bottom. John rushed out to help gather up the fallen, and Elizabeth ran across the room and hid her face shudderingly in the folds of her cloak.

"What's the matter?" asked Charles Stuart, shaking with amusement. "If you feel ill, I'll call old Bags back, Lizzie. He's a medical–in John's year, and they all say he's going to be gold-medalist."

"U-g-h!" Elizabeth sat up and regarded the bedroom door with disgust. "Human bones under the bed! Charles Stuart MacAllister, I do think medical students are the most abominable——"

"It's a fact," he agreed cordially. "When a man borrows your bones I think the limit is reached. It's bad enough when John borrows my ties and my boots."

He was speaking absently, and Elizabeth looked at him. He was glancing down at the magazine again, which was lying open on the table. She went straight to the point. "Stuart, you don't like my little verses."

He started. "Why, I–what makes you think so? I think they are beautiful–full of light and music and"–he paused.

"You looked disappointed when you finished," she persisted.

He was silent. "What was the reason?"

"I–I was looking for something I couldn't find," he said hesitatingly.

"What?"

"Its soul."

"Its soul?–'the light that never was on land or sea.' You are too exacting. Only real poets do things like that. I'm not a genius."

"You don't need to be. But one must live a real life to write real things," he said bluntly.

"And I don't," she said half-defiantly. She looked at him wonderingly, at his broad shoulders and his grave face, feeling as though this was the first time she had seen him. He seemed suddenly to be entirely unlike the old Charles Stuart who had always been merely a sort of appendage to John–a second John in fact, only not one-half so dear. It came to her like a revelation that he was not at all the old Charles Stuart, but somebody new and strange; and he was sitting in judgment upon her useless way of living! She picked up the *Dominion* and at a glance she saw the verses as he saw them. He was right–they were shallow, pretty little things, nothing more. Her lip quivered.

"Oh, I beg your pardon, Lizzie," he was saying contritely–"that's only one opinion– and I may be wrong."

"No, you're right," said Elizabeth, "only I didn't see it before."

They were interrupted by John's return. "Jean's calling you, Lizzie. She's got a pleasant little job for you downstairs. Don't be scared. I locked Bags and the skeleton into his room. He won't catch you."

Elizabeth, glad to get away, ran out and down to the next floor. Jean was standing at her room door, the green shade still over her wrinkled brow, her collar and belt both missing. She held up a card.

"Lizzie, could you go downstairs and interview the owner of this?" she pleaded, frowningly. "It's a caller. She's been sent by some new society your fashionable friends have organized in St. Stephen's. I do wish those idle people would leave busy ones alone. I haven't time to go down, and Mills simply won't be bothered."

Elizabeth took the card. "Miss Blanche Kendall," she read. "Why, this is the very thing Mrs. Jarvis wants me to join. Of course I'll go. What excuse shall I make?"

"Anything at all. I don't care."

"Very well. I'll tell her my brother has loaned his bones and my sister her clothing, and therefore they cannot come."

Jean did not resent the hint regarding her disorderly appearance. She disappeared, slamming the door with a sigh of relief. Elizabeth went hopefully downstairs. She was on the whole rather glad of the unexpected meeting. Miss Kendall she knew to be a very fashionable young lady indeed. Hunting up lonely students hardly seemed an occupation that would appeal to her. Who knew, the girl told herself, but she had been mistaken, and these young ladies were whole-hearted and sincere in their efforts. She entered the long, dingy parlor fully prepared to learn from Miss Kendall.

The visitor, a rather handsome young woman in a smart tailored suit, was sitting on the extreme edge of an uncomfortable chair, looking bored. She showed no sign of recognition as Elizabeth advanced smilingly. The latter was not surprised. She had met Miss Kendall only once–at a card-party–and Elizabeth had learned long ago that card-parties were not functions where one went to get acquainted with people. She remembered that Miss Kendall had sat at a table near her, that she had played with a kind of absorbed fury, and had gone off radiant, bearing a huge brass tray, the winner's trophy.

"Miss Mills?" she inquired, giving two of Elizabeth's fingers a twitch.

"No, Miss Gordon," said Elizabeth. "Miss Mills asks if you will be so good as to excuse her this evening. She has an unusual amount of work." She was about to add an apology for her sister, when Miss Kendall, looking frankly relieved, broke in: "Oh, it doesn't matter. You see, I'm sent by our Young Women's Guild–of St. Stephen's, you know; they are trying to call upon all the young women in this district who are away from home and likely to be lonely, and our president gave me Seaton Crescent. It will be perfectly satisfactory if I just report on them."

She opened a little elegant leather-bound notbook and consulted it in a business-like manner. "I mustn't miss anyone; Miss Withrow, our president, is so particular. Let me see. You are Miss Gordon,"–she put a mark opposite the name,–"one call; Miss Mills–two calls. I shall leave her a card. Then there are Miss Brownlee and Miss Chester–they are out, I understand, but I shall leave cards so I can count them too. Now, do you know of any others in this house who should attend St. Stephen's?"

Elizabeth's eyes were growing bigger every moment. This was an entirely new and original manner of comforting the lonely. Evidently Miss Kendall believed in bringing all her business ability to bear on her acts of charity. "Just what I thought they'd do," she said to herself. Then her love of mischief came to her undoing. Her long lashes drooped over her eyes.

"There are my brother and his friend, Mr. MacAllister," she said with wicked intent.

"Oh, I don't want young men," said Miss Kendall all unsuspicious. "There is another society for looking after them. MacAllister"–she consulted the notbook. "I think that was the name of the person who sent in another young woman's name–Turner. Is there a Miss Turner boarding here?"

Elizabeth wondered what in the world Charles Stuart had to do with it, as she ran over the list of boarders in her mind.

"I can't remember anyone of that name," she answered.

"Oh, well, never mind. I have enough, anyway," said the visitor with a relieved sigh. She dropped the little book into her hand-bag and closed it with a snap. Then she looked about her as if trying to find something to talk about. Elizabeth sat mischievously silent and waited.

The caller seemed to get little inspiration from the furniture. "I was sent to call by our Guild, of course," she remarked again, as though she felt it necessary to account for her presence.

"How nice of them," murmured Elizabeth. "Do you do much of this sort of work, Miss Kendall?"

"No, this is my first attempt, but I think I have taken it up pretty thoroughly. It comes rather heavy on one who has so many social duties as I have, but of course one does not expect these church calls returned."

"Oh," said Elizabeth demurely, "I thought one always returned calls."

"Oh, not necessarily, I assure you," the lady remarked rather hastily.

"You see, I never received a church call before," said Elizabeth meekly.

The visitor looked at her a moment almost suspiciously, but the air of childlike innocence was disarming. There was another long silence, while Elizabeth sat with folded hands and vowed that if the church-caller didn't speak before the clock struck twelve neither would she. She was wickedly hoping she was uncomfortable.

Miss Kendall seemed to suddenly note some incongruity between Elizabeth's fashionable attire and the life of a student. She looked more like a milliner or dressmaker, she decided. "Do you study very hard?" she inquired at last.

"Rather hard," was the sly answer.

"I suppose one must."

"Yes, one must." Elizabeth had suddenly decided upon her line of action. She remembered how, whenever Noah Clegg's daughters went a-visiting about Forest Glen, they would sit for a whole long afternoon with hands primly folded, and reply to all remarks by a polite repetition of the remarker's last statement, never volunteering a word of their own. She could recall a long, hot afternoon when her aunt and Annie had essayed alternate remarks upon the weather, the crops, the garden, church, Sunday school, and the last sermon, to the verge of nervous prostration without varying their visitors' echoing responses by so much as one syllable. Elizabeth felt that Miss Kendall deserved all the discomfort she could give her. She folded her hands more primly and waited. Her victim glanced along the chromos on the wall.

"It's been very warm for November, has it not?" she said at last.

"Yes, very warm," said Elizabeth, also examining the chromos.

"I suppose you go to church regularly?"

"Yes, quite regularly."

"Dr. Harrison is such a clever speaker, isn't he?"

"Yes, very clever."

"His sermons, I think, are quite profound."

"Yes indeed, very profound."

It reminded Elizabeth of the Cantata they had sung in the joyous old days at Cheemaun High School, where the chorus answered the soloist again and again with "Yes, that's so!" She wondered how long she dared keep it up and not laugh. She began to be just a little afraid that she might give way altogether and make Miss Kendall think she was quite mad.

But apparently the church call was drawing to a close. The caller once more consulted her notbook and arose. "Four calls," she said with a satisfied air. "I wonder if I couldn't put down five. You said there wasn't a Miss Turner here?"

"No, unless she came recently. Shall I inquire?"

"Oh, no thank you, I really can't spare the time. I have several other places to visit. I think she's a domestic, Mr. MacAllister said. One has to take all sorts, you know. I can count her, anyway, and here's a card for her if you happen to find her."

Elizabeth took the little bundle. She noticed that Miss Kendall's day was not marked in the corner, but instead the inscription, "St. Stephen's Young Women's Christian Guild."

"Those are our cards," said the visitor, noticing Elizabeth's glance. "Of course everyone understands by that, that it's not a social call one is making. You see, Miss Gordon, one must keep those things separate."

"Yes, I am sure one ought to," agreed Elizabeth with deep meaning, as she bowed the church caller out. She fairly soared to the top flat, convulsed with mirth. Jean would not appreciate the church call, she would not see the funny side of it, and might even resent it. But the boys would understand.

They did not fail her, they put away their books and gave themselves over to hilarity as she described the manner in which the Young Woman's Christian Guild of St. Stephen's had set about welcoming the homeless girls of Seaton Crescent.

"How 'll you explain your Dr. Jekyll-and-Mr. Hyde existence next time you meet Miss Kendall at a Green Tea?" asked John as the supper-bell interrupted the nonsense.

Elizabeth paused as she gathered up her cloak.

"John Gordon! I never thought of that! And I had orders to cultivate her society!" For a moment she looked troubled. "May a kind fate send her a short memory," she added. "Come along, which of you isn't too hungry to see me home?"

Neither was, and they both saw her safely to the door of the Seaton Court vestibule; and as she rehearsed the church call once more by the way, she quite forgot to ask Charles Stuart how his name happened to be mixed up with it.

Her eyes were still sparkling with fun, as she ran up the stairs and swept into Mrs. Jarvis's sitting-room.

"At last!" cried that lady looking up with a pleased smile, and at the same moment a tall man arose from a seat near the fire. He was a very fine-looking gentleman, faultlessly dressed and slightly pompous in manner. A certain stoutness of figure and thinness of hair told that he had passed his youth. He had, moreover, the air of a man who has reached a high rung on the ladder of success.

Mrs. Jarvis stretched out her hand and drew Elizabeth forward, the girl could not help noticing that she seemed pleasurably excited.

"Come, Beth, here is an old acquaintance. This is Mr. Huntley, Miss Gordon."

Mr. Huntley advanced with a look of genuine pleasure on his rather round face.

"Ah," he said, with a most flattering accent. "I am charmed to be presented once more to Queen Elizabeth."

CHAPTER XV
WHAT OF THE NIGHT?

Since that day in Cheemaun when Elizabeth had met Mrs. Jarvis, and unconsciously stumbled upon what Miss Gordon deemed her fortune, the girl had enjoyed her aunt's highest approval. She had made several holiday visits to the old home, and each time Miss Gordon had noted new signs of improvement. And now that Elizabeth had further distinguished herself by writing a poem, Miss Gordon's approbation broke out in an affectionate letter, that warmed the girl's love-craving heart.

The Gay Gordons, each after his own fashion, expressed his views of this new development of the wild streak, producing all sorts of opinions from Mr. Gordon, who memorized the pretty verses and hummed them over at his work and to Jean, who, while confessing that the little rhyme had no literary value, declared herself exceedingly glad that Lizzie was about to do something.

Mrs. Jarvis was the most highly pleased, and to add further to her joy, sent a copy of the *Dominion* containing the poem to her niece in Cheemaun. The Olivers had not been on the best of terms with their aunt since Madeline had been superseded by an interloper, and Mrs. Jarvis was not above enjoying her niece's chagrin.

Elizabeth heard of the effect of the poem from Estella. She wrote a rapturous letter, two pages of which were filled with congratulations, the other ten with a description of the perfectly horrid, mean way the Olivers were acting–except Horace–and the perfectly frightful time she was having with all her clamoring suitors. Horace was not excepted this time. She ended up by declaring she almost felt like marrying Horry just to spite Madeline–who still refused to notice her socially,–only he had been Beth's beau so long, she felt it would be cruel and wicked.

Elizabeth wrote renouncing all claim upon the youth, and signing over whatever rights she may have had to Estella. She sighed a little over Madeline's case, for they had been old school-mates, and Elizabeth felt keenly her position as usurper. Nevertheless, she was happier now than she had been since she left The Dale as Mrs. Jarvis's companion. She believed that her pen had found for her a purpose in life. Under all Elizabeth's gay exterior, unquenched by the idle life of fashion, there lay a strong desire to be of use in a large, grand way–the old Joan of Arc dream. When she had first entered the new world with Mrs. Jarvis, her dream had centered about Eppie, her forlorn little school-mate. The pathos of Eppie's old-fashioned figure and pale face had never ceased to touch Elizabeth's heart.

At first her conscience, trained by Mother MacAllister, had rebelled at the thought of accepting a luxurious home from the woman who had, through callous indifference, allowed Eppie to be turned away from her poor little log-cabin home in the forest. But Elizabeth could never have explained to her aunt her reluctance to accept the brilliant prospects before her, so she had gone into the new life determined to use whatever influence she could gain with her new companion towards bringing back Eppie and her grandfather to Forest Glen. But the years had passed, and, so far, she had accomplished nothing. Old Sandy and Eppie had disappeared, and even should she find them Elizabeth had little hope of help from Mrs. Jarvis. She could be indolently and weakly generous in the face of a pressing need, presented directly to her, but her young companion had always found her callously indifferent to any tale of distress that called for an effort of any sort.

And so Elizabeth's ambition had gradually waned, until she was in danger of developing into a mere woman of fashion. But now she had found a new avenue for her activities. She would produce a great song one day, something that would make the world better and that would command Charles Stuart's approbation, no matter how unwilling he was to give it. Accordingly she made a bolder flight into the realm of poesy, and sent this second venture to the *Dominion*. To her dismay it was promptly sent back without a remark. A third and fourth effort to gain an entrance to lesser publications, ending in failure, convinced her that once more she had made a mistake. The Pretender was right, she had not the divine fire. She tried prose next, but she could not weave a story had her life depended upon it, and as for those clever articles other women wrote, she did not even understand what they were about. No, she was a failure surely, she told herself. This little song was like her acting on the school stage in the old days at home. She had promised to be a star and had suddenly set in oblivion.

She gave up literature entirely, and once more that old imperative question, of what use was she to be in the world, faced her. She might have found opportunities in plenty in St. Stephen's Church, but the only young ladies she knew in the congregation belonged to the select Guild of which Miss Kendall was a member, and since her encounter with that lady Elizabeth had wisely avoided her. Besides, she felt that John and Charles Stuart would surely disown her if she were caught connecting herself with that society.

But the opportunities for self-examination and consequent self-dissatisfaction grew fewer as the winter advanced. Luncheons, receptions, bridge tournaments, and theater parties followed each other with such bewildering swiftness that Elizabeth seldom had time for serious thought. So busy was she that often a week flew past without an opportunity even to run over to No. 15, much to the satisfaction of Mrs. Jarvis, who was often jealous of its attractions.

There was a new reason, too, for Elizabeth's many engagements, other than her popularity. Ever since the evening early in the autumn when Mr. Huntley had recognized his little Queen Elizabeth of the Forest Glen woods, he had been paying her marked attentions. He was a wealthy man now, one of the city's most prominent lawyers, a large shareholder in one of the new and most promising railroads, and–as Mrs. Jarvis joyfully pointed out to Elizabeth at every opportunity–the best match to be met in their social circle.

At first his notice had flattered Elizabeth and pleased her. It was just what she had thought she wanted. There had been very little of such pleasant experiences in her life. She had been a spectator of many pretty romances, but had always stood on the outer edge of the enchanted land, longing, yet fearing to enter. Looking back she had to confess that Horace Oliver had produced her only romance, and now Horace was gone. Some of the young men she met in the fashionable world attracted her at first, and finally bored her. Often some one of them, captivated by her star-like eyes and her vivacity, would single her out for special favors, and be met with great cordiality. Then suddenly, to Mrs. Jarvis's disgust, Elizabeth would grow weary of him and take no pains to hide her feelings. The young men soon ceased to run the risk of being so treated. "Miss Gordon was eccentric," they said, "and besides had a sharp tongue." Elizabeth noticed wistfully that all possible suitors drifted away and wondered what was the matter with her.

But Mr. Huntley promised to be entirely constant, and his intentions grew more obvious every day.

He was almost a middle-aged man now, and not likely to have passing fancies. But here as elsewhere Elizabeth found herself behaving in an unexpected fashion. She told herself that Mrs. Jarvis was right, and that if Mr. Huntley asked her to marry him she would indeed be a fortunate young woman, and yet when he came to their apartments in Crescent Court she was always seized with a wild desire to run away to Jean and the boys.

Nevertheless she reveled in the idea of being loved, and as long ago she had striven to put her pretty teacher upon a pedestal for worshipping, just because a teacher was always a glorified being, so she sought to surround Mr. Huntley's rather pompous middle-aged figure with the rose mist of her girlish dreams. For Elizabeth wanted to be loved more than anything else in the wide world.

And so the winter sped away in days crammed with pleasure-seeking, and the light of Mother MacAllister's teaching had almost faded from Elizabeth's life. But just as it had grown too dim to be seen by mortal eye, there came softly stealing into her heart the first hint of that dawn which was soon to break over her spirit and melt the gathering clouds of uselessness and selfishness. Slowly and almost imperceptibly the day was advancing, just as it had risen that summer morning so long ago when her wondering child-eyes had seen it steal over The Dale. There was no light as yet. Forms of right and wrong remained dim and not yet to be distinguished from each other; nevertheless the first note of the approaching dawn-music was soon to be sounded. It was to be a very feeble note,–the cry of a bird with a broken pinion–but it was to usher in the day of Elizabeth's new life.

Spring had begun to send forth her heralds in the form of high March winds. It was a chilly afternoon, and Mrs. Jarvis, her attempts at youthfulness all laid aside, was sitting huddled between the grate fire and the steam radiator drinking her tea.

"Beth," she called sharply, "don't forget your engagement for this afternoon."

Mrs. Jarvis's tone told Elizabeth that the usual dispute regarding her goings and comings was at hand. Generally she managed to cajole her querulous companion into permitting her her own way, but prospects did not look very bright at present. She emerged slowly from the pretty blue bedroom looking very handsome in her rich furs and a gray-blue toque that matched her eyes.

"You mean that committee of Miss Kendall's? I'm afraid if I go I'll get tangled up in that awful Guild."

Since the day she had met Miss Kendall doing charitable work in Seaton Crescent, Elizabeth had managed by much scheming to avoid that young lady. But a few days previous a little note had come from her asking Miss Gordon to come to the committee rooms at the church to help arrange some private theatricals which the Young Woman's Guild purposed giving for an Easter entertainment. The proceeds were to go to the poor, and Miss Kendall felt sure Miss Gordon would be interested; besides, she had heard Miss Gordon had especial talent for the stage. As Miss Kendall knew nothing whatever about Miss Gordon, the latter had wondered where she got her information, until Mr. Huntley had enlightened her. He had dropped in the same evening with a dozen roses, and had intimated that he had helped Miss Kendall make out her list.

Mrs. Jarvis had been overjoyed, and now the day had come and Elizabeth was in some dismay as to how she was to get out of the predicament.

"Miss Withrow, the president, sent me an invitation to come to a meeting in the church. Some missionary man is to give an address. Now, wouldn't you rather I'd go there than to those giddy theatricals? The Withrows are quite as important as the Kendalls."

"Don't be sarcastic. It's very unladylike. I'm not so anxious for you to join the Guild, but I want you to go to Blanche's meeting. Mr. Huntley was telling me those girls are getting their heads full of romantic notions about slumming and all that nonsense. I know he doesn't like that type of woman, so you are as well out of it."

Elizabeth's long lashes drooped rebelliously.

"What has he to do with my affairs?"

"Oh indeed! What has he to do with them?" Mrs. Jarvis imitated her voice and manner. "He acts just now as though he had everything to do with you." She suddenly grew serious. "Mr. Huntley is a very fastidious gentleman, Miss Elizabeth, and you'd better not let him know anything about your eccentric tricks. It might spoil your chances."

Elizabeth's face flushed. "My chances of what, for instance?" she inquired.

Mrs. Jarvis laughed good-naturedly.

"Don't be absurd. Whatever you are you're not dull. Why do you persist in ignoring what is patent to everybody? Do you mean to stand there, Elizabeth Gordon, and tell me you never imagined yourself Mrs. Huntley?"

"Oh, as to that: there's no limit to what one can imagine. I've imagined myself Joan of Arc, often—and Mrs. Horace Oliver, and Jake Martin's third—supposing he dared outlive Auntie Jinit—and a circus rider, and a pelican of the wilderness, and any other absurd thing, without seriously considering taking up any of the afore-mentioned professions."

"Oh, you absurd young hypocrite. Run away now, and don't bother me. Go right over to the church at once and help Blanche. You always seem to miss every chance for getting better acquainted with her."

Elizabeth went slowly down the stairs, telling herself whimsically that the way of the transgressor was hard. She had not gone many steps before her spirit caught the mood of the radiant March day. There had been a light fall of snow in the morning, and the streets were beautiful for the moment under their fresh covering. The keen air and the dazzling sunlight brought a glow to her checks and a light to her eyes. She could not be troubled on such a radiant day by all the Miss Kendalls in Canada.

As she crossed the park, now a sparkling fairy garden, she was suddenly made conscious that a familiar figure was hastening along a crosspath in her direction; a comfortable-looking, middle-aged figure that moved with a stately stride. For an instant Elizabeth was possessed with a perverse feeling of irritation, as though he were guilty of the restrictions laid upon her. That he was the innocent cause of some of them could not be denied, for he was a very particular gentleman as to his own and everyone else's deportment, and the sight of him always raised in her a desire to do something shocking.

He smiled with genuine pleasure as he greeted her; though his manner was formal and a trifle pompous.

"And how is Queen Elizabeth this afternoon?" he asked. "As radiant as usual, I perceive."

She returned his greeting a trifle constrainedly, gave the requested permission to accompany her, and walked demurely at his side, her eyes cast down. She was wondering mischievously what he would say if she should tell him her reasons for wishing to escape her afternoon's engagement.

Their way led for a short distance along a splendid broad avenue that, starting at the park, stretched away down into the heart of the city. Its four rows of trees, drooping under their soft mantle of snow, extended far into the dim white distance.

"Toronto is a fine city," said Mr. Huntley proudly, "and just at this point one sees its best. Here are our legislative buildings, yonder a glimpse of our University, here a hospital, there a church and—-"

"And here," said Elizabeth, unexpectedly turning a corner–"another aspect of the same city."

She had turned aside into a narrow alley, which, in but a few steps led into a scene of painful contrast to the avenue. It was the slum district–right in the center of the beautiful city–the worm at the heart of the flower. Here the streets were narrow and dirty. Noisy ragged children, Italian vendors, Jewish ragpickers, slatternly women, and drunken men brushed against them as they passed.

"You should not have come this way, Miss Gordon," said Mr. Huntley solicitously, as he guided her across the black muck of the crossing, to which the snow had already been converted. "I hope you do not come here alone."

"I was never here before," said Elizabeth. "How terrible to live in comfort with this at one's back door, as it were." She shuddered.

Mr. Huntley looked slightly disturbed. "I am glad you are not one of those sentimental young ladies of St. Stephen's, who have been seized with the romantic idea that they can overturn conditions here. These people are better left alone."

Elizabeth was silent. They had just passed a wee ragged girl, whose blue, pinched face and hungry eyes made her sick with pity. The child was calling shrilly to an equally ragged boy who had paused on the sidewalk a little ahead of them. The youngster was absorbed in tormenting a feeble old man, whose little wagon with its load of soiled clothing he had just overturned into the mud of the street. The man was making pitiful attempts to gather up his bundle, but his poor old frame, stiffened and twisted with rheumatism, refused to bend. The urchin shouted with laughter, and his victim leaned against a wall whimpering helplessly. The sight of him hurt Elizabeth even more than the little girl's hungry face. She thought of her own father, and felt a hint of the anguish it would mean if ho should one day be ill-treated. The tears came, blinding her eyes so that she stumbled along the rotten sidewalk.

A young woman suddenly appeared from the door of a hovel that stood half-way down an alley just across the way. She had a ragged shawl over her head, her thin cotton shirt flapped about her meager limbs, and her feet were incased in men's boots. She ran swiftly to the old man, routed the urchin, and with many pitying, comforting words began gathering up the contents of the wagon. Elizabeth longed to stay and help and comfort them both; she listened eagerly, after they had passed, to catch what the girl was saying. "Poor grandaddy," she heard again and again. "Poor grandaddy, I shouldn't have let ye go alone."

There was something about her that drew Elizabeth to her. She wanted to stop and thank her for the assurance that love could blossom so beautifully even in this barren spot. Her voice, too, haunted her. Where had she heard that soft Highland accent before? It seemed to bring some vague memory of childhood. She glanced up at her companion, wondering if she dared step back and speak to the pair.

But Mr. Huntley did not seem to have noticed them. He was looking across the street with an air of half-amused interest.

"I'm rather glad you brought me around this way, Miss Gordon," he said, the amusement in his face deepening. "I own some property here that I haven't seen for years." He waved his cane in the direction of the row of houses across the street. Elizabeth looked back, the old man and the girl were disappearing down the alley into one of them.

"They are a hard lot, my tenants. If some of the young ladies of St. Stephen's experienced a little of the difficulty my agent has collecting rent, or came across one fraction of the fraud and trickery these people can practice, their philanthropy would cool slightly."

Elizabeth was too much moved to speak. It hurt her so to find him unsympathetic. To her unaccustomed eyes the signs of want on all sides were unspeakably pitiful, and in the face of it his indifference was callous and cruel. She struggled to keep back the tears, tears of both sorrow and indignation.

They had emerged into the region of broad, clean streets now, and her companion, glancing down at her, saw she was disturbed. He strove to raise her spirits by cheerful talk, but Elizabeth refused to respond. She looked so depressed he suddenly thought of a little surprise he had in store for her, which would be likely to make her happy.

"By the way, what is your brother going to do when he graduates next spring?" he inquired.

"I don't know," said Elizabeth, reviving somewhat at the mention of John. This was a subject upon which the brother and sister had had much anxious discussion. It was imperative that he should earn some money immediately, to pay his college debts, for this last year was to be partially on borrowed money.

"John's just worrying about that," she added frankly. "He'd like to get some experience in a hospital, but he really ought to be earning money."

"They want a young medical this spring up on this new North American line I'm interested in. There are hundreds of men on the construction. Ask him if he'd like that. It is a good thing, lots of practice, and more pay."

Elizabeth looked up at him, her eyes aglow with gratitude. To help John was to do her the greatest favor. She had heard him again and again expressing a desire for some such appointment.

"Oh, how can I thank you?" she cried, the light returning to her face. "It would mean everything to John. You are so kind." She gave him another glance, that set his middle-aged heart beating just a trifle faster.

They had reached the steps of St. Stephen's by this time, and Elizabeth's leave-taking was warmly grateful. Yes, she would be home in the evening when he called, she promised.

As she ascended the steps of the church she was reminded by the booming of the bell in the city tower that she was half an hour early. Why not run back to No. 15 and tell John the good news? His afternoon lectures had stopped and he would probably be studying. She turned quickly and ran down the steps. As she did so she was surprised to meet several young men and women ascending them. Surely they could not all belong to Miss Kendall's dramatic troupe, she reflected, as she hurried away.

John was in his room and alone, and when he heard Elizabeth's news he caught her round the waist and danced about until Mrs. Dalley sent up by one of her maids to inquire if them young men didn't care if the plaster in the ceiling below all fell down? The dancers collapsed joyously upon the sofa, and Elizabeth, looking at John's glowing face, felt what happiness might be hers one day if she had wealth enough to help her family to their desires.

"This is the bulliest thing that ever happened," cried John boyishly. "Say, he thinks all manner of things about you, Lizzie, I can see."

Elizabeth blushed. "Nonsense. It's your profound learning and great medical skill that attracted him."

"When did he tell you?"

"Just this afternoon. I was going to the church to a committee meeting of Miss Kendall's–the church caller, John, just think, haven't I the courage of a V. C.?–and he walked there with me–and oh, John, we came through Newton Street, and it's an awful place. I never dreamed there was such poverty right near us. Isn't it wicked to eat three meals a day and be well dressed, when people are starving right at one's door?"

"I suppose some of those poor beggars do have a kind of slim diet, but it's half their own fault. Don't you go and get batty over them, now. Mac has it so bad I can't stand another."

"Stuart? What about him?"

"He's got into some kind of mission business down in that hole; but don't tell him I let it out. He's the kind that would cut his right hand off if it hinted its doings to his left hand."

"Why, what does he do there?" Elizabeth's voice had a wistful note. This was just what she should have been doing, but Charles Stuart had never appealed to her for help. He knew better, she told herself, with some bitterness.

"Oh, all sorts of stunts–boys' club and Sunday school; everything from nursing babies to hammering drunks that abuse their wives. He keeps me and old Bagsley humping, too. It's good practice, but the pay's all glory. Bags has about a dozen patients down there now."

Elizabeth was silent; that old, old feeling of despair that used to come over her when John and Charles Stuart disappeared down the lane, leaving her far behind, was stealing over her. They had gone away ahead again, and she–she was no use in the world, and so was left to drift.

"I suppose he's going to be a minister after all, then," she said at last, rising and wrapping her fur around her slim throat. "Mother MacAllister will be happy."

"I don't know if he is. He's got all muddled up in some theological tangle. Knox fellows come over here and they argue all night sometimes, and Mac doesn't seem to know where he's at in regard to the Bible." John laughed easily. "Never mind, Betsey, I'm acting physician to the new British North American Railroad, and you're a brick, so you are!"

But the light did not return to Elizabeth's face. John followed her down to the door, bidding her an affectionate and grateful farewell.

"This is better than putting up my shingle in Forest Glen and living in old Sandy's house, eh?" he asked laughingly, as they parted.

Elizabeth smiled and nodded good-by. John had always prophesied dolefully that he would set up a practice in Forest Glen with her as his housekeeper. They would live in old Sandy McLachlan's log house, for he was sure he could not afford anything better, and it would suit Lizzie's style of housekeeping.

The reference to the old place cleared some misty memory that had been struggling for recognition in Elizabeth's brain. She stopped short on the street–"Eppie!" she said, almost aloud. Could it be Eppie she had seen on Newton Street, and could that old man be her grandfather?

CHAPTER XVI
"THE MORNING COMETH"

She dismissed the notion, the next moment, as absurd; but it returned again and again, each time more persistent; slowly she once more ascended the steps of the church absorbed in the thought.

At one side of the wide vestibule, a door led into a long hall. In one of the many rooms opening from it Miss Kendall was holding her meeting. The door was heavy and swung slowly. Just before Elizabeth opened it sufficiently to gain a view of the hall, she heard her own name spoken in Miss Kendall's decisive tones.

"Pardon me, Miss Withrow, but you are mistaken. The Miss Gordon you have reference to is a student or milliner or something; we certainly haven't asked her to join us. I know because I met her over on Seaton Crescent when I was calling on those tiresome boarders. Mrs. Jarvis's Miss Gordon is quite another person, I don't know her personally, but they say Mr. Huntley is quite enamored and—-"

Elizabeth shrank back closing the door softly. Here was a predicament indeed! The approaching swish of silken skirts sounded along the hall, and she ran noiselessly up the carpeted stairway looking for some place of concealment. The door leading into the auditorium confronted her, and shaking with silent laughter she pushed it open and slipped noiselessly within. A soft hushed movement like one breathing in sleep filled the great space. She paused, startled–the church was crowded.

Away up in the dim pulpit at the other end a man was speaking. Elizabeth dropped breathlessly and embarrassed into the pew nearest the door. She had no idea what this gathering was for or who the speaker was. Mrs. Jarvis attended the regular Sunday morning services in St. Stephen's, whenever a headache did not prevent, and Elizabeth accompanied her. But beyond this the girl had not the slightest connection with any of the activities of this religious body of which she was a member. Otherwise she might have known that this was a great gathering of students, many of whom were young volunteers for the army of the King that was fighting sin far away in the stronghold of heathenism. She would have heard, too, that the man up there in the pulpit, with every eye set unwaveringly upon him, was one who had stirred the very pulses of her native land by his call to the laymen of the church to a wider vision of their duty to the world. But poor Elizabeth knew very little more about this great movement than if she had been one of the heathen in whose behalf it was being made.

And perhaps because she had been so long shut away from the great things of life, for which her heart vainly cried, her very soul went out to the words of the speaker. He was nearing the end of his address, and was making his appeal to those young people to invest their lives in this great work for God and humanity.

Looking back upon that scene afterwards, it almost seemed miraculous to Elizabeth, that the first words of his message she heard were from that prophetic poem that had always moved her to tears in her childhood days when her father read them at family worship.

"The wilderness and the solitary place shall be glad for them, the desert shall rejoice and blossom as the rose. It shall blossom abundantly and rejoice, even with joy and singing." This was the promise to those who responded to their Master's call. The wildernesses of the earth, the sad and solitary places, were to be made glad and beautiful at their coming.

And then Elizabeth grasped the purpose of the gathering. She read it as much in the sea of eager upturned faces as in the speaker's words. She knew, too, that he was not speaking to her. She had no part nor lot in this great onward march of the world. She belonged to those who were clogging the wheels of progress. A feeling of intense envy seized her, all her old yearning for love and service came over her with twofold strength, and with it the bitter remembrance that she had wasted her life in worse than idleness.

The low, deep, appealing voice went on, and she bowed her head in humiliation. But surely he was speaking to her now. "Do you want to find Jesus Christ?" he was asking. "Have you lost your hold on Him? Then go out where the drunkard and the orphan and the outcast throng in their sin and misery–you will find Him there!"

For a brief space Elizabeth heard no further word. That message was especially for her. For she had lost her hold upon Him, and with Him, she realized it for the first time, she had lost the joy and power of life. She had been very near Him many times–when her father read of His love and sacrifice, or Mother MacAllister showed her the beauty of His service. The Vision Beautiful had been hers, and she had refused to go out at the call of the hungry, and so it had not stayed.

And now a new vision–the tormenting picture of what she might have made of her life was being shown her through the magic of the speaker's words. "The King's Highway," he called his address. "And an highway shall be there, and a way, and it shall be called the way of holiness. The unclean shall not pass over it, the wayfaring men, though fools, shall not err therein." He pictured to their eager young eyes, what that Way would be for the world, when they prepared it for the coming of their King.

"Would they make this way of holiness accessible to someone?" he asked. "To those wayfaring men who were sure to err unless guided thereto."

He ended with the Prophet's words, and the choir, away up in their brightly lighted gallery arose and burst forth into the glorious words that closed the vision.

"Then shall the redeemed of the Lord come to Zion with songs and everlasting joy upon their heads. They shall receive joy and gladness, and sorrow and sighing shall flee away."

Elizabeth could bear no more. She arose, the tears blinding her, and slipped quietly out. She had seen Jean looking over the gallery railing with serious eyes, and Stuart standing by a pillar with a group of fellow-students, his face pale and tense. She dared not risk meeting them or anyone else she knew. She hurried down the stairs and out along the street struggling for her self-control. Half consciously her footsteps turned in the direction of that little street where she had seen the girl that looked like Eppie. The tumult of self-accusation within drove her to immediate action. She would go down there at once and see that girl, and help and comfort her, and perhaps–even though she had wandered so far away, she might prove the speaker's words true–she might find the Vision return. Choking back her sobs she hurried along. The memory of the sad sight, that pitiful ill-clad girl striving to comfort the still more pitiful old man driving her forward as if with a whip.

The twilight had fallen and the dingy street looked even more gloomy. She was terrified by the glimpses of rough-looking men and slatternly women, by the loud voices and the sounds of violence that issued from many of the houses. But her fear did not once make her think of turning back. Her soul now recognized the fact that there were things more to be dreaded in the life of uselessness from which she was fleeing.

She turned down the dark alley from which she had seen the girl emerge, stumbling over heaps of garbage. Even in her terror she had a faint sense of grim enjoyment at the thought of how horrified Mr. Huntley would be could he know. She almost hated him for his solicitous care of her when she compared it with his indifference to these ragged shrill-voiced women about her. She paused at length before one of the low hovels and timidly knocked. At the same moment the door suddenly opened and a young man came lounging heavily out. By the light from the doorway Elizabeth caught a glimpse of a heavy brutal face, as he slouched past her. She started back, about to run, but stopped. Just beyond him in the doorway stood the girl she sought. The pale light of a flickering gas jet above her head revealed her face. There was no mistaking her now. Elizabeth forgot her fears and went forward with a joyful little run.

"Eppie!" she cried, "oh, Eppie! Do you know me?"

The girl stood staring.

"Is it?–Is it you–Lizzie?" she whispered.

"Yes–it's Lizzie. May I come in, Eppie?"

The girl shrank back as though afraid, but there was a pleading look in her hungry eyes, a gleam of something like hope that drew Elizabeth in. She stepped down into the chilly little room. The flickering gas jet shed a pale circle of light around the wretched place. At one glance every detail of the sordid surroundings seemed to be stamped upon Elizabeth's brain; the low bed in the corner under the sloping roof, where the old man lay, covered by a ragged quilt, the rusty fireless stove, with the water falling drip, drip upon it from the melting snow on the sagging roof, the old cupboard with its cracked dishes and its smell of moldy bread. And yet she looked only at her lost school-mate, at the hungry, frightened eyes and the white thin face. She saw, too, how the girl shrank from her, fearful and yet hopeful, and a great flood of pity surged over her. She took both the thin rough hands in her delicately gloved ones and tried to smile.

"Oh, Eppie!" she cried, "where have you been this long, long time, my dear?"

The effect of her words alarmed her. Eppie clutched her hands and burst into a storm of sobs. Frightened and dismayed, and at a loss what to do, Elizabeth blindly did the very best thing. She put her arms about the shaking little figure and held it close. She drew her down to an old box that stood by the damp wall, and the two old school-mates, so widely separated by fate, clung to each other and sobbed.

"Oh, Lizzie! oh, Lizzie," the girl kept repeating her friend's name over and over. "You always promised you'd come and see me, and I thought you'd forgot me–you being such a grand lady. I thought you'd forgot me!"

"Eppie," whispered Elizabeth, "don't! oh, don't! I wanted to find you–long ago–but I didn't know where you were. Hush, dear, don't cry so, you will make yourself ill. See, you will waken your grandfather."

She stopped at this, choking back her sobs. "It's because I'm so glad you came, Lizzie, and you such a fine lady," she whispered. "I hadn't nobody left." She sat up and wiped away her tears on her ragged apron.

"I seen you at that boarding-house where Charles Stuart was," she continued, "but you looked so grand I wouldn't let on to you I was there. I thought you wouldn't want me. And I wouldn't let him tell even Jean. But the woman wouldn't keep me, I was no good, and I was ashamed to tell Charles Stuart I'd gone, he was so awful good, and so me and grandaddy moved in here and I didn't let on, and I got washing; but the lady didn't pay me, and oh, Lizzie, grandaddy's sick and I–couldn't help it."

"Couldn't help what?" asked Elizabeth, puzzled over the incoherent recital. "Tell me all about it, Eppie."

"Tell me, dear," she patted her as though she had been a hurt child.

So Eppie began at the day they came to Toronto and told their whole sad history. They lived with her father for a time. He had written them to come, for he had a little grocery store and was doing well. He had been kind and good at first, and they had been happy. But he had began to drink again–drink had always been his trouble, and at last everything had to be sold and he went away West, leaving her and her grandfather alone. Then commenced a sorrowful story–the story of incompetence struggling with greed and want. They would have starved she declared only for Charles Stuart. It was he was the good kind lad. He had met her on the street one day last autumn and for a long while he had done everything to help them. He had found a place where grandaddy could board, and got work for her again and again. But she had always failed. "I tried, Lizzie," she said, sitting before her friend with hanging head, twisting the corner of her ragged apron pitifully, "but I'd never been learned how to do things, and I guess I was awful slow. When the ladies scolded I would just be forgetting everything, and then they would send me away. And when Charles Stuart got me a place at Mrs. Dalley's and I lost it, too, I was that ashamed I couldn't tell him. So we moved down here to this house, for I'd saved a little money, and grandaddy was pleased because he said it was a home of our own again, and he didn't seem to mind the water coming in on the bed. But the rent's awful dear, and the man that owns it he said he'd send me to jail if I didn't pay him next time. I hadn't any money last time, because the lady I worked for wouldn't pay me. Oh, Lizzie, don't you think rich people ought to pay folks that work for them?"

"Who didn't pay you?" asked Elizabeth, her eyes burning.

"Miss Kendall. She's a grand lady and works in the church and Charles Stuart asked her to let me work for her. But she'd always tell me to come back some other day when I went and asked her for money, and next week they're going to turn us out. Oh, Lizzie, do you mind yon Mr. Huntley that put grandaddy and me off our farm? He owns this house and now he's putting us out again! Grandaddy says God is good and kind and that He'll never forsake us. But I don't think He cares about us, or He wouldn't let all these awful things happen to us." She had been growing more and more excited as the recital continued. Her cheeks burned and she plucked nervously at her apron. Now a desperate look came into her eyes, her voice rose shrilly and Elizabeth gazed at her in terror.

"Did you see that man that was here when you came?" Elizabeth nodded, a new terror clutching her heart. Until now she had not realized that there might be far fiercer beasts of prey than even the wolves of poverty following Eppie's footsteps. "He's a bad man, Lizzie, but he's been kind to me. He gave me money yesterday or grandaddy would a' starved. Bad people are better to you than good people. He gave me money if I'd promise to go and keep house for him. And I'm going–to-morrow–and I'll get bad too–everybody round here's bad and I don't care any more—-"

She burst into violent sobbing again, and Elizabeth could only hold her tight and say over and over in helpless woe, "Oh, Eppie, my poor Eppie." For of the two girls clinging together in the damp little hovel, perhaps the more fortunate one was experiencing a greater depth of despair. A very chaos of darkness had descended upon Elizabeth's soul. She was taking her first glimpse of that world of misery and shame into which Eppie was being so ruthlessly driven, and her whole soul recoiled. To her excited imagination the girl in her arms was the sacrifice offered for her own comfort. It seemed as though the price of the boxes of roses and candy that were lavished upon her, had been wrung from those poor helpless hands now clutching her so desperately. And Mrs. Jarvis too; Elizabeth arraigned her before the ruthless tribunal of her awakened conscience. Why had she let all this happen, when she could have prevented it with a word?

Suddenly Eppie stopped sobbing and raised her head listening. Elizabeth looked at her and followed her eyes to the bed. The old man had made a slight movement, and uttered a strange, choking cough. His granddaughter ran to him with incoherent murmurs of endearment. Elizabeth following tenderly, the girl turned down the ragged coverlid, and laid her hand on his wrinkled forehead. There was the stamp of death on his peaceful old face.

"What's the matter?" whispered Elizabeth.

Eppie turned upon her wild eyes of terror. "I don't know. There's something wrong with him. Oh, what'll I do? What'll I do?"

"I'll get a doctor," cried Elizabeth, darting towards the door. Her heavy fur stole slipped from her shoulders, but she took no notice of it. She fled out into the night and went stumbling once more over the garbage heaps of the dark alley.

Mr. MacAllister had come in late for his supper that evening, and Mrs. Dalley's latest dining-room maid had served him with an air of cold reproach that almost gave that kind-hearted young man an attack of indigestion. He hurried away from the uncomfortable atmosphere, and found that his room-mate had gone out. He did not go to his books at once, but sat in their one easy-chair, his hands deep in his pockets, staring at his boots. John always declared the Pretender drew his inspiration therefrom, for after any prolonged study of those goodly-sized appendages he always arose and accomplished something startling. This time his meditation was longer than usual; his mind was on the lecture of that afternoon. Finally he arose and drew from the table a writing-pad. He wrote a long letter, and as he sealed it his dark eyes shone. For he knew that away up in a little northern valley, a woman with a sweet wistful face, who had waited for the message that letter contained, many long anxious years, was still waiting for it, and its coming would fill her heart with joy and thankfulness.

He had just finished when he heard his chum come thundering up the stairs. He looked up with laughing expectation. He knew by the manner of John's ascent that there was something grand and glorious doing.

"What's up now? You came up that stairs like an automobilly-goat. Is the house on fire?"

John leaped across the room, threw his cap upon the floor, and had poured out his good news before he got his overcoat off.

"Isn't that the dandiest luck?" he finished up. "I've just been down at Huntley's office. He telephoned just before supper. And I'm to have all expenses paid beside, and nothing but Dagoes and Chinamen to dope." He had taken off his boots by this time and was rummaging in the bedroom for his slippers, never pausing a moment in his talk.

"Huntley's a gentleman all right, isn't he? Of course, it's all 'cause he's so sweet on Lizzie; but I'm mighty thankful his sweetness came in my direction. A chap like you, with one of the best farms in Ontario at his back, can't have any idea what it's like to go to college on wind. Say, won't it seem funny to have little Lizzie married to that chap. She wouldn't confess to-day, but I could see there was something up."

He paused at last, for it was being borne in upon his joy-blended senses that his chum, who had always heretofore rejoiced when he rejoiced, was making no response.

"It'll be good practice for my first year, don't you think?" he asked rather lamely.

"Oh, yes, I suppose so." Charles Stuart's answer was even lamer.

John emerged from his room bearing the captured slippers.

"You're not sick, are you, old man?" he asked.

"Sick? No! What makes you ask such a fool question?"

"Why, you're looking perfectly green round the gills. You're not going out, are you?"

For the Pretender had sprung up and was dragging on his boots. He was finding it impossible to pretend any longer.

John watched him anxiously, all uncomprehending.

"Better let me take your temperature, Mac. Diphtheria's fairly booming in your year. Packard has it now."

"Nonsense! I'm all right. You meds. are always on the trail of death and disease."

"I thought you said you were going to plug to-night."

Charles Stuart was savagely dragging on his overcoat. "Well, I'm not, I'm going out."

"You haven't a pain or an ache anywhere, have you?"

The patient might have answered truthfully that he was conscious only of one great ache through his whole being, but instead he answered shortly: "Pain? Your granny! No, of course not!"

The door slammed soundingly behind him, and John sat gazing at it until the house shook with another tremendous bang, this time from the street door.

"Well, I'll be——" said the young man, and then paused, feeling how utterly hopeless it was to find a word expressive of his feelings. In all the years of their life-long comradeship he had never known Charles Stuart to behave in such a manner. "He's gone batty!" he said at last to the closed door, and then slowly and meditatively he returned to his books. "He's fixing for dip. all right," he added; "I'll have Bags in to overhaul him when he comes back." Then, with the satisfaction of a medical student who has correctly diagnosed and prescribed for a case, he settled himself comfortably in the easy-chair and went to work.

Meanwhile the supposed victim of incipient diphtheria was striding down the street as though pursued by that and every other fell disease. A worse malady had seized him, and he was calling himself a fool that he had been so blind to its symptoms. Life without the sunshine of Elizabeth's presence was a problem he had never faced. That he and she belonged to each other since the beginning of time had always been his deep-rooted conviction. And now he had lost her, and had realized it for the first time on the very day when he had found the true glorious meaning of life. His senses were numbed by the irony of his fate. He was conscious only of the fact that he had received a blow, and that he must move swiftly and more swiftly. He was whirling round a corner when he heard his name called sharply. He stopped short in mingled joy and fear. Someone was crossing the street towards him with headlong speed. It was she herself!–Elizabeth–coming to him with outstretched hands. He went swiftly to meet her.

"Lizzie! What is it?" he cried, catching the hands in his.

"Oh, Charles Stuart!" she cried with a sob of relief, "come–quick! I've found Eppie!"

CHAPTER XVII
DAWN CLOUDS

"And so you see; Aunt Margaret, I could not possibly have acted otherwise. I had to leave it all."

Miss Gordon sat a trifle straighter in her stiff chair. "I fear I must confess I cannot see it as you do at all, Elizabeth. You say yourself that Mrs. Jarvis would have been willing to pay Eppie's expenses up here, or support her in the city, and why you should have made her the cause of such an eccentric act I cannot understand."

Elizabeth looked out of the window in silent misery. Before her, Tom Teeter's fields stretched away bare and brown, with patches of snow in the hollows and the fence-corners. Rain had fallen the night before, a cold March rain, freezing as it fell, and clothing every object of the landscape in an icy coat that glittered and blazed in the morning light. But the sun and the fresh wind, dancing up from the south and bringing a fragrant hint of pussy-willows from the creek banks, were causing this fairy world of glass to dissolve. Such a glorious world as it was seemed too radiant and unreal to last. There was a sound of pouring water and a rattle as of shattered glass as the airy things tumbled to pieces.

The fences along Champlain's Road and the lane were made of polished silver rails that gave back the sunbeams in blinding flashes. The roofs of the houses and barns were covered with glass, the trees were loaded with diamonds. From the east windows of the dining-room where Elizabeth sat by the fire, she could see the orchard and the out-houses. They were all transformed, the former into a fairy forest of glass, the latter into crystal palaces. Even the old pump had been changed into a column of silver.

The breeze, dancing up over The Dale, set the fairy forest of glass swaying, with a silken rustle. On every swinging branch millions of jewels flashed in the sunlight. With a soft crashing sound some tree would let fall its priceless burden in a dazzling rain of diamonds. Crash! and the silver roof of the barn slid down into the yard, collapsing in a flood of opals. The whole world seemed unreal and unstable, toppling to pieces and vanishing in the rising mist.

To Elizabeth it seemed like her new radiant world of usefulness, which she had been building on her journey from Toronto. It was falling to pieces about her ears, before the breath of her aunt's disapproval.

The glorious freshness of the breeze, the dazzling blue of the sky, and the quivering, flashing radiance of the bejeweled world set all her city-stifled nerves tingling to be up and away over the wind-swept fields and the wet lanes. But she sat in the old rocker by the dining-room fire and clasped her hands close in her efforts to keep back the tears. This homecoming had been so sadly different from all others. She had not been welcome. The Dale and every dear old familiar nook and corner of the surrounding fields had seemed to open their arms to her and Eppie when John Coulson brought them out from Cheemaun three days before. Her father had received them with unquestioning joy. Mary and the boys had been hilarious in their welcome. Her aunt alone had met her with a greeting tempered by doubts. Notwithstanding the years of worldly success to Elizabeth's credit, Miss Gordon still lived in some fear lest the wild streak reappear. She had reserved her judgment, however, until her niece should explain, and the opportunity for a quiet talk had come upon the third morning after their arrival. As soon as breakfast was over, and the early morning duties attended to, Miss Gordon took her embroidery–Mary did the darning now–to the dining-room fire and called Elizabeth to her.

The old stone house was very quiet. Sarah Emily's successor, a shy little maid from an orphan home, was moving noiselessly about the kitchen under Mary's able supervision. Jamie was far on the road to Cheemaun High School, his books slung over his back, and Mr. Gordon was shut in his study. Eppie lay upstairs in the big airy room that had once been the boys'. Even where she sat Elizabeth could catch the echo of her racking cough.

Miss Gordon seated herself comfortably before the fire, bidding Elizabeth do the same.

They had not yet had a moment to talk about the future, she said pleasantly. There had been so much to say about poor little Eppie. But they must discuss Elizabeth's own affairs now. First, how long could she remain at home? She hoped Mrs. Jarvis did not want her to return immediately?

Elizabeth felt, rather than saw, the look of sharp inquiry her aunt bent upon her. There was no hope of putting off the explanation any longer. She turned towards her with a sinking heart. It had always been impossible to explain her actions to Aunt Margaret. And now, though she was a woman, Elizabeth felt a return of her old childish dread of being misunderstood.

She began carefully–away back at the resolution her young heart had made to use her influence with Mrs. Jarvis to help Eppie. Of her higher aims and aspirations she could not speak; and because she was forced to do so, to be silent concerning her yearnings for a higher life, and the revelation that had come to her that wonderful afternoon in St. Stephen's; because of this, even to her own ears, her story did not sound convincing. Her course of conduct did not appear so inevitable as it had before she faced her aunt.

When she had bidden Mrs. Jarvis farewell, declaring she could no longer endure the life of fashion and idleness which they lived, and had buried poor old Sandy and taken Eppie and fled home with her, she had been as thoroughly convinced as Charles Stuart, her aider and abettor, that this was the only line of conduct to pursue. To Elizabeth's mind it had appeared beyond doubt that, from the day her benefactress, acting through Mr. Huntley, had allowed Eppie to be driven from her home, that those two had been directly responsible for all the girl's misery. And this one case had revealed to her the awful train of innocent victims that must surely follow in the path of selfish idleness which Mrs. Jarvis pursued, or that of money-making followed by Mr. Huntley. And Elizabeth, too, was of their world, eating of their bread, accepting all the luxury that came from this wrong-doing. This was the thought that had stung her into such headlong action. She had told Mrs. Jarvis the whole truth, offending her bitterly thereby, and had escaped without even a word of farewell to Mr. Huntley. But now, in the telling of it all, she seemed to see herself each moment growing more culpable and ridiculous in her aunt's eyes.

And when she finished her story with an appeal, she was met by that old, old sentence that had been so many times pronounced upon her:

"I cannot understand you."

Elizabeth did not quite understand herself. She knew only that an inner voice–an echo from the thrilling words spoken in the church–had commanded and she could not but obey. The King's Highway was calling for her–she was needed to make it smooth for someone's feet. That voice had promised great things, too,–that the wilderness and the solitary places should be glad because of her coming, that the rose of Sharon should blossom by her side–that, because of her, some little of the sorrow and sighing of this sad world should flee away. And now, instead, there were thorns along the pathway, and she had brought distress upon one she loved.

If she could only explain, she said to herself in despair. She looked out of the west window away down Champlain's Road with its swaying, towering hedge of bejeweled elms, to the old farm-house against the pines of Long Hill. Mother MacAllister would understand without any explanation. If she were only telling Mother MacAllister!

"It seems so unnecessary, your leaving Mrs. Jarvis," Miss Gordon continued. "Someone else could have brought Eppie. And what we are to do with her I cannot tell. You cannot but see that she is consumptive, and it would be folly for us to allow her to be in the same home with Mary. Even you must understand that Mary is in danger of that disease, Elizabeth."

The girl's face blanched. "I will take complete care of her, aunt," she said hastily. "Mary need not go near her. But both Mr. Bagsley and Mrs. Jarvis's doctor said Eppie would soon get better with fresh air and good nursing."

"One never can tell with a disease like that. And as for good nursing—I see clearly that as usual the burden must fall upon me." Miss Gordon sighed deeply and hunted in her basket for her spool. "It is quite out of the question for you to undertake nursing her. I could not allow it in any case, but it would be unfair to Mrs. Jarvis. She must expect your return any day?" She looked up inquiringly, and Elizabeth's clasped hands clenched each other again. She made a desperate attempt to be brave, and turned squarely towards her aunt. The very necessity of the case drove her to take courage.

"Aunt Margaret," she said deliberately, "you do not quite understand yet. I–I cannot–I am not going back to Mrs. Jarvis–any more."

Miss Gordon dropped the linen square she was embroidering, but recovered it instantly. Even in the shock of dismay, she was dignified and self-restrained.

"Elizabeth," she said with a dreadful calm, "what is this you are telling me?"

"I cannot go back," repeated the girl with the courage of despair. "I am sorry–oh, sorrier than I can possibly tell you, Aunt Margaret, that I have brought all this trouble upon you. But I had to leave. I explained to Mrs. Jarvis how I felt–that it seemed as if we both had profited at Eppie's expense, and that as she had allowed Eppie to be turned out of her home, I felt as if she were responsible–as well as myself. And so I came away. I couldn't live that kind of life after seeing Eppie's home–and what she was almost driven to. Oh, Aunt Margaret, can't you understand that I couldn't!"

Miss Gordon was staring at her in a way that robbed Elizabeth of her small stock of courage. "Wait," she said, raising her hand to stop the incoherent flow. "Do I understand you to say that you–you insulted Mrs. Jarvis–and left her?"

"I didn't mean to insult her," whispered Elizabeth with dry lips. "I–I felt I was as much to blame as she–and I said so."

"And Mr. Huntley? What of him?" The girl looked up suddenly, a wave of indignation lending a flash to her gray eyes.

"Aunt Margaret, he owned the house Eppie lived in!" she cried, as though it were a final condemnation.

Miss Gordon waved her aside.

"And he was ready to offer you marriage. Mrs. Jarvis told me so in her last letter. Elizabeth,–do you at all comprehend what a disastrous thing you have done?"

Elizabeth looked out of the window in dumb despair. Miss Gordon arose, and, crossing the room, closed the door leading into the hall. In all the years in which she had seen her aunt disturbed over her wrong-doing, Elizabeth had never witnessed her so near losing her self-control. The sight alarmed her.

Miss Gordon came back to her seat and threw her work aside. She faced her niece, clasping and unclasping her long slender hands, until her heavy, old-fashioned rings made deep marks in the flesh.

"Elizabeth," she said with an effort at calm, "the only possible excuse that can be made for your conduct is that you must have been out of your mind when you acted so. If you realized what you were doing, you have acted criminally. You have brought this consumptive girl here, and endangered Mary's life, just when I felt she was beginning to be strong. You have destroyed John's prospects. He cannot possibly accept this position, since you have treated Mr. Huntley in this fashion. You have utterly ruined your own chances in life. And what chances you have had! Never was a girl so fortunate as you. But you have all your life deliberately flung aside every piece of good fortune that came your way. And wait,"–as Elizabeth strove to speak–"this is not the worst. You have never known that we live here in The Dale merely by Mrs. Jarvis's favor. Your father has no deed for this property, no more than old Sandy McLachlan had for his. He might claim it by law, now,–but if Mrs. Jarvis asks us to leave, we must do so. Thank Heaven, some of the Gordons have pride! And that she will ask us now, after the outrageous manner in which you have met all her generosity, I have not the slightest doubt. We shall all be turned out of our home, and you will bring your father's gray hairs down with sorrow to the grave."

She arose and walked up and down, wringing her hands. Her extravagant words and actions were so pregnant with genuine grief and despair, that they smote Elizabeth's heart with benumbing blows. Mary, John, her aunt, and now the best beloved of all–her father! She was bringing ruin upon them all! Totally unaccustomed to deliberate thinking, she was unable to view the situation calmly, and took every accusation of her aunt's literally.

"Aunt Margaret!" she cried desperately, moved more by the sight of the stately woman's abandon than by the thought of her own shortcomings. "Oh, Aunt Margaret,–don't! It may not be so bad! And can't you see I didn't mean to do wrong? Oh, I truly didn't. You always taught us to do our duty first. We knew it was the sense of duty that kept you here when you wanted to go back to Edinburgh. And I felt it was my duty to bring Eppie and come away. Oh, if you could only have seen the place where poor old Sandy died! And Eppie need not stay here. Tom and Granny Teeter want to take her–and the Cleggs, and,–oh, if you'll only forgive me!" Elizabeth broke down completely. She had made a horrible mistake somehow–she did not understand how, any more than she had understood in her childhood how she was always bringing sorrow upon her aunt.

Miss Gordon came and stood over her. She was once more calm and self-contained. "I can never forgive you, Elizabeth," she said deliberately, "until you have become reconciled to Mrs. Jarvis. Go back to her and beg her pardon for your conduct, and then come and ask mine."

She gathered up her work, and in her stateliest manner walked from the room. Elizabeth's first impulse was to fling herself upon the sofa in a passion of despair, but the remembrance of Eppie saved her. She sat a few minutes fighting for self-control, and praying for help, the first real prayer she had uttered for years. When she was sufficiently calm she went up to the room where Eppie lay with the March sunshine streaming over her pillow. Her eyes brightened at the sight of Elizabeth, but instantly the old look of dull despair came back. "You're a little better to-day, aren't you, dear?" Elizabeth asked, striving to be cheerful. Eppie nodded. "Yes, I'm better," she said drearily.

"And it's the loveliest day, Eppie. Why, we have glass trees in the lane, and it's so sunshiny. If you'll only hurry up and get strong, you'll be in time to pick the first May flowers that grow down by the old place."

"I think I'd rather not see it, Lizzie," said the sick girl. "Grandaddy and me used to talk by the hour about comin' back to Forest Glen. And I always wanted to get back that bad it made me sick. But now I think I'd sooner not see the old place, because he can't see it too."

Elizabeth's forced calm was forsaking her. The tears welled up in her eyes.

"Ye're not well yourself to-day, Lizzie," whispered Eppie. "What's troublin'?"

"Nothing you can help, dear," said Elizabeth hastily. "See, I'm going to get you some milk and then you must sleep." She fled from the room, and down the hall towards her own little bedroom. At the head of the stairs she met Mary carrying a covered dish. Mary was not ignorant of the turn affairs had taken, and her sympathy was all for her sister, for she would have welcomed any disaster that brought Lizzie home.

"I've made Eppie a custard," she said comfortingly. "I'll give it to her and you can go to see Mother MacAllister–she'll help." There was a secret bond of sympathy between the sisters that enabled Mary to divine that whatever was the nature of Elizabeth's trouble, Mother MacAllister would prove an excellent doctor.

But Elizabeth took the bowl. "No, I must attend to Eppie myself. Aunt Margaret does not want you to be with her. Never mind me, Mary dear, I've made a big muddle of things, as usual, but it can't be helped now. I shall go and see Mother MacAllister as soon as Eppie goes to sleep."

It was afternoon before Elizabeth found an opportunity to leave. Eppie's cough was painful and persistent, and Miss Gordon kept her room prostrated with a nervous headache. But late in the day both invalids sank into slumber, and finding nothing to do, Elizabeth flung on her coat and hat and fled downstairs.

She paused for a moment at the study door as she passed. Her father was sitting at his desk, over his accounts. Elizabeth approached and gently laid her hand upon his shoulder. It was a very thin, stooped shoulder now, and the hair on his bowed head was almost white. The mental picture of him being driven from The Dale through her act rose up before his daughter, and choked her utterance. Unaccustomed to any affectionate demonstrations as the Gordon training had made her, she could not even put her arms about his neck, as she longed to do, but stood by him silent, her hand on his shoulder.

"Well, Mary, child," he said in his absent way. Then he glanced up. "Eh, eh, it's little Lizzie? Well, well! Tuts, tuts, of course you are home again." He patted the hand on his shoulder affectionately.

"Are you glad to have me home, father?" whispered the girl when she could find her voice. It was a foolish question, but she longed to hear him say she was welcome.

"Glad?" he said. "Tuts, tuts, there's been no sunshine in the house since 'Lizbeth left. Eh, eh, indeed, I think I must just be sending word to that Mrs. Jarvis that I can't spare you any longer."

Elizabeth smiled wanly. She could not trust herself to speak again. She wanted to tell him she had come home to stay, and all that her homecoming meant. But she could not bear to trouble him. She merely patted his hand and slipped away before the tears could come.

The radiant morning had been succeeded by a dull afternoon. Every opal and diamond of the opening day had vanished. Low sullen clouds drifted over the dim-colored earth, and the wind was chill and dreary. Elizabeth's mood was in perfect accord with the grayness. She was about to give herself up to melancholy when, as she plodded up the muddy lane, she was hailed cheerfully from the road. The speaker was Auntie Jinit McKerracher, as she was still called, though correctly speaking, she had been for some time past Auntie Jinit Martin. Evidently her life as mistress of the red-brick house, from which she had just come, had been a success. Auntie Jinit looked every inch a woman of prosperous independence. Though the low clouds threatened rain, she wore a very gay and expensive bonnet, adorned with many pink roses that scarcely rivaled the color of her cheeks. The dress she held up in both hands, high above her trim gaiter-tops, was of black satin, much bedecked with heavy beaded trimming. From all appearances Auntie Jinit had, to use her own phrase, been "up sides" with Jake Martin, since her second marriage.

"And is yon yersel', Lizzie lass!" she cried heartily. "An' hoo's the pair bit lamb the day?"

"Eppie? Oh, not much better, Auntie Jinit. I'm afraid sometimes poor Eppie will never be better."

A sympathetic light shone in Auntie Jinit's bright eyes, and a shrewd, knowing pair of eyes they were. Not much escaped them, and her visit to The Dale the day before, coupled with Elizabeth's disappointed appearance, told her plainly that all was not well between the girl and her aunt.

"Tuts, lass," she said, "the warm weather 'll be along foreby, an' she'll pick up. Ah'll send oor Charlie ower wi' a bit jug o' cream ivery morn, an' it'll mak the pair thing fatten up a wee."

"Thank you, Auntie Jinit," said Elizabeth, the kindness bringing the tears to her eyes. "You're so good."

Mrs. Martin glanced at her sideways again. She had seen little of Elizabeth within the last few years, but her regard for the girl had never changed. She was as proud of her as though she had been her own daughter. Her eyes rested fondly on the slim, erect figure in the long gray coat, the smart, blue-gray velvet toque that matched the deep eyes beneath, and the soft, warm coils of the girl's brown hair. Lizzie was a lady and no mistake, Mrs. Martin declared to herself, a lady from her heart out to her clothes; and if that stuck up bit buddy at The Dale, who thought herself so much above her neighbors, had been worrying the lass, she, Auntie Jinit, was going to find out about it.

"Ye'll need help in lookin' after her," she said, feeling her way, "an' Mary's no able to gie it."

"That's just the trouble," said Elizabeth, responding to the sympathy. "I wouldn't mind caring for her myself entirely, but Aunt Margaret–I mean we all feel a little afraid for Mary–she's not strong. And, to tell you the truth, Auntie Jinit," she added hesitatingly, "I don't quite know what to do with poor Eppie."

"Hoots, lassie." Auntie Jinit's voice was very sympathetic. She was beginning to understand fully. "There's mair folk than ah can name that's jist wearyin' to tak the bairn. There's Tom Teeter—-"

"But granny could never give her proper care, auntie, and it wouldn't be right to burden her."

"Weel, there's Noah Clegg, an' there's yer ain Mother MacAllister, aye, an' there's Jinit Martin, tae. We've a braw hoose ower by yonder, jist wearyin' to be filled. Ah'll tak the bit lass masel," she finished up suddenly, and closed her firm mouth with a resolute air.

Elizabeth looked at her in amazement and admiration. Jake Martin's house was the last place in Ontario she had supposed one would choose as a refuge for an orphan. Certainly Auntie Jinit had worked a revolution there.

"But there's Susie, Auntie Jinit, she's not as strong as Mary."

"Ah'll mind Susie, niver you fear, ma lass—-"

"And–Mr. Martin?" hesitatingly.

Auntie Jinit laughed a gay, self-sufficient laugh. "Ah'll mind him tae," she said firmly. "Ah've sed to Jake mony's the time–there'll be some awfu' jedgment come upon this house, Jake Martin, because ye turned a bit helpless bairn an' a decreepit auld buddy oot o' their hame. An' Jake kens ah'm richt. He's been a bit worrit aboot it, an' ah'll jist pit it till him plain that if he taks Eppie it'll jist avert the wrath o' the Almichty."

Had Elizabeth's heart been a little less heavy, she must have enjoyed immensely this slight revelation of the change in affairs at the Martin home. Auntie Jinit had indeed worked a transformation there. The house was well-furnished and comfortable. The younger children were receiving an education; Charlie, one of the older sons, had returned to help his father on the farm; Susie, under the care of the best doctors in Cheemaun, was slowly creeping back to health and strength, and Mrs. Martin herself was the finest dressed woman who drove along Champlain's Road of a Saturday with her butter and eggs.

Something like a smile gleamed in Elizabeth's eyes, as she looked at her, tripping along by the muddy roadside.

"So don't ye worry, ma lass," she said. "It's a braw fine thing ye did, bringin' the pair stray lamb back to the auld place, an' berryin' the auld man; an' it's no fit ye'll be carryin' the burden. Beside, ye'll be leavin' us a' sune, ah doot. Yon braw leddy 'll no be able to spare ye lang."

Elizabeth slowly shook her head. "I don't intend going back," she whispered.

"Not gaun back!" Auntie Jinit's very figure was a living interrogation mark. But her penetrating glance saw the misery in the girl's face, and her pity, always more active than even her curiosity, made her pause. She tactfully changed the subject. She could afford to wait; for all things that were hidden within the surroundings of Forest Glen were certain to be revealed sooner or later to Mrs. Jake Martin.

"It's a raw day," she said. "Ah didna like to venture oot, but ah thocht ah'd jist rin ower an' see pair Wully. He's no weel, an' he wearies for me whiles. Ah tauld Jake if he wesna jist himsel, ah'd bide wi him the nicht." She gave a sidelong glance as she said this, half amused, half defiant. But Elizabeth had not been home long enough to understand the full meaning of the words and look. These periodical illnesses to which "pair Wully" was so strangely subject had a peculiar significance in the Martin household. It was reported throughout the neighborhood that when Jake grew obdurate, as he sometimes dared, even yet, his wife, by some process of mental telepathy, became convinced of the notion that pair Wully would be jist wearyin' for her, he wasna' weel onyway, an' micht jist slip awa' afore she saw him; and away the devoted sister would hie, leaving the forsaken husband and his home to whatever ill-luck fate might send. As his house was faultlessly and economically run when its mistress was there, and fell into ruinous neglect in her absence, Jake generally succumbed at an early date. Wully's physical condition having a strange correspondence to Jake's mental state, they always recovered at precisely the same time, and Auntie Jinit returned triumphant. On this present occasion, the proposed papering of the Martin parlor had caused a serious indisposition in the Johnstone home, and Auntie Jinit was on her way gayly thither, prepared to nurse her brother until the paper was ready to be hung. She anticipated a struggle over Eppie, but Auntie Jinit knew her power and was ready for the fray.

She kissed Elizabeth affectionately as she left her at the MacAllister gate, bidding her be cheery, it would all end right, and tripped away down the road to her brother's home. Elizabeth found Mother MacAllister sitting in her accustomed seat by the kitchen window. She had more time to sit there now, for Wully Johnstone's only unmarried daughter had come to be the helper in the MacAllister kitchen when Sarah Emily became the wife of Peter, and declared she couldn't put up with anybody's penoeuvres when she was cooking a dinner.

Mother MacAllister's eyes rested fondly on the girl as she laid off her coat and hat. Lizzie was still to her the little daughter she had lost, and her homecomings brought her joy second only to that of her own son.

"And you'll not be looking yourself, lovey," she said tenderly when Eppie had been inquired for. "Is it a trouble I could be helping?"

Yes, it was just for help she had come, Elizabeth explained, and sitting on her old seat, the milking-stool, at Mother MacAllister's knee, she told her all, how she had left Mrs. Jarvis, and the life of fashion they had lived, because she had been given a glimpse of another life—one employed in the King's service. And she had seen also the life that the unfortunate ones of the earth led, the cruel misery they suffered, and it had all seemed to her the direct result of her own self-indulgence. She had fled from that selfish life, and now her act was likely to bring disaster upon those she loved best, and she was in doubt. Perhaps she had done wrong. Had she? And was it possible a right act could bring such dire results?

And then Mother MacAllister went, as she always did in times of perplexity, to the story of the One Who had suffered all man's infirmities and knew as no other knew how to sympathize with man's troubles. She read of how He turned away from worldly power and triumph and chose a life of poverty, and a death of shame, because He loved, and love gave all. And sitting there, listening, with swelling heart Elizabeth lived again that radiant evening when Mother MacAllister had first shown her a glimpse of what His service meant. And this was a renewed vision, a lifting of the clouds that still obscured the dawn. She went home with a feeling of exaltation in her heart. "Inasmuch as ye have done it unto the least of these, ye have done it unto Me," Mother MacAllister had said in parting. Lizzie had done right and she must leave the consequences with Him. He would see that it came out all right. As she paused to open the sodden gate leading into The Dale lane, she glanced back at the old farm-house against the dark background of pines. Above the long hill the wind had opened a long golden rent in the gray skies. Elizabeth smiled. It was a beautiful omen, and hopeful.

She soon discovered that she needed all the light that her vision of love and duty could shed upon her pathway; for the ensuing days proved dark ones. The possibilities of coming disaster hung over her head, and her aunt's attitude of aggrieved reproachfulness was torture to the girl's loving heart. To add to her suffering, Miss Gordon insisted, martyr-like, in taking charge of Eppie. Elizabeth strove to assist, but she was always doing things wrong, and her aunt sighed and declared she only added to her burdens. Offers of a home for Eppie had come from all sides, but at first Miss Gordon refused each one. For, after all, the lady of The Dale was made of fine material. Never could she be brought to turn an orphan from her door, and her stern sense of duty drove her to nurse the girl with all the care and skill she could command. But hers was a nature that, while it was capable of rising to the height of a difficult task, failed in the greater task of carrying the burden bravely.

So Tom Teeter, the Johnstones, the Cleggs, and the MacAllisters were forced to content themselves with sending gifts of cream and fresh eggs and chicken-soup and currant jelly to the poor little guest at The Dale, until her hosts were embarrassed by their riches. But Auntie Jinit's offer was not to be so put aside. For what was the use of vanquishing a husband if one could not display the evidence of one's triumph? The new gay paper on the parlor wall witnessed to brother Wully's complete recovery from rheumatism, but the crick in his back, brought on by his brother-in-law's stormy refusal to take old Sandy McLachlan's child into his home was long and persistent. It had vanished at last on a certain evening when Jake sheepishly presented himself at the Johnstone home to inquire when his truant wife was coming back. This was always the enemy's sign of capitulation. Auntie Jinit sailed home with flying colors, and the next morning presented herself at The Dale and demanded that Eppie go home with her.

Not even Miss Gordon dared deny her, and so Eppie went to her new home–one where every care a motherly heart could contrive was given her. But Elizabeth's position was no less uncomfortable after Eppie was gone. Her aunt treated her with stately politeness, her manner saying plainly that she was merely waiting for her erring niece to confess herself mistaken, and ready to make amends. But Elizabeth still clung forlornly to her resolution. She gained some comfort from seeing Eppie growing strong and rosy, and much from Mother MacAllister's counsel.

Annie and John Coulson sympathized, too, though even Annie could not quite understand.

Just one event broke the monotony of Elizabeth's days before John's homecoming. This was a visit from Estella and Horace. They drove out one sunny afternoon and remained to tea. Horace wore an apologetic air, as though he felt guilty of having jilted Elizabeth, and Estella's manner was of the same quality, with a dash of triumph. On her way upstairs to remove her wraps, Estella explained in an ecstatic whisper that they were really and truly engaged, and didn't Beth think she had the loveliest diamond ring ever? Horace was such a dear, and the only thing that marred her perfect happiness was–well, of course it was a delicate matter–but neither she nor Horry could ever be quite happy until Beth said she would forgive them.

Too amused to resent the imputation, Elizabeth granted a free and full pardon, and then the true purport of Estella's visit was revealed.

"What on earth has happened between you and Aunt Jarvis?" she asked, sitting down on the edge of the bed and fluffing up her light hair before the mirror. "You see I call her Aunt Jarvis already–I might as well, you know, we'll be married so soon. Whatever has happened, Beth; was the old crank nasty to you?"

"Oh, Stella! No, she was always good and kind, but I–oh, I can't explain, only it was all my fault."

"Well, then, you'd better get to work and make it all right, you silly thing. Madeline's just out of her head with joy about it. She's quite the nastiest thing that ever lived, Beth Gordon, even if she is to be my sister-in-law. Neither she nor old mother Oliver have called on me, or noticed our engagement in any way, and Madeline's getting ready to go to the Old Country with Aunt Jarvis–instead of you, Beth, and if you let her I'll never, never forgive you. We'd just love to take our wedding-trip to the Old Country–I mean to go abroad, nobody in Cheemaun ever says the Old Country now–but we can't. Mr. Oliver's as stingy mean with poor darling Horry as ever he can be. And if Madeline goes I'll–Oh, Beth, whatever did happen to make you act so?"

Elizabeth explained that she could not possibly interfere. She was not to return to Toronto. Mrs. Jarvis probably did not want her any more. Then, to quit the uncomfortable subject, she suggested they go down to her aunt and Horace.

"My, you're so close," grumbled Estella, rising and shaking out her silk skirts. "I came out here on purpose to get it all out of you. But I'll do it anyway–see if I don't."

"Do what?" added Elizabeth, half-alarmed.

Estella laughed gayly. "Never you mind, Betsey dear. I can be as mum as yourself, never fear. It'll be a good turn for you, anyway," and she kissed her old schoolmate with genuine affection.

The subject was not referred to again, as Estella occupied the remainder of her visit talking about her trousseau, and she left without Elizabeth discovering just what she intended to do.

The days passed slowly and painfully, and the next event was John's homecoming. Elizabeth had looked forward to it, with something of the feeling a ship-wrecked mariner experiences when he sees an approaching vessel.

But John's presence did not bring the comfort she had fondly expected. He said not one word of reproach; but his sister could not help seeing he was deeply disappointed over the loss of his position. He had received no further orders from Mr. Huntley regarding his appointment, and had hesitated to approach him. He would send for him, the lawyer had said, when all arrangements were completed, but no summons had come yet, and John was feeling very much depressed indeed.

"Oh, John," groaned Elizabeth, as they wandered in the lane one warm spring evening, "I wish–I can't tell you how I wish I hadn't spoiled this chance of yours. But I can't see how I could have acted otherwise."

"It's all right, Lizzie," he said comfortingly. "Don't you worry. Of course, I can't see just why you went and busted up things in such a wholesale manner. But I know you felt it was the thing to do, and I can go somewhere else. I may get in with Dr. Harper here in Cheemaun."

"I feel I did right," Elizabeth said mournfully, "but it seems to have turned out all wrong. What does Jean say?"

"Jean?" John laughed. "She wasn't saying anything to anybody but old Bags when I came away. Boys, oh! If I didn't forget. She cautioned me to break the news that they were engaged."

"Engaged! Who?"

"Why, Jean and Bagsley."

"Jean and–and what?" screamed Elizabeth. "Not the bone man?"

"Yes, why not? He's all right I tell you, Lizzie. Finest chap in our year. Going to be gold medalist, sure."

"But how on earth?–what in the world?–John Gordon, are you telling me the truth or is it a joke?"

"Both. Mac and I nearly took hysterics the night Bags told us. We never suspected it. He never met a girl on the street without shying, and how he and Jean made it up is a mystery. But it's all right, and Aunt Margaret'll be tickled to death. Say, you must tell her. Go and do it now like a good kid. I'm going over to have a chat with Tom."

But Elizabeth would not let him go. She had not recovered from the shock. For the first time since her return home she felt her old spirits return. As yet, to Elizabeth, all love-making was something of a joke, and this was undoubtedly the funniest thing that had ever happened in Cupid's line. She deluged John with questions. What had put it into the bone-collector's shaggy head? And having got it there, where did he get the courage to propose? He must have done it by telephone, and long-distance, too. Or did he come stumbling into Jean's study and inquire in awful tones, "Miss Gordon, will you lend me your heart?" and then dash out and fall downstairs? And even if one could imagine his offering himself, how could anyone who knew Jean conjure up a picture of her stopping her mathematics long enough either to accept or reject? What a "come-downer" it would be for Jean to be merely married!

The brother and sister laughed together, in the disrespectful way that younger brothers and sisters have, and Miss Gordon, seated at her sewing by the open parlor window, heard Elizabeth's gay voice with rising resentment. The care-free laughter seemed to her but another indication of the girl's defiant indifference to her wishes.

Elizabeth entered, radiant with her news, but the sight of her aunt's face smote her. Miss Gordon had aged under her disappointment, and looked pale and dispirited.

"Is your head aching, Aunt Margaret?" the girl asked timidly.

"No, I thank you, Elizabeth," was the answer in the tones of stately politeness which Miss Gordon always used towards her wayward niece. "I am merely worried. But I have become accustomed to that lately."

She sighed deeply, and glad of a diverting subject, Elizabeth delivered John's report of Jean. The effect was most gratifying. Her aunt grew immediately alert and full of eager questions. Elizabeth had very little to tell. She wisely kept her own impressions of the young man to herself, but she dwelt upon the glowing report of Dr. Bagsley both John and Charles Stuart had given, not forgetting to add that he had greatly helped the latter in his philanthropic work.

"Jean has really done very well, then," Miss Gordon said, her face suffused with a pleased flush. "I really did not look to her for a good match. But Jean will always be a success, no matter in what sphere she is placed."

Elizabeth was silent. She could not picture Jean as a great success at cooking the bone-man's dinner, though perhaps he never ate anything. Mary was coming up the garden path from the lane, and as she looked at her she wondered why girls always seemed to be trained for some other life than that which fate brought them. She herself should have been a nurse, and so prepared to care for Eppie, and to do that work upon which she had now determined. Mary was perfectly fitted for a home-maker, and the chances of Mary's marrying were very small, and Jean was a mathematical machine and knew no more about housekeeping than Dr. Bagsley himself might be expected to know. It was such a puzzling world–especially for girls.

"Two letters for you, Lizzie," Mary cried. "Jamie's been to the post-office. One's a gentleman's handwriting, I can tell," she added, teasingly, "and the other's from Mrs. Jarvis. I know her writing."

Elizabeth took the letters tremblingly. She recognized Mr. Huntley's hand on the first, and the second was indeed from Mrs. Jarvis. She was painfully conscious that her aunt was watching her keenly as she opened the latter. The contents were even more of a surprise. It began, as Mrs. Jarvis's letters invariably did, with an account of her sufferings. Such prostrating headaches she had endured. Dr. Ralston had declared she was on the verge of a nervous collapse, and must leave the city as soon as she was able to travel. She did not wish to reproach Beth, but there could be no doubt as to the cause. It had been so all her life. Those to whom she had given most, for whom she had made the greatest sacrifices, were always the ones who turned against her. First her husband, then her niece and Madeline, and lastly Both, whom she had believed really loved her. But–and here Elizabeth received her surprise–she was ready to forgive. It was her way–her weakness, indeed, but she always forgave those who used her most cruelly. Yes, she would take Beth back if she would say she was sorry. That she was truly repentant Miss Raymond had assured her. Horace and his pretty fiancée had called to see her when they were in the city the day before, and Mrs. Jarvis had understood from them that Beth loved her in spite of her strange, cruel actions, and was ready to return. The doctor had prescribed a sea voyage, and just as soon as she could get a little strength to do some shopping, she would start for Europe. She was going with a party–Mr. Huntley was to be one of them–and Beth must come too. Yes, she really must. Mrs. Jarvis was ready to forgive and forget. So was Mr. Huntley, she felt sure. Of course, he was grieved and hurt at Beth's conduct. He could not understand why she had gone away without a word of farewell. She herself had smoothed matters over as well as she could, but the worry of it all had got on her nerves. She did not pretend to understand what strange notions Beth had got into her head. As though she and Mr. Huntley and Blanche Kendall were responsible for all the poverty in Toronto. Well, there was no use discussing the matter further–it only made her nerves worse–and Dr. Ralston had said any more worry might prove fatal. But she felt that the sea-voyage would perhaps help her. Beth must write at once and say what she would do, for Madeline would come if Beth forsook her. Madeline had written, indeed, offering her services. There was more about the headaches and nerves, but it ended with words of genuine affection, that brought the tears to Elizabeth's eyes. To fight against love was the hardest task for Elizabeth. Almost everyone she cared for, John, her aunt, Mrs. Jarvis, and Estella, warm-hearted and loyal as she was in spite of many faults, seemed arrayed against her to force her to yield.

The other letter was in Mr. Huntley's best formal and semi-pompous style. He, too, began in a slightly aggrieved tone. He did not know until lately that Miss Gordon was not coming back to Toronto at once. He had fancied that some slight announcement of her departure was due him, but, of course, she knew best. Her brother, too, had gone without acquainting him of the fact. His appointment was still open, and he would be expected to be on duty within a week's time. Of course, Dr. Gordon might not care to accept the position now; Mr. Huntley had gathered from Mrs. Jarvis that somehow Miss Gordon was offended with him. He was not conscious of any offense given, and hoped to hear from her that their relations were as friendly as when she had left the city. In which case he hoped to meet Dr. Gordon at his office not later than Thursday, when the final arrangements for his work would be made.

Elizabeth scarcely noticed the polite closing of the letter. Her heart was beating to suffocation. She was dazzled by the prospect that had suddenly opened before her. To accept meant to gain everything the world could give to make her happy; her home secured, John established in his profession, her aunt content. Then she thought of the sermon in St. Stephen's Church with its call to a higher life, of Mother MacAllister's words concerning One Who had Himself trod a thorny path and Whose true disciple must be content to follow.

She looked up and saw her aunt's eyes fixed upon her in intense eagerness.

"Your letter is from Mrs. Jarvis?" Miss Gordon could not keep the painful anxiety from showing in her face.

"Yes," faltered Elizabeth. She did not offer to show it, as had been her habit in the old days. Miss Gordon turned away with a hurt, grieved air. "Of course," she said coldly, "I must not ask for your confidence, Elizabeth. I find it hard to remember that you do not consult me any more in your affairs."

"Oh, Aunt Margaret!" cried the girl brokenly. It was the cry of a motherless child appealing for its rights to the one who had, in spite of all deficiencies, filled a mother's place in her life. "Here,–read them both. I do want your advice." She shoved both letters into her aunt's hands as she spoke. Then she rose and fled upstairs to her little room. Something told her that in that act she had put away from herself the power to choose; that she had turned her back upon the Vision.

CHAPTER XVIII
DARKNESS

And so, once more Elizabeth failed. This time the world did not recognize the failure as such, and it was regarded by her family, and especially by her aunt, as the highest success. But Elizabeth knew; that wiser inner self, always sternly honest, called her action by its right name. On the very evening she wrote Mrs. Jarvis, promising to return, she felt the full bitterness of failure. For at family worship her father read from the life of that One whom she had, for a brief time, tried to follow. The Man of Nazareth had been showing His disciples how His pathway must lead to the cross, and "from that time many of His disciples went back and walked no more with Him." The sorrowful words kept repeating themselves over and over to Elizabeth after she had gone to bed–"went back and walked no more with Him"; and though she had that day chosen wealth and worldly prosperity, in place of hardship, poverty, and discomfort, she sobbed herself to sleep.

As the days passed and preparations for her departure went forward, she struggled to regain her habitual cheerfulness. John had gone West, full of joyful ambitions, her home and her father's peace were assured, her aunt was once more kind and happy. But Elizabeth could not be content. Too honest to compromise with her conscience, she allowed herself no false hopes in regard to making her life with Mrs. Jarvis a useful one. She could not bear to look into Mother MacAllister's eyes the day she told her of her altered plans. For the joy over Charles Stuart's new life had made those eyes shine with a beautiful new radiance, and the girl was grieved to see it dim. And just what Charles Stuart himself would say when he returned and found her gone, was a speculation that could not but be disturbing.

By working hard, visiting here and there, writing letters, and spending much time with Eppie, she managed to make the few remaining days pass. When left alone she found her only refuge from pangs of regret was in keeping herself extremely busy. For this reason, having the big stone house to herself one morning, she set to work at the housecleaning. Annie and the babies had been with them for a day, and had gone home, taking Mary and Miss Gordon with them for a day's shopping. Elizabeth, whose fickle allegiance was always given to the latest arrived Vision in Annie's family, missed the soft cooing little voice and adorable antics of Baby Betty, to the verge of heartache. She realized that on this quiet day she must do something strenuous.

Her first task was to see her father happily at work in his garden, and her next was to send her little maid to the Martin farm to help Auntie Jinit with her late spring soap-making. Not that Auntie Jinit needed help, but the Gordons strove in every way to show their friendliness towards their kind neighbor. Thus safe from the shocked protestations that were sure to follow upon her engaging in anything useful, Elizabeth set feverishly to work.

She would thoroughly clean the room Eppie had occupied, she resolved. Arraying herself in a dress of Mary's which was much too long, an apron of the little maid's that was much too short, and a huge dust-cap of her aunt's, she set vigorously to work, washing, scrubbing, and cleaning windows. There was some grim satisfaction in the hard physical labor, her last chance, she felt, to do something useful, some satisfaction, too, in wondering what the fastidious Mr. Huntley would say, could he see her.

She had finished the hardest part of her task and was just tacking up with loving hands an old photograph of Annie's first Vision, in a long, white robe, when she heard the front door open suddenly, and knew by the bounding step that Sarah Emily had arrived. Ever since her marriage Mrs. Peter Johnstone regularly visited The Dale, at short intervals, and in spite of many broad hints from her former mistress, she had never yet become sufficiently formal to knock at the door. "Come right up, Sarah Emily," Elizabeth called over the balustrade.

"I knowed you'd be alone, Lizzie," said the visitor, mounting gayly. "I seen the rest o' the folks goin' off in all directions, an' ses I, 'I'll scoot over an' slap up a batch o' biscuits or somethin',' for I knowed you couldn't get any dinner. For the love o' the crows, you ain't housecleanin'!"

"Doesn't this room look as if I were?"

Sarah Emily sniffed the damp clean odor. "Well, I never. If this ain't a come-downer for a lady like you!" She turned and regarded the girl with affectionate reproach. "What d'ye do it for?" she continued, puzzled.

"Because I like it, Sarah Emily. I'd like to go on doing it all my life."

Sarah Emily laughed. Of course this was only Lizzie's nonsense, and she didn't mean a word of it.

"You're a pretty one," she declared, assuming her old air of authority, which came to her easily in the presence of the Gordon children. "Here, if you ain't gone and cleaned up the whole place an' that stove-pipe not moved."

Elizabeth uttered an ejaculation of dismay. "Oh, I forgot. Can't we do it yet?"

"Course we can!" said Sarah Emily cordially. "Come along, I'll show you!"

She flung aside her shawl and soon Elizabeth was in her old subordinate position. Sarah Emily took matters in her own hands. She proceeded to remove the stove from the study below and the pipes from the room above, flying upstairs and downstairs in her old authoritative way, much to Elizabeth's amusement. At her peremptory summons Mr. Gordon came in from his garden to lend a hand, evidently under the impression that Sarah Emily had never left, and was merely attending to her customary duties. There was much running to and fro, and banging of stove-pipes, and a great deal of talk and laughter, for Sarah Emily was always in the gayest spirits if she happened to be at The Dale during the absence of its mistress. Besides, she was a born commander, and shouted orders to her two subordinates with the greatest enjoyment.

All went smoothly and swiftly until the work was almost accomplished, when a delay occurred. Mr. Gordon was downstairs removing the stove-pipes from the study. Above, Sarah Emily, mounted upon a chair, was supporting the long black column that ran into the chimney, while Elizabeth, down on her knees, was preventing another column from descending into the room below.

"Now, you down there!" shouted Sarah Emily, "you carry out them pipes to the barnyard, so's the sut won't fly onto them clothes on the line, an' me an' Lizzie 'll hold these till you get back."

Mr. Gordon, obedient to the voice from above, took the pipes, and his retreating footsteps could be heard along the passage leading to the kitchen. While they waited his return Sarah Emily beguiled the time with a story of how she circumvented that there Pete, who had determined to sell the brindled cow to a butcher in Cheemaun. But she showed him who was boss, so she did. Though married Sarah Emily still kept up her show of cruel indifference, and never lost an opportunity of telling how she trampled upon her husband. The neighbors, however, knew that she waited upon Peter hand and foot, and that he was growing fat and arrogant. So Elizabeth did not know just how much the brindled-cow story was colored by the story-teller's imagination. She responded with a tale of the city, such as Sarah Emily liked, full of finely dressed ladies, and flower-bedecked drawing-rooms. Then Sarah Emily recounted once again her experiences when she worked as maid for Mrs. Oliver and first became acquainted with high life and Mrs. Jarvis. This last circumstance she thankfully declared to be the beginning of Lizzie's good luck.

But in spite of much entertaining talk, it soon began to be borne in upon the minds of the two that both time and the stove-pipes were hanging rather heavily on their hands. Elizabeth shifted her cramped position and wondered what could be keeping father; and Sarah Emily braced herself against the wall and declared some folks were slower than a seven years' famine. It was impossible to leave their places, for the pipes would collapse into the study below, so that there was nothing to do but wait, Casabianca-like. Elizabeth misquoted something about the noble two who held the pipes in the brave days of old. But Sarah Emily did not understand the allusion, and the joke fell very flat. Her arms were cramped too, and her sense of humor was becoming dulled.

They waited and called and waited, until at last Elizabeth became alarmed, fearing something had happened to her father. Still holding her uncomfortable burden, she rose to her feet, whence she could command a view from the windows overlooking the kitchen-garden. One glimpse she caught and uttered a shriek of laughter, which threatened dislodgment of the stove-pipes. For there, far down the garden, near to Tom Teeter's fence, peacefully hoeing in his potato-patch, stood her absent-minded father!

But Sarah Emily did not laugh. Declaring that Lizzie's pa was the most forgettable man that ever pestered the soul out of a body, she managed to place herself so that her strong arms supported both sections of the pipe and dispatched Elizabeth after the truant.

Mr. Gordon flung up his hands in dismay at his daughter's appearance, and fled back to the house full of apologies enough to appease even Sarah Emily, who was by this time both cramped and cross. Elizabeth followed more slowly, filled with laughter. It was impossible to hurry indoors on such a morning. The orchard path was bordered with soft grass, vividly green. The bluebirds hopped and twittered in the branches above, and on every side the undulating fields stretched away, shimmering in the warm sunshine. When Elizabeth looked back in later years at the picture of herself walking gayly down the orchard path on that radiant morning, she wondered how she could have laughed, and how it was possible that not the smallest premonition was given her of the storm of anguish so rapidly approaching.

As she reached the end of the orchard path the rattle of wheels attracted her. She looked up to see John Coulson driving slowly down the lane. She ran through the house and out to the garden gate in glad surprise, full of questions. What had brought him out here at this hour? And why did he come alone? And what did he mean by leaving Baby Bet at home? And what did he do with Mary and Aunt Margaret? And didn't he think she looked fetching in this cap and apron?

And then some subtle change in John Coulson's kindly manner made itself felt. She slipped her hand into his arm as they went up the garden path.

"Is anybody sick, John Coulson? How is baby?"

"She's all right, dear. No, Annie isn't ill, nor anyone–only–I–have something to tell you, Lizzie. Come in, I want to see you alone."

The study stove-pipes were still being removed, and Elizabeth led her brother-in-law into the parlor. Her heart seemed clutched by a cold hand. Something was the matter, or why should John Coulson call her Lizzie, and look at her with such sorrowful eyes.

"John Coulson!" she cried, clutching his arm, "I know something's happened. Oh, is it baby?"

No, it wasn't baby, he answered her again, but he led her to the sofa and sat beside her, holding her hand. And then he told her–Elizabeth never knew just how he broke the news, whether it had been gently or suddenly. She only knew that he had come to tell her that John was dead; that John had been killed by an explosion of dynamite, at the blasting of a tunnel on the British North American Railroad.

She listened quietly to the faltering words, and when they were ended she said nothing. She sat looking at her brother-in-law, her hands hanging inertly, and thought how strange it seemed to see a big, strong man like John Coulson with tears running down his face. It seemed strange, too, that she was not sorry that John had been killed. Often in earlier years she had tormented herself by imagining the death of some member of the family, and her heart had scarcely been able to bear the anguish of such a thought. And now John was dead, and she did not mind. She felt sorry for John Coulson, of course, he seemed so very, very sad. He was looking at her with such anguished eyes, that she patted his arm comfortingly.

"Poor John Coulson," she said. "Why, we won't need to call you John Coulson any more, will we?–only John." Then she arose and called her father and Sarah Emily, so that they might be told, and went quietly upstairs to finish the task she had left.

But she did not go to work. Instead she sat down in the chair upon which Sarah Emily had stood, and tried to reason herself into some feeling of grief. Why, she had not even felt like shedding a tear, and Aunt Margaret would be home soon, and she would think her so cold and cruel. She must really try to cry a little when Aunt Margaret came, even though she didn't feel sorry that John was dead. The stove-pipes had been removed, and she sat by the empty pipe-hole listening idly to the sound from below. She could hear John Coulson's low, deep voice, and Sarah Emily's loud lamentations. She wished she could act like Sarah Emily, it seemed so much more sympathetic. Her mind seemed to have become possessed of a keenness never felt before. She thought out every detail of the changed circumstances John's death must bring, forgetting nothing. It would mean that she could not leave home quite so soon, she reflected, and even wondered how Mrs. Jarvis would feel when she learned that Elizabeth must wear black.

And all the time she was feeling ashamed that she could sit so callously making plans, while even now John's dead body must be on its way home. But then she did not feel sorry. She wondered if there had ever before been anyone bereaved who had been so heartless.

The sound of wheels reached her alert senses, and she arose and went to the window overlooking the lane. She saw a carriage come down with her aunt and Mary in it, and Charles Stuart driving. She did not think it strange that he should be there, but only wondered if he felt sorry about John. Evidently Mary did, for she was sobbing convulsively, and Aunt Margaret walked so slowly that Charles Stuart gave her his arm up the garden path. Elizabeth arose and softly closed the door, lest her aunt come and find her. She was not sorry that John was killed.

She came back to her seat by the pipe-hole and again listened to the sounds of lamentation from below. Then the study door closed and she could hear only the voices of Charles Stuart and John Coulson. She peeped down and saw Charles Stuart's face. He was sitting by her father's desk, and he did not look sorry, only angry. His face was ghastly pale and his eyes burned red as he stretched his clenched fist along the top of the desk. Elizabeth leaned down and deliberately listened in the hope that she might hear some details of the accident, that would make her feel sorry.

"Oh, John Coulson," the low, anguished voice was saying, "it's devilish work this money-making. It's blood money that man Huntley is getting, and he declares he knew nothing about it–and I suppose he doesn't, but he'll take the money, you'll see! And Mrs. Jarvis has shares in it. And–and Lizzie—-"

His voice broke. There was a deathly silence.

"This must never reach her ears, Stuart, nor any of them. It would kill Aunt Margaret." That was John Coulson's voice, and Elizabeth held her breath to catch what this was she must not hear. If it were so terrible, surely it would make her feel just a little regretful concerning John.

"No, no," Charles Stuart answered. "They'll never know, and the public will never know. The man who did the dastardly thing will see to that. And his company, headed by Huntley, will shield him."

"Can't they be exposed?" John Coulson's voice was a mere whisper.

"Exposed! Not they. The papers say it was merely an accident, with only one white man killed. That is Huntley's story too, and who cares that a hundred or so Chinamen were blown to pieces? Nobody is going to be so crude as to announce that they were put out of the way when the company was done with them, to save big arrears in wages. And nobody can prove it. They'll make a fuss about John—-" The voice broke again. Elizabeth did not wait to hear more. She arose and went quietly down to the study. She opened the door and stood facing the two men. She did not feel one pang of grief as yet, but she wanted to make things plain. She wanted to explain to John Coulson and Charles Stuart that it was not the President of the British North American Railroad that had killed John, but she, his favorite sister; because it was she who in her stepping aside from the path of her plain duty had sent him to his death. This she was determined to tell, but somehow the words seemed so slow in coming. She stretched out her hands in an attempt to explain herself. Then she saw Charles Stuart spring towards her out of a mist, and there fell over her a great darkness.

CHAPTER XIX
SUNRISE

Long before the sun appeared above Arrow Hill Elizabeth was dressed and sitting at her bedroom window watching the lane. For she had promised Auntie Jinit that she would be off to the creek at the earliest hour to gather violets and lady's-slippers and swamp lilies to decorate the tables for the wedding breakfast. Charlie Stuart had promised to call for her at sunrise, but she was too excited to rest.

For this was Eppie's wedding-day. Poor little Eppie had found her home at last–her old home too. Jake Martin, at his wife's instigation, had handed over to his son the little farm that had once belonged to old Sandy and there Charlie and Eppie were to start their new life. And so just as the stars were sinking into the faint blue vault of heaven, and the earth was rising slowly from its shroud of darkness and sleep, Elizabeth had arisen and was now dressed and waiting for Charles Stuart long before he could be expected.

The grand forward march of day had commenced; very slowly and majestically it was approaching, and the waking earth stirred at the sound of its footsteps. From every bush and tree looming up from the grayness, from every field spread out in dark waving folds, and from the black swamp beyond uprose the welcoming chorus. Elizabeth was reminded of that early dawn she had witnessed so long ago when she had sat at this same window watching for Charles Stuart. That was the morning she had seen Annie steal down the orchard path to meet her lover, the morning she had experienced her first hint of that desire, now strong within her, to sing of the glories of earth and sky.

She leaned forward over the window-sill, listening to the great chant earth was raising to heaven. Up behind the black trees of Arrow Hill shone a faint crystal transparency–the airy curtain that yet obscured the wonders of the dawn. A mist gathered in Elizabeth's eyes. Those words that had come to her in that dawn years before returned:–"Who coverest thyself with light as with a garment; who stretchest out the heavens like a curtain." Slowly, imperceptibly, that garment of light was growing brighter, changing to a faint luminous gold as the gray earth changed to a deep blue.

Down the drive lane, near the creek stood the old elm, its topmost branch still towering into the heavens, its lower limbs sweeping the earth. Remembering how it had come to life that other morning, Elizabeth leaned farther out to listen. And as it slowly took form, gathering itself from the blue background, there arose the musical accompaniment to its birth, the loud rapture of a robin's morning hymn.

It paeaned the waking note to the watcher as well. Elizabeth's soul soared up with it in ecstatic worship, voiced in the notes of a new song, that came from her heart as freely as did the robin's. For years her fettered spirit had been struggling to express its music, but the repression of her early life, disobedience to the call to higher and nobler things, and later a crushing sorrow had stifled her voice. But now she was free. She had not been disobedient to the heavenly vision. Her soul had turned at last to meet the dawning need, valiant for doing. It had arisen at last, warm and radiant, and she was permitted to sing its welcoming chorus in notes that were to make her name known throughout the length and breadth of her native land.

The dawn had come to Elizabeth through storm and darkness. She never quite recovered from the blow that had driven her back, wounded and faint, to the path of duty. Never a day passed that she did not miss the dear companionship of John, did not listen half-unconsciously for his footsteps, never a night she did not remember with anguished heart the manner of his death. But a year had passed, helping to heal the wound, and Elizabeth had found happiness in service. One year more and she would be a graduate of a nurses' training school, and a brilliant graduate too, her superior officers predicted. For at last Elizabeth was succeeding. And so her useless days left, she had chosen her life this time without hesitation. Mrs. Jarvis had gone, bidding her an affectionate farewell, and leaving in her hands the title-deeds to The Dale. Her going closed the door of that side of Elizabeth's life. She was to be some use in the world at last. And because she had found a place that satisfied the highest instincts of her nature, the long-stifled song came welling forth.

The faint gold of the east was turning to a soft rose, the blue of the earth was growing brighter. And keeping pace with the growing light, the earth-chorus was swelling into a storm of music. Elizabeth thought of that dawn of her childhood days, and of her struggle to grasp its meaning. Now she knew. Its message came to her in the words of a hymn. They were the words they had sung in Forest Glen Church the day they laid John in the grassy graveyard:

"But lo! there breaks a yet more glorious day,
The saints triumphant rise in bright array,
The King of Glory passes on His way,
Hallelujah!"

The King of Glory had come, and the gates of Elizabeth's soul had lifted up their heads that He might enter.

She slipped noiselessly from the room, taking care to waken no one, and descended to her father's study. There she seated herself at the desk and strove to put upon paper the great hope and longing and happiness that were filling her heart.

Charles Stuart was whistling at the garden gate before she noticed him. She ran down the path to meet him, brushing the dew from the border of mignonette with her light gown.

"What a glorious day Eppie's going to have!" she cried, plucking a rosy sweet-pea that nodded over the gate.

"I wish it was our day," Charles Stuart said enviously. "Two years more to wait, Lizzie."

She smiled up at him hopefully. "But we'll make them beautiful years," she whispered. "See," she held up a sheet of paper. "I've done it again."

He took it, but did not look at it immediately. For Elizabeth was as radiant as the morning, and his eyes could not turn from her so soon. He did not need to be a Pretender any more either, for the love-light in his eyes was answered by her own.

As they walked down the lane with the sunrise gleaming in Elizabeth's uncovered head, he read her verses.

"Has it a soul?" she asked mischievously.

There was a mist in Charles Stuart's deep eyes as he turned towards her.

"Lizzie! It has an immortal soul! It's a musical morning-glory! It has come at last, hasn't it?"

"It was my own fault that it was so long in coming," she said. "But I think it was waiting for you, Stuart."

Charles Stuart's answer was not verbal, but it was more expressive than the most eloquent words.

They plunged gayly down the bank of the creek, hand in hand like two children.

"Oh, oh," cried Elizabeth, "just look at the forget-me-nots! I'm going to make a wreath of them for Eppie's hair."

Far up the creek, a cat-bird, hidden amongst scented basswood blossoms, was singing a gay medley of purest music. On either side the banks were hidden in a luxury of reeds, water-lily leaves, blue forget-me-nots, and gay bobbing lady's-slippers. And between, the winding stream shone pink and gold in the sunrise.

Charles Stuart stood watching his lady as she filled her hands with blossoms.

"You love this place, don't you, 'Lizbeth of The Dale?" he said.

"Love it? There is no spot on earth like it."

"And how can you bear to leave it all to come away with me—and to a foreign land, too?"

She raised her face from her rosy bouquet and looked into his eyes. And Charles Stuart smiled, knowing he had said a very absurd thing indeed.

They sat down under an overhanging willow, and talked of the days that were past, and the yet more interesting days to come.

"I remember I used to discuss the possibility of my being a foreign missionary with Mother MacAllister," Elizabeth said, "in sun-bonnet days. But I did not think the dream would really come true."

"I remember, too, that when your contemplation of unclothed heathen and boa-constrictors was too much for your courage, you used to remark despairingly that you supposed you would just stay at home and marry Charles Stuart."

Elizabeth laughed. Her ideas concerned with marrying Charles Stuart had undergone a radical change in the past year.

From the tower over the Martin woodshed a big bell clanged out a startling interruption. They sprang up, looking at each other guiltily. Auntie Jinit had threatened to so remind them of their duty if they remained too long at the creek. For such a pair for stravagin' over the fields as Lizzie and Charles Stuart, she declared she had never seen, and she was thankful Eppie wasn't given that way.

They scrambled gayly up the bank. "They're ringing the wedding-bells already," cried Elizabeth. "There go Mary and Jean; they promised to set the tables—and brother Bone-Bagsley too—the dear! We must hurry."

Nevertheless they still lingered. When they reached the top of the slope, they stood for a moment in the rosy sunlight and, with a common impulse, looked back.

"It's almost a year ago," whispered Elizabeth.

"Yes, almost a year," answered Charles Stuart.

Down the bank past the mill, and up the opposite shore ran the little stony path they had so often trodden in schooldays. It crossed The Slash, now a trim clover-field, and disappeared into the cool depths of Forest Glen. But they could follow it still in imagination. It passed Eppie's old-new home they knew, went down the lane, skirted the highway, and curved round into the grassy churchyard where John lay.

They turned at last and went up the lane together. There were tears in Elizabeth's eyes, but the words of a song were on her lips:–

"And when the strife is fierce, the warfare long,
Steals on the ear the distant triumph song,
And hearts are brave again and arias are strong,
Hallelujah!"